All Our Perfect Imperfections

A Wounded Warrior Legacy Novel

Nika Rhone

With deepest gratitude to the military and first responders who keep us safe, and run toward danger when duty calls. Thank you for being on the wall.

And to those who raise and train guide, service, and therapy dogs, thank you for everything you do for the wounded warriors who sometimes return from that wall in need of support.

"We are all wonderful, beautiful wrecks. That's what connects us—that we're all broken, all beautifully imperfect."

Emilio Estevez

Prologue

TODAY WAS THE DAY that just might break him.

It could have come at any point in the last weeks or months since his son had died serving his country. Every day that passed had added another ballast stone of grief and despair. Another pound of excruciating weight pressing down on the delicate framework holding what remained of his family together.

Bowing it.

Stretching it to its very limits.

But today's stone, bearing the burden of a twenty-first birthday that would never come, could be what finally shattered the whole damaged thing into tiny, unmendable pieces.

The possibility sent a familiar twist through David Winchester's gut as he stood in the open doorway to his son's room. The one his wife wouldn't allow a single thing to be touched in. Couldn't even bear to enter. Or have others go into.

Not even him.

Which was why he stood there now, in the moonlit dark of the early hours after midnight. Not wanting to upset Carol any more than today was already going to rip at her. But wanting—no, *needing* to be there. In the place his boy had grown from sweet child to inquisitive teen to compassionate young man. The place that enshrined his life, rather than his death.

That place they'd visit in the morning. So Nicole could lay flowers on it as she wished her big brother a happy birthday.

"Damn it, Mikey." Swallowing back the bitter grief threatening to roll up his throat like a molten tide, he stepped into the room.

Guided by memory and moonlight, he walked past the neatly made bed to the battered oak desk set against the wall. The one Mikey had done his homework on. Built model cars and airplanes and rockets on. Poured over books and watched countless hours of online videos on, learning everything he could about how to care for injured animals.

"That damn rabbit," he murmured, running his fingers over the uneven spots where years of model glue mishaps had marred the desk's surface. Mikey's focus had shifted the day he brought the bunny with the lame leg home and declared he was going to help it get better. He'd gone from wanting to build things, to wanting to fix them.

No, *needing* to.

It was like some switch had been thrown inside him, deep in his DNA. Showing him exactly what it was he wanted to do with his life. Who he wanted to be.

Who he was *meant* to be.

Heady epiphany for a ten-year-old to have. But like everything else in his life, Mikey accepted it and moved forward with absolute confidence. That was one thing his boy hadn't lacked an ounce of. Neither had he been short on compassion.

Actually, he might have possessed a bit too much of it.

Which was how they'd ended up with a mini wildlife hospital in their garage. And why Mikey spent his summers mowing the lawns of not one, but three of their elderly neighbors for free. And why he'd taken all the money he saved for a car and donated it to Make a Wish for a local kid diagnosed with cancer to go to Disney.

And why they'd be laying flowers on his grave today instead of lighting candles on his cake.

The grief made another burning appearance in his throat. This time, he let it come. Let the fiery tears form and spill as a soft, pain-filled sob escaped along with them.

His son. His boy.

God, it still didn't seem real.

Standing in this room, untouched by time since his last visit home on leave, it was almost possible to pretend it wasn't.

But he'd seen the body. Watched the casket lowered into the cold, hard ground. Listened to the lonely echo of Taps as it stretched out over the endless field of white stones lined in precise rows of military attention.

Mikey was gone. Really and truly gone.

And somehow, they all had to find a way to go on without him. To make sense of his loss, his sacrifice, and the almost immeasurable hole he'd left behind. Not only in their family, although god knew that one was fucking cataclysmic. But in the world itself.

A world Mikey would have made a much better place. Not just by his mere presence in it, but because he'd been bound and determined to make sure it *was* one. Better. Safer. Happier. One simple act of selflessness and compassion at a time.

Too bad that's what got him killed.

The hushed dark of the room and its lingering cobweb of memories were suddenly suffocating. He escaped, the door closing behind him with a quiet click of finality.

Maybe Carol had been right to let sleeping ghosts lie.

Socks shushing whisper soft on the smooth hardwood floor, he went to the kitchen sink, where he stood in a puddle of moonlight spilling through the window to the backyard. He grabbed a glass and filled it, downing the tepid water in an effort to settle both his stomach and his head.

And wished it was something stronger.

As soon as the thought entered his mind, he shoved it out again. Dipping into the bottle of scotch in the top cabinet wouldn't do anything except give him a wooly head in the morning. And give Carol a reason to pull away from him even further than she already had if she woke up and smelled it on his breath when he got back into bed.

He loved his wife. His heart ached at how hard their son's death was hitting her.

But he also resented her for it, too.

Just a little.

Because the anger and grief which formed a protective shell around her heart didn't just hinder her grieving process by keeping her emotions in. Choking her on them. It also kept both him and Nicole out. Stopped them from all grieving together, as a family.

Sometimes it didn't just feel like he'd lost a son.

It was like he'd lost his wife as well.

Like he'd lost everything.

Maybe even a piece of himself.

Fuck it.

No way was he falling back to sleep with that thought in his head. Not without a little help.

As he snapped on the small pendent light over the sink, the sound of Sadie's tags jingled up the stairs from the basement where they'd set up the whelping den for her and her litter. Looking sleepy and confused, the golden retriever padded over to him. She head-butted his leg in greeting, then leaned against it as he gave her soft ears an indulgent rub.

"Didn't mean to wake you, Sadie-girl," he said softly, then chuckled at the groan of ecstasy he got when his fingers hit just the right spot. "Yeah, you don't care, do you? Not when there's an ear rub to be had. And a treat." He turned the last word into a question.

One Sadie knew well. Abandoning her ear rub, she pranced over to where her snacks were kept and looked back at him, feathery tail swishing in anticipation.

He chuckled again. "That's what I thought."

After choosing her favorite peanut butter-flavored treat from one of the plastic containers in the bottom cabinet, he said, "Sit." When Sadie's furry butt plopped obediently to the hardwood, he almost said *shake*.

But something made him say, "Salute" instead.

After a brief hesitation, probably because she hadn't heard the command in a while, Sadie brought her right paw up into the air near her head. It was more of a high-five, really. But Mikey had taught her the trick when he'd come home after boot camp three years ago, and it had made him laugh. So as far as David was concerned, it was a damn salute.

"Good girl." The words came out husky as he fed her the treat, which she took off to devour in the corner.

More than ready for his own treat, he opened an upper cabinet, pulled the whiskey bottle from the top shelf, and splashed a small amount into his water glass. The smokey scent of fire and peat filled his nose as he took the first sip.

It was a decent label, but still burned all the way down to his belly.

From there, the heat spread in all directions like branch lightning, all jagged and bright, warming places he hadn't realized were so cold. Eyes closed, he savored the sensation for a long moment.

Damn, but it felt good to feel warm again. Like a comforting hug from the inside.

It was an illusion, of course.

All of that comfort and calm would be gone come morning, leaving behind only the same aching pressure of loss as before. But for tonight, for right this minute, it was exactly what he needed. To get to sleep. To get past the grief.

To get through the never-ending guilt that came with outliving your child.

That. That was the heaviest stone in the load to bear.

One even the grief counselor they were seeing hadn't been able to help him deal with. To *live* with. Because there were days when the thought of going on living without his boy seemed almost impossible.

But he had no choice. His daughter needed him.

Needed *both* of them.

But until Carol could find her way past the wall she'd built inside herself, it was up to him to help Nicole navigate something no fifteen-year-old should ever have to.

Any more than a parent should.

His arm came up again, this time to gulp, not sip. But before the glass reached his mouth, a sharp pain in his little toe made him jerk in surprise.

"What the fuck!"

The last thing he expected was to see one of Sadie's puppies latched onto his sock. Its needlelike teeth made another prick on his toe as it tugged again, chunky little retriever body wriggling with delight at its prize.

Wincing, he crouched down and gently disengaged the pup's bear-trap grip.

"How the hell did you get up here?"

He looked around, half expecting to see the other seven puppies making their own break for it from the basement. Luckily, this seemed to be the only escapee. Cooper, according to the color-coding system they used on the collars to tell the pups apart.

Thank God. The last thing he needed was to be corralling a herd of recharged little speed demons through the house in the middle of the night.

Just as it was about to lunge for the sock again, he put the glass down and scooped the puppy into his arms.

"Oh no you don't." Instantly, Cooper changed targets and started furiously licking his nose instead, filling his next breaths with the unique scent of puppy spit.

Before the licks could turn to nibbles, because they definitely would, he shifted his hold so the dog couldn't reach his face anymore. Which he wiped as best he could on the sleeve of his tee with a grimace.

"Okay, it's back to bed for you, pal. You've got a big day tomorrow."

A vivid memory of saying almost the same thing to Mikey when he was about four or five echoed in his head. He'd snuck out of his bedroom on Christmas Eve because he said he'd heard Santa and wanted to catch him leaving presents.

Who he'd almost caught was David, with Mikey's big-boy two-wheeler he'd just taken out of hiding in the basement. Only the fact Mikey had those Spiderman slippers, the rubber-soled ones that squeaked like sneakers on a gym floor with every step, had given enough warning to head off disaster.

Much like Mikey, the puppy put up a whiny protest about being sent back to bed. Small whimpers erupted when David walked toward the stairs, alarmingly loud in the thick quiet that blanketed the house.

"Shh, stop that before you wake up your littermates."

Or Carol. Then he'd have to explain why he was wandering around at one in the morning.

Guilt tickled his gut as he glanced at the scotch on the counter.

Okay, maybe he wouldn't have to explain.

Which was actually worse.

Turning from the basement stairs, he gave the pup a gentle squeeze. "Fine, you win. Just be quiet, okay? You can stay up a little while longer, just until you get sleepy." Which for puppies could be anywhere from five hours to five seconds flat. This was Sadie's third litter, so he was getting pretty savvy as to how they worked. But sometimes there were still things that caught him by surprise.

Like how a 3-month-old chonker like Cooper had managed to get past the board blocking the doorway downstairs only Sadie should have been able to hop over.

"Maybe we should have named you Houdini instead of…"

Instead of after one of the men Mikey had died trying to save.

Pain won out over guilt, sending him straight for the scotch. As soon as he reached for the glass, though, Cooper took the opportunity to squirm in his loosened grasp, little legs kicking in an effort to get down.

"Oh, no you don't. You've already proven you're a runner. You're staying right where you are, pal."

But squirmy puppies were just as hard to hang onto as squirmy kids. Both required a two-handed grip. Leaving him SOL about the drink.

Probably for the best, anyway.

He'd spent a lot of nights right after the funeral staying up late, wandering the house or staring out the window. Just him, his whiskey, and his thoughts. Too many nights.

Too many whiskeys.

Too easy to slip into old habits of self-medicating himself to sleep.

Turning his back on temptation, he slowly paced the perimeter of the kitchen, rocking the puppy in rhythmic cadence to his steps. The same way he'd walked with Nicole when she'd had an ear infection and couldn't stop crying, And Mikey when he had five of his baby teeth all coming in at the same time, making him so miserable they hadn't thought he'd ever sleep again.

Or that they would.

It had been a long time, but somehow his body still remembered. The speed. The sway. The soft flow of words meant to distract and calm. It all came flooding back. Along with the reminder of why this puppy, this litter, was so different from the others.

So important.

"You don't know it yet, but you're going to be doing big things, little man," he crooned softly as he walked and swayed. "You, Bailey, and Samson. All of you will be helping out some very special people who need a hand adjusting to their new lives. Or maybe it would be a paw." He grinned when the pup yawned. "Yeah, Mikey felt the same way about my dad jokes."

The kids had loved them when they were little. Not so much when they'd gotten older and outgrown the silliness of the puns and groanworthy punchlines.

"Everyone just grew up so damn fast. I miss when we all spent the weekends as a family. Going to the beach. Playing board games. Making s'mores in the backyard. They were young for like a minute, then, poof! They're all grown up, off doing their own grown-up things. Driving. Dating. Joining the army and heading off to the other side of the world."

Dying.

He stopped, throat tightening, making it hard to breathe.

"Damn it. I miss him so fucking much."

The puppy whimpered, as though tuning in to his emotions. Face pressed against the warm, soft fur, he breathed through the unexpected pocket of grief. Listening to the steady beat of Cooper's heart helped quiet his own racing one, but nothing could slow the memories. A whirlwind slideshow of his son's life. His accomplishments.

And his failures. He was human, after all, not a saint.

No one ever talked about those, though.

Who wanted to speak ill of the dead?

Although honestly, no one spoke about him much in any way these days. Not outside of grief counseling. Every time he or Nicole would start to reminisce over a Mikey story at dinner or while watching something on tv that reminded them of something he'd said or done, Carol would shut up, shut down, and more often than not leave the room entirely.

So, he talked about his son less and less. Until he barely spoke of him at all, just to keep the peace.

Maybe that had been a mistake.

Maybe he needed to talk more, not less. Maybe they all did. Remembering Mikey with love and fondness, and even some gentle roasting for the not-so-perfect things he'd done, rather than burying his memory along with his body.

Cooper shifted restlessly in his arms. Taking the hint, he started walking again.

And talking.

"Mikey might have been a whiz at building and repairing things, but you know what he was absolutely terrible at? Cooking. Couldn't get the hang of it no matter how hard he tried. He could follow a recipe to the letter, and it would still somehow come out tasting awful. And yet every year for Mother's Day he'd insist on making his mom breakfast in bed. And every year she choked down probably the worst meal in the history of food with a smile."

He glanced down at the pup.

Its eyes were finally starting to droop, so he kept going.

"I asked her once how she could do it. Eat something so bad, right down to the last bite, and do it with such honest happiness. You know what she said? That the only thing she could taste on the plate was love. And love was worth any sacrifice. Even indigestion."

Laughter, warm and healing, bubbled up.

"It may have been made with love, but I was still glad when he just got me a new tool when Father's Day rolled around every year. What that boy did to bacon was criminal. But he kept trying, I'll give him that. He never gave up on something he set his mind to doing. No matter how hard, no matter how long. He stuck with it. He wasn't afraid of trying and failing, only of not giving it his best shot."

Another glance.

Eyes almost shut now.

Come on, pal. Fall asleep already before my arms do.

For a little dude, this chonker was freaking solid. He might not be the alpha of the litter, but he'd probably end up the biggest.

"He was tenacious, our Mikey. And fearless. Which is probably why he was such a good medic. He'd have to be both, running out under fire to help treat the wounded and get them to safety. He saved so many people over the years. Not that he ever told us about it. But his lieutenant, he said it in the letter he wrote after...after."

He cleared his throat.

"It wasn't an email, either, but an honest-to-god handwritten letter. Telling us how much Mikey meant to the men he served with. To him. As a soldier, and as a friend. And about how many times Mikey had gone into harm's way to save his men. Sometimes against some really bad odds."

Until he'd played those odds once too often.

And lost.

He still managed to save three severely wounded soldiers that day. Men who'd made it out alive after they were ambushed because of his bravery. The same three men—Cooper, Bailey, and Samson—three of the puppies in Sadie's litter had been named for.

To honor Mikey's sacrifice.

The same puppies headed to the non-profit foundation, Another Step Forward, to be trained as service dogs to help injured soldiers lead easier lives.

To honor his legacy.

Both were Nicole's ideas. As were the letters she wrote to accompany each of those pups after they graduated from the program in about two years. Letters to be given to the wounded vets they'd be paired with.

Telling them about Mikey.

Something no doubt inspired by the letter from Mikey's platoon leader, which he knew she'd made a copy of for herself. He wasn't sure if she took comfort from rereading the man's words, or if it was one final connection to her brother she couldn't let go of.

A connection she'd wanted to ensure lived on through her own letters.

And maybe...maybe she just needed to talk to someone about him, since he and Carol had all but shut down that possibility at home.

His guilt at that thought lined up perfectly with the bottle of whiskey as his rambling circuit of the kitchen led him full circle back to the counter where it sat.

Waiting.

Beckoning.

He stopped, but rather than reach for the glass of amber oblivion, he opened the drawer below it instead. The one where Carol had shoved Nicole's letters after he'd given them to her to read after he had. He wasn't sure if she ever did.

He was betting on not.

The purple envelopes—his daughter's obsessive color of choice for everything these days—stood out against the usual odds-and-ends inhabiting every junk drawer across America. Stray rubber bands. Fast food menus. Birthday candles.

That last hit him like a cold slap.

It was a brand-new box, cellophane wrapping still intact. No doubt bought months ago in anticipation of celebrating of their son's milestone day.

Today.

He swallowed down a groan. Had Carol seen those when she'd tossed the envelopes into the drawer?

Of course she had.

Oh, sweetheart, why didn't you say something? I was standing right there. You could have told me. Leaned on me.

They could have leaned on each other.

But she was still locked in her own bubble of grief, and he'd given up trying to reach her through it. Not wanting to push her too hard, and maybe end up pushing her away.

Or maybe he was just afraid of failing, and giving up had been easier.

Kind of like sneaking into his son's room in the middle of the night had been easier. Avoidance over confrontation. The coward's path out of any difficult situation.

Oh, Mikey. You'd be so disappointed in me.

But not in Nicole. She'd found her own way to push back against the silence. Putting her thoughts and feelings onto paper to share with not just the people who got the dogs, but with him and Carol as well. Making her voice heard without having to speak a word.

He looked at the envelopes with a new appreciation.

Clever girl.

It seemed Mikey wasn't his only child with a tenacious nature.

Or a need to fix things.

His hands itched to pick one up and read it again, but they were full of puppy. Who was finally, thank you God, asleep.

With great care not to jostle and wake him, he carried Cooper downstairs, Sadie following at his heels. She hopped neatly over the board across the doorway to the game room they'd temporarily converted to the puppy den. The one that should have been too high for Cooper to get over.

A mystery solved as he stepped over it himself and nearly tripped on one of the dog toys laying against it on the other side. The black rubber chewing tire wasn't huge. Only around six inches across and three inches thick. But standing on top of it must have given the pup just enough extra height to let him scramble over the board and follow his mother upstairs.

Forget Houdini. Cooper was a little MacGyver in the making.

"You are definitely going to be a handful for your person, pal," he said softly as he laid the pup's boneless body down near one of his siblings. Then stood for a moment listening to the quiet breathing of puppies, the way he used to stand and listen to the kids sleeping when they were babies.

A soft wave of melancholy rolled over him.

This was the last time they'd all be together. Tomorrow Cooper, Bailey, and Samson were going to the service dog foundation. The breeder was coming next week to take the alpha pup as his stud fee. Four more would go to their new homes then as well, with half the money their sale brought in donated to animal shelters.

That was Mikey's doing.

He'd protested when they decided to breed Sadie to help bolster the family vacation fund. Hated the idea of bringing more dogs into the world when there were so many already in need of a loving home. Splitting the profits with the local shelters had been the compromise.

It still amazed him how skilled a negotiator his son had been to get them to agree. But then, he'd always been good at the things he was passionate about.

There was one puppy staying with them this time. A spicy little female they'd named Ginger, who they hoped would keep Sadie company and distract her from the fact her favorite person was never coming home again.

The humans weren't the only ones who loved and missed Mikey.

After putting the tire on the other side of the door to prevent a second escape attempt, he went upstairs. His feet led him back to where the whiskey waited.

He chose the letters instead.

Not that he needed to read them again. His daughter's words had been so special, so incredibly insightful, they were already seared into his memory. But he wanted to see them one last time before they disappeared into strangers' hands tomorrow, just like the puppies.

He opened the top envelope and withdrew the folded sheet of purple stationery inside.

Dear Serviceperson,

First, I want to thank you for your service. If you're reading this, it means that you were wounded in some way and are in need of a service dog, and for that, I'm truly sorry. But if you're reading this, it also means that you're getting one of the dogs that was born to my brother Mikey's dog, Sadie, and for that I'm glad. You see, Mikey was a medic in the Army, and he was killed trying to help some wounded soldiers just a few weeks before he was supposed to come home.

I'm sorry to say I was really angry with my brother when I first heard what he'd done. I guess it's selfish of me to think he should have cared more about keeping himself safe than risking his life for other people. But the more I thought about it, the more I realized there was no way he could have done anything else. Mikey was always the kind of guy everyone could rely on. He was smart, and funny, and the best big brother anyone could ever have. I loved him lots, and I'm going to miss him even more, every single day of my life.

I'm not telling you any of this to make you sad. I just wanted to explain about my brother, and why the dog you're getting is so special. My brother spent the short time he had on this Earth helping others. I can't wish him back to life, but I can wish this: that his generous spirit live on in the love and comfort you receive from your service dog. Take each day you have together as a gift, and maybe once in a while think about Mikey. I know when I do, I'll be picturing him smiling down on you, knowing that his legacy, and Cooper, are in good hands.

Wishing you a happy and fulfilling life,

Nicole

As they had before, his daughter's words brought him to tears. Only now he realized it wasn't from sadness. Or not only sadness. It was also from the love and hope that sang from every line she'd written. Every feeling she'd shared.

Mikey had been loved, and that love would never die, as long as they nurtured it by keeping him alive in their hearts.

Life changed. Went in new directions.

Sometimes you just had to trust in where it was taking you.

He refolded the letter with care. As he placed the envelope on top of the others, each the same except for the puppies' names, he briefly considered leaving it on the counter instead for Carol to see. And immediately rejected the idea.

That would just be one more bit of passive inaction.

No, he'd actually *talk* to her in the morning. About reading the letter. About a lot of things. Maybe it wasn't too late to fix what he'd let stay broken for far too long.

But he did take the box of birthday candles from the drawer before he shut it.

The whiskey went in the cabinet, what was left in his glass down the sink. From now on, his comfort would come from bringing his family back together, not a bottle.

It wouldn't be easy. Might even be painful. And messy. But Carol was right.

Love was worth any sacrifice.

And like Mikey, he wouldn't stop trying, no matter how hard it might get to fix things. He'd see it through to the bitter end.

No matter what, he'd do his son's legacy proud.

Chapter 1

"Oh, please tell me he's here to interview for the job!"

With a frown, Camille followed her friend's hungry gaze down the hallway they'd stopped in to talk about the upcoming Field Day. *Wowza.* The man walking across the elementary school lobby toward the glass front doors was tall, lean, and had a face just rough enough to keep him from being pretty.

And he definitely wasn't there to interview for the first-grade teaching position needing to be filled for the fall term. She'd remember *that* resume crossing her desk.

"Sorry to disappoint you, but no."

Joelyn sighed. "Too bad."

Shooting her a sidelong glance, Cam said, "You're a happily married woman."

"Doesn't mean I can't still enjoy the scenery."

As much as she wanted to argue, she really couldn't. The man was certainly easy on the eyes, with a little kick of something extra. Something dark and spicy that made a woman's libido sit up and take notice. Eighty-year-old women probably stopped and stared in the grocery store when he walked by, it was *that* potent.

The thought brought a grin twitching to her lips. Until the guy turned and bent over slightly to listen to what the little girl walking beside him said.

No.

Amusement was stripped away as alarm surged in to take its place. Pink top, pink backpack, pink sneakers. Carly Aiken. A first-grader who'd had an unholy obsession with the color all year.

And she was about to walk out the front door of the school with a total stranger.

Not on my watch.

"Excuse me, sir!"

Cam broke into a fast walk toward the two of them that was just short of a run, the words of her predecessor ringing in her head despite the circumstances. *Principals do not run through the hallway no matter the provocation. They remain calm and dignified at all times. It instills confidence in those around you.* "Wait a moment, please. I'd like to talk to you."

She knew he heard her, because his head swiveled in her direction even as he was scooping Carly up in his arms. Alarm gave way to fury as he looked around wildly before bolting toward the door.

Screw dignified.

She broke into a run, yelling over her shoulder to Joelyn, "Call the police!"

Thankful for her sensible low-heeled shoes, she still slid a little on the polished tile floor before she hit the push bar on the heavy glass-and-metal door and shoved.

Only to come to a stumbling halt a few steps outside.

She'd expected to have to chase the bastard through the parking lot to his car.

Instead, he was hunkered down at the side of the cement walkway next to the child he'd just snatched, rubbing her back as she retched into the flowerbed. He glanced at Cam over his shoulder, acknowledging her presence, then went back to murmuring words of comfort as a second round of retching ensued.

What the...

Joelyn came barreling through the door, cell phone in hand. "They're on their..." She took in the tableau with the same confusion on her face Cam was experiencing.

It wouldn't stop Cam from doing her job, though, and that was ensuring Carly's safety.

"Sir, I need you to step away from the child right now."

She bristled when he shot her an exasperated look and ignored her order, instead slipping the straps of the pink Disney princess backpack down and off Carly's hunched back. "Sir, get your hands off her and step away."

The guy reached into a pocket in his khaki cargo pants, making her heart trip into high gear. But rather than a weapon, he pulled out a pack of tissues, peeled one off, and handed it to Carly. "Here you go, sweetheart."

Only after Carly had taken it to wipe her mouth did he finally stand up.

And up.

She swallowed as she took in just how large and intimidating the guy actually was. A good six inches taller than her own five-eight, with arms under a dark t-shirt that looked like they could crush boulders into dust with one flex.

Or middle-aged principals.

Good lord, had she really thought for even a second he was sexy? More like dangerous. If he tried to grab Carly and run again, she wasn't sure even she and Joelyn both jumping on him would be enough to stop him. Or even slow him down.

She squared her shoulders. It didn't matter. She'd do whatever she needed to. No one was hurting one of her kids.

As she was mentally calculating the best way to get Carly away to safety, the girl stood up, wrapped her thin arms around the guy's right leg, and looked up at him, sniffling. "I'm sorry, Daddy."

Everything froze.

Daddy?

Glacial eyes the blue of the deep sea warmed as he looked from Cam down to Carly, one large hand stroking over her now lopsided blonde ponytail. "It's okay, peanut. Everyone gets sick sometimes."

"But...I made a mess." Her lower lip quivering, she looked on the verge of tears. That was when Cam noticed the black t-shirt the guy was wearing had indeed been christened with a swath of vomit across the front.

"What, this?" He made a *pfft* sound. "That's nothing compared to some of the puke-ups you had as a baby."

"Daddy, eww."

"It was like a firehose, just, *everywhere*." He gestured with his hands in an exaggerated spraying motion.

"Dad-*dy*!" She sounded scandalized, but was giggling at the same time. Which, judging by the loosening of tension around his eyes, was what he'd been going for.

He gave Carly a smile and a wink, which earned another giggle. Only then did he turn his attention to Cam.

The force of his complete focus tingled like it was full-body contact.

Oh boy.

She was right. This man was dangerous.

Just not in the way she'd originally thought.

Shaking herself free of the sensation, she asked, "You're Carly's father?"

"Yes, ma'am. Judd Aiken." He reached out a hand, then reconsidered as they both saw it wasn't exactly clean. He gave her a quick grin instead.

She didn't return it.

The last name was right, but all she knew about Carly and Boone Aiken's father was that he was divorced from their mother, Dana, and lived in another state. There were usually good reasons for that. None of which left her comfortable about him leaving school grounds with Carly until she cleared a few things up.

Before she could ask her first question, Carly tugged on her father's pants—one thing Cam was willing to concede was the relationship, especially when faced with their almost identical blue gazes. "Daddy, my mouth tastes gross."

"I have some water in the truck."

Cam took a protective step closer. If he thought he was going anywhere with that child before she got some answers, he was sadly mistaken. He gave her another of those exasperated looks. Only this time tinged with a hint of respect.

"Carly, honey, stay here with your teachers while I go get it, okay?"

"Miss Richards isn't a teacher, Daddy," Carly said in what was probably supposed to be a whisper. "She's the *principal*."

"Ah." Lines crinkled the tanned skin around his eyes as he grinned, showing he'd spent a lot of his life in the sun. "Then you stay with Miss Richards and..." He shot an inquiring smile at Joelyn, who immediately appeared flustered.

"Joelyn. Baker. Mrs. Baker. And I *am* a teacher. Second grade."

Cam practically rolled her eyes at her friend's giddy reaction. "Jo."

To his credit, if Judd was amused, he didn't let it show. He just palmed a big hand—the clean one—over Carly's little head again and said, "Be right back."

As soon as he walked away, Cam moved to the girl and led her a few steps from the pungent fragrance of vomit wafting from the daisies. "Carly, honey, you know you're not supposed to leave school with anyone except your mom or your grandparents."

"And my dad. Mrs. Ryan said so." Her face set itself in stubborn lines that only increased the resemblance to her father.

Cam looked over at Joelyn, who was already typing on her phone with a muttered "Checking." If the school nurse had released Carly into her father's care, he must have been on the approved pick-up list.

And Cam had just made a huge mistake.

Sure enough, when Joelyn's phone dinged and she read the text, her expression confirmed what Cam already suspected. She returned her friend's "oops" face with one of her own.

"Cooper!"

The girl's excited squeal brought Cam's attention back to her, and the massive golden retriever heading their way. The dog made a beeline for Carly before Cam could intervene, plopping its furry butt down with a swish of its feathery tail. It accepted the exuberant hug Carly wrapped around its neck with what could only be called stoic patience.

That didn't stop Cam's hands from itching to snatch the little girl away.

When Carly released the dog, Cam noticed for the first time the bottle of water held delicately in its jaws. When Carly said, "Release," it let her take it from him, tongue lolling as she patted his head and thanked him and called him a good boy.

"Cute trick," Joelyn said.

"It's not a trick," Carly said in a very matter-of-fact tone. "It's a skill. He has lots of them."

Joelyn couldn't hide a smile. "Impressive skill, then."

It was. The dog was clearly well trained.

That didn't mean having it off-leash on school grounds was okay.

She turned to tell the dog's owner exactly that, but he wasn't there. Then she saw him by the dirt-streaked white quad-cab truck in one of the nearby visitor parking spots. The driver's side rear door was wide open as he did something in the back seat.

An apology was in order, and she'd prefer doing it in private in case things got unpleasant. She looked at Joelyn and tipped her head toward Carly in an unspoken request to keep an eye on the girl. Then she squared her shoulders and marched over to the truck.

Admitting she was wrong wasn't something she had to do very often. Which meant she only hated it even more when she did. But she'd made an assumption. An incorrect one, as it turned out. Now it was time to pay the piper.

"Mr. Aiken, I just wanted to—"

Everything else stuck in her throat as she stepped around the open door and saw what he'd been doing behind its shelter. The soiled tee had been stripped off, and he was using a small terry towel dampened from the bottle of water in his other hand to clean off whatever vomit had soaked through to his skin.

And there was a lot of skin.

Deep golden brown, from the slightly loose waist of khaki cargo pants that dipped below his belly button, all the way up his ripped abs to his muscular pecs and broad shoulders. Dark and even enough to make her rethink her assumption of a tan in favor of a natural skin tone like her own, courtesy of her Vietnamese mother.

Judd froze for a second as well, then continued cleaning himself off with short, efficient movements. "Yes?"

"I'm so sorry." She spun, giving him her back. Partly to give him his privacy. But also because heat from an embarrassed blush was flaming along her cheekbones as she realized just how long she'd been staring at his naked chest.

Brilliant, Camille.

Gawking at a student's father. Could she be any less professional?

"It's not a problem." Thankfully, there was no amusement in his voice, which would have only made everything worse.

"I, ah, okay." If he was willing to ignore it, so could she. "I wanted to apologize, but it can wait until you're, um, finished." And dressed. She wasn't sure she'd be able to form coherent sentences with the distraction of all that nakedy goodness staring her in the face, unprofessional or not.

She was only human, after all.

"I'm done," he said a minute later.

She turned slowly in case his idea of being done and hers differed, and breathed a silent sigh of relief. His chest was now covered by a gray t-shirt. Although the sleeves were cut off, leaving his muscular arms on full display. His biceps bunched and flexed as he zipped the soiled tee into a plastic bag and shoved it in the backpack on the seat, which was probably where he'd also gotten the towel and bottles of water.

Biting her lip, she forced herself not to drool.

"I don't see what you have to apologize for," he said, clearly unaware of the riot he was causing with her hormones. "You were just doing your job, looking out for the welfare and safety of one of your students." He zipped the backpack closed and turned to face her. "I should be thanking you for being vigilant on behalf of my kid."

Wow. Totally not what she'd been expecting.

"That's...thank you. Parents aren't usually so understanding when it comes to things like being chased down and spoken to like a criminal." She gave a self-deprecating smile, going for a little levity.

Dark shadows crossed his expression.

"Most parents don't know the kinds of bad people there are in the world." He visibly shook himself from his thoughts and offered a rueful grin. "Besides, in hindsight, I guess my actions could be interpreted as somewhat questionable."

"You mean picking up a child and running out the door with her? Yes, a little bit."

"In my defense, I was going to wait and talk to you. But Carly said she was about to throw up and I didn't see any bathrooms or garbage cans nearby, so I figured outside was the next best choice."

Ah, so that explained the wild-eyed look he'd given around the lobby right before bolting for the door. "Context really is key. But I still need to apologize. It's my job to know what's going on in my school. I should have been aware you'd been added to the emergency pick-up list."

"I wasn't. I mean, not until today. It was more of a last-minute thing when the nurse called Dana about Carly having a stomachache. She asked me to come pick her up since her folks are out of town and she didn't want to lose a day's pay if she didn't have to. She called the nurse back to okay it."

"There's only a week left of school, but you might want to have her add you to the authorized list so you don't have any problems in the future. If you're going to be here that long, I mean," she added, realizing she was making assumptions again. He could very well be there for only a few days' visit.

"I'll be here for a while. I'll mention it to her, thanks."

There was no reason she should be happy at that news.

Professional, Cam.

"She can call the office anytime."

"Thanks. So, is it okay for me to take Carly home now?"

"Yes, of course." Cam glanced over to where the girl was showing off some of the dog's other tricks—*skills*—to Joelyn. "That's a very large dog you have."

Judd's hand froze on the truck door for a split second before he closed it. "Yeah, Coop's big for his breed. But a real gentle giant. You don't have to worry about him with Carly. He loves the kids."

"Still, he shouldn't be unleashed in public."

A muscled ticked in his jaw. "It won't happen again, ma'am." He started walking, then stopped, the stiff line of tension easing somewhat from his body. "Sorry. You're right. He's just so dam...darn smart I sometimes forget he's still a dog."

She didn't let it show, but that "ma'am" annoyed her more than the snippy attitude had. At forty-two, she knew she was at least a few years older than he was. She just hadn't realized how much it would bother her *he'd* noticed it, too.

Which it shouldn't have. At all.

Scrambling for another, safer topic as they walked, she said, "That was good before, getting Carly to laugh. Kids, especially little girls, can get pretty upset about throwing up."

The lightning grin she was already coming to recognize flashed across his lips. "It was just the god's honest truth. You know what baby projectile vomiting is like."

She barely held back a flinch from the blow his words landed.

So much for a safer topic.

"Yes. I think every one of my nieces and nephews has gotten me at least once." She managed what she hoped was a credible smile, but by the pensive look he gave her, it might have fallen flat. Thankfully, he turned his attention to his daughter, leaving Cam feeling like she'd dodged a rather large landmine.

"Hey, peanut, how's your tummy doing?"

"It's still all gurgley, but I don't feel so sick anymore."

"Well, that's good. You ready to go home?"

"Uh-huh." She slipped a tiny hand into his.

It was a simple gesture. One she saw play out dozens of times every single day. But for some reason, this time it twisted something painful in her chest. Hard enough she had to look away from the adorable picture the little girl and big man made together.

And saw the Sheriff's car pulling up to the curb a few yards away.

Son of a biscuit.

"Oh, no. Jo..." She looked at her friend, who gave her wide eyes back.

"I called and told them it was a false alarm, I swear."

They all watched as Uriah Dixon unfolded his large frame from behind the wheel of the white Ford Explorer. It took a moment, because there was a lot of him to unfold. At close to six-foot-six, he was the tallest man Cam had ever met, and the rest of him matched the height. Despite crossing the half-century mark earlier that year, celebrated at a big to-do thrown by his wife and attended by probably half the town, he was still in excellent shape.

Or so she'd thought until she had Judd Aiken's chiseled physique to compare him to.

She glanced over at Judd to apologize for what was sure to be an additional delay in getting his daughter home, but the words never left her mouth. The charming, doting father of a few seconds ago was gone, replaced by a steely-eyed stranger.

He hadn't moved an inch, but she could sense the difference in him somehow. The tension. The watchfulness. It was probably her imagination, but he seemed like a coiled spring ready to launch at a moment's notice.

Uriah took the time to settle his cowboy hat just so, covering the gleam of his shaved ebony dome from the noonday sun, before walking toward them. It was difficult to tell with the mirrored sunglasses, but he appeared as focused on Judd as Judd was on him.

Oh boy, just what they didn't need.

Two alpha males butting heads for no good reason.

She smiled and started talking before he reached their little group, hoping to diffuse the situation. "Everything's fine here, Sheriff. It was a simple misunderstanding about who was picking Carly up when she had a stomachache. They should have called to let you know not to bother coming."

"Just doing my job, Miss Camille." His deep baritone rumbled so low it was almost a growl. "Besides, I'm always happy for an excuse to come check in with our littlest citizens." He took off his sunglasses and smiled down at Carly, who was leaning against her father's right leg again. She returned it with a shy one of her own.

The warm smile turned cold and professional when Uriah shifted his attention back to Judd. "And you are?"

"Judd Aiken. Carly's father."

"Is that right." He looked over at Cam as though for confirmation. She nodded. "Well, then, you wouldn't mind showing me some ID, now would you, son?"

Oh, for the love of Pete.

"Uriah, is that really necessary?" she asked, even as Judd pulled out his wallet and flipped it open.

"Just doing my job," he said again.

He took the offered wallet and examined the driver's license under the plastic window. "Coronado, California, huh?" He shot an assessing look at Judd as though that meant something. When Judd continued giving him the same bland expression he'd been wearing, Uriah grunted and handed the wallet back. "In town for long?"

"Daddy's staying the whole summer!" Carly's excited announcement had Uriah giving her another broad smile. "We're gonna go to the park, and the movies, and ride our bikes, and play dolls, and everything!"

Judd's expression finally broke, turning soft as he looked down at his daughter. "You bet, peanut. We sure are."

"Is that right. So, I guess that means you're staying with the family while you're here?"

"No. I'm renting a place."

Uriah tipped his hat back an inch with his thumb. "Well, now, rentals aren't exactly thick on the ground here in Slow Creek. Where'd you manage to find one to rack out in?"

Pressing his lips into a tight line was the only indication Judd was unhappy about answering. "Mr. Garvey is letting me stay in the camper on his place."

"That rusty piece of junk?" Uriah's eyebrows shot up in surprise. "I don't think it's moved from next to that old barn of his in years."

Cam vaguely remembered the white and green camper Old Man Garvey used to tow behind his pickup when he took his horses on the rodeo circuit when she was a kid. "His camper has to be thirty years old, at least. Probably closer to forty, since it was pretty beat up even back when I remember him still using it."

Judd shrugged. "I've lived in worse."

Uriah gave a significant glance down at Carly, as though questioning the wisdom of bringing a child into that environment.

Judd's lips compressed even tighter. "It's not pretty, but it's clean. And safe. I made sure of it." Looking down, he palmed his hand over his daughter's head like she was the most precious thing in the world to him. "Besides, it's only temporary, until I can find something else." His lips twisted into a mocking grin. "Like you said, rentals aren't exactly thick on the ground here. Beggars can't be choosers."

His dark eyes narrowing slightly said Uriah hadn't liked having his words thrown back at him. "I'll keep my eyes open for you."

It sounded more of a threat than a promise of help. But if Judd took it that way, he didn't let it show.

"I'd like to take my daughter home now, Sheriff, if that's okay with you." It was worded as a question, but it didn't sound like one.

Cam jumped in before Uriah could take offense.

"Yes, I think we've kept her standing out here in the sun for too long as it is." She gave Uriah the kind of look students usually wilted under when she turned it on them. "Wouldn't you agree, Sheriff?"

He didn't exactly wilt, but after a second he tipped his head as though conceding. He smiled down at Carly. "You feel better now, Carly." He gave Judd a long look, then said, "Ginger ale is good for settling their tummies. Soda crackers, too."

"Thanks." Judd nodded to Cam and Joelyn. "Ladies."

Cam said, "I'll let Boone know why his sister won't be on the bus after school, so he doesn't get worried."

"Thank you." He gave her another of those lightning grins she felt all the way to her toes. With a hand gesture, he collected the dog, who had been sitting so quietly she'd forgotten it was there. It took up a position at his left side, heeling perfectly, while Carly walked hand-in-hand with him on his right.

The girl looked back over her shoulder and waved.

Cam returned it with a smile.

"I better get back in. The bell's about to ring for lunch." Joelyn gave Uriah a smile. "Nice seeing you, Sheriff."

"You too, Miss Joelyn."

Cam waited until her friend was inside to ask, "Honestly, Uriah, was all that really necessary?"

"Camille, I will *always* do whatever it takes to make sure these kids are safe. There are too many stories in the news these days about bad people doing bad things in schools. It would be foolish to think it could never happen here in Slow Creek."

A chill skated up her spine at his grim words. The shootings that had become much too commonplace for a sane society were her worst nightmare. "Funny, Judd said almost the same thing." She didn't realize her slip of the tongue in using his first name until Uriah gave her a speculative look.

"Well now, I suppose he probably would." He glanced at the truck, where the man in question was buckling Carly into her booster seat. "You just be careful, now, y'hear?" He touched two fingers to his hat and lumbered away before she could ask what he'd meant by his comment about Judd.

Mr. Aiken, she reminded herself as she gave one last look in his direction before heading inside. She always addressed parents formally, even in her head, unless she had a personal relationship with them. And even then, she didn't use first names for anything related to school issues. It helped establish the proper roles they each had to play.

Especially when it came to things like discipline. Which, for the kids of a friend, could get a little sticky. But for some reason, this particular parent was short-circuiting her usual automatic compartmentalization.

Probably because he was the only one whose naked chest she'd ever ogled.

Closing her office door, she gave a little laugh at herself and her pathetic libido. "You are in drastic need of a date, woman."

Unfortunately for her, single, interesting men near her own age were as thin on the ground in Slow Creek as rentals apparently were.

It had been a good four months since she'd even been out to dinner with someone. Twice that since she'd been interested enough to go out more than once with the same man. And as for the last time she'd been intimate...well, it was so far back she'd need a search party to find the actual date.

Letting her guard down enough to get naked and vulnerable with a man after her divorce had so far been nearly impossible.

After sending a message to Boone Aiken's third-grade teacher to let him know his sister had gone home sick, Cam thought about Uriah's odd reaction to where Ju—Mr. Aiken was from. Out of curiosity, she Googled Coronado, California.

Tons of hits came up. It was a small city on a peninsula in San Diego Bay boasting excellent beaches, surfing, a golf course, shops, bars, and the famous Hotel del Coronado. All the things a tourist could want.

It also was home to the west coast Navy SEAL Teams.

She sat back in her chair with a surprised huff as a few things clicked into place. The physique. The watchfulness. The coiled strength.

Holy cats.

She'd been right the first time. Judd Aiken was one very dangerous man.

Chapter 2

CLOSING THE BEDROOM DOOR behind him with a soft *snick*, Judd breathed a sigh of relief. It had taken longer than expected to get Carly changed, into bed, and fed some ginger ale and saltines. But as soon as her head hit the pillow, it had been lights out.

Thank God for small miracles.

It had been more than three years since he'd had to deal with one of the kids being sick. He didn't enjoy it now any more than he had then. He was a man used to being able to fix things. See the problem, work the problem.

Little girls with tummy aches didn't fit that model, though. And his inability to make things better left him feeling both inadequate and frustrated.

Walking to the kitchen, he tried not to notice the shabbiness of his ex-wife's small two-bedroom house, but it was hard. It was clean, at least, or as clean as a home with two small children could ever be. But beyond the kid clutter was an air of general neglect that reached back a lot further than the two years Dana had been living there. Things she should have insisted the land-lord take care of before moving in.

Then again, as the sheriff had so accurately pointed out, rentals didn't exactly come up all that often in this town. And after a year of living with her parents, Dana had been desperate enough to get into her own place that she'd settled for a two-bedroom instead of three, rationalizing the kids wouldn't need their own rooms until they were a little older.

Although judging by the explosion of pink everywhere in the small bedroom he'd just left, he had a feeling that time might come a lot sooner than she'd planned. Boone loved his sister to pieces, but no eight-year-old boy wanted posters of mermaids and unicorns on his walls, even if they were on "her side" of the room.

Floorboards creaked under the faded, worn linoleum in the kitchen as he walked to the sink. Pausing, he carefully rocked his weight back and forth on one spot a few times. It wailed and groaned like a ghost in a graveyard, but at least it didn't feel rotted through.

Yet.

Satisfied no one would put their foot through the floor in the immediate future, he grabbed a glass from the drying rack on the counter. He filled it from the dripping faucet and sank onto a slightly off-balance wooden chair at the kitchen table with a sigh of relief.

For the first time since he'd gotten Dana's pleading call to pick up Carly from school, the tension knot in his gut finally eased. She was home and she was safe. Mission accomplished.

Not without a few small hiccups along the way, though.

Well, one small one.

And one great big one named Uriah Dixon.

Judd wasn't sure what to make of the man. He'd come off almost like a caricature of what someone might expect a small-town hick of a sheriff to be, with his big gun, big hat, and slow drawling midwestern accent.

But none of those affectations could hide the sharp intelligence that shone from the man's hawk-like eyes, or the balanced way he held his huge body. If he didn't have some military service in his background, Judd would be very surprised.

He'd also be surprised if the man didn't follow up on his threat—and it had been one—to keep his eye on Judd while he was in town. Not that he was going to be doing anything wrong. But knowing his every move might be weighed and judged by the one person who actually had the authority to make his time here difficult didn't sit well. Especially since he'd done nothing to warrant the attention.

Except be an outsider, of course.

Small towns were alike all over the world, whether it was in northeast Kansas or northeast Afghanistan. Anyone who hadn't lived their entire lives there would always be viewed with a great deal of suspicion and mistrust.

With a soft whine, Cooper laid his furry muzzle on Judd's thigh. He dropped a hand onto the dog's head and stroked the silky fur, the simple motion soothing his growing agitation. It might not be his primary training, but Coop was still a hell of a barometer when it came to Judd's moods. Knowing exactly when he needed a little distraction whenever his thoughts turned too far inward.

Which was much too often these last few months.

Cooper whined again before moving away, only to come back with the ratty tennis ball he'd brought into the house from the truck. He dropped it in Judd's lap and sat, tongue lolling in a happy dog smile.

He had no choice but to laugh. As far as Cooper was concerned, there was nothing a good game of fetch couldn't fix.

"Sorry, bud, not now. But I promise we'll play when we get home." It was one of the few good things about his temporary living arrangement. With the horses long gone from Garvey's place, there was plenty of open pasture space where he could let Cooper run to his heart's content. He was a big dog, close to eighty pounds of fur and muscle, but he was damned fast for his size. And he loved to chase things.

All things.

Balls, frisbees, squirrels. Anything and everything that moved. Which meant he'd need a yard, or at the least a nearby dog park, wherever they ended up.

Something else to keep in mind while weighing his options about the future.

Which right now was a great, big ball of unknown.

The dog was still watching him with anticipation, so he tossed the tennis ball from hand-to-hand and gave in. "Okay, just one. Ready?"

Cooper danced back a few steps, body quivering, eyes laser-focused on the target. There wasn't a lot of room in the tiny kitchen, so he was careful to bounce it with minimal force, rebounding it to about six feet in the air.

"Get it!"

The shallow bounce wasn't much of a challenge to catch, but that didn't stop Cooper from prancing over with his prize as though he'd done the impossible. Judd laughed again, but refused to take the ball.

"Later, Coop. If we break anything, Dana will have both our heads."

Though she didn't really need an excuse to get annoyed where Cooper was concerned. She'd never been a dog lover, and took every opportunity to express her displeasure when he brought the dog with him to see the kids.

He's too big, he sheds everywhere, he could pee on the floor.

It had only been two weeks, and she'd found a new complaint each time he'd been over. Unfortunately for her, the kids had fallen in insta-love with the hairy mutt, so she'd given in to his presence, albeit with ill grace.

Not that he would have considered leaving the dog behind, even if she hadn't. They were a team. With very few exceptions, wherever Judd went, so did Cooper.

Uttering a resigned groan, Cooper sank to the ground at almost the same time Judd's phone rang. A quick look at the screen had him wondering if there was a secret nanny cam hidden in the house he wasn't aware of. "Hey, Dana."

"How's Carly?"

He checked his annoyance and let the lack of greeting go. "She's sleeping."

"Has she been sick again? Is she running a fever?"

"No, and no. She's exactly the same as when you talked to her half an hour ago." A knot of something angry lodged in his gut. "I may be a little out of practice, but I am capable of taking care of my daughter."

"I know, I know. Sorry. It's just...I don't like not being there when she needs me."

Now you know how I've felt for the last three years.

He pushed the bitter sentiment back down into the deep place he kept all the pain and disappointment about his marriage and divorce. Both had been contentious, but the one thing they'd always agreed on in everything was the kids came first.

Which was why he'd let her carve his heart out by taking them fourteen hundred miles away after they split up.

"Well, you'll be home in"—he checked the time—"forty minutes. You can see for yourself she's fine."

"Actually..."

He waited, knowing there would be a request attached to that drawn-out word. There always was.

"I have the chance to pick up a supper shift here at the diner, so I was hoping you'd be able to stay and be there when Boone gets off the bus, and maybe make them something to eat, if it's not too much trouble."

Too much trouble. Like he was a stranger.

Although he supposed in some ways, he was.

"It's fine, Dana. I'm happy to spend time with my kids. That's why I'm here." The heavy silence from the phone echoed the same uncertainty she expressed when he'd first told her his plan to come spend the summer in Slow Creek.

"Okay," she said finally, sounding more resigned than relieved. "Thank you. I should be home around seven, seven-thirty the latest, so you don't have to worry about getting them to bed. And if Carly doesn't want to eat anything, don't try to make her. She'll probably just throw it up again, anyway. Oh, and if Boone's feeling sick when he gets home—"

"Dana, I've got this."

"Of course you do." The muttered comment didn't sound flattering.

After listening to her go over what was in the house for the kids' supper and what they could and couldn't watch on tv, he dropped the phone on the table and cupped a hand around his neck, massaging the tension knot beginning to build there.

He'd forgotten how easily his ex could make him feel like he was nothing more than a glorified babysitter. As if he hadn't helped raise their kids during the five years before their marriage disintegrated.

Granted, he might not have always been there as much as he wanted to be. Or that she wanted him to be. But that was the way his job worked. She'd known what she was getting into by marrying someone on the Teams.

In fact, it had been her main objective in going to the local watering hole he and a lot of the other guys frequented. To bag herself a SEAL. He hadn't figured it out until after Boone was born, but any of them would have suited her purpose that night. He'd just ended up being the lucky guy she locked onto.

Although unlucky might be more accurate.

Even so, he wouldn't trade having his kids for anything in the world. They were worth every second of grief and frustration he'd gone through with Dana. These past eighteen months without seeing them except via Zoom had been absolute hell.

For more than one reason.

Packing that thought away, he whistled up Cooper. After a quick check on Carly, who was still sleeping the sleep of the boneless dead as only kids could, he took the dog into the postage-stamp sized backyard. By the time Coop had sniffed the perimeter of the fence twice and picked a spot that met his approval to pee on, the warm humid afternoon air had settled like a suffocating wool blanket over Judd's entire body.

After only a few tosses of the ball for Cooper to chase, it was like his body had sprung a leak. Damn, since when was Kansas supposed to feel like the freaking Amazon?

Pulling the hem of his t-shirt up to wipe his damp face brought to mind the expression on the principal's face when he unwittingly flashed his abs at her. He hadn't meant to. It was why he'd ducked behind the truck door in the first place.

But the flicker of naked admiration in her gaze before turning away had sparked something. Something he'd worried had been buried so deep it might as well have been gone forever.

Thank God.

That zing of arousal had taken him off-guard, though. And made him glad she'd done an about face, because he wasn't sure his body wouldn't have given him away, loose pants or not. And it wasn't just her interest that had done it.

Camille Richards was one incredibly attractive woman.

Deep chocolate eyes with a subtle tilt. Sleek brown hair that reminded him of polished mahogany. And that voice...the slightly husky undertone could make a man think of late nights and aged whiskey.

As a whole, she had definitely sparked his interest.

With a thick line of sweat soaking the waistband of his skivvies, he whistled Cooper inside. There was no air conditioning, only a small table-top fan on the counter that did nothing but blow the humid air around a little when he turned it on. He needed to get out of his cargo pants and into a pair of shorts before he melted entirely. And he had to take care of the sweat that had already soaked him before it became an issue.

Which presented its own set of problems.

After checking in on Carly, he ducked out quick to the truck for the backpack that went everywhere with him these days. Another kid check, then he took the go-bag into the lone bathroom, which smelled of hairspray and baby shampoo. One brought on a surprising rush of nostalgia, while the other made him sneeze.

With the door open a few inches so he could hear if Carly woke up, he dropped his pants and sat on the closed toilet lid, easing them over the sneaker attached to the foot of his prosthetic left leg. The other pant leg he kept hooked around his right ankle in case he needed to yank them back up fast.

Depressing the one-way valve, the suction holding the socket in place hissed as it loosened. With a careful tug, he pulled the carbon-fiber limb off and propped it against the tub out of the way.

Next off was the sock that aided in keeping everything snug and comfortable. As he'd expected, it was damp and would need to be changed out.

Finally, he peeled off the silicone liner that protected his skin from the inner shell of the socket. Inverting the liner, he carefully patted it dry with a clean towel from his pack before doing the same to his residual limb.

He'd been warned, but it still surprised him how much sweat could accumulate between the liner and his skin in such a short amount of time.

Somewhere past the cracked bathroom door, a phone rang. It took a second to realize it was his, and he'd left it sitting on the kitchen table.

"Shit."

If it was Dana calling back again, she'd panic if he didn't answer and probably call out the police *and* fire departments. Putting all his pieces back on would take too long. And trying to answer the phone as he was would mean hopping halfway across the house since he didn't have his crutches.

Not exactly the introduction he wanted to give his daughter to his legless state if she should wake up.

"Cooper!" It only took a few seconds for the door to be nudged open by the retriever's nose. "Cooper, get the phone. Get the phone, bud."

He was off like a shot. Nails scrabbled on wood, then linoleum. There was a soft thump, probably as he put his front paws up on the chair whose legs weren't quite even, then the click of his return trip.

Even knowing the dog was trained to do exactly this task, it still amazed him after all these months when Coop pranced into the bathroom, head high like a conquering hero, the still-ringing cellphone held with delicate care in his mouth.

Thank God for OtterBox covers.

"Release." Taking the phone, which was surprisingly dry, he rubbed the dog's head with a rushed but enthusiastic "good boy!" before answering with a barked "I'm here. What?"

The low chuckle on the other end of the line told him it wasn't Dana after all. "There's that charming personality I've missed so much."

A wry grin curved his lips at the sound of his friend's voice. "Fuck you."

"Only if you buy me dinner first."

"Dinner, hell. You can be had for nachos and a dollar beer."

"What can I say, bruh? I like to spread the good times around."

The familiar banter relaxed something inside enough for him to laugh. Kevin Gillman had been his number three on the Team, not to mention his best friend. The native Californian gave off typical surfer dude vibes. Only a lucky few got to know the steel core under the shaggy sun-streaked hair and pooka shell necklace.

"It's good to hear your voice, man."

"You, too." Gil paused. "So, how are things going up there?"

Judd gave another laugh, this one a little less amused. "I'm sitting in my ex's bathroom with my pants around my ankle, drying off my stump. What do you think?"

There was another pause. "If that's some kind of code for post-sex cleanup, that's way too much info, dude, but it's good to know you're back in business."

Only Gil could twist a simple comment into something perverted without even trying. It was his superpower.

"I didn't have sex with Dana, you ass."

"Well, that's a relief. So, you already found someone new to bang the drum with? Outstanding."

An image of the sweet little principal's face popped unbidden into his head. For about a second. All it took was one look down at his ruined leg for reality to reassert itself. As interested as she'd seemed when faced with his naked upper body, she'd never have the same reaction if she caught a peek of his lower half.

He pushed her firmly out of his mind. "I'm not here to get laid. I'm here to spend time with my kids, and figure out what comes next."

"Yeah, about that."

Judd waited, but he had a feeling he knew what his friend was going to say.

"Zee was sniffing around again. Asking about you. Where you were, what you were doing, how he could get in touch with you since you didn't answer his calls."

"What did you tell him?" Although he could probably guess.

A familiar snort confirmed his suspicions. "What do you think? I told him to go pound salt in someone else's sandbox, you weren't interested." There was an uncertain hesitation. "You're not, right?"

"Hell, no." But the reply was more automatic than convincing. In the months since Ray Zebrowski had tracked him down at Walter Reed and given his best job pitch, he'd had a lot of time to contemplate his situation. What seemed unthinkable then had gotten a little more appealing after the ink on his medical retirement papers had dried and the reality hit that he no longer had a career.

Or a home.

"Dude." There was a wealth of disappointed censure in the word.

"I'm not planning to do anything right now." But he'd have to make some choices about his future, and soon. Because whatever he decided wouldn't just impact him. He had Boone and Carly to think about.

Speaking of...

"Listen, Gil, I'd love to talk more, but I have to get myself put back together before Boone gets off the bus, or Carly wakes up. Can I call you later?"

"So, I'm guessing that means you haven't let them see your stump yet."

"They're little kids, Gil. They don't need to see something this ugly." Just the thought made his gut cramp. They'd been curious about the high-tech above-knee prosthesis when he'd shown it to them. But he wasn't sure either of them had fully grasped the correlating reality that his own leg was gone.

Exposing the scarred remains to them wasn't a step he was ready to take.

Not yet.

Maybe not ever.

The sigh Gil huffed out was long and annoyed. "You're not giving them enough credit. Kids are pretty damn resilient."

"Oh, so you're a fucking expert on kids all of a sudden?"

"No more than you are." There was a heavy silence between them. "Judd, man, I'm sorry, that was out of bounds."

His temper flared, then sputtered out just as quickly.

Gil was right. What the hell did he really know about kids, including his own? His contact with them since the divorce had been limited. Occasional visits when he could afford the airfare, supplemented by Zoom calls from whatever part of the world he was deployed to. After his injury, the first face-to-face time he'd had with them in eighteen months was two weeks ago when he drove into town.

That didn't exactly give him great parental insight into their psyches.

"I know I'll need to talk to them about it eventually. But I need to ease into it, when the time is right. And that's...not yet."

"Fair enough. But at the risk of pissing you off even further, I just want to say I think this is more about you than it is them."

He *would* have gotten pissed. If Gil hadn't been right.

Again.

After all the people who had seen and handled his damaged leg since he took those bullets—doctors, nurses, physical therapists, prosthetists—he should have grown indifferent to the awkward sense of embarrassment it brought him to bare it. Desensitized to the ugliness. And while he'd been at Walter Reed, he mostly had.

But it seemed when faced with the possible reactions of the people whose opinions mattered most to him, he was a total chickenshit coward.

Dropping the towel over his scarred left thigh, which now ended several inches above where his knee should have been, he shoved the problem down into a box and locked it shut for now. Compartmentalizing was something he'd always been good at, even before the SEALs had gotten their hands on him.

Growing up the way he did had made it a necessity.

"Be sure to add a nickel to my tab." The phrase referred to the Peanuts comic strip and the Lucy character's therapy booth, and had become shorthand among the unit for when someone was straying into unwelcome emotional 'touchy-feely' territory.

"Roger that, Bravo Two."

It was hard, but he didn't let himself flinch at the use of his old call sign. "I'll talk to you later, Gill Man."

"Later, dude."

He put the phone on the edge of the tub and took a deep breath to settle his nerves, which itched like a cat's fur stroked the wrong way. Talking to the men he once considered family was now an uncomfortable chore, with both sides doing their best to pretend nothing had changed. That they were all still as tight as they ever were.

Except it had. And they weren't.

Removing the towel, he glared at the reason. It was so easy to go over all the what-ifs. What if he'd moved right instead of the left when the shooting started? What if their intel had been better? If he'd been faster getting back to the extraction point? Slower? There were a hundred different things that could have gone differently that day. That might have changed the outcome for him.

But the fact was, none of them mattered. His leg was gone. Despite the incredible advances made in prosthetics which allowed him to walk again with relative ease, nothing would ever change that fact.

Just like nothing would ever give him back his place as Bravo Two.

Oh, he could have remained in the Navy despite the prosthetic. Even stayed with the Teams. Hell, they'd all but begged him to consider a position as an instructor. But it had seemed too much like living the punishment of Tantalus, where food and drink were always within sight, but kept forever just out of reach. He'd be a SEAL, but not. Forced to watch his men deploy to dangerous places while he stayed behind.

Not to mention how he'd be viewed by the men he was training. As a cautionary tale of how easily their lives could go to shit in the blink of an eye.

Annoyed with himself for falling down the rabbit hole of self-pity he'd thought left far behind, he carefully rolled on the now-dry silicone liner. After making sure all the air bubbles were out, he added on a soft, dry sock from the half-dozen different thickness options in his pack. By the time he snugged the socket back onto his residual limb, the sweat was already beginning to build again.

Just another fun day in his new fucked-up normal.

He stood, rocking to test the fit and suction. Satisfied with both, he changed his cargo pants out for the baggy black work-out shorts in his pack and breathed a sigh of relief.

After checking on Carly, who was evidently a little tornado while she slept judging by the twisted covers he straightened, he still had ten minutes to kill before Boone would get off the bus.

The phone in his pocket buzzed with an incoming text. When he pulled it out to look, he found a picture of Gil and two other Team members, Sandoval and Clay. Taken at night on the beach around a bonfire, his three closest friends were laughing their asses off at the camera, a beer in one hand while the other was raised in a single-fingered salute. The message *wish you were here* was typed below.

Yeah. He wished he was, too.

Everything he'd worked for the past seventeen years. Everything he'd poured into being the best at what he did, one of the elite. Someone who made a difference in eradicating evil from the world. All of it was gone. He wasn't a SEAL anymore.

And without that, who the hell was he?

He took a picture of his own hand gesture and sent it back, knowing it would give Gil a good laugh. His friend had been trying to cheer him up by making him feel included, but all it had done was drive home—again—he wasn't a part of that life anymore. That he wasn't a part of anything anymore.

And he had absolutely no idea what was supposed to come next.

Chapter 3

Controlled chaos.

It was the kindest description Judd could think of as he surveyed the writhing mass of people who'd taken over the elementary school's playground for Field Day. There had to be a hundred kids running every which way. Plus probably twice as many parents mixed in, along with what seemed a totally inadequate number of teachers overseeing things to keep it all from collapsing into utter bedlam.

And yet, somehow, they made it work.

Not too surprising, actually, considering the woman who was playing Overwatch on the entire thing.

She was wearing another of those awful brown outfits again today, only slacks this time instead of a skirt. "Dowdy" was the word that came to mind. The clothes weren't ugly, exactly. But the color kind of washed her out, and the pants were cut so they fell straight from her waist, no hint of hips or butt visible.

Granted, she spent her days around kids and had to dress appropriately for the job. But it was still a crying shame to camouflage herself so thoroughly when there was probably a sweet little body under all that boring material.

Somewhere.

While teachers organized and ran the various games for each of the age groups, Camille Richards walked the battlefield with her clipboard. Observing. Directing. And twice that he'd noticed, gently admonishing a few parents who were taking their kids' competitions a little too seriously. Not that he was watching her or anything.

Okay, he was watching.

He hadn't meant to. It just seemed whenever he wasn't cheering on one of his kids passing water balloons chin-to-chin or balancing an egg on a spoon as they ran, his gaze automatically homed in on wherever she happened to be.

And it shouldn't.

He hadn't left the woman with the best first impression of him. And despite the momentary flash of interest on both their parts, he'd already decided it wasn't something he should explore any further.

That *wouldn't* be explored further.

And yet, he couldn't seem to stop himself from tracking her through the crowd no matter how many times he reminded himself of that fact.

Maybe Gil was right and he needed to get laid.

And there he went, zeroing right back in on his sweet little principal again as soon as the thought hit his brain. And dick.

Damn it.

He had to get over this fascination with her before someone noticed. Like his son, who was running up to him, excitement shining in his eyes.

"Dad! Dad! Come on, we have to go now or we'll miss it!" He grabbed Judd's hand and towed him toward the back section of the playground. Cooper, who'd been dozing at Judd's feet since he'd found this little slice of shade by the bleachers, popped up and trotted with them, leash jangling softly.

"Miss what?" Not that he cared. The fact his son was so enthused about having him go anywhere was enough to have his heart near to bursting with happiness.

"The three-legged race. Come on!"

With a laugh, he allowed his son to pull him along. Thankful every step for all the work he'd put in on making his gait seem as normal as possible as they wove their way through the crowd. Stairs and unstable terrain like sand and gravel were the only places there was still a noticeable hitch in his movements.

With time, he'd conquer those as well.

Nothing else was acceptable.

As they reached the area where the race was being held, Dana came rushing up to them, expression harried. "There you are! Boone, come on, we have to line up now or we'll miss it."

Boone stared at the beckoning hand she held out to him. His gaze flicked from her to Judd and back again. "But...I was going to do it with Dad."

Dana froze for a split second before her expression went from surprised to uncomfortable. "Oh no, honey, that's really not a good idea." She shot Judd an almost apologetic wince, like she was embarrassed for him.

Which was when it finally hit him.

He looked over at the starting line where contestants were lining up, brightly colored lengths of ribbon cinching their legs together. All of the teams were made up of a child and a parent.

Son of a bitch.

He hadn't seen that one coming.

Boone clung to his hand, refusing to give in. "Why not?"

"Well..." The question seemed to stump Dana for a moment. "Because it just is. Besides, we had a lot of fun doing it together last year, remember?"

"Dad wasn't here last year. But he's here now." He stared up at Judd, eyes pleading. "Please, Dad?"

Emotions rose up to choke him as he looked down at his kid. Pain. Regret. Frustration. No, he hadn't been here last year to watch his kids having fun. He'd been at Walter Reed, learning how to walk again.

Not that they'd told the kids anything other than vague generalities about his injury and prolonged hospital stay. But it seemed all Boone remembered was his dad hadn't been there the way he'd promised to be. And now he was cashing in his IOU, not really knowing what he was asking.

Before he could figure out a way to gracefully decline without either hurting Boone or damaging the fragile bond that had been growing between them these past few weeks, Dana spoke up for him.

"Oh, sweetie, your father can't really do those kinds of things anymore."

Anger flashed through him, scalding enough to make him speak without thinking. "No, it's okay. I'll do it." He wasn't sure who was more surprised, him or Dana.

"You will?" The shock in her tone only strengthened his resolve.

"Sure. Why not?"

"Well, because..." She made a vague gesture at his leg, never quite looking at it even though the prosthesis was hidden beneath his pants.

His lips tightened along with his gut. "It'll be fine."

He had no idea if it would be fine.

Just like he had no idea how this would even work. But he was willing to give it his best shot. Because his son wanted to do this with him, and he'd be damned before he let the boy down. Even at the risk of publicly humiliating himself.

Which was a very real possibility.

Ignoring Dana's sputtered protests, he pressed the leash into her hands and gave Cooper his stay command before following an exuberant Boone to the starting line. He recognized the teacher who handed him the red ribbons and gave a quick nod and smile.

"Nice to see you again, Mrs. Baker."

Her eyes widened, as though surprised he'd remembered her name.

"Good to see you as well, Mr. Aiken. Good luck," she added with a wink before walking down the line of contestants, checking everyone's legs were properly secured.

He looked at the two lengths of cloth in his hand and debated his options of which leg to use them on. Logic dictated he keep his undamaged right leg free to use for balance and power. But something inside him cringed at the idea of putting his son in such direct contact with his prosthesis. Not that Boone had ever shied away from touching it.

Or tried to pretend it didn't exist, like Dana.

"Dad!" Boone tugged on his arm, eyes pleading for him to hurry up and tie them together.

Deciding to avoid the possibility of wrenching the prosthesis loose—at least, that's what he told himself—he quickly secured his right leg to Boone's left, making sure the ribbons weren't too tight. They walked in a circle to get the feel for it, his hand on his son's thin shoulder while Boone's arm circled his waist and clung to his belt loop. Awkward, but doable.

They took their places. Looking down the ragged line of parents and kids, he had a single moment to wonder what the hell he was doing. Then they were off, and his thoughts shifted to the task at hand.

Namely, not falling flat on his face.

It took a few strides to find their rhythm, but once they did, it was a lot easier than he'd expected. Probably because he wasn't running full out. More like trotting at a slow jog to match Boone's shorter stride. About halfway to the finish line, he stopped thinking about falling over and started thinking they might actually be able to win this thing.

That hubris was his undoing.

His body wanted to run. His brain was telling him to slow down. Somewhere between the two, he managed to screw up the rhythm they had going, and the next thing he knew, they stumbled and seemed certain to go down.

Somehow, he had no idea how, he kept them on their feet, but the dull pull through his groin muscle promised he'd pay for it later.

The stumble cost them the win. They still managed to cross the finish line in third place, though, before the inevitable happened and they got tangled up in each other and went down laughing. Judd lay on his back, eyes closed, his arm cradled under Boone where he'd cushioned his landing, letting the sound of his son's delighted laughter soak into him like a balm.

God, he'd missed this.

A wet nose pressed against Judd's cheek, startling him out of his moment of reverie. Cooper followed up by licking his chin, whining softly until Judd sat up and pushed him gently away. "I'm fine, you big dope. Stop."

Dana came puffing up at a run, annoyance etched on every line of her sweat-sheened face. "Your stupid dog wouldn't listen to me at all. He just pulled the leash right out of my hands and ran off."

He had a feeling she hadn't tried all that hard to hang onto it.

"It's okay. He's just doing what he's trained to do if I fall." Something he probably should have warned her about beforehand.

Oops.

"I told you you shouldn't have done it," she grumbled, pushing back a long lock of hair drooping over her eyes.

"Did you hurt your leg, Daddy?" There was deep childlike concern on Boone's face, spoiling the excitement of a moment ago. Making Judd wish Dana had kept her grumpy comments to herself.

"Not even a little." His groin muscle was another story. He'd be uncomfortable for a day or two at least, but consider the pain well worth it. "Good job, buddy! That was a great race. Thank you for letting me be your partner." He was relieved when the smile came back to Boone's face.

"With some more practice, I bet we coulda even won."

Judd grinned. "I bet we coulda." He tousled his son's hair, barely resisting the urge to hug him instead. He didn't have a clear memory of how he'd been at Boone's age, but he was pretty sure that kind of public show of affection around his peers wouldn't be welcome.

Of course, that was before affection of any kind had been replaced by a barren wasteland of intolerance and indifference.

"Mr. Aiken, while I appreciate you had your dog properly leashed this time, it's still unacceptable to let it run...oh. Oh! I'm so sorry. I...I didn't realize..."

The stumbling apology told Judd what he'd see before he followed Camille Richards's wide-eyed gaze to his legs. Specifically, the left one, where his baggy cargo pants had hiked up in the tumble, revealing the carbon fiber prosthetic limb beneath.

Just perfect.

The one time he was comfortable enough not to be paying attention, and *she* had to be there for the show.

He yanked his pant leg down, but the damage was done. Looking up at his sweet little principal, it was just like he'd feared. There wasn't an ounce of heat or interest in her dark eyes. All he saw was pity and concern.

Fuck my life.

"My apologies again, ma'am." He focused on untying the ribbons, hoping she'd take the hint and leave.

No such luck.

She stood there, watching as his fingers fumbled through the simple procedure of undoing the knots he'd tied. They should have come free with a tug. But they somehow had become more Gordian than Bowline, refusing to budge.

The ankle one finally came free, but the one below his knee tightened into a tangled, angry mess, growing worse with every tug he gave.

And because he clearly hadn't had enough humiliation for one afternoon, she knelt down to help. "May I?"

He wanted to say no. *Hell* no.

But he waited too long, and she took his silence as consent.

With nimble fingers, she started working on the knot he'd made, picking it loose like a pro. He did his best not to look down her blouse, which had gapped a little as she leaned forward, giving a teasing peek at the cleavage beneath.

Especially since his son was still sitting right next to him.

That would have been all kinds of wrong.

Instead, he stared at the fall of straight, shiny brown hair as she bent her head in concentration. And wondered briefly if it was as soft and silky as it looked. And what it would feel like gliding over his naked body.

The ribbon loosened and fell away.

"There!" With that satisfied exclamation, she grinned at him, only to have it falter as she met his gaze. He had no idea what she saw there, but it was enough to make her break eye contact with a nervous laugh as she stood, brushing nonexistent grass from her slacks. "All done."

"Thank you." He had to force the words out, caught between conflicting emotions that made him want to growl for different reasons.

"Yes, well, I guess twenty years of dealing with knotted shoelaces can come in handy once in a while." She flashed a quick little smile.

Boone, on his feet the moment he was free, bounced in place. "Dad, we have to go get our prize. C'mon!"

If only it were that easy.

Doing his best to ignore not just the fact he had an audience, but who that audience was, he pivoted himself so he was on all fours. Without being given any command, Cooper immediate-ly stationed himself at Judd's left side in case he was needed for balance.

Which he sincerely hoped he wouldn't.

With care for the grassy terrain, he brought his right foot flat on the ground, checked his balance, then pressed up to a standing position. A slight burn tugged his groin muscle again as his left leg came under him to its fully extended position. It wasn't quick or smooth, and definitely not pretty. But he didn't wobble, so he counted it a success.

"Dad!" Boone grabbed his hand and started tugging.

Laughter bubbled up at his son's impatience. Clearly, *he* didn't care if Judd was as graceless as a pregnant cow. "All right, all right, I'm coming. Hold your horses." To Camille he said, "Thanks again," before letting Boone pull him away.

"Mr. Aiken."

Fuck.

Denied his quick exit, he stopped and turned to look back. She held up the end of Cooper's leash. He took it with a rueful grimace. "Right. Sorry."

"No, I'm sorry. I didn't realize...Cooper, is it? That he was working. My apologies for giving you a hard time about having him on school grounds."

It shouldn't have bothered him she'd realized Coop was a service dog. But it did. No, it was the fact she realized he *needed* one that rubbed him on the raw. He'd kept Coop's status as low-key as possible, choosing only to put it on his collar and not have him wear any kind of vest or harness.

Most of the things he helped with were done in the privacy of their home, anyway, when the prosthesis was off and his mobility became more limited. In public, he preferred not to draw any extra attention to himself if he could help it.

"Don't worry about it." The words came out gruffer than he intended. He gave her a quick nod goodbye and gratefully let Boone pull him to where Mrs. Baker was getting ready to hand out the awards for the race.

Dana walked with them. Hell, he'd forgotten she was even standing there.

When Boone was handed the blue ribbon with the big "3" on it, he waved it like a flag. "Dad, look!"

Something that went beyond pride spread like warm jelly in his chest.

He gave a thumbs up before clapping. "Great job, kiddo."

Dana smiled and clapped as well. "Well, at least it completes the set with his first and second place ribbons from the last two years."

The years she'd done the race with him.

The softly spoken reminder stung, as it was likely meant to.

Boone didn't seem to care about not finishing higher, though. Watching his son high-five every other kid who'd raced, winner or not, filled Judd with a sense of pride no first-place ribbon could ever match. For all her other faults, Dana was raising their kids right.

"You shouldn't get his hopes up, you know."

He tipped his head in Dana's direction, brow raised in question.

"He thinks you're staying."

"I am."

"For the summer. What happens after that?"

"I don't know yet." And for a man who always had a plan, that was hard to admit.

"Well, you'd better figure it out before you break their little hearts."

Without giving him a chance to reply, she collected Boone and headed over to where Carly and the other first graders were getting ready to run some kind of race that involved carrying tablespoons of water.

Following behind, Cooper at his side, he forced down the anger her snapped words caused. Reminding himself she was looking out for their kids' best interests only helped a little. The last thing—the very last thing—he wanted to do was hurt them. But he'd be damned if he gave up this time with them, not after losing the past three years.

Unfortunately, Dana had primary custody. Which meant he needed to tread carefully. She hadn't brought it up, but if she wanted to she could curtail his visitations to only what the custody agreement allowed him.

It would be a shitty thing for her to do. But then, Dana had a nasty streak that came out whenever she felt slighted. Something that had kept her from forming any close friendships with the other Team members' wives back at Coronado, and helped pave the rocky road to their divorce.

One of the things, anyway. The divorce papers may have simply listed "irreconcilable differences," but she'd been very clear it was his emotional distance that made her finally pull the plug. Not that they'd ever been some big love story.

In the end, though, the reasons didn't matter. What did was that Dana held almost all the power over his ability to see the kids. So, he'd bite his tongue and do his best to play nice even when she lashed out. He had three years to make up for in two short months. He wasn't going to risk a minute of it fighting with her about past grievances.

But...

If she decided she wanted a war, then he'd give her one. And one thing she needed to remember about SEALs was, they fought to win.

"To another successful Field Day." Joelyn clinked her wine cooler bottle to Cam's as they relaxed in Jo's living room later that evening.

Success was a relative term. But since there had been no injuries requiring more than a Bandaid or ice pack, Cam decided they'd come pretty darn close. Any Field Day without stitches was a good one.

She sipped the pomegranate and raspberry drink, letting the icy-cold sweetness slide down her throat like a bubbly tide and released a satisfied sigh. It always felt liberating to be done adulting for the day.

"To two more days." They clinked bottles again.

Two days before the official start of summer break. Students weren't the only ones counting down. Teachers were just as anxious for that final bell to signal two whole months of freedom.

For Cam, though, it marked the start of another summer counting back down to the first day of the fall term.

It wasn't that she didn't enjoy summer break. She did.

For a few weeks, anyway.

After that, she started getting a little twitchy. She wasn't good with too much idle time on her hands. She liked to be *doing* something.

Which was why her summers always began with a complete house cleaning. Top to bottom, inside and out. She scrubbed every nook and cranny. Donated things she hadn't worn or used since last year's cleanup. And finally, picked one room in the house to paint a new color and shifted the furniture around, just to keep it fresh.

Not that there were a lot of rooms to redo; her bungalow was on the small side, with only one medium-sized bedroom and a somewhat compact bathroom. She would have preferred a second of each. Especially for when she was called on to do an emergency foster by children's services, which thankfully wasn't very often.

But since she hadn't requested alimony, something everyone called her crazy for, the tiny home was all she could afford. So, she made it work.

That was what she excelled at.

All the cleaning and refreshing usually took an entire month to complete. Which left her with a whole other month to fill. In the past, she'd spent a lot of that time with her nieces and nephews. Going to the lake, or the park, or just staying home playing board games and watching movies on her big pull-out sofa with tubs of super-buttery popcorn.

But most of them had reached the age where they had better things to do with their summers than hang out with their Auntie Cam.

The kids had their friends. Her brothers and sister had their spouses. Her parents had each other. Cam was the only odd-woman out in their extended family unit, and it was becoming an uncomfortable position as the years slid by with what felt like exponentially-increasing speed.

She took a long sip of her wine cooler.

Then nearly spat it out again when Joelyn casually asked, "So, how much about what people were saying about you and the mysterious Judd Aiken is true?"

"What?" She coughed and patted her mouth with the back of her hand. "What are people saying?" What *could* they be saying? She'd spent all of five minutes in the man's company all day.

"That he has some kind of bionic leg that came off during the three-legged race, and you helped him put it back on afterward."

"Oh, for the love of..." *Unbelievable.* "Where do people get this stuff? No, his leg didn't fall off."

"Oh." Joelyn looked disappointed. "But he's really missing one?"

"I don't know if it's his whole leg, but yes, he has a prosthesis."

And what a shock *that* had been.

She'd seen him walk, run, carry his daughter, and participate in a three-legged race. And through none of it would she have ever guessed he didn't have two healthy, fully functional legs. Not until his pants had rucked up halfway to his knee.

At least now she knew why he'd been the only other adult there today besides herself wearing long pants in this ridiculous un-May-like heat.

Which meant he was very likely sensitive about it.

She winced on his behalf. Probably nobody would believe the story about his leg falling off. But that wouldn't stop everyone from talking about it anyway. That's the way small-town gossip worked.

If he'd been trying to keep it private, the cat was well and truly gone from that bag and streaking through town like greased lightning.

"I wonder how it happened," Joelyn mused, fingers tapping against the bottle sweating in her hand.

"If he wants anyone to know, he'll tell them." She tried to put enough censure in her tone to quell her friend's legendary curiosity right there. But it was clear from Jo's expression she had more to share on the subject.

And, weak woman that she was, she didn't try to stop her.

"I heard from Bethany Turner, who heard it from Marjorie Manning, that Dana Aiken told *her*—in confidence, mind you—her ex was some kind of special Navy commando or something."

"A SEAL," Cam murmured. Uriah had been right.

"Yes, that!" Joelyn took a drink, brow furrowing. "I wonder if that's why they got divorced. You know, because he lost his leg."

Indignation rose on Judd's behalf.

"That would be a pretty shallow reason to leave someone you're supposed to love through sickness and health." She should know.

"Well, maybe it was more than that. Maybe his leg wasn't the only thing that got, you know." She lowered her voice despite the fact her kids were passed out in their beds upstairs. "Damaged."

An awful thought, but a possibility.

Then she remembered the predatory heat filling Judd Aiken's eyes when she'd looked up from untying the knotted ribbon. He'd banked it almost instantly, but she'd still had to look away. It was either that or melt right on the spot into a very inappropriate puddle of gooey middle-aged hormones.

"What?"

Cam started at the question. "What?"

"That look." Joelyn leaned forward like a bloodhound catching a scent. "You thought of something. What?"

Nothing she was going to mention, that's for sure.

"I just don't think it's appropriate to be sitting here speculating about the...parts of one of the parents, that's all." Especially one she was already inexplicably drawn to, despite her strict personal code of conduct.

Joelyn made a face, but slumped back with a sigh. "You're probably right. Besides, it's not like it really matters to either of us if he's able to...you know."

Was it her imagination, or did Jo give her a searching side-eye look as she said that?

"No, it's not." This time, she knew she didn't imagine the disappointment that flashed over her friend's face. Cam barely stifled a groan. "Whatever you're thinking, just stop. I don't need to get mixed up in some messy thing with a parent, even if he is divorced.

Maybe especially because he's divorced. It would be the worst kind of mistake."

"Of course it would." Jo paused. "But if you did…"

This time, the groan came out. "Jo…"

"Sometimes messy can be good."

"And sometimes messy can get your guts ripped out and stomped like grapes." Especially when the person doing the ripping and stomping was the one person who knew you better than anyone else in the world.

And knew exactly where your most vulnerable spots were.

Remorse wiped all amusement from Joelyn's face. "Sweetie, I know he hurt you bad, but don't let that idiot ex of yours ruin the rest of your life."

"I'm not letting him ruin anything. I've dated, haven't I?"

"Not a lot. And not with any real interest."

Both true.

But after Ty's betrayal, anything more than casual companionship had seemed too risky. If she was ever going to open herself up to a man again, he would have to prove himself worthy of her trust first.

So far, none had.

"When the right guy comes along, I'll know." Probably. Maybe.

She hoped, anyway.

"And besides, he isn't sticking around. He mentioned he was here for the summer to spend time with his children. The last thing I need is to get involved with someone who already has one foot out the door."

She winced inwardly at the unfortunate choice of words.

"Or maybe it's exactly what you need. No, hear me out," Joelyn said when she tried to object. "You've pretty much exhausted the potential dating pool here in Slow Creek. Why not expand your horizons a bit and take advantage of what the good lord has so thoughtfully provided?"

She couldn't help but chuckle. "Oh, so now he's a gift from God? To have an affair with? A little blasphemous, don't you think?"

"God, fate, whatever. He's here. You're here. Why not just see where it goes?" She gave Cam a sardonic look. "You can't tell me you don't find him attractive."

No, she couldn't. The man had punched buttons in her body she'd forgotten still worked, all from a look.

One hot, hungry look.

She pressed the icy bottle to her forehead and tried to blame the flush she felt on the alcohol hitting her system, but what was the use in lying to herself? She found Judd Aiken extremely attractive and intensely virile.

And she wasn't the only one, either. She'd witnessed more than a few longing gazes being sent his way earlier today.

Not that he seemed to notice. He would just be walking by, and heads would turn in what they probably thought was subtle scrutiny. He was like human catnip for women. And like anything that potent should be indulged in sparingly.

Like for a summer, some inner voice whispered.

It was a bad idea.

But as with most bad ideas, a tempting one.

Needing to derail Jo's sudden interest in her love life, as well as her own heretofore silent inner hussy, she grabbed at the only thing she could think of.

"There's one little problem with your summer fling plan. Weren't you just wondering about whether or not he might be, uh, incapable?"

Surprise was chased across Joelyn's face by chagrin. But rather than be dissuaded, she instead adopted an innocent smile double-dipped in pure devilry.

"Well, there's nothing to say that would stop *you* from enjoying yourself even if it's true, now is there?"

"You're terrible." But she laughed when Jo only waggled her eyebrows suggestively in reply. "Anyway, school's almost over, and after that, I'll probably never run into Judd Aiken again."

"But just think. If you do, it'll be as Camille and Judd, not Principal Richards and Mr. Aiken. Imagine the possibilities."

On the drive home, she couldn't seem to think about anything else.

Which was a slippery slope she should stay well clear of. For all the thrill she might get from a brief affair of any kind, she had to consider the pitfalls as well.

Slow Creek was a small town with a big gossip network. Anything she did would be noted and remarked upon, no matter how much it might be nobody's business. She'd worked long and hard to get to the position of respect and authority she held in the community. The last thing she needed was to do something that might tarnish it.

Especially since it was all she had left.

By the time she pulled into her driveway, her resolve had firmed. No flings. No affairs. No Judd.

That last might cause a twinge of regret in her chest—okay, and maybe a little lower—but she didn't waver. Ignoring the attraction might be the coward's way out, but the gossips had gnawed on the carcass of her marriage for ten long months. She just didn't have it in her to go through that kind of humiliation again.

Chapter 4

When Judd noticed the sheriff's car coming down the long dirt driveway, the only surprise was that it had taken him so long to actually show up at the Garvey place.

An entire week had passed since the not-so-subtle "I'll be watching you" threat. Uriah Dixon had struck him as a conscientious man. The kind who kept a close eye on his community not because it was his job, but because he truly cared about the people living there.

There wasn't a doubt in his mind if the sheriff decided Judd was a problem, he'd have no qualms about using the full power of his office to make that problem go away. It wouldn't be the first time he'd dealt with a petty dictator with the power of authority to back him up.

But it would be the first he wasn't sure he could win.

With that in mind, he kept his expression neutral and put his concentration back on the board he was cutting down to size.

Like everything else on the property, the tools he'd scrounged together were in rough shape. He'd set the electric saw aside for later so he could repair the cord chewed partway through by something. Probably whatever was rustling in the dark corners of the musty shed when he'd been rummaging around in there.

That left him with a couple of well-used hammers, a rusty hand saw, and a set of wobbly sawhorses to work with.

Not ideal, but good enough to get the job done, even if it took a little extra effort.

And after two weeks of being in Slow Creek, he was ready for some physical activity, despite the unseasonable May heat. His body was used to daily routines and grinding workouts. The loss of his leg hadn't changed that, only modified how he went about them.

Either he was going to have to figure a way to improvise some kind of gym while he was here, or suck it up and go join a real one. Otherwise, he'd screw up his ongoing recovery and end up feeling like absolute shit long before the end of summer.

By the time he finished the cut and stopped to brush at the sawdust clinging to his sweaty forearms, Dixon was walking toward the sawhorses under the shade of a massive oak tree that had to be a hundred years old if it was a day.

He wasn't in uniform this time, which was a little surprising. But even in faded shorts and a dark blue t-shirt boasting the logo of the high school football team in bright yellow, he was no less imposing.

And it wasn't just his size.

Judd had known plenty of hulk-sized men during his years in the Navy, and seen more than a few backed down by someone smaller but with a more potent personality. Dixon, however, had a formidable combination of both attributes. Which meant treading lightly until he found out why he was there.

Although he had a pretty good idea.

"Afternoon." Dixon's greeting was amiable, but his expression was as neutral as Judd's.

"Afternoon, Sheriff. What brings you out this way?" Judd held the plank out and looked down its length, checking for any warping.

"Well, now, funny thing you should ask. It seems I got this call someone was buying up a truck full of lumber using old Wilt

Garvey's account. So I thought I'd just mosey on over and have a look-see what that was all about."

Yup. He'd been right.

"Just doing some repairs for Mr. Garvey, is all." He hefted the board and three others from the stack he'd cut to his shoulder and brought them to the front porch. It was currently a checkerboard of weathered boards and empty spaces where he'd removed the rotted ones.

"And in case 'someone' didn't mention it, Mr. Garvey called and gave them the okay to charge everything to his account."

Which hadn't been his intent when he'd offered to do the work. But the old man had puffed up his bony chest and refused to accept what he considered charity, practically spitting the word like it tasted bad.

Going to his right knee, he dropped his load and placed one of the boards into a gap. After testing its fit, he slipped the hammer from the loop on his cargo pants and snagged a few nails from the brown paper bag of them he'd bought with the lumber.

The pants were hot as hell, but necessary to help keep stray sawdust from getting into places it shouldn't. Especially the joints. Any repair work needed on the prosthetic would require a trip all the way down to the Topeka VA.

With several sure strokes, he drove the nails in, securing the board to the joist below. The underlying structure had seen its own better days, but was sound enough to last a few more years, at least.

Dixon waited until the hammering stopped before speaking again.

"Well, now, as a matter of fact they did mention that. Like they mentioned all of the work he said you were going to be doing for him. Which got me to wondering just how much you might be charging old Wilt for all this *help*."

Not letting it show how bad the implication he was taking advantage of the old man burned, he selected the next board and set it in place. "Not a thing."

"Is that right."

He pounded the nails in, putting his annoyance into every swing, which vibrated up his arm like a small electric shock. "Yeah, that's right."

"Pretty generous of you."

He said *generous*, but Judd heard *suspicious* loud and clear.

"It needed to be done. I have the time to do it. It's not a big deal." He fitted the last two boards in place. "Besides, he was nice enough to offer me a place to stay. And he's not charging me nearly as much as I would have paid if I stayed at the motel I was at out by fifty-nine if he didn't. Not to mention the travel time back and forth he's saving me. So, I figure the least I owe him is a little sweat equity in return."

"Well, now, I've been wondering about that, too. How was it you two met in the first place? It's not like old Wilt gets to town much these days."

"He was at the real estate agent's office when I went in to find a place to rent for the summer. The one by the diner."

"Nathan Baxter." Just the way the sheriff said his name told Judd what he thought of the man. For once, they were in agreement. "Wilt's great-nephew."

Something Judd already knew, since Wilt had gone on at length about his last living blood relative in the two and a half weeks he'd been living there.

Seemed he wasn't too fond of good old Nate, either.

"Well, after none of the few rental listings he had fit both my needs and budget, he promised to keep looking and give me a call if something new came available." Although he'd wondered at the time if that "unfortunate lack of inventory" might have had more to do with him being an outsider than any actual scarcity of rentals.

"When I left, Mr. Garvey followed me out. Said he had an old camper on his place I maybe could rent if I was interested, and didn't mind roughing it some."

"So, he invited a total stranger to come live here, just like that?" If there was a word a step beyond skeptical, Dixon's voice was that. "I can't see him being so hard up for money. In fact, I know he's not."

Judd shrugged and drove in the last few nails.

"Could be it was more about him being hard up for company." He pushed to his feet, pleased the groin muscle he'd strained a few days ago during the race didn't even twinge. "Or it might have been to tweak his nephew's nose," he added with a quick grin, remembering the old man's gleeful cackle at the thought of depriving Baxter of a possible commission.

That got a snort of what might have been laughter. "Yep, that I can see."

As he grabbed a few more boards from the cut pile, Judd said reluctantly, "And I suppose it might have also had to do with him seeing the Trident on my keychain."

The silver disc with the emblem of the SEALs was the only reminder he'd allowed himself to keep from his former life. Everything else, including pictures and souvenirs of the places he'd been around the globe, was packed away in storage back in Coronado.

Dixon gave a slow nod. "Now *that* I can see making a difference to him, since Wilt was a Marine back in the day."

"The day" being the Korean War.

Wilt had shared a few stories about it over beers at the kitchen table since Judd moved in. One of those times he'd been drunk enough to bring up the battle of the "Frozen Chosin" where he'd lost several toes to frostbite during the seventeen-day siege. Something he'd had no qualms about showing off, seeing as how Judd "knew his own self" what it was like to give up a body part for your country.

Judd shook the memory off.

"We got a slice of pie and some coffee at the diner, talked for a while, and he offered me the camper for a more than decent price, so I said yes." He placed the boards beside the next section of gaps.

Dixon followed him onto the porch this time. "Sounds like it was fate, then. Him being there the same time as you."

A shiver ran down Judd's spine.

Fate was a bitch he hadn't had much luck with lately.

"Just right place, right time, is all. I wouldn't lean on that if I were you," he cautioned as Dixon started to put his weight on the railing.

With a frown, Dixon wiggled the wood. It moved back and forth like a loose tooth. "I didn't realize things had gotten so run down around here." The frown deepened as he took a longer look at the porch, where a good third of the boards had been rotted enough to need replacing. "Nathan said he was making sure the place was being taken care of."

Judd couldn't tell if the frustration in his voice was directed at the negligent nephew, or at himself for letting the welfare of one of his town's senior citizens slide down the slippery slope of neglect. Either way, the evidence spoke for itself.

Nathan wasn't just a weasel.

He was a liar as well.

A small nugget of satisfaction filled him at the thought of the visit Nathan would no doubt be getting from Dixon sometime real soon to discuss that revelation.

As he was pounding in the next board, Dixon strode down the steps, maybe to go do that very thing. Instead, he returned a moment later with the second hammer in one hand and a stack of boards in the other. Snagging some nails from the bag, he deposited everything next to a large gap at the other end of the porch.

The two men exchanged a wordless look of understanding before they set to work, not stopping until they'd gone through the entire stack of cut boards.

Taking a much-deserved break in the shade of the oak, Judd grabbed two cold waters from the cooler there, tossing one to Dixon. At the sound of the cooler being cracked open, Cooper snapped to attention from where he'd been napping like a big golden shadow and trotted over to investigate.

Judd dumped the tepid water out of the plastic bowl on the ground and refilled it from his bottle before downing the rest in a few long swallows of blissful coldness. Cooper slurped up half before giving Dixon a curious sniff. Not seeing any food in evidence, he settled for a few ear scratches from both men before he laid back down.

"Good lookin' dog." Dixon finished off his water with a gulp. "Heard he was a service animal of some kind?"

His lips pressed tight in annoyance before he let out a resigned puff of air. He should be used to small-town grapevines, where everyone knew everything a minute before it happened. It had been the same way in the Teams. There was nothing nosier than a bunch of guys living in close quarters with too much time on their hands.

"He is."

After a pause, Dixon asked, "One of those emotional support kind of ones?"

"Nope." Not exactly a lie, since it wasn't Cooper's primary training. He wasn't trying to be an ass, but hell, if Dixon was going to be nosy, Judd was at least going to make him work for it.

"Son, I'm trying not to be insensitive here—not always one of my best things, if you believe what my wife has to say on the matter. So, I'd appreciate it if we cut through the bull. The law says I'm not allowed to ask outright. Which is why all I'm gonna say is that nothing chaps my butt more than people who slap a service dog label on the family pet and use the ADA laws to thumb their noses at those who have an honest-to-God need for them."

Any desire to continue giving the sheriff a hard time evaporated at his words. He couldn't even get pissed off at the insinuation. It hit a little too close to his ongoing insecurities about how real his actual need for a service dog truly was.

How many times had he asked himself over the past months if he was being a selfish bastard? If he was taking a dog someone else might have had a greater need for than him?

Take each day you have together as a gift.

The words from the handwritten letter he'd been given the day he left the Another Step Forward training facility with Cooper were ones that popped into his head often.

Because having Coop *was* a gift. He hadn't realized it at the time. But after leaving Walter Reed hospital, he'd been entirely alone. No family. No career. No home.

No purpose.

Being paired with the dog had kept him balanced while he got his bearings, both mentally and physically. Which was probably why the shrink had strongly encouraged him to apply for the program before he okayed Judd's discharge.

"Coop's a mobility assistance dog," he finally said, voice gruff as he looked over at the mutt in question. He was already asleep again. "He's trained to help me if I fall and can't get up on my own, or if I need him to pick up things I've dropped or are in another room if I don't have my"—*leg*—"crutches. To go get help if I pass out or fall and knock myself stupid. Those kinds of things."

The emotional support he got in additional to all that came from Coop just being Coop. Dogs had the most amazing sense of empathy he'd ever witnessed, and he thanked God every day for it. Even on the days he and the Big Guy weren't exactly on the closest terms.

"Is that right." Dixon poured a little of the cool water into his hand and splashed it over his shaved head. "Well now, sounds like he's a good one to have around."

"He is." The best.

"So, I'm guessing that means you're not just on leave, then?"

Several different emotions threatened to rise up and choke him. He pushed them down and locked them away. "Medically retired."

"Any idea what you're gonna do now?"

No, and it was making him twitchy.

"Still working that part out."

"You planning on working it out here in Slow Creek?"

He had no fucking idea.

His kids were here, sure. But what was here for him besides them?

"Would it be a problem if I was?" The eye contact between them sizzled with challenge until Dixon shook his head.

"Nope. Don't think it would."

The tension dissipated. Judd wasn't one for explaining himself to people, but he figured if Dixon would make a bad enemy, he might make an even better ally.

So, he did what didn't come naturally and offered up some personal information.

"I get a decent check every month, even after child support, but nowhere near what it was when I was getting jump and special duty pay. I need to find something to supplement it so I can help get my kids into a better place and plan for their futures. But I've only ever worked on a cattle ranch and been in the Navy, and the way I am now, I'm not much good for either of those anymore."

Not that he'd step foot back on the ranch even if he had a gun to his head. That was a part of his life he had not just locked away, but welded shut and concreted over.

Permanently.

Dixon nodded. "I hear ya. I've got two boys. All grown now, with families of their own, but I still remember sweating out how we were going to pay for college without getting in debt to our eyeballs. Being a parent is a hard row to hoe, but a rewarding one."

The look Dixon gave him made Judd tense, expecting a nosy question about Dana or the divorce. Instead, he said, "It's good you've got their interests uppermost in mind, son. Says a lot about you."

The praise caught him off guard. He dropped his gaze and stared down at the hand wrapped around the water, knuckles scarred from a lifetime of hard use. "They're the best thing I ever did." And he'd do whatever he had to for them.

Unlike his own father, who'd thrown him to the wolves.

Before unwelcome emotions started to rise again, he got awkwardly to his feet and headed for the pile of uncut boards still stacked near the sawhorses. The porch wasn't going to fix itself, and he was done with sharing.

Without a word, Dixon joined him, installing the boards as Judd cut them, until the last hole was filled. Tired and dripping with sweat, both men retreated to the shade and sucked down more water as they sprawled on the grass.

The front door to the house opened and Wilt Garvey stepped out. With his headful of white hair and a frame slightly stooped from the burden of age and arthritis, it was hard to see the decorated soldier he'd once been.

Until you looked into his eyes. Which still burned with intelligence and a wealth of knowledge only eighty-nine years on this earth could bring.

Despite having just dropped to the ground, he got up again and walked over to join Wilt as he stood surveying the repairs. Dixon followed. The new boards were almost obscenely bright against the older, weathered ones which had passed muster to stay. But a year or two being exposed to the elements would fix that.

A pang hit at the thought the old man might not be around by the time that happened.

"Well, now, you did a fine job, Judd, a fine job. And Uriah, seems like you put in a good bit of work, too, judging by the look of you." He glanced from one to the other, one bushy eyebrow raised. "Didn't realize the two of you were friends, though."

Dixon gave one of those big, aw-shucks grins. "You know what they say, Wilt. A stranger's just a friend you haven't met yet."

Judd wasn't so sure about that. In his former line of work strangers usually just wanted to kill him. But the sheriff's words lit something deep inside him. Where he'd felt empty and alone these past months, since leaving the hospital and the men he'd come to consider like family through their shared injuries and recovery journeys. Yet another part of his life he'd had to pack away and leave behind.

He hesitated, then gave Dixon a nod of acknowledgment for the sentiment.

He'd been shooting for an ally, but having this man as a friend wasn't a bad prospect, either. Not bad at all.

"Well, come on then, boys, grub's ready. Plenty for everyone." Without waiting for an answer, he shuffled back into the house, screen door banging behind him. Cooper's head popped up at the sound, one ear flopped back, giving him a goofy just-woke-up look.

Judd grinned. God, he loved that silly mutt.

"Coop, bring the bag."

Practically vibrating with eagerness, the dog was up and at his side in seconds, carrying the backpack by the loop on top the way he'd been trained. Judd took it and gave him a vigorous chest rub and some praise, ending with a high-five, something they'd been working on the last few weeks.

As he went inside with the go-bag slung over his shoulder, he told himself he'd given the command rather than walk the few yards to get it for Coop's sake. The dog needed to feel useful just as much as he did.

Cooper was trained for helping tasks, and it was obvious he was proud of himself when he accomplished one of them. So, Judd made sure to give him a few to do every day, even if he didn't really need them done.

But he couldn't deny a little bit of it had been showing off, too.

"You go on ahead and clean up first," he said to Dixon, who was taking in the run-down condition of the inside of the old farmhouse. And looking none too pleased with what he was seeing.

It wasn't being polite so much as knowing he'd need to use the bathroom for a lot longer while he dried off his leg and liner. The last thing he needed was to rush through the process because the other man was waiting and tear the damn thing.

Once that had been taken care of, he changed into the shorts from his go-bag with a sigh of relief. After a quick wash of his hands, arms, and face in the chipped porcelain sink, he felt a hundred times better.

He'd spent his Navy career in some of the grittiest, most unhygienic places on the planet. Showers and soap nothing more than a distant wet-dream, pun intended. They'd had to laugh about it, because by the end of some missions the collective funk coming off every one of them had been enough to gag a skunk.

But now, any bit of sweat or dirt bothered him. Either could royally fuck up the integrity of his residual limb to the point he wouldn't be able to wear the prosthetic leg until whatever irritation it caused had healed.

He didn't like it, but necessity had transformed him from mud-crawling warrior to fussy-ass clean freak.

Joining the other two men at the kitchen table, he surveyed the pile of thick sandwiches on the platter at its center with profound appreciation. Stomach rumbling, he grabbed one with rare roast beef and Swiss cheese, adding a generous helping of homemade potato salad and a pickle to his plate.

As he reached for the pitcher of lemonade to fill his glass, though, he noticed Dixon watching him with an unreadable expression. He glanced at his plate. It couldn't be because he'd taken too much food. Dixon had helped himself to twice as much.

"Don't be looking at the boy like that, Uriah. It's just a leg."

"Sorry," came the rumbled reply as Dixon's gaze jerked guiltily back to his food. "Didn't mean to stare."

It was only then Judd realized he'd gotten comfortable enough around Dixon that he hadn't even considered what his first reaction might be to seeing the prosthesis on full display. "No problem. It's a pretty cool piece of technology." He stretched his left leg out so the other man could get a better look.

With that invitation, Dixon gave up all pretext of subtlety and studied the carbon fiber prosthetic with open interest. Finally, he sat back, shaking his head.

"That's a helluva thing."

"It surely is," Judd agreed, picking up his sandwich and taking a bite. The seasonings from the roast beef exploded on his tongue, sharp and spicy.

Heaven.

Talk between bites revolved mostly around baseball and led to a heated debate about who was most likely to make it to the World Series that year. Wilt and Dixon had a heavy prejudice towards the Royals, being the local team. Judd threw his support behind the Padres, whose home field was right across the bay from Coronado in San Diego.

He and the guys had gotten tickets to games whenever they'd had the chance. He'd even taken Boone to his very first major league game there for his fifth birthday.

Dana had him served with the divorce papers a month later.

Not that he'd been entirely surprised. Things had been strained between them for a while by then. He just hadn't expected her to choose the easy way out rather than trying to work through things with marriage counseling first.

Although in hindsight, he probably should have.

Dana had always balked at having to work hard for anything. She'd been head cheerleader, prom queen, and the star of the high school drama club. She'd gone to Hollywood with expectations of becoming instantly rich and famous.

When that didn't happen, she went with Plan B instead: marrying someone to take care of her. To this day, he wasn't sure she hadn't lied about being on birth control so he'd be well and truly stuck when the stick turned pink.

"You like to fish?" Dixon asked.

Glad to be pulled from the downward spiral of his thoughts, he nodded.

"Some. Why?"

"The VFW runs a tournament every Memorial Day weekend. Everything caught gets donated to the big fish fry at the town picnic Monday, but the winner gets a trophy and bragging rights for the next year. I happen to know there's still a few spots open, if you were of a mind to go."

Dana and her parents were taking the kids to the big water park in Kansas City to celebrate the end of the school year. Something booked months ago, he'd been informed, and it would just be "too awkward" for him to tag along. So, he had no plans for the weekend.

That didn't mean he wanted to spend it stuck on a boat with a bunch of strangers pretending not to stare at his leg the same way Dixon had.

"I don't know," he said slowly, not wanting to give insult to the well-intentioned invitation. "I was thinking I'd get some more work done around here. The railing still needs to be fixed, and then there's the roof to take a look at…"

Wilt snorted. "Hell's bells, another few days ain't gonna make any difference. Go, have fun. They're pulling some nice-sized catfish out of the lake from what I hear. That's some good eatin'." He smacked his lips.

"Does that mean you're going?" Judd asked.

"On a boat? Hell, no. Me and my puny bladder will be fishing off the dock with all the other old farts."

He wavered. The prospect of another day of solitude with no one but the dog to talk to held less appeal than spending it with a bunch of nosy people he didn't know.

"I don't have any equipment."

Wilt waved the excuse away. "I got plenty."

If it was in the same shape as everything else around the place, that wasn't exactly helpful. But what the hell.

"Sure, why not. Thanks."

Leaving Wilt to relax in front of the tv after the meal, Judd and Dixon carried two old hand-carved rockers out front. They went back where they'd been on the porch before it got too dangerous to sit on.

Hands on his hips, Dixon gave a nod as he surveyed their work. "Looks good."

"Thanks for your help. I figured it'd take me at least a full day or two to get it done by myself."

"Glad I came by." They exchanged wry grins, since the reason Dixon had come out was to see if Judd was some kind of grifter. "I'm happy to come back and help with the railing when you get to it."

Ignoring the instinctive refusal that rose to his lips, he nodded. The last eighteen months of recovery had relied solely on his determination. His willpower. His headspace. Success or failure had been his responsibility alone.

It was time to start remembering how to be part of a team again.

"That would be great, Sheriff. Thanks."

"It's just Uriah when I'm not wearing the badge." He hesitated. "Can I ask you something?"

"I guess." It didn't mean he'd answer.

"You seem to get on real well with old Wilt. He likes you, likes the dog. He's got plenty of empty bedrooms."

"And?" Judd asked when no question came.

"I guess I'm just surprised he didn't offer to let you stay up here at the house instead of in that crappy camper of his."

Judd sucked on his lower lip as he considered what to say.

He settled on the truth.

"He did ask, about a week ago. I decided to stay where I was."

Brow furrowed, Dixon asked, "Why?"

"I like the privacy."

And not just when it came to removing his prosthesis. From out there, the old man couldn't hear when he screamed out during one of the nightmares that still hit from time to time. Waking to the agony of phantom pain in a leg that was no longer there.

Understanding lit Dixon's dark eyes. He nodded. "It gets better. With time."

Having seen the Army Ranger tattoo on Dixon's arm while they'd been working, he didn't need to ask how he could possibly know such a thing. "God, I hope so."

After waving the other man off with a promise to be at the lake early Sunday morning, Judd checked on Wilt, who was snoring away in his ratty brown recliner. Not wanting to wake him, he decided to leave off starting any more repairs for another day. Instead, he sank into one of the chairs on the porch and just...rocked.

Relaxing wasn't his best thing. But as the minutes rolled by, a sense of peace started to seep into him. Coming to Slow Creek had been a gamble. But the way things were shaping up, it looked like it might just have been the smartest decision he'd made in a long while.

With school out after today, he had two whole months to spend with his kids, making up for lost time. It was going to be great.

As long as he didn't piss off Dana.

And there was always the minefield of her parents to maneuver through as well. Where his ex had been fairly reasonable since he showed up, her folks were another matter.

They still blamed him for knocking up their little girl and ruining all her big dreams of stardom. Every time he saw Edith Leffler, her thin nose quivered and stuck up in the air like a rat scenting some bad cheese. Richard wasn't much better, though he was careful to be civil in front of the kids.

Who had no idea their grandparents would like to see their father strung up by his balls from the nearest tree.

At least he didn't have to worry about getting trapped on a boat with Richard on Sunday, since they'd all be at the water park. Although he supposed he should be prepared for the possibility of running into them at the town picnic the next day.

Unbidden, a picture of the other person he might run into came to mind.

Camille.

He didn't know what it was about the woman, but she'd been haunting his thoughts for days now. Sometimes his dreams as well.

Waking up with her on his mind and his hand on his dick this morning hadn't been one of his finer moments. Camille Richards was a classy woman. She deserved more than being masturbatory material for a horny, broken-down wreck like him.

But as he rocked, breeze on his face, dog at his feet, Judd couldn't help hoping he'd run into her again. Their last two meetings, he hadn't exactly shown at his finest.

Maybe the third time would be the charm.

Chapter 5

"Aunt Cam, Aunt Cam! Look at me!"

Shading her eyes, Camille watched with a knot in her stomach as her sister's oldest son, Owen, climbed up the rope and wood structure set up in the park as part of the Memorial Day picnic activities. AKA something to keep the kids occupied while the adults ate and socialized with their friends and neighbors.

At twelve, Owen was just entering the gawky beginning stage of puberty. Not that you could tell from the way he scampered up the series of rope ladders and swaying bridges as if he'd been born doing it.

Not so for his brother. Only three years younger, Elijah had the athletic coordination and grace of a newborn calf. All wobbly-legs and huge eyes, he was gamely following in Owen's footsteps despite looking like he'd rather be anywhere else on the planet.

She could sympathize. It was tough trying to prove you were just as good as your siblings. The same rivalry had sprung up between her and her sister, although it had been an academic rather than athletic one.

Which was a good thing, because in that arena, Cam was about as talented as poor little Elijah seemed to be.

After both boys were safely back on the ground, they collected their stickers for making it to the top. She then herded them over to where her family was congregated and turned them over to their parents with a grateful sigh. She loved being Auntie Cam. Loved spending time with them, especially since in a few more years they'd be like their older cousins and prefer their friends' company to hers.

But at the same time, it was always a relief when she could return them in the same condition she'd gotten them in: intact and unbloodied. She didn't envy their parents the strain of that twenty-four-seven responsibility.

A small pinch of regret tightened her chest.

What a liar.

She envied the hell out of them.

Rubbing her breastbone to relieve the uncomfortable sensation, she made her way over to her father, who was in animated conversation with her older brother, Vincent. Like her, he'd inherited their father's Scandinavian height and their mother's Asian coloring. But it was even more obvious the two men were related by the almost identical stubborn expressions on their faces.

Though Hank Richards's hair had long gone silver, his face lined and a little saggy in the jawline, she could still see the handsome young soldier her mother fell in love with during the final years of the Vietnam War. Even the cane he'd started using whenever he left home lately couldn't detract from the aura of strength and dependability he seemed to exude.

Kind of like another soldier she'd recently met.

Annoyed with herself for once again letting *that* man into her thoughts where he had no business being, she tuned in to the ongoing conversation. Only to realize it was the latest round of arguments over what colleges Vincent's son should be applying to. Despite the fact John was only sixteen, it had been the hot topic of debate in the family for months now.

Sadly, his father was the only one who seemed to care what John wanted.

Before she could retreat, Vincent saw her and latched onto her presence as a way to extricate himself. "Dad, didn't you want to talk to Cam about something?"

"Coward," she murmured as he brushed past her in escape.

Not that she was really annoyed at him. Much.

As the two oldest of four, she and Vincent had taken the brunt of their parents' pressure for academic excellence to the exclusion of all else. So, she understood his desire to keep from doing the same to his own children.

She just wished he hadn't thrown her under the bus in the process.

"You need to talk to your brother about this crazy idea of his," her father said in a frustrated tone. "Art school. What is he thinking? That kid has the brains to be an engineer. Or an architect!"

She threw up her hands in a 'stop right there' gesture

"I'm not getting in the middle of this one." Mostly because she was on Vince's side. John *could* be an engineer or architect if he wanted to. But he didn't. He wanted to be an artist, something her father was having a hard time wrapping his head around.

Hoping to divert him, she asked, "You needed to talk to me about something?"

"What? Oh, right." His annoyed expression shifted to a smile she was all too familiar with. "Camille, sweetheart."

"What did you do, Dad?" But that look said it all. She groaned in frustration. "Please tell me you didn't set me up on another blind date."

"Camille..."

"How many times do we have to have this conversation? I don't need you to find me a man. I don't *want* you to find me a man."

He managed to look wounded. "I don't know why you're being so dramatic. All I did was invite someone to stop by and say hello so he could meet you. Is that so wrong?"

She counted to ten before she could grind out, "Yes, Dad. It is."

"If it's wrong to want to see my daughter settled and happy before I die, then fine. I'm a horrible person."

"You're not horrible, and you know it. And you're not dying anytime soon, either. But you need to stay out of my love life."

She could almost hear Joelyn asking *What love life?*

"He's a very nice young man. What would it hurt to just talk to him for a while? Get to know him a little?"

From the stubborn angle of his jaw, he wasn't going to admit he was in the wrong. Which meant retreat was her best option before this turned into a full-scale argument.

Where's a sibling and a bus when you needed one?

"Sorry, Dad, but I'm not interested." She gave him a quick peck on his wrinkled cheek. "It smells like they've got the fish fry going. I'll go get you a plate."

"I can get my own damn plate," he muttered. He gave her a brooding look. "Not all men are like that piece of primordial ooze you married, you know. Don't discount the whole barrel because of one rotten apple, Camille."

She forced a smile. "Ty has nothing to do with anything. I simply prefer to handle my own personal life."

But as she walked away, doubt made her stomach churn.

Jo had said almost the same thing. *Was* she letting her bitterness about Ty influence how she reacted to other men? Could it be that when he'd destroyed her trust in him, she'd lumped all men into the same untrustworthy category by default without even realizing it?

"That still doesn't give him the right to try and interfere." The grumbled words ended in a small squeak as she ran into a solid wall of muscle.

Strong hands grasped her arms to steady her.

"Sorry. Are you okay?"

Looking up, she was caught in the concerned gaze of none other than Judd Aiken. That funny little buzz started in her belly, the one she hadn't felt in far too long.

And despite knowing he was the very worst person for her to feel any kind of sexual attraction for, she let herself revel in it for a few seconds. Until she realized he was waiting for her to say something.

"Um, I'm fine. Thanks. And I'm the one who should be sorry, I wasn't looking where I was going."

"No harm done."

The low rumble of his voice did amazing things to her insides. As the concern in his eyes morphed to something more heated as she watched, she could practically hear Jo screaming at her to not waste the chance fate had handed her on a big, yummy platter.

But before she could make a decision, he released her arms and took a half-step back. Far enough to be out of her personal space, but still close enough she could smell his slightly woodsy scent with every breath.

Still close enough to be tempting.

And oh boy, was she tempted.

Then the sounds of kids laughing intruded, reminding her where they were, and she took a half-step back of her own, breaking the moment. Scrambling for something normal to fall back on, she smiled down at the dog sitting patiently at Judd's left side.

And froze at the sight of the prosthetic limb on full display under the baggy cargo shorts Judd was wearing today. It was only a split second before she recovered from her surprise, but she knew he'd noticed.

"I'm glad you're wearing shorts," she blurted before pressing her lips together in mortification. "I mean, I'm glad you decided to be comfortable. Because you're hot. I mean, because it's hot! Outside. Today. So, you'd be hot. In pants." She clamped her lips shut, the heat from an embarrassed blush starting to creep up her neck.

Forget the bus. Where was a hole when you needed one?

Judd's lips twitched.

For some reason, his amusement made her feel better instead of worse. "Are you laughing at me?"

He shook his head, but his eyes gleamed with mirth. "I wouldn't dream of it."

"Hmph." But her own lips twitched as well. "So, are you having a good time?"

Judd's broad shoulders moved in a small shrug. "Dana was supposed to bring the kids, but I got a text they're running late." There was a hint of frustration in his words.

Probably because the only reason he was at the picnic in the first place was to spend time with his children, she realized. Outside of Mr. Garvey and herself, he most likely didn't know anyone else here. No wonder he was wandering around by himself.

That, at least, she could do something about.

"Well, I was just heading over to the food, if you'd like to join me." There was the briefest flicker of heat in his eyes again before it was gone, making her wonder if she'd only imagined it.

"Sure. Thanks." As they turned toward the area where huge grills had been set up, he asked, "How about you? Are you having a good time?"

"Of course." When he gave her a quick side-look, she added, "Why wouldn't I be?"

Those broad shoulders went up again. "You just seemed upset by something when we, ah, ran into each other."

They shared a quick grin over the literalness of that before she gave a shrug of her own. "Not upset so much as annoyed. My dad has boundary issues when it comes to family. He thinks we should all do what he says because he knows what's best."

Judd's expression hardened. "People who say they're doing what's best for someone are usually more concerned with what's best for themselves."

The vehemence in his tone surprised her. "That's awfully cynical."

"But true."

She wanted to argue, but the look on his face said he was speaking from personal experience. "Maybe for some people," she conceded. "But I know my dad only has everyone's best interests at heart when he meddles." Something harder to remember when it was *your* life he was trying to orchestrate. "If it wasn't for him pushing me, I never would have become a teacher like him."

They reached the line that snaked past the grills and tables of food and grabbed paper plates and forks. Blackened catfish, corn on the cob, homemade salads and slaws, and jalapeno corn bread still warm from the oven. The combination of delectable aromas sent her salivary glands into overdrive.

As they shuffled along tables groaning with more offerings than could fit on one plate, she was caught off guard by how many people greeted Judd. Not just by name, but with honest pleasure. Some complimented how well-behaved his dog was. A few even teased him about the size of the lone fish he caught the day before, when he'd evidently joined in the annual fishing tournament.

After politely declining several invitations from people to join them, they headed toward an empty table tucked forgotten under the shade of a towering maple tree. As they sat across from each other, she shook her head.

"I didn't realize you knew so many people in town already."

"I mostly just met them yesterday while we were fishing."

And they were already acting like Judd was an old friend. Amazing. She gave a wry grin. "I guess I didn't need to worry about you having to eat all alone, did I?"

"Was that the only reason you asked me to join you? Because you felt sorry for me?"

Caught in his intense stare, another of those little frissons ran through her. She moistened her suddenly dry mouth. "No. No, it wasn't."

His expression remained serious, but his lips curved the smallest bit at the corners, giving him a look of piratical satisfaction. "Good."

Watching as he tore into the corn with straight white teeth that would do any wolf proud, the frisson slid into a full-on burn. Dropping her eyes to her own food, she let out a shaky breath. She was in some serious trouble here. In trying to protect herself from her father's meddling, well intentioned or not, she'd run from the frying pan and jumped right into a fire of her own making.

A sizzling, sexy fire.

And the truth was, she wasn't the least bit sorry. Maybe, just maybe, it was time she let herself get a little singed again.

That thought swirled through her brain as Judd opened the backpack he'd been carrying and pulled out a collapsible bowl. After pouring in some water from his bottle, he set it next to the table for Cooper. Who lapped half of it up before laying back down with what almost sounded like a sigh of contentment.

She shook her head at the dog's manners. "I can't believe he hasn't begged for a single piece of food. My brother Daniel's beagle would have been climbing my leg for handouts by now. And my cat would have been front and center as soon as the plates hit the table to see if anything was worth his time."

Because cats didn't *beg*. They demanded their due.

"Service dogs go through a shi—um, a lot of training before they're certified. Hundreds of hours. Coop won't be distracted by food, animals, or people if he's working."

"And when he's not working?"

"He's pretty much like every other dog. Squirrels are his kryptonite."

"Well, you'll get plenty of those here." She looked at the surrounding trees. "So, even if one ran right down onto the table and danced a cha-cha in front of him, he wouldn't react if he was in work mode?"

Judd's lips twitched, but tilted his head a little as though giving it due consideration. "We've only been together for about six months, so we're still getting to know each other. But from what I understand, it would take something pretty extraordinary to make him break training. I'm not sure if a dancing squirrel fits that criteria, but knowing Coop, I'd have to say no." He paused. "Although he might hate me for not giving him his release command to go teach the smart aleck rodent a lesson." He reached down and ran a loving hand over the dog's head and neck.

There was a wealth of affection in his expression that said his relationship with this dog went a lot deeper than it simply being a service animal performing a task. She started to lean down, then caught herself, remembering proper etiquette. "Is it okay if I pet him?"

Judd nodded and uttered a soft word to the dog. Cooper rose to his haunches, tongue lolling, and leaned into her tentative touch just like her cat Jasper did when he wanted more. Grinning, she obliged.

"You're just a big old mush, aren't you?" she cooed. When the dog swiped its tongue across her face in enthusiastic agreement, she laughed and turned away.

And found herself staring straight into Judd's heated gaze. Her breath stuttered slightly in her chest at the intensity she saw burning in those indigo depths.

Okay. She wasn't the only one feeling the heat. Good to know.

But she still had no idea what she wanted to do about it.

No, that wasn't true. She knew what she *wanted* to do. It was more a question of what she *should* do that was tripping her up.

She remained hyper-aware of the man at her side as they tossed their trash away and walked back toward the more crowded part of the open grassy field. The silence stretching between them was so charged she wasn't sure there wouldn't be an actual spark if they happened to touch.

Something she very much wanted to find out.

So, she didn't.

Instead, she kept just enough distance between their swinging arms as they walked so they wouldn't accidentally brush, but she could still feel the movement of air from his body with every step. Talk about self-torture. What was she trying to prove, anyway? That she was strong enough to resist temptation?

For god's sake, why was she fighting this so hard? She was a single adult. He was a single adult. What more did she want?

Of course, he was a much *younger* single adult than she was.

Something her increasingly overheated libido didn't seem to give two figs about.

Just as the rope of sexual tension had her body swaying closer to his, there was a high-pitched childish squeal of "Doggie!" Reminding her—again—they were in the middle of a park crowded with not only her friends and neighbors, but the children she was supposed to be setting an example for.

Embarrassment she'd forgotten that for even a second morphed to worry as the little girl who'd spotted Cooper came running up and threw her arms around the dog's neck before anyone could stop her.

Cooper stood stoic under the embrace. His eyes locked on Judd as though asking what he was expected to do about the little person clinging to him like a spider monkey.

It might have been amusing if it hadn't actually been so serious.

No matter how well trained the dog was, her every instinct screamed to grab the child away. But she clenched her fists and held back, trusting in Judd to be able to handle the situation with the same skill he had during the Field Day events when the children threatened to mob Cooper on first sight.

With a command that kept Cooper in place, Judd squatted into a modified crouch near the child. "Hi there. I see you like dogs."

Turning her head so she could see him, the girl smiled, showing a missing tooth. "She's pwetty."

Judd's expression softened further with a patient smile.

"Actually, she's a he. His name is Cooper. Would you like for him to say hello?" The girl nodded vigorously, sending her blonde ponytail wagging. "Okay, good. Why don't you come right over here." He quirked his finger.

Cam let out a quiet breath of relief as the girl gave up her hold on the dog without a fight and moved to Judd's side. Even crouched down as he was, he still towered over her, but the child showed as little fear about the strange man as she had the strange dog. There wasn't an ounce of caution on display.

Outrage flared. What was wrong with her parents? Hadn't they taught her about stranger-danger? That caused another thought, making her look around. Where *were* her parents, anyway?

"What's your name?"

"Sally." The missing tooth made it come out with a lisp.

"Well, Sally, I'm Judd, and this furry guy is Cooper. Say hello, Coop." Responding to a hand signal, the dog raised its right paw for a shake.

Giggling, she took it. "Hello, Cooper."

"Would you like to pet him?" When she nodded, he said, "Okay, but remember to be gentle." He guided her little hand to the dog's head and let her stroke the fur a few times.

"He's soft."

"He is," Judd agreed. "But Coop's a pretty big guy, so you want to be careful you don't startle him. So, next time you see him, or any other dog, just ask first before you hug him, okay? He might knock you over without meaning to, and it would make him feel bad if he hurt you by accident."

With a small frown, Sally said, "Okay."

"Good. Let's shake on it." He held his hand out. When Sally did the same, he used just two fingers to give it a gentle shake. Then he said, "Cooper, you too."

The girl giggled again as she gave the dog's paw a good shake, impressing Cam with how deftly Judd handled everything.

As Judd looked around, he asked, "Sally, where are your parents?" The only answer he got was a sulky lower lip sticking out. "Do they know where you are?" Nothing. He glanced up at Cam questioningly.

She shook her head. "I don't know who they are. I don't recognize her." The child looked to be about five, but she must be younger, because Cam was certain she hadn't attended kindergarten this year. Although she did look somehow familiar. Maybe she was someone's little sister?

Before she could ask if Sally knew her last name, a loud male voice barked out, "SallyAnn, how many times have I told you not to go running off like that?"

Everything inside her froze.

No. It couldn't be.

But it was.

Staring at the man approaching with angry strides, green eyes to match his daughter's flashing with irritation, she suddenly understood why Sally had seemed familiar. Pain like she'd never felt before stabbed her straight through the heart.

"Hello, Ty."

She thought she'd managed a calm, even tone, but judging by the sharp look Judd threw her way, she might have missed the mark.

Not that Ty noticed. He barely spared her a glance before focusing back on his daughter, who had stuck her rebellious lip out even further.

"What were you thinking, young lady? We turned our backs for one second, and you were gone. You scared your mother half to death!"

"But I wanted to see the doggie." The whine in her words warned tears weren't far behind.

"That doesn't make it okay to go off by yourself when we don't know where you are."

There was a sniffle. "I'm sorry, Daddy."

With a sigh, Ty shook his head. "Go on, your mother is waiting for you."

Cam tried to resist looking in the direction he gestured, but it was as impossible as stopping the earth's rotation or the setting of the sun. Some force beyond her control made her look to where a lovely blonde, very pregnant woman stood holding the hand of a toddler who was the spitting image of his father. Lucky for her, the boy hadn't seen the dog yet. But the woman saw Cam, and had the grace to look uncomfortable.

With another sniffle, Sally said, "Bye, Cooper."

"Cooper, wave goodbye." Judd winked at Sally as the dog raised a paw up high. Sally managed a watery smile as she waved back. After a last disgruntled scowl at Ty, she trudged toward her mother, head down, yellow SpongeBob sneakers dragging through the grass with every step.

Ty gave Judd an angry glare and jabbed a finger at him. "Keep your dog away from my kid."

"Ty!" She couldn't believe it. "Judd and Cooper did nothing wrong. Sally was the one who came up and grabbed the dog."

"So, what, you're blaming a little kid?" Ty's bluster faltered as Judd rose from his crouch, towering over him by a good handful of inches.

A small, petty sense of satisfaction filled her.

"Nobody's blaming anyone for anything," Judd said. "But you should really teach her not to run up to strange dogs like she did.

Not all of them are as well trained as Cooper. They can be startled and bite when they don't mean to."

"If your dog bites my kid, I'll sue your ass off!"

"Like that would help her live with the scars." Disgust hung heavy in Judd's voice. "You've got an adorable daughter. Trust me, you don't want her to have to spend a lifetime paying for a split-second bad choice."

Ty bristled. "Was that a threat or something?"

Stepping next to Judd, Cam snapped, "Ty, don't be an ass. He's saying protect your daughter." She got a glimmer of satisfaction at seeing him rear back in surprise.

She'd never talked to him like that in front of other people, not even during the divorce. All of their fights had been in private, behind closed doors. "Why are you even here? You don't live in Slow Creek anymore."

Thank God.

If she'd had to see him and his perfect little family every day, she just might have lost her mind.

"I grew up on this tradition, same as you. Why wouldn't I come?" Something cruel flickered in his eyes. "Besides, my parents wanted to spend time with their grandkids."

As a coup de grâce, it was a masterful stroke.

Feeling like her insides had been scooped out like one of the gutted fish on the grill, she forced a smile to her face. "Why wouldn't they?" Grandchildren had been what her in-laws talked about most during their marriage.

And the one thing she hadn't been able to provide.

It wasn't until Judd's arm came around her shoulders she realized she'd started to sway. She hated leaning on anyone for anything. *Hated* it. But this once she allowed herself the weakness and accepted the support of his solid strength, letting it steady her.

Ty watched them both, eyes narrowing. "So, you two are...together?" He made it sound inconceivable, giving the knife another deft little twist.

Judd squeezed her shoulder lightly when she took a breath to answer. "And why would that be any of your business?"

Gaze darting from Judd to Cam and back, Ty smirked. "Well, I guess it's an even match, since you're both, you know...defective." His gaze dropped to Judd's prosthesis, then rose back to Cam, malicious triumph shining bright. "You did tell him, didn't you?"

Gritting her teeth, she ground out, "Just stop."

Judd leaned toward the other man, his entire demeanor transforming from laid-back to deadly between one heartbeat and the next.

"I'd watch my mouth if I were you, son. And just so we're clear, that one *was* a threat. One I'm perfectly capable of making good on, defective or not. Now, do you really want to get your ass kicked by a one-legged man, or would you rather walk away while you can with what little dignity you still have intact? I can oblige either way."

Face going ashen, Ty swallowed hard. "Asshole."

Judd bared his teeth. "Back atcha."

"Just go away, Ty. Go back to your family and leave us alone."

Ty made a sound of disgust. "Whatever. Have fun with your broken little boy toy, Camille." With an angry glare at Judd, he turned and stalked off.

Only when he was lost to sight in the crowd did she allow herself to let out a shuddery breath. Then another. She wasn't going to cry, damn it. Not over him. Never again.

Judd tightened his embrace, keeping her against his side and turning them in the opposite direction. "Let's go for a walk."

It was only then she noticed all the people trying to look like they hadn't been watching the drama between her and her ex unfold. None were close enough to have heard what was said, thank god.

But that wouldn't stop them from speculating. Especially if they saw her lose her composure and burst into tears.

Having people think she still wasn't over Ty was the last thing she needed.

By the time they made their way onto the path winding through the trees to the duck pond at the center of the park, her nerves had calmed. Her anger, on the other hand, was still white-hot.

Ty had always resorted to taking cheap shots when they fought, especially at the end of their marriage when everything had so spectacularly fallen apart. But she hadn't been prepared for him to go right for the jugular. In front of Judd, no less.

The bastard.

"Thank you," she murmured as they walked. "It's probably petty of me to admit, but I enjoyed watching him look like he was going to wet himself."

Judd gave a snort of laughter. "Believe me when I say it was my pleasure." He paused. "I'm gonna go out on a limb and guess that was your ex-husband?"

"Guilty as charged. But in my own defense, he wasn't always that much of an ass." She bit her lip. "I'm sorry he said that. You're not, you know." She couldn't bring herself to say the word. But the momentary stiffening of his body told her he knew exactly what she was talking about.

He didn't agree or disagree. Instead, he said, "Can I ask you something?"

Her gut twisted. Of course, he'd want to know what defect of hers Ty had not-so-subtly hinted at. "Sure." How could she say no, after what he'd just been subjected to because of her?

"Would you like to have dinner with me sometime?"

"Ah..." Caught off-guard by it not being the question she expected, she was left floundering for words for a few, brief seconds. But it was long enough for a shuttered look to fall over Judd's expression. His arm slid from her shoulders.

"Sorry, I shouldn't have put you on the spot like that. Just...forget it."

"Yes."

He sent her a questioning glance.

"Yes, I'd love to have dinner with you." She hated the doubt filling his eyes, knowing she'd caused it. Her with her hesitation, and Ty with his 'defective' jab.

Judd hadn't seemed affected by it then, but now she could see how wrong her assumption was. He'd just hidden his reaction better. Something she had a feeling this man did more often than anyone around him might think.

"Okay. Good." The words were right, but his body language remained stiff and wary.

Not sure how else to prove she was being honest, she reached for his hand and laced her fingers through his. It was a few worrisome heartbeats before his hard, calloused fingers finally curled around hers in return. Relieved, she smiled up at him as they left the trees and found themselves at the pond.

"Aunt Cam! Aunt Cam! Come feed the ducks with us!"

She didn't know whether to groan or laugh. "My nephews," she said by way of explanation and apology. Waving back at the boys, who were standing in line to get a handful of food pellets, she was torn. As much as she loved spending time with them, she wasn't ready to let her private interlude with Judd end just yet.

Selfishly, she wanted a little more time being Camille and not Aunt Cam.

Before she had to make a choice, Judd's phone chirped in his pocket. With an apologetic grimace, he dug it out and read the text. "Dana's finally here with the kids." He looked as torn as she felt, so she let him off the hook and made the decision for them both.

"Go, spend time with them."

"Are you sure? I feel like I'm abandoning you."

"Don't be silly. They're your kids. They come first." She understood that, even if she did feel the teensiest bit abandoned. But she was an adult. She'd suck it up like one.

She'd had a lifetime of practice at it.

Judd looked relieved. "Yeah, they do." He hesitated, then opened a different screen on his phone. "What's your number?" He typed it in as she recited it, and the phone in her pocket rang. "Now you have mine. Call me if you still want to have dinner." He started to turn away, then stopped. "I had a good time today. Thank you."

"Me, too."

A little lick of heat flickered in his eyes before he banked it. "See you around, Camille." With a wink and a grin, he headed back the way they'd come through the trees, Cooper at his side as always.

She bit her lip as she watched him go. *If* she still wanted to have dinner? Like there was any doubt. But even as she thought it, they started to trickle in like a rushing tide.

What would people think if they saw her out on a date with the father of two of her students? With someone so much younger than her? Was it worth the possible heartbreak when he was only going to be in town for the summer? What would it do to her reputation?

Her job?

Feeling like she'd made a huge mistake, she pulled out her phone and sent a quick text. Only her fingers typed something entirely different than she'd meant them to.

Does Friday @ 6 work for you?

She stared at the screen in disbelief. Good god, what had she done?

Maybe he'd say no. Maybe he'd already have something planned with his children. Maybe she'd still have a way out.

The seconds ticked by. Then a minute. Just as she was telling herself he was busy and probably wouldn't even see the text until later, her phone chimed.

Sounds perfect.

She let out a laugh that was half surprise, half terror. Well, there it was. Right or wrong, she was committed. No take-backs, no do-overs. She was having dinner with Judd Aiken on Friday. She'd either just made the best decision of her life.

Or the most foolish.

Chapter 6

"I really appreciate this."

Head bent over the lug wrench as he strained to loosen the last nut on Dana's flat tire, Judd grunted in reply.

"Really, I do."

He grunted again.

Damn, who put this one on, the fucking Hulk?

"I don't know what I would have done without you."

"Called Triple A?" *Tug.* "The garage?" *Tug.* "Your brother?" With a frustrated growl, he put everything he had into it until his arms were quivering with the strain. He was using too much upper body and not enough lower, but what choice did he have?

Dana already had trouble looking at his prosthesis. The last thing he needed was to have it loosen and come off if he torqued his leg the wrong way and the suction valve leaked. Unlikely. Maybe even impossible. But he couldn't bring himself to take the chance.

Which probably made him an idiot.

Finally, when he thought he might pop a nut himself, the lug gave and the wrench moved a quarter-turn.

About fucking time.

As he shook out his arms, he glanced up at Dana, who was hovering off to the side, watching him work.

She gave a small shrug as though just realizing he expected an answer. "No one else was around, and I don't have Triple A anymore."

"Why the hell not?"

"Because it costs money, Judd. Calling for a tow truck from the garage costs money. *Everything* costs money! There just isn't always enough to go around. Sometimes the kids and I have to do without."

It was a comment designed to prick at his guilty conscience, but he managed not to flinch. Instead, he gave a pointed look at the pink summery dress she was wearing, which was clearly new. "And sometimes I guess you don't."

Dana ran a hand over the front of the dress before crossing her arms over her chest in a defensive gesture he knew all too well. One she used because it showcased her plump breasts. She'd won a lot of arguments when they first got married with that move.

"I deserve something nice once in a while. This is the first new dress I've bought in a year."

That might very well be true. But it didn't help his temper when he thought about what could have happened if his kids had been in the car when it broke down. What if they'd been out in the middle of nowhere? If she hadn't had him to call for help?

All the horrible things that could happen to them stranded at the side of the road, alone and helpless, filled his imagination and turned his guts liquid.

"I'll pay for the damn Triple A," he growled, shoving the jack under the car. Not that he was exactly rolling in cash, either. But for the peace of mind about his kids, he'd find a way to cover the added expense.

It didn't take long to swap out the flat tire for the spare, which wasn't looking all that healthy either. A quick inspection of the remaining tires showed they all had the bare minimum of tread left to be considered safe to drive.

His frustration grew. In their five years together, Dana had ignored anything to do with the cars because he'd taken care of it.

What the hell had she been doing for the last three years since the divorce? Putting in gas and hoping for the best?

He put the flat and jack in the trunk, giving the space a quick once-over for any sign of a roadside assistance kit, jumper cables, or first aid kit. There was nothing. With a sigh, he closed the lid and walked to the sidewalk where Dana stood.

Her face glimmered with sweat, but he didn't let her 'poor me' expression stoke his guilt the way it usually did. He'd offered to let her sit in the air-conditioned truck while he worked. She'd taken one look at Cooper sitting in the backseat and declined.

If she'd expected him to take Coop out into the heat so she could sit in cool, dog-free comfort, she'd been wrong. His days of putting her first were over.

His kids were a different matter.

"You're all set. But I wouldn't drive far on the spare." He opened the back door of his truck and grabbed a towel out of his go-bag to wipe his grimy hands on. Dana moved closer, into the blast of cool air pouring out around him.

"It'll have to last 'til Monday. That's when I can get to the garage to get the other one fixed."

"It's not worth the cost of a repair. You need new tires."

"I can't—"

"I'll pay for them, damn it."

She bristled. "I'm not asking for charity."

Hot, tired, and—he checked his watch with a curse—late for dinner, he didn't have time to play to her ego. "And I'm not offering it. This is about knowing my kids are safe when they get in the car. If that means buying you a new set of tires, then I will."

He'd have to dip into his dwindling savings for it, but what else could he do?

Those calls from a private number he didn't recognize, the ones he'd been ignoring because he knew damn well who was on the other end, suddenly got a little more tempting to answer.

Tears glimmered in her cornflower eyes. "You're right. It's for the kids. Thank you," she added, putting her hand on his arm, fingers curling around his biceps.

It was the same thing she'd done all those years ago in the bar when they'd first met. Then, her touch on his bare skin had caused an explosion of instant lust. Now, he just wanted to shake her off so he could get going.

"Sure." He tossed the dirty towel on the floorboard, gave Cooper a quick scratch, and stepped back to close the door. Which forced Dana to step back as well, breaking their contact. "You're good to go. Just let me know how much for the Triple A and tires, and I'll get you a check."

"Oh. You want *me* to buy the tires?" She blinked her eyes, doing a good impression of a helpless kitten. When he knew for a fact she could be a spitting she-bitch when she wanted to. Another familiar weapon from her arsenal. And another to fall flat.

God, had he really ever been that stupid?

Sadly, the answer was yes.

"It's your car, so, yeah." He tried not to sound unkind, but it still came out with a little hint of "duh" to it.

"Oh. Okay." *Blink, blink.* "I guess I can ask my dad to go with me, to make sure I get the right ones."

And once he knew Judd was footing the bill, he'd be sure to pick out the most expensive set he could find, just for spite.

Gritting his teeth, he acknowledged he'd been out-maneuvered.

"Never mind. I'll go to the garage tomorrow and take care of it."

Blink. "Oh, would you? That would make it ever so much easier, Judd, thank you." *Blink, blink.*

"Sure." He looked at his watch again. Damn it. "I have to go."

"Could you maybe follow me home first? To make sure I get there okay with the spare on?" *Blink, blink.*

He gave her an 'are you serious?' look.

"We're less than a mile from your house."

"Which means it'll only take a few more minutes of your precious time." When he looked at his watch again, she asked with a trill of laughter, "Oh come on, what are you, late for a date or something?" Her amusement faded when he didn't answer. "You have a *date*?"

Her incredulous tone stoked his temper.

"Imagine that. I guess not everyone finds my injury as repulsive as you." Triumph bloomed at the small flinch his direct hit scored, only to be replaced by a familiar sense of weary guilt. "I'm sorry, I shouldn't have said that. But I really do need to go. I'll call you tomorrow to let you know when you can drop your car off at the garage for the tires."

"Sure. That would be fine." The stiff words only made him feel worse, but he resisted the urge to apologize again. He'd spoken nothing but the truth, even if he could have phrased it better.

There had been a lot of apologizing during their marriage. On his part, anyway. Much of it for things he shouldn't have had to apologize for. Sometimes it had just been easier to take the blame to smooth things over.

But they weren't married anymore.

And he'd be damned if he got sucked back into old patterns which had been bad even when they'd been new.

Once in his truck, he sent Camille a short text apologizing again and saying he was on his way, then waited until Dana pulled away.

When he realized what he'd just done, he cursed loud enough to have Cooper stick his cold nose into his ear from the backseat, checking to see if he was okay. With a sigh, he gave the dog a reassuring hug before giving the command to settle onto the seat and putting the truck in drive.

It seemed when it came to Dana, he couldn't stop from falling into his default mode of taking care of her. Not even when he knew he was being played. It was frustrating as hell. And something he definitely needed to work on, or it was going to be a very long, aggravating summer.

The directions Cam had given him to her house were easy to follow. Parked in front of the quaint little bungalow with the white picket fence, he had a moment of pure 'what the hell am I doing?' that almost kept him from getting out of the truck.

"You have a date?"

He hadn't really thought of it that way until Dana said it.

Until then, it had just been dinner with Cam, a nice woman he enjoyed spending time with who didn't treat him like a freak or a cripple. Someone who hadn't known him *before*. Before the FUBAR of a mission. Before the surgeries and eventual amputation.

Someone who didn't remember the intact, able-bodied, un-scarred man to constantly measure the current wrecked version against.

A date, on the other hand, brought up all kinds of other thoughts. Romantic thoughts. Thoughts he shouldn't—*couldn't*—have. Not about Cam. Not about any woman. Not when he had nothing to offer anyone.

Not physically. And definitely not emotionally.

His disastrous marriage had proven that.

Rows of red and yellow flowers flanked the brick walkway to the white front door in perfect formation, not a single weed or wilted bloom in sight. It was almost *too* perfect. Too disciplined. As he knocked on the door, he surveyed the freshly mowed front yard with a puckered frown.

Why did all that manicured uniformity bother him so much?

Maybe because it reminded him of the prim, skirt-to-her-knees Miss Richards he'd first met at the kids' school. And he much preferred the not-wound-as-tight Camille he spent time with at the picnic. The one whose modest shorts had still showcased the delicious curve of her ass when she leaned across the table to grab some cornbread. It had been...eye-opening.

And arousing.

Okay, maybe he understood why she wore the baggy camouflage at work.

The door opened, and he got the little punch to his solar plexus that seemed to happen every time he saw her. Her dark brown hair was loose, the ends curling just over her shoulders. The unrestrained style suited her. As did the tiny bit of makeup she wore, the liner winging up slightly from the corners of her eyes, complimenting their natural tilt. A thin silver chain glittered around her neck. That was it. No other accessories or adornments.

And still, she took his breath away. Especially when she smiled. *Oh, man.*

He was so screwed.

"I'm really sorry," he said for probably the third time since he'd first called to tell her he might be a few minutes late. Funny how it didn't bother him to keep apologizing to *her*. "It should have only taken me ten minutes, but the lug nuts were a bi—um, pain to get off." His hands flexed at the reminder, sending a sharp twinge up his arms.

Cam's smile turned to a wry grin. "I told you, it's fine. And you don't have to keep censoring yourself around me like that. I may work with kids, but I still know all the grownup words. I even use a few of them myself on occasion."

Oh, he doubted she knew *all* of them. Not even close. SEALs were pretty damn creative when it came to their profanity. It was almost an Olympic sport for them. But Neanderthal bastards that they were, they still tried to have *some* kind of manners when they were around other people. Especially women.

Still, it was good to know she wouldn't flip out on him if he happened to let a stray 'fuck' fly once in a while.

"Come on in while I grab my purse."

"Are you sure that's a good idea? Didn't you say you had a cat?" He gave a pointed look down at Cooper, who'd whined like a baby about being left in the truck again, even for a few minutes. He wouldn't bother the cat, but the cat might not be as tolerant.

"Don't worry. Jasper took off for my bedroom the second you rang the bell. He's pretty stand-offish with strangers, so he won't be coming out anytime soon."

He didn't miss the wince as she stepped back to let him in. "Are you okay?"

"Oh, yeah. I just twisted my ankle a little this morning. It'll be fine."

As he followed her into the house, he watched with a critical eye as she limped along in front of him in her low-heeled sandals, telling himself he was assessing her injury. *Not* staring at the incredible legs below the swishing hemline of her summery blue skirt.

Manning up enough to admit he was full of shit, that he was absolutely checking out her legs, he refocused his gaze on his surroundings. And was immediately struck by the coziness of the space.

The living room was small, but didn't feel closed in despite the long sectional sofa that took up almost two whole walls. Twin bookcases sat against the third wall, shelves filled almost to capacity with a mix of books and framed photos, flanking a decent-sized tv. Which was currently playing one of the shows he recognized, where people bought run-down houses and fixed them up into their dream homes.

There had been a lot of television watching during his initial recovery.

Cam picked up the remote and turned it off before pivoting back toward him. "I hope you—" She broke off with a soft hiss of pain.

Reflexes he didn't realize he still had got him to her side just as her right leg crumpled. "Easy, now. I've got you." He eased her onto the sofa. "Okay?" She nodded, although her face was still pinched. "I'm going to check your ankle, okay?"

Another nod, this one more hesitant.

Going to his knee, he slipped off her sandal and gently ran his hands around the slightly swollen joint. It didn't seem misshapen, which was a good sign.

"Any numbness or tingling?"

"No." She hissed through clenched teeth as he pressed lightly on the ankle bone, then yelped as he did the same to the soft tissue.

"Sorry, sorry," he murmured, caressing the tender spot in sympathy. The feel of her silky skin was a distraction he couldn't ignore no matter how inappropriate it was. "It definitely seems like it's the tendon and not the bone, but you'll want to have a doctor check it out if the pain and swelling don't subside in a few days. Have you been icing it?"

"A couple of times, yes."

"How about wrapping it?"

"Um...no."

"Stayed off it and kept it elevated?"

"Mostly?" She dragged the word out, making it sound almost like a question. That told him she 'mostly' hadn't done either one.

With more reluctance than he should feel, he put her foot back on the ground and stood. "First things first. You need to get this up." He surveyed the available options before grabbing one of the decorative pillows on the sofa that looked like it would be about the right thickness. Then dragged the ottoman over from the other end of the sectional.

"Oh, you really don't have to..." Cam sighed as he gave her what Gil had always called his "you're doing this so why are you wasting my time arguing" look. "Oh, all right."

Good to know it still worked.

After situating her foot on both ottoman and pillow, he asked, "Where's your ice pack?"

With a resigned look, she gestured toward the kitchen. "Plastic baggies are under the sink. Ice is where it usually is."

Like the living room, the kitchen it opened onto was small but cozy, with dark blue cabinets on the bottom, lighter ones on top, gray stone countertops sandwiched in between. Hand-drawn crayon pictures hung from magnets on her fridge.

Most were childlike, similar to the ones Boone and Carly had gifted him with that were taped all over his cramped living space. But one was a pencil sketch of a cat done with a level of skill that set it apart as exceptional.

Curbing his curiosity, he focused on the task at hand and grabbed what he needed, bringing the improvised ice pack back to the other room.

In his short absence, Cooper had wormed his way up onto the sofa at Cam's side. Head on her thigh, his eyes were closed in pleasure as she slowly petted him. It was stupid to be jealous of a dog. But watching her run her hand along Coop in long, slow strokes, he wanted to know what it would feel like to have her touch *him* like that.

Hell, he'd probably have the same besotted expression his damn dog did.

Leaving the mutt to work his soothing magic, Judd draped the bag of ice as gently as he could over Cam's ankle. "How does that feel?"

"Like I should know I'm too old to let my nephews try to teach me to ride their Hoverboard," she replied with an embarrassed laugh. "It's fine. You really didn't need to make such a fuss, but thank you."

Maybe not. And yet, he had a feeling she was enjoying it, despite her protests.

He knew he was.

"I'm sorry I'm making us even later for dinner," she continued, worrying at her lower lip. "I'll just keep this on for a few minutes, and then we can go."

"Absolutely not. You're keeping off that ankle for the rest of the night."

"Oh, but dinner—"

"Is not worth risking your health for," he said firmly. "If you don't take care of it properly now, it could take weeks to heal up instead of days."

As it always had when his doctors and physical therapists used it on him, the threat of a longer recuperation did the trick. Cam sank back into the cushions with a disappointed frown.

"I guess we can always do dinner another night," she said with a sigh.

He could have just agreed. He probably should have.

But honestly, he was as reluctant to miss out on their evening together as she seemed to be.

Before he could think better of it, he said, "Or I could go get some take-out and bring it back here. Well, you do have to eat," he added when she looked surprised by the offer. "And this way I'll know you're staying off your ankle."

He thought she'd argue again. Instead, she gave a small smile.

"That would be nice. But you don't have to go out for food. I'm sure there's something in the kitchen I can put together...that *you* can put together," she amended when he hit her with the look again. "Can you grill a hamburger?"

He snorted. "I'd have my man-card revoked if I said no."

As he'd hoped, that made her grin. "Then I think we're in business."

Under Cam's directions, it didn't take long to gather what he needed for their impromptu meal after he washed his hands. She knew where every single thing in her kitchen was by memory, right down to what shelf in the refrigerator the pickles were on.

It reminded him of how he'd always packed his gear, everything in the same place every time so he knew where to reach for it even in total darkness.

Neat. Organized. Efficient.

A nice change from the barely controlled chaos of Dana's house.

Once he had everything assembled on the counter, he said, "Okay, just point me toward the grill and tell me how you want your meat." He realized how that might have sounded, and added quickly, "Cooked. How you want your meat cooked."

Laughter danced in her eyes. "Medium, please. But I'm coming outside with you."

Selfish bastard that he was, he didn't argue. He would much rather have her company while he cooked than not. The problem was going to be the logistics of getting her from here to there without putting weight on that ankle.

Once upon a time, it would have been a no-brainer. Just pick her up and carry her out. Now? He wasn't a hundred percent certain he could.

Frustration gnawed at him with vicious, ego-grinding teeth. "I can't..."

Fuck.

With a last pat for Cooper, Cam shooed him off her lap and removed the bag of ice from her ankle. "If you let me lean on you, I can hop out there with no problem." She swung her leg down and reached out her hands to him. "Help me up?"

Fuck, fuck, fuck.

Bracing himself, he took her hands and helped her lever up to her good foot. The right one she kept tucked up as she looped her arm around his waist, leaning into him as she found her balance. He hesitated the briefest second before his arm went around her shoulders.

Damn, she smelled good.

"You sure about this?"

"Piece of cake."

Cake, hell. More like humble pie.

In what felt like a parody of the three-legged race with his son, he helped her toward the sliding glass door at the back of the house one careful hop at a time. All the while praying he didn't end up dumping them both on their asses the way he had with Boone.

He waited while she unlocked the door and slid it open, then eased her down one hop to the slate patio—

—and stepped into a cacophony of colors and scents and sound that nearly took his breath away.

Gardens overflowing with wildflowers rioted around the entire perimeter of the small yard. Blues, whites, yellows, pinks, all mixed together with no rhyme or reason. Like someone had tossed handfuls of seeds in the air and let them grow wherever the wind took them. It was everything the perfect rows of flowers in the front of the house weren't: wild, free, uninhibited.

Which begged the question: which garden represented the *true* Camille?

Or was it both? The public-facing calmer half, balanced by the more carefree private side only an intimate few got to see?

The woman just became ten times more interesting.

"Your yard is incredible."

"Thank you." Cam wore a pleased, almost shy smile as they hopped to the teakwood table a few yards away. She gave a sigh of relief as she sank into one of the cushioned chairs. When he turned another one toward her, she made a face but put her injured leg up without a fight. "It's my favorite place to come sit with a book."

He could see why. The tall hedges kept the yard completely private and hushed, except for the sound of some frogs and crickets starting up their evening serenade. It was the kind of place you could relax and turn your mind off for a little while.

Something he hadn't been able to do in far too long.

After a few trips to the kitchen bringing the assembled items out, he dropped three burger patties on the decent sized gas grill. As they sizzled, he couldn't help remembering his earlier slip-of-the-tongue about meat. He shot a quick look in Cam's direction.

And found her staring at him with a surprisingly hungry expression before she bent to pet Cooper, who had planted himself at her side again.

Hungry for food, you ass.

Any other explanation was ridiculous. Despite the burst of attraction that pinged between them at the picnic, Camille was an educated, classy lady. What interest would she have in a broken-down piece of obsolete equipment like him?

"So, you've been here for a few weeks now, right? What do you think of our little town?" Her polite tone matched the neutral expression on her face when she looked up at him.

Yep. He'd been imagining anything else. Which meant he needed to strangle the wayward thoughts he kept having about wanting to put his hands on her body again and explore more of that satiny soft skin.

Every. Luscious. Inch.

Giving himself a mental bitch-slap, he focused on the question and the burgers. "I like it here. I mean, obviously I've been here before when I came to see the kids. But I was never around long enough to really pay attention to the town itself, or the people. It's a nice place, though. A good place to raise kids."

"Even when it's so far away from where you are? No, sorry," she said, waving her hands. "Forget I asked that. It's none of my business."

No, it wasn't. And if it had been anyone else who asked, he would have told them to fuck the hell off.

But this was the woman who'd all but thrown herself in front of someone who was bigger and stronger to protect his daughter. Her, he didn't mind answering.

"It's a fair question. I guess the short answer is, I wanted to do what was best for Boone and Carly." God, how he hated that phrase. But in this case, it was true.

"After Dana and I broke up, they couldn't stay in base housing anymore, and it would've been tough to find something affordable in the San Diego area. Plus, even if she got a job, most of the money would have gone to daycare. Then her parents offered to let her move in with them until she got on her feet. The kids would have a home and family, and Dana would have a support system to help raise them. It seemed like the best answer for everyone."

"Everyone except you."

Judd shrugged, ignoring the burn in his chest that always came with the reminder of what he'd lost. "Dana and the kids come first."

"*Dana* and the kids?"

"Because she's their mother. Not because I still have any feelings for her."

"Are you sure about that?"

From the tone of her voice, she was no doubt thinking about how he'd put everything on hold to go running the second Dana called about being stuck with a flat.

How he'd put *her* on hold.

He grimaced. "Dana's always been...needy. I guess I still have some habits to break when it comes to her. But I can tell you with one hundred percent certainty there are no feelings left between us."

No good ones, anyway. Those had all been burned to ash long before the divorce papers were ever drawn up.

He scooped the burgers onto buns and brought the plates to the table. "Dinner is served," he said, laying the food in front of her with a flourish. He sat and they both doctored their burgers, him with ketchup and pickles, her with a dollop of barbeque sauce.

Watching her wrap her mouth around the burger to take a bite shouldn't have been erotic. Shouldn't have made his body sit up and take notice. But it was, and it did, in a very primitive, uncomfortable way.

And yet, he couldn't look away.

When she caught him staring, he cleared his throat. "It's okay?"

Swallowing, she nodded and wiped the corner of her mouth with a napkin. "Your man-card is safe."

He shifted in his seat. If she only knew.

The next few minutes were spent in silence as they took the edge off their hunger.

One kind, anyway.

"This potato salad's really good," he said between mouthfuls. In a blue ceramic bowl rather than a plastic container, the delicate balance of tangy and sweet was perfection. "Homemade?"

"Yes, and thank you. I have a lot of time on my hands during the summer, so I end up doing a lot of cooking. And reading. And knitting. And wow, that sounded like I was describing my grandmother." She didn't seem pleased by the realization.

"A couple of my teammates learned to knit." He waggled his fingers. "They said it was good for digit dexterity."

"Oh, come on," she scoffed, stabbing at her potato salad. "A bunch of macho guys sitting around in a knitting circle? You're just trying to make me feel like less of an old fogey."

"I swear, it's the truth. And trust me, Camille, you are a lot of things, but old is definitely not one of them. In fact, I think you're almost kind of perfect." He caught her surprised gaze as it snapped to him. Okay, maybe that was a little more direct than he'd intended.

Tension pulsed between them for several long heartbeats.

Cam broke first. "I...um, thank you."

Stupid, stupid, stupid!

As unsettled as she also seemed, he tried to pretend the moment hadn't happened while mentally kicking his own ass. "Anyway, I guess knitting is harder than it looks. Gil never quite got the knack, but Sandoval's pretty good. He makes a lot of scarves and blankets. So many he started giving them away."

To local churches and shelters, but that was Sand's private business.

Cam looked like she was going to say something, seemed to rethink it, then asked, "How about you?"

"Me?"

"Are you a closet knitter, too?" The question was accompanied by a teasing grin.

"Nah. I gave it a try, but my hands are too big and clunky." He put one on the table next to hers to demonstrate. What he didn't expect was for her to reach over and run her fingertips over his scarred knuckles. Down digits that had almost all been broken at one time—some more than once.

He swallowed hard as she turned his hand over and repeated the exploration on his palm. "And too rough." The words were squeezed out as he struggled to keep his body from reacting to her touch as she lightly rubbed the many scars and callouses she encountered. "They're pretty ugly, actually."

"Oh, I don't know." She laid her palm against his and gave his words back to him. "I think they're almost kind of perfect."

Looking at her smooth, delicate hand on top of his scarred, battered one was the strangest sort of aphrodisiac. Desire, hot and thick, welled up despite his best efforts to hold it at bay. He licked his lips. "Camille?"

"Mmm?"

"I think I'd like to kiss you."

She looked up at him, and this time there was no mistaking the hunger he saw there for anything other than what it was.

Pure, unadulterated lust.
"I think I'd like that, too."

Chapter 7

WHAT AM I DOING?

The panicked question floated up through the layers of lust and need, only to sink again the moment Judd's mouth touched hers. The kiss was neither too soft nor too hard, but the perfect combination that put it in the Goldilocks zone of just right. She reveled in the feel of his firm, warm lips against hers.

It was so, so good, but she wanted more.

So much more.

Reaching up, she cupped his jaw with her hand as she ran her tongue along the seam of his lips in an appeal for entry. With a groan that made her inner muscles quiver with anticipation, Judd opened for her, letting her invade and plunder at will before returning the favor with equal fervor.

They dueled, sparred, nipped and nibbled. Neither giving quarter as they continued to stoke each other's passions higher and hotter. He tasted hot, and spicy, and deliciously masculine.

Wanting—needing—even more, she tried to pull him closer, but her position with her injured ankle propped on the chair thwarted her efforts. She broke the kiss with a frustrated groan. "I need to move my leg down so I can get closer to you."

Her words seemed to break the spell holding Judd in as much thrall as it was her.

"Damn, I forgot about your ankle. I shouldn't have started this." He began to ease away, but she looped her arms around his neck, refusing to let him go.

"No. Don't stop. I may never have the nerve to do this again."

It was an embarrassing admission, but she was so aroused at this point, she didn't care if she had to beg. She had to have just a little bit more of him.

Something dark and wicked passed through his eyes.

"Well, in that case, we need to do this right." With gentle hands he pulled her upright until they were both standing, steadying her with hands on her hips. Then nudged her until her butt was pressed against the table. She didn't understand what he wanted until he pushed the remains of their meal out of the way.

Ah.

Smart man.

Edging her rear onto the table until she was comfortably seated on it, she was glad for choosing the billowy skirt with all the excess material. Not just because she knew it made her legs look good. But because it allowed Judd to nudge his way between those legs with ease, giving him full access to her body.

Better yet, giving her full access to his.

Perfect.

She ran her hands up his chest, reveling in the firm muscles. She wished his shirt was gone so she could see as well as feel the contours of his rock-hard body as she explored. Now *that* would certainly be worth the price of admission. She should know, since she'd already gotten the sneak-peek preview.

Her fingertips curled over his shoulders and pulled him as close as he could get without actually being inside her.

Her inner muscles spasmed at the thought.

Looking up into eyes almost black with desire, she whispered, "I believe you said something about doing this right?" She gave a challenging tilt to her chin. "So? Let's see what you've got."

The look he gave her in return was so hot and raw she was surprised her lips weren't scorched as he swooped down to take her mouth with his.

Clearly rising to the challenge, this kiss blew the other two away. It zoomed right past hot, slid through passionate, and rocketed straight into full-out carnal. Oh, the things this man could do with his mouth!

His hands weren't idle, either.

They were gentler, though, almost hesitant, as they roamed her back and shoulders. As if testing the boundaries of what she would allow. She had a feeling if she made the slightest sound of protest, he'd stop everything he was doing.

And she didn't want him to stop.

No, she wanted him to bring those big hands of his around and cup the breasts aching to be touched and caressed.

Hoping to encourage him to be bolder, she ran her own hands down the long line of his back. When she reached his belt, she hesitated, but was too far gone under the spell of desire for her usual inhibitions to ruin this for her.

She wanted this man. Wanted to touch him. Wanted him to touch her. For the first time in what seemed like decades, she simply *wanted*.

And damn it, she was going to take whatever he was willing to give.

Even if it was for just this one night.

Hands plunging further south, she cupped the firm globes of his ass through his pants and squeezed lightly. As Judd groaned into her mouth, his lower body jerked forward, thrusting the hard bar of his erection against her.

Oh, yes please.

She squeezed again, getting the same unconscious response.

As she'd hoped, her brazenness fueled his own. His hands edged down, thumbs skimming the sides of her breasts, leaving her aching for more. When he did it again, she whimpered, wondering what it would take to get him to really touch her.

By the third fly-by caress, she realized he was doing it on purpose. Teasing her with anticipation. Stoking her arousal. As if she needed any more stoking. She was so stoked she was ready to go off like the whistle on her tea kettle when it hit full boil.

It was time to take things into her own hands.

Literally.

Dipping lower on his ass, she ran her fingers along the crease where his cheeks met his thighs. He shuddered. When her fingertips grazed his inner thigh, his breath stuttered. When they drifted lower on their way back around to the front and the real prize, dragging along his upper thighs—

—he stepped back, breaking all contact with her. Hands, mouth, body, all hot and hard one second and gone the next.

Leaving her blinking in confusion. "Judd?"

He dragged a shaky hand through his hair. "I'm sorry."

"Why? What's wrong?"

"I let that get out of hand. It was just supposed to be a kiss. I forgot..."

"Forgot what?"

Instead of answering, he shook his head and said again, "It was just supposed to be a kiss."

Cold started to seep into her despite the warm evening. She crossed her arms protectively over breasts that were still achy and swollen. "Says who? I don't remember putting a limit on what was going to happen."

"But I did. I swore it would be..." He shook his head again.

"Just a kiss?" When he gave a sharp nod, she threw her hands up in the air. "For god's sake, why?"

"Because I can't give you more."

"I beg to differ. I felt how much more you have to give." Her gaze dropped to where she could see the firm evidence of it still pressing against the front of his pants.

Good. At least she wasn't the only one suffering.

"That's not...*fuck!*" He fisted his hands at his side as though trying to contain whatever emotion was driving him. "What I'm trying to say is, I haven't...*been* with a woman since..." His hand flexed open against the top of his left thigh.

The chill blew away in a rush of understanding. "Since you lost your leg."

His hand curled into a fist again. "I knew I couldn't...that I shouldn't...but damn it, you were just so beautiful and sexy, and I thought, if I could just have one taste..." He gave a harsh laugh. "God, what an idiot."

As much as she wanted to revel in the fact he thought she was beautiful and sexy, she tucked those words away to pull out and roll around in later.

First things first.

"You're not an idiot. And I'm telling you it doesn't have to be only a taste." She tried to touch him, but he'd moved to where he was just out of reach. Her hand fell back into her lap. "I've seen your prosthesis, remember? At the picnic. Did I give you the impression it made any difference to me?"

If anything, his fist clenched even tighter. "You haven't seen everything. You wouldn't want to."

"Why don't you let me decide that for myself?"

"Okay, then *I* don't want you to."

Well, there wasn't much she could do about that.

Except maybe try to talk him down off the ledge he seemed to be teetering on. Eyes dark with lust just moments earlier were now showing too much white. Like a skittish horse about to make a break for it. She had a cold, hard feeling if she let him go now, she'd never see him again.

And darn it, she wanted to see him again.

"Then I guess I'm the one who should apologize to you," she said, shoulders sagging. "I was the one who wasn't satisfied with only a kiss. I pushed for more, and I shouldn't have. I should have been happy with the fact someone like you would even want to kiss someone like me."

"Someone like you? What's that supposed to mean?"

"Old. Boring. Plain." Ty's venomous words hissed through her brain. She swallowed against the bad taste they left in their wake. "Defective."

"Jesus." He stepped forward, cupping her jaw with his hand. "You are none of those things. And I swear, I'll punch your ex's lights out if I ever hear him call you that word again. You. Are. Perfect."

Bitter laughter spilled from her lips. "Almost kind of perfect. That's what you said before."

"I didn't mean—"

"I know. But you were right, anyway. And so was Ty. I am..." She bit off the word as Judd narrowed his eyes. "I couldn't..."

God, this was harder than she'd expected.

"We never had children, Ty and me. We wanted to. We tried. It just never happened for us. The doctors couldn't point to a reason. They said we were both healthy, both capable. And still, after six years of trying, nothing. But then he went and got his mistress pregnant in like, ten seconds flat, so it was pretty obvious the problem was with me, not him."

The look on Ty's face when he told her he was going to have a baby with another woman still haunted her. He'd been so happy. So damn smug.

"See? It's not me who's the problem, Camille. It's all you. You're the one who's broken."

Then he'd dropped the divorce papers on the kitchen table next to her morning coffee and walked out. To go be with his new family.

Anger darkened Judd's expression. "You know that's not true."

"You saw the proof of it yourself the other day."

It took a few seconds for the pieces to click. "Sally."

"Sally." Cute, adorable Sally. Who in a kinder, fairer world could have been *her* daughter. But wasn't.

Would never be.

"That doesn't prove anything." Judd nudged her chin so she had to look at him. "And even if it's true you can't have children, it doesn't make you defective." He spat the word with contempt. "You are not the sum of your reproductive parts."

"And you're not the sum of your limbs. Oh, no you don't," she gritted out when he tried to back away again. She looped her legs around his to hold him in place.

Only to yelp in pain when she moved the injured ankle she'd forgotten about in a way it didn't like. "Son of a biscuit!" This time when Judd tried to pull away, she let him go, but he only moved to check on her ankle.

Despite the concern in his eyes, the hint of a grin flirted with his lips. "Is that one of those grown-up words you know so well?"

"Oh, hush." She might have been amused if her ankle wasn't throbbing so badly.

"Hurts?"

She nodded, pressing her lips together to hold back the "Of course it hurts, you dolt!" that wanted to come out.

Judd straightened from his examination. "Come on, let's go get some more ice on it, then."

After they made their slow way into the house, she found herself right back where she'd begun. On the sofa with her leg propped on a pillow, a new ice-filled bag draped over her ankle, Judd's dog curled up at her side like a furry therapy ball.

She wanted to protest when Judd started clearing the table. It was one of the biggies her mother had ingrained in her: guests don't clean. But there was no way she would have been able to do it herself, and they both knew it.

So she sat and stewed as she watched him move around her kitchen. Putting things back in the fridge. Wrapping leftovers. Even rinsing dishes and loading the dishwasher, since he refused to leave them in the sink as she instructed.

As annoying as it was, it was also kind of nice.

Intimate, even.

Other than family, he was the first man to be in her kitchen since she'd moved in. Watching him move through the space like he owned it made her wonder if he'd take command the same way in other rooms in the house.

One room in particular.

Whoa, down girl.

What was it about this man that made her lose all control of herself this way? Kissing him? *Fondling* him? It was like logical take-it-slow Camille had been hijacked by horny take-it-now Cam.

And yet, the only thing she could find it in her to regret was how she'd managed to bring everything to a screeching halt just when it was getting good.

Really good.

Her breasts gave a dull throb, echoing her disappointment. As unobtrusively as she could, she pressed a hand to them, trying to ease the ache. She had no idea where things might have gone if Judd hadn't put on the brakes, but her body still wanted to find out. Her brain was still riding enough of the dopamine high to want that, too.

Unfortunately for all of her, Judd had drawn a pretty clear line in the sand, and she didn't know how to go about crossing it. Or even if she should try. He was clearly dealing with issues related to his injury.

What if she did or said something wrong? The last thing she wanted was to make whatever he was going through even worse.

Maybe it was best if she let things end between them now, before that happened.

The water stopped running in the sink, breaking her attention from her vacillating thoughts and back to the man causing them. As Judd dried his hands on the red-and-white checkered dishtowel, it was like she could feel them on her body again. Touching. Stroking. Kneading.

Her breasts gave another throb of longing, echoed further south between her thighs.

She barely held back a moan.

At least, she thought she had, until Judd walked toward her, concern on his handsome face. "Are you okay?"

No, I'm hot and bothered and want to climb you like a rose trellis.

Managing a smile, she nodded.

"Fine. Just a twinge when I moved." He didn't look like he was buying it. Needing to redirect them both, she said, "Thank you for cleaning up. You really could have left it for me to do in the morning."

"And now you don't have to worry about it. Consider it my thank you for dinner."

"Which you cooked. Next time, I have to cook for you."

Why on earth did she say that? Hadn't she just decided letting things die a natural death between them might be for the best?

A quick peek up at Judd showed he wasn't sure what to make of the offer, either. He was staring down at her, chest rising as he took a long, slow breath, then let it out just as slowly.

"I'd like that." From his gruff tone, she might have thought it a lie. Until she saw the glimmer of something else in his gaze before he looked away.

Longing.

For her? Sex? Food? She couldn't tell from that tiny glimpse.

But she knew she needed to find out.

"Make sure you wrap that ankle up when the ice comes off," Judd said, his tone back to business-as-usual. "But not too tight, and don't leave it on overnight. But try to prop it up on a pillow when you go to bed."

Was it her imagination, or had he stammered, just a little, on the word 'bed'?

"Got it. Thank you."

A tiny frown marred his face. "I hate leaving you here all alone when you're hurt. Are you sure you'll be okay?"

Ask him if he'd like to stay the night to make sure, take-it-now Cam whispered.

Well, she wasn't doing that.

No matter how much she wanted to.

"It's sweet of you to worry, but it's just a sprained ankle. I'll be fine."

"Okay. Good."

There was an awkward silence.

Hoping she wasn't reading him dragging his feet to leave the wrong way, she said, "You know, it's still early. Would you like to stay a while? Maybe watch a movie, or play cards or something?" It looked like his interest was piqued, so she sweetened the pot a little. "And did I mention there's pie?"

"Pie?"

"Mmhmm. Cherry. Baked fresh this morning." Two of them, in fact. Both for the church bake sale the following afternoon, but he didn't need to know that. She'd still have time to make a replacement if he said yes.

After another of those long, slow breaths, he gave a tiny nod. "That sounds...real nice. Yes, thank you, I'd like that. A lot."

Their gazes caught, and the slow burn began to amp up again.

Wetting his lips, Judd shifted his gaze to Cooper, who was watching him with keen eyes from her side as though waiting for a command. "I, um, I'm just going to go grab his water dish from the truck."

When the door closed behind his escape—because that's what it was no matter how you sliced it—she took a deep breath of her own. One nowhere near as calm and even as Judd's had been.

"Good lord, that man is *potent*." She couldn't remember the last time just being around someone had made her body light up like a Christmas tree. It was both exhilarating and a little bit embarrassing. She wasn't some hormone-charged teenager, after all. She was forty-two. Almost forty-three. She should be beyond this kind of uncontrollable lust.

It took longer than it should for Judd to return.

Was he out there trying to talk himself into staying, or going? She hoped the former. Sexual tension and uncontrollable lust aside, she was enjoying his company. Much more than she'd expected to.

Her body snapped to attention the second he stepped back inside, the black backpack he'd been carrying at the picnic bumping against his leg as he turned to shut the door. It took every ounce of willpower she had to pick up the tv remote and start scrolling through movie options rather than simply stare as he went to the kitchen and filled the collapsible water dish he took from the pack. Especially when he bent over to put it on the floor.

Not that there wasn't a stolen peek or two.

She didn't have *that* much self-control.

Cooper abandoned her to go take a long, sloppy drink. She snuck another look while Judd's attention was focused on wiping up after the dog, pants pulled taut over his muscular backside.

Potent? The man was downright lethal.

How was she ever going to hide her reaction to him? All he had to do was be in the same room, and her body started tingling like a live wire. And she'd committed herself to another few hours in his company.

Brilliant move, Camille. Not masochistic at all.

She went back to flipping through the guide on the tv screen. "What kind of movie do you want to watch?" Because that would be a lot safer than cards or a board game, where they'd have nothing else to do but talk to each other while they played. With a movie she'd be able to concentrate on something other than the man sitting next to her.

Or at least pretend to.

"Anything's fine."

So untrue. Half the movies she scrolled past were rom-coms, which was the last thing she needed to watch with him.

"How about a comedy?" That seemed safe.

"Sure." He walked into the living room. "But you should probably wrap that ankle up first. If you tell me where it is, I'll get the ace bandage for you."

"I think there's one in the medicine cabinet in the bathroom."

There was. But when Judd came back with it, he was shaking his head. "This is too short."

She lifted one shoulder. "It's the only one I have, so it'll have to do."

"Hang on." Grabbing his backpack, he unzipped one of the compartments, reached down deep, and pulled out several different sized rolls of elastic bandages. He chose the one still in plastic. "Here we go. I thought I had a new one in there."

A new one? Why did he have any of them? Who carried around half a dozen elastic bandages? The question was on the tip of her tongue, but she forced it back.

None of your business, Camille.

Pulling off the wrapper, he went to one knee beside the footstool and removed the bag of half-melted ice. "This isn't looking too bad," he murmured as he made a quick examination of her ankle. "You'll probably be able to walk on it by tomorrow."

The urge to squirm in her seat as his strong fingers ran over her bare skin was almost impossible to resist. Her brain knew it was a purely clinical touch. Her body had other ideas. "That—" She cleared her throat and tried again. "That's good to hear."

His gaze shot up to hers as his fingers froze where they were. Several long, blistering seconds passed before he snatched his hand away. "Sorry. I shouldn't have...here." He thrust the rolled bandage at her. "Why don't you take care of this while I, um..."

"Get the pie?"

"Right. Yes. Get the pie." He lurched to his feet, grabbed the ice bag, and retreated to the kitchen.

Cam blew out a silent breath. She really needed to get her hormones under control, or it was going to be a long, frustrating night.

For them both.

By the time she'd wrapped up her ankle, Judd was back with two plates loaded down with generous slices of gooey, flaky cherry pie. Since she could keep scrolling for an hour and still not make a decision about what to watch—she'd done it more than once—she just clicked on the movie she'd stopped on without paying attention to the name.

They both settled onto the sofa as it started. After the 20th Century Fox fanfare, the title flashed on the screen accompanied by a crack of thunder. *Young Frankenstein.* As the stars' names ran over the black and white image of a castle to the accompaniment of haunting violin music, she wanted to sink between the cushions and hide.

Of all the comedies out there, she'd managed to pick probably the only one in the world that dealt with stitched together body parts to watch with an amputee.

Kill me now.

Biting her lip, she said, "I'm sorry, I didn't even ask if you wanted to...we can watch something else." Anything else. *Please.*

"Are you kidding? This is one of my favorites. Mel Brooks is a genius." He must have seen some of the discomfort in her face, because he gave a soft, understanding smile and patted her hand. "It's fine, Cam. Really."

And it was.

It took maybe half the movie, but she finally managed to relax and enjoy herself. A great deal of that enjoyment came from just listening to Judd laugh. It was a low, masculine sound that originated deep in his belly and set off a corresponding tingle deep down in her own. Not a sexual kind of tingle this time, though. It was more...interest.

Real interest.

And that wouldn't do. Not at all.

She'd almost talked herself into believing a quick summer fling with Judd Aiken might be okay. Because a limited affair with a built-in end date was safe.

Interest, on the other hand, wasn't.

Interest encouraged thoughts of a future, and for the two of them, there wasn't one. She didn't know exactly when, but one day soon, Judd would leave Slow Creek and go back to his real life somewhere else.

She just needed to be sure he didn't manage to take a piece of her heart with him when he left.

Chapter 8

THIS WAS A STUPID idea.

He pulled in front of Camille's tiny bungalow, throwing the truck into park a little harder than necessary, and just sat there.

A really stupid idea.

It had started out innocently enough. A simple phone call to check and see how her ankle was feeling this morning. Much better, as it turned out. She'd thanked him for his part in that. Between the ice, bandage, and elevation, his prediction had come true and she was able to walk on it again, albeit gingerly.

The conversation should have ended there.

Would have, if he hadn't been feeling like a moony-eyed teen who didn't want to be the first to hang up with the girl he liked. So, they'd kept talking. And somewhere along the line she'd mentioned she was going to some charity bake sale thing this afternoon.

With a sigh, he unclamped his hands from the steering wheel and got out.

He should have left well enough alone. But no. He'd had to go and open his big mouth and volunteer to drive her. Since it was her right ankle she'd injured and he didn't think she should be driving just yet.

Oh hell, who was he kidding?

It had been an excuse to see her again, and he'd grabbed it with both hands. Only after she'd accepted did he realize he'd not only committed himself to being in her company—again—but worse, in public this time.

Which was why this was such a stupid idea. Because if last night was any kind of barometer, he couldn't be within two feet of the woman without having a very real, very physical reaction to her.

Trying to put a muzzle on his dick was a challenge he wasn't sure he could win.

Get comfortable being uncomfortable.

That had been the advice his BUDS instructors shouted as they had the men link arms and sit in the freezing cold surf of the Pacific during training. Sometimes for hours at a time, as the crashing waves pounded over them like a frigid firehose.

He had a feeling it would be just as appropriate for how his day with Cam was going to go.

The door opened before he could ring the bell. As it had yesterday, the sight of her reached somewhere deep inside him and gave a twist. Damn, she sure was pretty. Today's summery dress was a bit more conservative and a lot less flirty than last night's had been. But the blue-green material still hugged all her curves the right way and made her dark eyes even darker.

A quick look down showed she'd gone the smart route and put on flat shoes that looked a little like ballet slippers.

"Hi."

"Hi."

They stared at each other for a few long seconds before Cam broke the awkward silence. "Let me just get the pies and we can go. I'll be right back."

"Can I help?"

"Actually, yes. If you wouldn't mind carrying them out so I can lock up."

With a sense of déjà vu, he followed her to the kitchen, where an orange tabby was chowing down on a bowl of what looked like stinky wet tuna. When Judd came into the room, the cat glanced over its striped shoulder at him and froze.

"Well, hey there, Jasper." He kept his voice light and unthreatening. But the second he made a movement in the cat's direction, it took off like a shot.

Cam uttered a sad sigh.

"Please don't take it personally. The folks at the shelter said he came out of an...unpleasant situation. When I first brought him home, he ran every time I tried to touch him, too. It took a lot of patience and coaxing to finally get him to trust me. He's not exactly a cuddlebug, but at least he tolerates me petting him. Sometimes," she added with a wry grin. "But new people still make him nervous."

"I'm impressed you'd want to take on a cat that was so badly damaged."

"How could I not? Someone had to care what happened to him. It wasn't his fault he was abused."

Something dark and ugly stirred at her words.

He shoved it back down. Hard. "We should probably get going."

Once Cam was settled in the truck, pies secured on her lap in their plastic travel containers, they were off. He followed her directions to the parking lot behind the building shared by the local VFW and American Legion. Tables had been set up in a line on the strip of grassy lawn in the front facing Main Street.

After unloading Cooper from the backseat, he took the pies from Cam. He followed her to the tables and the cluster of women fluttering around them, setting out cakes and pies and plates of cookies as they chattered and laughed and bragged about whose treats looked best and which were going to sell first.

It all sounded good-natured on the surface. But there was a hint of true competitiveness in a few of the women's joking words.

Two of the gray-haired matrons who'd set their wares on opposite ends of the same table were exchanging what had to be the sharpest barbs coated in sugar he'd ever heard. Leaning close to Cam as they walked past, he asked in a low voice, "If those two hate each other so much, why don't they just stay away from one another?"

Cam grinned. "They don't hate each other. Miss Lottie and Miss Thelma are the best of friends. They're just highly opinionated about which of them is the better baker."

Opinionated? He could easily imagine the two women pulling out their rolling pins and facing off like geriatric gladiators.

"So, which of them is right? Who's better?"

"Oh, no. That's a fight I'll never step in the middle of," Cam said with a light laugh.

They reached one of the tables with open space on it, and he put down the containers so Cam could take out the pies. They'd survived transport in perfect condition, and his mouth watered at the scent of cherries and warm sugar that exploded as she opened the second container. Which was strange, because the first pie hadn't smelled that good when she took it out.

Which was when it dawned on him it was because this one was still warm.

"You had to make another pie this morning because you fed me the other one last night," he murmured near her ear. "Didn't you?"

"What if I did?"

"Then I'd say thank you, but that you didn't have to. I would have stayed even without the pie." The admission was out before he could think through the implications.

Of which there were many, by the way her eyes widened and her lips parted in a tiny O of surprise. "You would?"

He hesitated, then nodded.

What the hell. Go big or go home.

"I enjoyed the pie, but I enjoyed spending time with you more."

"That's..." Her tongue darted out to moisten her lips. "I did, too."

Gaze tracking the movement, he felt a dangerous stir of interest. Now wasn't the time for it, but he couldn't help remembering how her tongue had felt as it dueled against his while they kissed. The hot, sensual caress of those lips. The press of her body tight against—

"Camille, hello!"

He snapped out of his inappropriate flashback and focused on the bleached blonde standing in front of the table, clipboard pressed to her well-endowed chest as she smiled at Cam. For a split second, he thought he was looking at his ex. The hair, the blue eyes, the perky smile—whoever this woman was, she was almost a dead ringer for Dana as she'd looked nine years ago when he first met her.

It was freaky enough to wash away every wisp of heat that had been building and yank him back to the reality of where he was. And what he absolutely should *not* be thinking about right now.

"Oh, hello, Heidi." There was a surprised quality to Cam's tone that said he wasn't the only one who'd been too distracted to notice the woman's approach.

When the blonde turned that mega-watt smile in his direction, he could swear he heard the theme music from Jaws playing.

"And who is this handsome young man you've brought with you?"

Since he was obviously a good several years older than her, the only reason to call him that would be to point out he also happened to be a few years younger than Cam.

A point she felt the sharp tip of, judging by the way her spine stiffened.

"Where are my manners?" Cam murmured, although the flash in her eyes said she wasn't the one whose manners were lacking. "Heidi, this is Judd Aiken, and his dog, Cooper. Judd, meet Heidi Pruitt. She's the president of the Booster Club, which is running the bake sale."

"Just one of many fundraisers we'll be holding. It's so important to do what we can for the children." The words came out as though she were giving a speech. A finger tapped against her lips as she stared at him, a look of concentration wrinkling her brow. "Judd. Judd. Where have I...oh!" Her eyes widened. "*Aiken*. You're Dana's Judd."

"Not anymore."

He hadn't meant to imply anything other than he and Dana were well and truly not a couple any longer. But the way Heidi's baby blues darted from him to Cam as her smile broadened said she'd read another meaning into his words. Possibly the one she'd been fishing for all along.

"Oh. Oooh! Well, isn't that...interesting."

It would have only taken a word to set her straight. But her earlier barb about his age, and by implication Cam's, still pissed him off. So did the way she said *interesting*, like it was somehow incomprehensible he might be involved with Camille.

Remaining silent instead, he stared her down until she started to squirm.

"Well, I have lots to do to make sure today's a success, so I'd best be off. It was nice to meet you, Judd." Her gaze flicked to Cam and back. "So very, very nice."

"You really have to teach me that stare of yours," Cam said with soft amusement as Heidi walked briskly away, clipboard still clutched to her chest like a shield. "It's one handy little weapon."

The thought of his sweet, classy Camille being able to look mean enough to back anyone other than a six-year-old down made his lips twitch. "Somehow, I don't see that working for you."

Wait, *his* Camille?

No, no, no. He scrubbed the thought from his brain. She wasn't, would never be, his. No matter how many times he seemed to forget that fact.

Luckily—or unluckily—the other women took Heidi's introduction as their opening. They all started coming over, greeting Cam as though they hadn't seen her in weeks, then waited expectantly for her to present Judd to each of them in turn.

Social situations weren't his forte. But he held his ground, doing his best to be polite and remember not to scowl at them.

By the time the last introductions were done, he was feeling like the only animal in a petting zoo as they all circled him, chattering with eager smiles. He'd faced down attacking insurgents that hadn't made him as twitchy.

The only saving grace was they were all too polite to come right out and ask anything about his leg. Although he caught more than one of them giving it a glance, as though trying to see through his pants to the prosthesis below.

At least, he *hoped* it was his leg they were stealing peeks at. The other possibility was too disturbing to consider.

Camille, bless her, came to his rescue right before he broke ranks and bolted for the parking lot. "Oh look, our first customers."

The simple comment had all the women hurrying back to their respective tables. He threw her a grateful look, which she returned with a sly wink before she turned to say hello to the couple approaching from the sidewalk.

He moved himself and Cooper out of the way. Leaning against a nearby tree, arms crossed, he observed as foot traffic quickly picked up as word spread the bake sale was open for business.

There was no reason for him to stay. He'd done what he set out to do, make sure Cam got to town safely. She didn't need him again until it was time to take her home.

He should probably head back to Wilt's place and get started stripping off the rotten roof shingles he'd marked earlier in the week. The weather had cooled to what was normal for early June instead of the crazy heatwave they'd endured for almost a full two weeks. Now was the perfect time to tackle that particular repair, before summer came back for real.

He should go.

But he didn't.

Instead, he stayed under the tree, content to watch as Camille interacted with people, from the other Booster Club ladies to the people who showed up to buy something to show their support. She seemed to know everyone. And it didn't surprise him a bit when one of her pies went almost immediately.

Although he did feel a twinge of jealousy toward the lucky people who were taking it home with them.

It wasn't until Cam shifted her weight off of her bad ankle he realized he was staring at her ass. And that she had no chair.

Neither of those would do.

He straightened and looked around, assessing his options and assets before zeroing in on the VFW hall behind him. It was probably where the folding tables had come from, so it was the most likely place to have the chairs to go with them.

The door was unlocked. He mentally shook his head as he went inside, Cooper on his heels. People were much too trusting around here for their own good.

Or maybe he was just too cynical.

Stacked against the far wall of the main room was exactly what he was looking for. There was no one there to ask, so he did what he was used to doing and took charge. He grabbed one of the chairs, then paused, considering all of the other ladies also standing outside in the sun. He grabbed a few more.

He was making his second trip when Uriah entered the building. Dressed today as he had been the first time Judd saw him striding up the front walk of the school like an old-fashioned gunslinger in his sheriff's uniform and Stetson, his expression wasn't hard to read.

He was annoyed.

Judd decided to beat him to the punch. "Just getting some chairs for the ladies."

"Something that should have been done when they put out the damn tables this morning." Uriah's mouth turned down in a deep frown. "They were supposed to set up a few of the tents for them, too, so they wouldn't be in the sun all day. Damnation." He slapped his hat against his leg. "I hate it when people drop the ball like this."

Judd silently agreed. In his world, a single task left overlooked could spell catastrophe for a mission. Even death. Granted, chairs and tents didn't fall into the same category, but his years in the Teams had permanently set his bar extremely high.

If you have a job, do a job. No whining, no excuses, no exceptions.

"Thanks for stepping in and getting the ladies their seats. That was mighty nice of you, Judd."

He raised a shoulder. "Not a big deal."

"Maybe not, but I still appreciate it." Uriah sighed. "I'd also appreciate it if you'd give me a hand setting up those tents before you go. Hate to ask, but it'd be a lot easier with two doing it than one."

"Sure. Let me get the rest of these chairs out first."

It took next to no time for them to drag the pop-up canopies out of the storage room and get them set up over the tables. The ladies were singing their praises by the time they were done, and tried to ply both men with sweets in thanks.

They politely declined.

"Thanks again for your help," Uriah said, wiping sweat from his shaved head with a handkerchief before replacing his hat. "It's a good thing you happened by when you did and noticed."

Not about to lie, Judd fell back on his default response of saying nothing. For most people, it was enough to make them drop a subject.

Unfortunately, Uriah wasn't most people.

Raising one dark eyebrow, he gave Judd a searching look. "You didn't just happen by, did you? You came for a reason." He laughed. "Screw the intimidating stare, son, I've been doing it a lot longer than you. I'm immune."

Glancing over at the women, it didn't take him long to figure out. "Are you sweet on Miss Camille, is that it? You came by to see her?"

Not hard to deduce, since she was the only one unmarried and under the age of sixty sitting there. Still, he resented Uriah's quick assessment of the situation. Obviously, he wasn't masking his attraction as well as he'd thought.

And that could be a problem.

"She sprained her right ankle yesterday. I offered to give her a ride so she wouldn't have to drive on it yet." The truth, if not all of it.

"And just how did you come to be in a position to know she hurt her ankle?"

Damn it.

Well, no use dancing around it. Uriah clearly wasn't going to let this bone go.

"She told me when we had dinner last night."

"Dinner. Is that right." Uriah crossed his arms, drawing attention to his thick biceps and broad chest. A subtle move that would have most people feeling a bit intimidated by his size and strength, if the shiny badge on that chest wasn't enough to do it alone.

Fortunately, Judd wasn't most people, either.

"Camille's a grown woman, Sheriff. She can take care of herself. But I can promise you this. I'd never do anything to hurt her."

"Maybe so. But there's a lot of ways to hurt a woman. Someone like Camille won't do well having her affections toyed with."

The fuck?

"I'm not toying with her."

"Does that mean you've decided you'll be staying on in Slow Creek, then?" When Judd didn't answer, Uriah shook his head. "Unless you're sticking, son, you need to be real careful. Camille may be a grown woman, but she can still get her heart bruised."

He ground his teeth together. "I won't let that happen."

But could he honestly promise that?

Hadn't he spent the last two days telling himself the exact same thing? That he had nothing to offer her? How he should be keeping his distance rather than getting even more wrapped up in her and her life?

And yet, the first thing he did after Uriah drove off was go to her side. Not just to check on her, or because he was bored. But because he enjoyed being near her. Talking to her. Hell, everything about her.

He knew all of what Uriah said was true, yet selfishly he didn't care. Not enough to step away and leave her alone.

God, he was an asshole.

"Uriah looked a little upset when he left." Cam turned her concerned gaze on Judd as he leaned over her. "Is everything okay?"

"He was just annoyed things didn't go as planned." For both the set-up and his warning. "How's your ankle feeling?"

"Fine, now that I'm sitting down. Thank you for that." Her smile lit up his insides in dangerous ways. "In fact, it's feeling so good I was thinking maybe we could try dinner again. Tonight, maybe."

"Yeah?"

Oh, real smooth.

"Yeah. What do you think?"

The heat in his belly kindled brighter. "I think"—*I want to kiss you*—"I'd like that. A lot." With supreme effort, he reined in his out-of-control thoughts and straightened before he gave in to the impulse.

And looked right into the confused face of his ex-wife standing in front of the table.

It was a strange, frozen tableau as the three of them looked at each other while Fate, that sly, savage bitch, sat back and laughed her fucking ass off.

"Daddy!" With a happy cry, Carly and Boone both zipped around the table and tackle-hugged him from each side, breaking the moment. He stiffened slightly when he realized Carly was leaning against his left leg, then forced himself to relax. If she wasn't fazed by the contact with his prosthesis, he'd try his best to do the same.

He hugged them back. "Hey, munchkins! This is a nice surprise."

And it was. He almost never saw them on the weekends. Those were Dana's days off from the diner, and she'd been adamant that during his summer visit Saturday and Sunday would remain hers and hers alone with the kids.

He hadn't been thrilled. But compromise was key to having access to them the other five days of the week. When her parents didn't make plans for them and ice him out, of course. They'd been adamant about having their time with the kids as well.

"Mommy said we could pick out something to buy for dessert." Boone's words were slightly muffled from his face being pressed into Judd's side.

"'cause it's going to help the boots," Carly added.

The chuckle was right there, but he swallowed it down and smiled instead. "I think she said booster, baby, not boots."

Giving a one shoulder shrug that looked suspiciously like his own, she tilted her head to look up at him. "We're looking at all the cakes they have before we decide. I want to get the prettiest one."

"And I want to get the biggest," Boone said.

Cam grinned. "Well, you certainly have some great choices to pick from."

"Hi, Miss Richards," Carly said shyly. Spotting the dog where he was half-dozing under the table near Cam's feet, she added, "Hi, Cooper!"

The retriever's tail thumped on the grass but he stayed put at Judd's hand signal. It wasn't the time or place to let dog and kids get rambunctious.

"Hi, Miss Richards. Coop." Boone looked at his sister. "Come on, let's look at the rest of the tables before all the best stuff is gone!"

As the kids darted off, a vacuum filled the space they'd been.

Unable to avoid it any longer, he acknowledged his ex. "Hello, Dana."

"Judd." She still seemed a little baffled. "What on earth are you doing here?"

"Helping out." It wasn't going to get any less awkward, so he said, "You know Cam, uh, Miss Richards, don't you?"

"Of course. Nice to see you." She gave Cam a distracted smile, like she barely registered her presence.

"Nice to see you, too, Mrs. Aiken." There was a cool distance in Cam's tone. He wasn't sure if it was for Dana or him.

Fuck me sideways.

"Helping out?" Dana gave him her 'get real' frown. "*You* made a cake?"

"I didn't say I baked something. I was here to—Carly, don't you put your finger in that icing. Miss Inez spent a lot of time making that, and no one wants to eat something with your fingerprints all over it."

Two tables down, Carly pulled back her little hand from the cake with the ornate pink-and-white frosting, guilt written all over her face. "Sorry, Daddy." When he tipped his head, she hung hers and added, "Sorry, Miss Inez."

"I'd forgotten how you could do that," Dana murmured.

"Do what?"

"Know what's going on around you, even when you aren't looking."

It was true. His peripheral vision was outstanding, and he was always hyperaware of his surroundings. He'd learned very early not to get caught unawares by anything.

Or anyone.

It was where his Team nickname of Oracle came from. All seeing, all knowing.

And yet, he hadn't seen Dana or the kids until they were right on top of him. Because all of his focus had been on Cam, and the way she made him feel. She made him forget everything else. Including why he shouldn't be feeling that way for her.

And that was even more dangerous than being caught off guard.

He shrugged. "Kids. Cake. It wasn't hard to guess what might happen." It wasn't meant as a rebuke. But as soon as he said it, it was clear she'd taken it that way.

Lips pressed into a thin line, she said, "Then I guess I should go help *my* kids make a choice before they do anything else wrong."

"Dana..." He sighed as she stalked off. Oh yeah, he was going to end up paying for that somehow.

Cam's fingers curled around his and squeezed. He squeezed back, grateful for the silent show of support. "Sorry about that."

"It's fine." Her thumb slid over the back of his hand in reassuring strokes. "If we're comparing exes behaving badly, mine was way worse."

The tension in him eased. At least she wasn't pissed at him for putting her through his Dana drama. "Yeah, well, yours is a—" He cleared his throat. "Jerk."

"I think you mean a dick. And yes, he is."

A bubble of laughter rose as he stared at her in surprise. "Guess you *do* know some of those grown-up words."

"I know *lots* of grown-up things."

The twinkle in her eyes hinted at what those things might be, sending a blast of heat right where it didn't belong while standing on full view in the middle of town. The moment was thankfully broken as a young couple pushing a stroller approached the table. He let himself fade into the background as Cam smiled and greeted them by name.

Her pleasure was clearly genuine. But he thought he caught just the barest hint of something in her eyes as the young mother went into rapturous detail of her little boy's most recent efforts to crawl. Something maybe a little bit...sad.

Which reminded him of the previous night's interrupted discussion about her supposed "defect," not being able to get pregnant. It had been clear from the anguish in her tone, her hunched-in body language, it was a devastating issue for her.

She wanted to have a baby. Badly.

How did she do it? How did she handle being around other people's children all the time and not fall into a sucking vat of jealousy and despair? He knew he still had a damn hard time watching able-bodied men doing all the things he might never be able to again. Performing the job he *knew* he'd never do again.

But Cam loved on her nieces and nephews. Worked in an elementary school. And seemed to know just about every child she came across by name, as well as their siblings if they had any. She embraced the very thing she'd been denied for herself, and did it with honest joy.

That kind of inner strength, of grace in the face of having your own body betray you. It was extraordinary.

And a little humbling.

Not long after the couple moved on, his kids came running back to tell him what cake they'd gotten. He pretended to be surprised, although he'd already seen Miss Inez hand her flower-covered monstrosity over to Dana. And even if he hadn't, the smear of pink icing on Carly's mouth would have clued him in.

Going awkwardly to one knee next to the table, he hugged first his daughter, then his son goodbye. As Boone pulled away, Judd said softly, "You're a good brother for letting her get the pink one. I'm proud of you."

Boone rolled his eyes, but the smile on his face said how much the praise meant. He surprised Judd by throwing his thin arms around his neck for another hug before pelting off after his mother and sister.

Once again, Cam reached out to him in comfort, putting her hand on his shoulder where he knelt beside her chair. A spasm of loss hit him as he watched them go.

God.

It was hard enough knowing he wouldn't see them again until Monday. What was he going to do when summer ended? They'd go back to school and he'd go...away. He still didn't know where, or what he'd be doing. Only that he wouldn't be seeing his kids almost every day like he was now.

And that was suddenly fucking unacceptable.

Maybe Uriah had been on to something.

Maybe it was time to start thinking about the future.

And what it might look like if it happened right here.

Chapter 9

"You have to tell me *everything*!"

Wincing at the screech, Cam pulled the phone from her ear. Joelynn's call wasn't the first she'd received after her afternoon outing with Judd. It wasn't even the third. More like the eighth, and it wasn't quite suppertime yet. The gossip mill still had several good hours of grinding left before it would be considered too late to call to "just say hello."

And then casually ask about "that nice young man you were with today."

Surprisingly, though, none of the callers had been her family. And she knew they knew about Judd, since her sisters-in-law, Aubrey and Addison, had both stopped by to drop off something for the sale. She'd introduced them to him herself.

Which made the silence on the home front doubly disconcerting.

She shifted on the kitchen chair, fingers tracing the chilly sweat beading on her glass of lemonade. "There isn't really much to tell."

"Did he propose?"

Cam pulled the phone away again, this time looking at it like it was crazy. Or at least the person on the other end was. "Of course not! Why would you even ask something so ridiculous?"

"Well, I heard it from Felicity Newcomb, who heard it from Isabelle Sanchez, that she saw him go down on one knee next to you—"

"To hug his kids!"

"—and you had your hands all over him—"

"I touched his shoulder!" Because he'd looked so sad and lost after they left.

"—and that you were looking at him like you wanted to crawl into his lap and kiss his face off."

Okay, so they'd gotten one out of three right. Not that she was going to admit it. Not even to her friend. Maybe especially not to her.

She went on the attack instead.

"What's wrong with everyone? Don't they have anything better to do than to willfully misinterpret everything they see to make it more salacious than it actually is?"

"Ooh, you're hiding something!"

"What? Why would you say that?"

"Because you always start using your big pretentious words when you're feeling insecure. Plus, you didn't bother to deny it."

Dang it.

"I'm not hiding anything. I just don't think it's anybody's business how Judd and I feel about each other."

"So, there *are* feelings! I knew it!"

Double dang.

"I meant, *if* we had feelings for each other. Which I have no idea if he does or not."

"But you do," Jo guessed.

She sighed. "I don't know what I feel. I mean, he's very sweet. And nice. And considerate. And he makes me feel...safe."

A frustrated groan came through the phone. "Camille, he's not a puppy you brought home from the pound. How does he make you feel *as a woman*?

"Good. He makes me feel good about myself."

"And?"

"And..." *Hot. Bothered. Horny.* She picked up the Board of Education bulletin that had come in the mail to fan herself with. "Reckless." What else could you call arriving at a function run by the worst gossips in town escorted by a man?

Especially *that* man.

"You want him!" Jo crowed.

What was the use in denying it anymore?

"God, so much."

Almost too much. It had been next to impossible to stop her stupid body from going all hot and sensitive every time he drew within a few feet of her today. She'd never reacted to anyone this way before. Not even her ex-husband.

"Well, halleluiah, the drought is over!"

Needing to redirect Jo before she started asking question Cam had no desire to answer, she asked, "Did your gossip connection happen to mention Dana Aiken was there today, too?"

"No!" Jo sounded horrified and intrigued all at once.

"Yup. Walked right up while Judd and I were talking."

"Awk-ward!"

"Extremely." But enlightening as well.

Judd may have told her last night he had no feelings left for his ex, other than as the mother of his children. But feelings, deep feelings, weren't always so easily snuffed out. Sometimes a few glowing embers remained long after the fire was extinguished, just waiting for the right moment to be coaxed back to life.

Which had made seeing Judd and Dana together so nerve-wracking, but also so important. She'd been terrified that when she looked into Judd's eyes, she would see some hint of longing or wistfulness or *something*.

And there had been...nothing.

Well, frustration maybe, and a little bit of wariness. But nothing even remotely like pining for a lost love. The realization he'd told the truth had made her almost dizzy with relief. It had even taken the sting out of the way he called her Miss Richards rather than Camille.

Oh, she understood his reasons to err on the side of caution there. Now. But in the moment, it had sounded as if he was distancing himself from her. Like it was the first nail in the coffin for their budding...whatever this was.

"Was she a bitch?"

"No." Surprisingly enough. "That was Heidi Pruitt, being her usual charming self." The woman's catty innuendo still made her stomach curdle, even hours later.

"Oh, lord, what was the Clipboard Queen's problem this time?"

Her lips twitched. Ever since Heidi had lost her bid for president of the PTA, she'd put all her efforts into running the Booster Club. To the point she micromanaged every detail to a neat and orderly death by checklist, earning her the hated nickname.

Mostly, she was harmless. But every once in a while, someone would get the subtly sharp edge of her tongue the way she'd experienced today. Which had surprised her, since Heidi had usually been respectful of Cam's position as principal.

She told Jo about the encounter, leaving out the little dig about Judd's age and focusing instead on the way she'd practically salivated over him. Especially after finding out who his ex-wife was.

"As if she didn't already know," Jo scoffed.

"What do you mean?"

"Didn't you know? Dana Aiken and Heidi Pruitt were best friends back when they were still Dana Leffler and Heidi Lang."

"I've never noticed them being particularly chummy." They both had kids close to the same age, but she couldn't recall them spending time together at school functions.

"Probably because when Dana left town after graduation, Heidi went and married Dana's high school sweetheart. And is by all accounts blissfully happy, living with Kyle and their three kids in their big, expensive house on the north side of town."

While Dana was divorced and waiting tables at the diner just to make ends meet. Yeah, she could see how that might throw a kink in the friendship dynamic.

"How do you know all this? More of your gossip buddies?"

"No. Because I was still substitute teaching back when they were seniors, and I spent a few months in the high school when one of the teachers went out on maternity leave. Those girls and their snooty little clique were hard to miss. Or forget." She put a shudder in her voice. "They're one of the reasons I decided to stick to elementary level teaching."

Dana and Heidi had gone to high school together? That would mean they were about the same age, although she'd always taken Dana as being older. And since Heidi had been gushing during Field Day about how her husband wanted to throw her a huge party to celebrate the big three-oh in the fall and just *everybody* was invited, that meant...

She sucked in a sharp breath as the math worked itself out.

It meant she was a solid twelve years older than Judd's ex-wife.

Suddenly, Heidi's subtle age dig made more sense, especially if she'd known who Judd was all along. The only thing she still wasn't clear on was who the dig had been meant for, Judd or herself. Not that it mattered. Either way, the numbers didn't lie.

Compared to Dana, she was practically an ancient crone.

"So, when are you seeing him again?"

She ran a nervous hand over the brand-new lavender gauze skirt she'd changed into. Trying too hard to look younger than she was, maybe? The possibility eroded some of the confidence putting it on had given her.

"We're supposed to have dinner tonight"—another squeal—"but I'm wondering now if that's such a good idea, considering how much people are already talking. I didn't realize simply letting him drive me to town would become such a huge event. I'm sure he won't appreciate all the attention being focused on us."

"*He* won't?"

"Okay, I'm not thrilled with it, either."

Massive understatement.

Becoming the focus of public gossip wasn't something she wanted to go through again. Ever. Being talked about and pitied for her husband's infidelity, desertion, and quick marriage to the mother of his love child had been bad enough.

Being laughed at for becoming the clichéd divorcée taking up with a younger man would be so much worse.

A heavy sigh came through the phone. "Camille, I'm going to tell you this because you're my friend and I love you. Screw 'em."

She laughed. "What?"

"I mean it. Stop worrying so much about what other people think of you. People will talk no matter what. That's what gossips do. Don't miss out on something—on some*one*—who could be the best thing to happen to you in years just because of them."

It sounded so easy when she put it like that.

But Jo wasn't the one who'd spent months hearing the whispers following her everywhere she went. Who'd felt eyes looking, judging. Trying to find the fatal flaw that had driven Ty into the arms of another woman.

A younger woman.

"Cam?"

She jerked her thoughts from that sad bit of irony. "I know. You're right. You're absolutely right."

Knowing didn't make it any easier, however.

When Judd arrived an hour later, most of the fizzy excitement she'd felt the previous two times he showed up at her door had been supplanted by a nauseating sense of dread. Even so, when he gave her one of those lightning-quick grins as she opened the door, she knew she couldn't cancel.

Whatever happened, whatever the consequences, she was going to keep their date.

She was so focused on mentally preparing herself for an evening of being on display, they were already on 59 heading south before she realized they'd left Slow Creek behind five minutes ago. "Where are we going?"

"Villa Roma."

That was all the way down in Lawrence.

"Oh, I just assumed we'd be going into town."

"I wanted to take you someplace nicer than the diner or the pub, so I asked Uriah for a recommendation for an actual restaurant." He shot her a hooded look. "I hope you don't mind?"

Mind? That they were going somewhere no one knew them? Where they wouldn't be stared at or talked about all night long?

"Not at all." She smiled, her first real one of the evening. "It sounds perfect."

Mood lightened, she followed Judd's conversational lead, keeping things light as they discussed the bake sale and the more memorable moments of the day. Most notable had been when Miss Lottie's and Miss Thelma's cakes had been bought at the same time by the same person, thereby throwing their rivalry into an unexpected tie.

"I honestly thought they were going to chase the poor woman down and ask her which of the cakes she decided to buy first," Judd said with a chuckle.

"Just be glad they didn't think of it."

After they parked, Judd helped her down, then attached the leash and let Cooper out of the backseat. For the first time since she'd met him, his stride was slower than normal as they crossed the unpaved parking lot. Almost tentative.

When he caught her watching him with a hint of concern, he grimaced.

"Gravel still gives me a little trouble with my balance sometimes. I need to practice on it more." It was clear from the stiffness of his expression admitting something as simple as small stones could challenge him wasn't easy.

Her first instinct was to wrap her arm around him to offer support.

But some shred of caution warned it would be the worst thing she could do. Instead, she simply stayed extra vigilant until they made it to the concrete walk leading to the restaurant's front door.

So did Cooper. Who walked close to Judd's other side in a way that made her wonder if he was supposed to be wearing some kind of balancing harness for Judd to grab onto. It was one of the things mobility service dogs were trained for. At least, according to the website she found after she'd given in to her burning curiosity shortly after learning that's what Cooper was.

Why wasn't he being allowed to do his job?

A side-long look at Judd's clenched jaw as he held the door for her said not to ask. But she had a pretty good idea. Because Judd didn't normally require that level of support. At least, not anymore. Every time she'd seen him, he'd walked as smooth and steady as anyone who had two good legs.

But the gravel had been an unexpected reminder to them both that he didn't.

And it was clear he wasn't happy about it.

The inside of the restaurant was small, holding at most twenty tables, half of them intimate two-tops. Done in dark wood, stucco walls, and checkered tablecloths, it felt like it was trying a little too hard for a rustic Italian vibe. But if the food was as good as she'd heard, she could overlook the cheesy décor.

Behind the host stand, a dark-haired man in his thirties gave her his best smile. "*Buonasera.*" His smile moved to include Judd as he followed her in. Only to falter, then fall from his face completely by the time the door had shut behind Judd and Cooper. "I'm sorry, sir. Dogs aren't allowed in the restaurant."

"This is my service dog."

Judd's tone was calm and relaxed, but she could sense the thin line of tension running through him as the man gave him a disparaging look from head to toe, ending with a sneer.

"Oh yes, you definitely look like you need one."

Shocked at the unexpected rudeness, she sputtered, "Are you serious?"

The sneer turned in her direction. "Please. If you're going to lie, at least try to look the part."

"You mean like this?" Judd jerked his pant leg up enough to expose the black and metal prosthetic limb beneath it.

The sneer froze. "Uh…"

"Or I can go take my leg off entirely and come back on my crutches if you'd prefer." Judd smoothed his pants back into place, never breaking eye contact with the other man, who was starting to look a little sick.

"No! That is, uh, of course not. That's not…I just thought…"

"No, you assumed."

The man's prominent Adam's apple bobbed as he swallowed. "I'm sorry, sir. You just look so…healthy."

"Not everyone's scars show. Remember that next time."

"Yes, sir."

She touched Judd's arm. It reminded her of a piece of petrified wood. "Do you want to go?" He looked like he wanted nothing more than to say yes.

Which was how she knew he'd say no.

"No, we'll stay. I promised you a nice dinner." The look he shot at the other man had him scrambling to grab up two menus.

"If you'll follow me, please."

As they made their way through the narrow aisle between the tables, she could feel the eyes of the people they passed on them. She didn't know if any of them had heard the conversation, but more than a few were eyeing Judd and Cooper with varying degrees of curiosity and annoyance.

Since he was so good at knowing what was going on around him, there was little doubt Judd was aware of them, too. But he gave no indication it bothered him.

After leading them to a table, the host waited until they were seated and Cooper settled underneath it out of the way before handing them their menus. "Please, order whatever you like. It's on the house."

Judd shook his head. "No need."

"Then a drink, at least. Please." He gave them a pained look. "I really want to make amends."

"All right, fine." Judd sounded like he'd rather drink gasoline.

Relief crossed the host's face. "Thank you." He signaled to a hovering waiter, who took their drink order.

Once they were alone again, she wasn't sure what to say. She took her cue from Judd, who was studying his menu with the silent intensity of someone trying to crack a top-secret military code. But as she looked over the choices, she couldn't miss the whispers from the nearby tables.

...can you believe the nerve...

...why did they let them in...

...someone should complain to the manager...

With every snide comment, her shoulders rose closer to her ears and she clutched the menu tighter, until she thought the laminated pages would crack.

"I'm sorry," Judd said in a harsh whisper. "I shouldn't have said anything. We should have just left."

She looked at him in surprise. "You most definitely should have spoken up. You and Cooper have every right to be here. Why would you say that?"

"Because you're upset."

"For you!" And she realized it was true. The hot, squirming feeling twisting through her gut had nothing at all to do with finding herself once more on public display. Every bit of it was from righteous indignation on Judd's behalf.

How dare these people whisper and judge things they knew nothing about! She sent a nasty glare at the loudest offender, who quailed under her gaze and ducked his head to concentrate on his food.

She started when Judd dropped his hand over hers.

"I was wrong. You've got a pretty good glare going there yourself, Teach," he murmured with amusement.

"How can you find this funny?"

"I don't." His thumb rubbed over her hand, the caress sending a shiver through her nerve endings. "Come on. You're never going to enjoy your meal. Let's get out of here."

It felt like conceding defeat, but he was right. There was no sense staying and choking down an expensive meal just to prove a point. One most of the mutterers and whisperers wouldn't get, anyway.

With great reluctance, she nodded and closed the menu.

Back in the truck headed for home, they rode in silence for a few minutes before she asked, "Does that happen to you a lot?"

"First time. But then, I don't eat out much." He glanced over his shoulder toward Cooper in the backseat. "I didn't realize it might be a problem. Guess I should've left him home tonight. Sorry."

"No, you shouldn't. And you have nothing to apologize for."

"Sure I do. I promised you dinner, and didn't deliver." He shook his head. "For the second time."

"No, last night was my fault, remember?"

"Oh, I remember." The glance he gave her said he remembered *everything* about last night. Every kiss. Every lick. Every touch.

A pulse of heat thrummed through her in response.

Resisting the urge to fan herself, she cracked the window a little wider instead. "Do you like barbeque?"

"Love it. Why?"

"Because I'm going to introduce you to the best little barbeque shack west of Kansas City."

Following her directions, he drove them to a tiny little dive tucked in the middle of nowhere a few miles outside of Slow Creek. After pulling into one of the few open spots in the dirt parking lot, Judd turned off the engine and sat for a moment, staring at the rundown building with a hint of surprise on his face.

"I know it doesn't look like much," she said, remembering her own reaction the first time she'd been there. "But trust me, the food is five-star."

"If there's one thing I've learned, it's to eat where the locals do. They always know the best-kept secrets."

The Shack wasn't a secret, exactly, but more a word-of-mouth discovery. Not a lot of people driving by would stop based on its appearance alone, which was run-down and small enough to match its name.

Inside and out.

The booth the twenty-something Daisy Duke shorts-wearing waitress led them to was like all the others, looking salvaged from old diners that had closed down or been mercifully renovated to join the current century. Vivid red vinyl clashed with faded turquoise, with a few mustard yellows thrown in to give the space a truly awful color palette. The tables in the middle of the room were also mix-and-match wood, metal, and peeling laminate.

And all were crowded with people and overflowing with food.

She didn't miss the tension running through Judd as they took their seats, Cooper tucked in at their feet. She could feel it in herself as well. Waiting. Listening. But the only one who even seemed to notice or care there was a dog was the waitress, who asked if Judd wanted a bowl of water for him.

He declined with thanks and a warm smile that had the waitress looking a little flustered as she took their order.

"You should go easy on that smile. It's as potent as the glare." When Judd gave her a confused look, she laughed. "Do you honestly not know you just put that poor girl's hormones into hyperdrive?"

The confusion deepened. "All I did was smile."

"Exactly."

Confusion melted into consideration. "Do I put your hormones into hyperdrive when I smile at you?"

A warm shudder rippled through her. "Oh, yes."

Something flared in his eyes, hot and hungry as a slow smile stretched his mouth. One with specific intent. "Good to know."

For the third time that day, she wished for something to fan herself with as her body responded to the naked desire in his expression. Instead, she grabbed a chip from the basket on the table and shoved it into her mouth.

Why, oh why, had she just admitted that? Bad enough he could turn her on like a light switch. Did she really have to let him know it?

After downing another chip, she licked the salt from her lips, hoping their drinks would be there soon. A soft sound jerked her gaze back to Judd. No longer smiling, he was focused with laser-like intensity on her mouth. It took a few seconds to catch on. She flicked her tongue out to her lips again. His breath stuttered.

Oh, yes.

A sense of pure feminine power filled her. She bit her lower lip, eliciting a groan. "Hyperdrive?"

"Freaking warp ten," he answered hoarsely.

Knowing they were equally susceptible to each other somehow evened the playing field. It did nothing to lessen the sexual tension that had sprung up between them, however. Never before had eating a rack of baby-back ribs glistening with thick barbeque sauce seemed so much like foreplay.

Every bite, nibble, and especially lick was a new level of mutual torture. Knowing they were both thinking the same things, all the things they wanted to do to each other, right there in the middle of a crowd of people who had no clue, just ratcheted the hotness factor even higher.

It was the most erotic meal of her life.

The ride back to her house was made in complete silence. It was as if both of them were afraid any talking, even a single word, would break the heady spell pulling them closer and closer to the inevitable conclusion between them.

As she unlocked the front door, her pulse accelerated. This was it. If she didn't say *stop* in the next ten seconds, this was really going to happen.

Tonight.

Right now.

Her and Judd, naked and sweaty, tangling in her plain blue cotton sheets. Once they went inside, it was all but inevitable.

Pushing the door wide, she stepped in without a word.

Judd followed with Cooper. Closed it and turned the lock, his motions slow and deliberate, his gaze never once leaving hers. They stood there for a moment, both breathing hard. Then she lunged at him. Or he lunged at her. It didn't matter who moved first, just that they were finally touching.

Kissing.

Devouring.

A moan rumbled up her throat when he grabbed both globes of her butt in his strong hands and pulled her tight against his erection. It was just as big and hard as she remembered. Just as good. Her head dropped back as he thrust against her.

God.

Taking immediate advantage of the access to her neck, he kissed his way down the sensitive skin there to the tendon that ran along the side.

And bit.

She couldn't hold back the gasp that gentle laying of teeth elicited. Any more than she could stop the dampness soaking through her panties. Needing more of him, she slipped her hands under the hem of his polo shirt and shoved it up. Relishing the feel of hot, naked skin under her fingertips.

Judd yanked the shirt over his head and tossed it aside, leaving him bare from the waist up. The last time she'd seen him this way, propriety and the fact they were fifty feet from the school had forced her to turn away.

Now, there was nothing to stop her from looking her fill.

Good lord, he was beautiful.

Bronze skin flowed over broad shoulders and muscles that twitched and quivered like a racehorse in the starting block as she ran her hands over them. Her fingers grazed two lines of black ink over his left pectoral, partially hidden by the sparse dark hair growing there. A string of numbers.

No. Dates.

Putting her discovery aside for later, she drew her nails lightly over his nipples. They tightened into hard buds as he sucked in a breath, making her smile. Next her fingers ran over abs defined enough to earn the descriptor ripped. Down along the thin line of hair from his sternum past his belly button and straight to parts further south currently guarded by his belt buckle.

Undeterred, she bypassed the blockade and settled her hand on his erection through his pants with a sense of possessive triumph. Giving a gentle squeeze, she ate the groan from his mouth. His erection jumped and pulsed beneath her palm.

Clearly, it wanted out. What could she do but oblige?

But when her fingers went to work on the buckle, he covered them with his and broke from the kiss. "Cam...I'm not...I don't think I'm ready to be naked. Not yet." From the pain in his voice, it wasn't just being physically bared to her that terrified him.

She pressed a tender kiss to his lips. "It's okay. We can do this at your pace. In fact…" She gauged the distance to the wall behind him. "Do you trust me?"

Keeping eye contact the way you might with a dangerous animal, Judd nodded. He let out a small *oomph* as she used her body to force him back two steps until he touched sheetrock. He kept watching as she slipped to her knees in front of him, brushed his hand away, and slowly undid the buckle. It wasn't until she was pulling down the zipper that he laid his hand on hers again to stop her.

Smiling up at him, she said, "Trust me."

Slowly, and with obvious reluctance, he set her free.

He wore his pants loose, so it didn't take much to tug them down to expose the top of his gray boxer briefs. His erection strained against the stretchy material, the flushed tip peeping from beneath the elastic waistband. With care, she pulled the briefs down just enough to free it and took him in her hands, then into her mouth.

This time, they both groaned.

Oh, yes.

He was hot and hard against her tongue and tasted salty and delicious. She swirled her tongue against the sensitive bundle of nerves under the rim before taking him deep to the back of her throat, again and again, until he was calling out hoarsely for mercy.

Smiling around his erection, she eased back, but only a little. She wanted him just this side of wild. It would keep him from thinking too much.

Hands tangled in her hair, forcing her to look up at him. Eyes of burning midnight met hers, and she knew he'd reached his breaking point.

"Bed." He growled the word. "Now."

Letting him slide from between her lips with one last lick, she smiled up at him, triumph singing through her veins. "I thought you'd never ask."

Chapter 10

I thought you'd never ask.

Ask? There was no asking. He'd demanded, lust clearly stealing his higher brain functions and ability to speak in anything other than single syllables.

He didn't care.

All that mattered was getting her naked. Getting inside of her.

Now.

They stumbled into the bedroom, still touching, continuing to stoke the flames. Neither of them wanting to give what was burning between them the chance to cool by even the smallest fraction.

This was incendiary, and they were both willing to be scorched by it.

After flicking a switch for the bedside lamp, Cam led him to the bed. She sat and tugged him toward her, caressing his cock as she licked her lips in anticipation.

The primal part of him growled *yes, take it!* But if he went into that talented mouth again, it would be the end of him.

And he had other plans for his naughty little principal.

Big plans.

"Uh uh uh." While his lizard brain howled, he gently loosened her hands from him and pushed them to the bed. "My turn. Lay back."

With a soft moan of anticipation, she did as he commanded.

"Take off your panties. Not the skirt," he barked when she reached to pull both waistbands down together. "Not yet. Just the panties."

He wanted to make this last.

It was impossible to look away as her hands inched her gauzy skirt up over her thighs with agonizing slowness. His mouth watered with every inch of bare skin she exposed. Then very nearly dried up and choked him when he saw the proof of her desire dampening the crotch of the lilac lace panties she started to ease off with her thumbs.

Fuuuck.

It was slow torture.

His hands ached from the tight fists he made to keep from ripping them off her himself. When the panties reached her knees, she let them slide down the legs that hung over the edge of the bed, and pool around her ankles.

She must have kicked off her shoes somewhere, because her delicate little feet were bare when he slid the panties off over them.

No longer constrained, her legs parted easily as he knelt between them, the skirt still hiked up, baring her to his greedy gaze. "You are...*god*. So fucking beautiful."

The scent of her arousal teased at him, honey and spice, making him hungry to find out if she tasted as delicious as she looked.

She was too far away. Grasping her thighs, savoring the silky feel of her skin, he tugged, bringing her right to the edge of the mattress. Right to his mouth. Which hovered above her for a few seconds, savoring the anticipation.

A few seconds was all either of them could stand.

"*Please,*" she begged.

With a groan of surrender, he pressed his mouth to her. Licking along the slick walls. Lashing at her clit with his tongue until she was a writhing, gasping ball of need. All it took was sliding one finger inside her to send her over the edge.

As she screamed, her body pulsed around his finger, making his cock give a sudden pulse of its own.

It wanted to be there, inside her. *Now.*

Exerting every ounce of willpower he still retained, he bided his time. Let her milk every last bit of pleasure from her orgasm while he watched. It wasn't until she finally collapsed against the bed and stopped twitching, breathing in ragged gasps, that he eased back from her.

"So fucking beautiful," he repeated.

Watching her come had been like seeing the sun rise after a long, dark night in one of the hellholes he'd been deployed to.

Glorious and awe-inspiring.

"I don't think I've ever felt this good." Cam's words were slurred, causing him to grin at proof of a job well done.

"I'll take that as a challenge." After kissing her inner thighs, he got back to his feet.

"Oh, please do."

Hands on the sagging waist of his pants, he started to shove them down.

Only for reality to slam into him like a rocket-propelled grenade as his fingers brushed the uppermost part of his silicone liner. He froze.

He forgot. How could he have fucking forgot?

Cam writhed on the bed, hands reaching for him. "Judd, please. I want you."

He wanted her, too. Wanted to strip away the remaining clothes between them, crawl on top of her, skin to skin with nothing between them but well-earned sweat. Love her until they were both too exhausted to move. But—

He couldn't.

Couldn't take that last step.

He swallowed so hard it made an audible click. "I..."

"Leave them on if you need to," she said with patient understanding in her eyes. "It's okay. Just please don't stop."

Staring down at her, sprawled wanton on the bed, skirt up around her waist, thighs wide in invitation, knowing what he wanted—what they both wanted—he was terrified of not being able to perform as expected. A familiar panic boiled up inside.

Not now, not now!

Pulling on his SEAL training, he concentrated on his breathing to fight the anxiety attack back. In four seconds, hold four, out four, hold empty four. In, hold, out, hold. It took three repetitions, but the buzzing in his ears finally receded and his fingertips stopped tingling.

And Cam watched him through it all with her calm, patient gaze.

Fuck my life.

"Better?" she asked quietly.

Not trusting his voice yet, he gave a jerky nod.

She held her arms out to him again. "Just lay with me and hold me, if that's what feels right for now. I shouldn't have pushed you. I'm sorry."

She was apologizing to *him.*

Unbelievable.

"I want to be inside you so badly I can barely think straight," he rasped out. "I want to do this with you. I do. I'm just...hitting a lot of firsts here. And I'm not sure what will work the way it used to." Or not.

Besides him.

Because he'd just proven he wasn't the man he used to be.

Fucking pussy-ass anxiety attacks.

"Then we find a new way that you feel comfortable with." She looked up at him through her lashes as she bit her lower lip. "Think of the fun we can have experimenting."

His cock, which had started to deflate, perked back up at the suggestive tone of the offer. "Think so, huh?"

"Know so." Her reddened lips, still bearing the indents from her teeth, turned up in a smile. Only her eyes remained solemn as she waited for him to make a decision.

Man the fuck up, Aiken.

"Can we..." He flicked a glance at the bedside lamp.

As much as he wanted to see her face, watch her writhe and shudder and gasp her way through another orgasm, he wasn't certain he could perform if he knew she might see what he wasn't ready to show her. Not yet.

Maybe not ever.

He pushed the voice of weakness aside with a violent shove.

This was about here and now. See the problem, work the problem. When it was over, *then* he'd worry about the future.

Silently, Cam rolled to her side and switched the lamp off, throwing the room into a dusky twilight. Rather than lay back down, she stayed seated on the edge of the bed. Once more, she reached out her hand to him. "Kiss me."

That, he could do.

Sinking down beside her, he covered her mouth with his. He let all the desperate desire bottled up inside loose in that kiss. Devouring her. Worshipping her. Begging her, even though he wasn't sure for what.

She met him kiss for kiss, nip for nip, driving him higher and hotter with every stroke of her tongue against his. The taste of her was intoxicating.

Breaking away for air, she gasped, "Touch me."

With pleasure.

Hands plunged up under her blouse to the silk-clad mounds of her breasts. He ran his thumbs over the hard points of her nipples, dragging a moan from her throat.

Needing more, he reached around and undid the clasp, shoving the bra up and out of the way. His fingers closed on the perfect handfuls just as her hands pressed to his bare chest, scoring his skin lightly with her nails.

With gentle pressure she urged him onto his back. Kissing. Touching. Building the heat between them back to the point of ignition. She was on all fours beside him now, and he took full advantage, bringing his mouth to her right breast and suckling a gasp right out of her.

He switched sides, giving the left the same attention, before claiming her mouth for another deep, carnal kiss.

Once again, she broke away with a gasp. She stared down at him, chest heaving for breath as fast as his was. "Trust me."

He'd followed where she led so far. Consumed by the desire whipping between them, he groaned out a response, even though it hadn't been a question. Or maybe it had. "Yes."

Her expression was lost in shadows, but he was certain she smiled.

In one fluid motion, she slid her leg over his body so she was straddling him, a knee on either side of his hips. His cock was trapped between them, so close to her damp heat it was like being poised on the lip of a volcano.

He was in both heaven and hell.

If she moved up, just a little, he could be inside her.

And if she moved down, she might see the top of his prosthesis liner.

When she started to shift, he stiffened, but all she did was lift herself enough to free her bunched-up skirt. It billowed out around them like a lavender cloud, hiding where they were so close to being joined from view.

And everything else along with it.

Which was why he didn't panic when she rose on her knees and reached beneath her skirt to readjust the open flap of his pants.

Worried she was being jabbed by the buckle or zipper, he lifted his ass to shove both pants and briefs down a few more inches.

His aching balls appreciated their freedom.

Especially when Cam's slender fingers slid over them in a caress of tactile discovery. She cupped them and gave a gentle squeeze that pushed a grunt from somewhere deep in his belly before continuing her quest up his shaft. Then she was raising herself up again, holding him firmly in one hand as she sought the right angle to take him inside.

With a slow groan, she sank onto him. The sensation so damn good it nearly blew the top of his head off. She was so tight and wet and— "Condom!"

Cam froze. "Oh my god, I've never...I'm healthy. And I can't...can't get pregnant. Remember?"

He'd heard that before. About nine months before Boone was born. *Of course I can't get pregnant. I'm on the Pill.* Right. Well, he was in no position to take that kind of chance again. "I'm healthy, too. But we should probably stop and get one, anyway."

"I hope that means you have one with you." Her words were edged with desperation. "Because I don't."

Neither did he.

"Fuck!" They had to stop.

But he couldn't.

Couldn't be here, be right inside the snug heat of her like this, and pull out now. Not for anything other than her telling him to.

Besides, hadn't she tried for years to get pregnant without succeeding? What were the odds this one time, out of all those others, that she would? One lousy time should be safe, damn it. That bitch Fate owed him one.

"Do you want to stop?" he gritted out. He would if she said yes.

It would kill him, but he would.

She hesitated only a second. "No. Do you?"

"No." Lizard brain had won this round.

"Thank god." She leaned forward to kiss him.

Then she began to ride. Rising up, she sank down again with an undulating motion, her inner walls clasping him tight. Let him go with great reluctance. Welcomed him back again with every stroke. Tighter, wetter, hotter than her mouth, it was the most incredible sensation he'd felt in...forever.

Reaching up under her blouse and loosened bra, he palmed her bare breasts. Without prompting, she slipped both off and tossed them away, giving him easier access. The light was too dim to see the color of her nipples. They were tight and puckered under his fingertips, and no doubt dark with arousal.

He urged her closer to take one in his mouth.

With a soft mewl of pleasure, Cam's inner muscles spasmed around him, nearly sending him to the point of no return. Through sheer will, he forced his orgasm back.

Not yet.

He wanted more.

Needed to give her more.

When the tempo of her up-and-down glide changed abruptly from slow and smooth to fast and jerky, he knew she was close. Thank god. He wasn't sure how much longer he could hold out.

Reaching under the skirt, his thumb found her hard little clit and stroked it in time with her rise and fall. Up. Down. Harder. Faster.

She gasped, writhed, then came apart for him. Head thrown back on a long, guttural groan as her inner walls contracted and pulsed with every wave of the orgasm.

With a cry of his own, his control disintegrated and his own pleasure rushed over him like a tsunami of sensations. Molten. Colossal. Miraculous.

Drained, they lay panting on the bed, Cam collapsed forward across his chest, her breath soft and warm against his neck. They'd need to get up and deal with the messy consequences of bareback sex soon. But not right now. Not yet.

First, he had to sort through all the thoughts and emotions bombarding him about what had just happened.

Making love to a woman was something he'd all but accepted might never happen again. Oh sure, the doctors had said he was fully capable, physically. The shrinks had told him any impediment to the act was in his head. The physical therapists and other amputees at Walter Reed had assured him where there was a dick, there was a way.

He hadn't thought any of them were lying, exactly.

But he hadn't really believed them, either.

Until Camille.

Like that sun dawning over the desolate dark, she'd given this part of his life back to him. Proved the doctors were right, and he was still a whole man. Showed him he could still pleasure a woman. Still feel pleasure.

So much pleasure, he was surprised his heart hadn't fucking exploded from it.

A heart she might just have laid claim to a piece of.

He couldn't say any of that. Especially not the last part, which was only now starting to sink in. So, he said something ridiculous instead.

"I really love this skirt."

A puff of laughter warmed his neck. "Really? And here I wasn't even sure I should wear it tonight."

"Wear it? Hell, you should bronze it and hang it on the wall." He ran a hand over her damp back, relishing the softness of her. "I thought you looked like a beautiful Romani queen when you opened the door."

A vision of her flashed through his mind. Not of that moment, but of her perched atop him, breasts bare, riding him for all she was worth. "Make that Romani goddess."

"A goddess, huh?" She sounded both amused and pleased.

"Oh, yeah."

"Does that mean you'll worship at my feet?"

He ran a hand down her arm in a soft caress. "Your feet, your knees, your nose..."

"My nose?" she repeated with a laugh.

"I'll worship any part you'd like."

She snuggled her head tighter into the crook of his neck. "Mmm, I think I like the sound of that."

So did he.

As much as he wanted to stay just like this, wrapped up in her arms and body in the dark for the rest of the night, eventually the need to get cleaned up became a pressing concern.

Cam beat him to it.

She pushed herself up, hands on his chest, and gave him a long, slow kiss. "I need to use the bathroom. I'll be right back." She hesitated, then tapped a finger against his sternum and said with mock sternness, "Don't go anywhere."

Any answer he might have given was lost in the sensation of her pulling off of his still partially erect cock. Resisting the urge to grab her back, he rested on his elbows and watched her shimmy out of the skirt which had been such a godsend. Only when the bathroom door clicked down the hall did he fall back onto the bed with a groan.

Don't go anywhere? Hell, he wasn't leaving without a gun to his head. And probably not even then. He had every intention of—

His thoughts stuttered to a stop.

Of what? Climbing under the covers with her? Spending the night holding her, touching her, worshipping her body?

A low, humorless laugh escaped him. It was hard to believe, but he'd actually managed to forget again, just for a minute, why he couldn't have those things. Not yet, anyway. But maybe one day...

Hope was a dangerous thing.

It could carry you through hell, but also destroy you if you let it. He'd had hope he wouldn't lose his leg. Hope his marriage wouldn't implode. He'd spent years hoping someone would rescue him from the nightmare of his life on the cattle ranch.

Hope could be just as big a bitch as Fate sometimes.

By the time Cam returned to the bedroom, he'd cleaned himself up with some tissues and pulled everything back into place.

Sweat was pooling in uncomfortable amounts under his liner. His go-bag was out in the truck, but he didn't feel like explaining to her why he needed to get it. It would have to wait until he got home.

Which was probably going to be soon, judging by Cam's disappointed expression when she saw him standing there fully dressed. Or, as dressed as he could be, since his shirt was still out by the front door somewhere.

She, on the other hand, was gloriously naked.

A disparity that had her reaching for the silk robe draped on the chair by the closet. "You're leaving?"

"Not this minute. Unless you want me to."

"But you're not staying."

He didn't pretend to misunderstand. "I can't. Not...yet. I'm sorry."

"Okay." She managed a smile as she walked toward him, tying the sash. And kept right on walking until she was flush against him, arms looped around his waist as she looked up at him. "It's okay."

Staring into her open, honest eyes, he believed her.

"Thank you." He set his lips to hers. Softly. Reverently. Trying to put all of the emotions he couldn't find the right words for into the kiss.

When it was done, she blinked slowly, like someone coming out of a trance.

"Wow." She pressed a kiss to his chest. "You're very welcome." Looking up through her lashes, she asked, "Would you be averse to a little cuddling before you go?"

Going anywhere near that bed with her, even clothed, was a dangerous temptation. But it was too close to the fantasy about how the night might have gone if he wasn't such a broken mess to pass it up.

To risk stealing just a small taste of what he couldn't have.

He nodded and let her tug him to the bed. The pillow his head sank into smelled like her. The sweet scent mingled with the earthier aroma of sex still in the air, a combination that had his cock twitching in renewed interest.

This is so dangerous.

Tucked in against his right side, Cam let out a contented sigh. He wanted to do the same. She felt exactly right there. Almost perfect. The only thing that would make it better was if he didn't have to get up and leave.

Her hand found its way to his chest, toying with the sparse hair there before stroking over the same spot on his left pec several times. He knew without looking what she was running her fingers over.

"My kids' birthdays. So I could keep them close whenever I deployed. Safer than carrying a picture." You never wanted to give the enemy a weapon to use against you if you were captured. Even a tat of their names would have been dangerous.

"You missed them." It wasn't a question, but a commiseration.

"Like you wouldn't believe." He blew out a sigh. "I had no idea it was going to be this hard."

"Them moving here after the divorce, you mean?"

His skin quivered as she ran her finger over the ink again in a whisper-breath touch. "Yeah. At the time I thought, I'm used to being away from them a lot, anyway. How much worse could it be?"

Turned out, a whole lot worse.

He hadn't realized how precious every crumb of time he spent home with them between deployments was until he was left with nothing but phone and Zoom calls. Hard to tuck your kid in or get a goodnight hug over the computer.

"You were away a lot because you were a SEAL?" She looked a little embarrassed at his surprised start. "I heard a rumor."

Of course she had. Damn small towns.

"Yes, I was a SEAL." The past tense still tasted bitter. "And yes, that's why I wasn't home much. Being on the Teams meant being deployed for a mission at any time, being gone for sometimes weeks or even months. And not being able to talk about what you did when you got back."

"It sounds like that kind of life can be really rough on families."

"It is." To the tune of a ninety percent divorce rate, according to the attorney who'd handled his. Not very encouraging numbers. But Team guys kept getting married anyway, always hoping they'd be the ones to beat the odds.

Fucking Hope again.

"If you had it to do over again, would you still let the kids move to Slow Creek?"

"Definitely."

"Even knowing how hard it would be for you?"

"I may not be the best father in the world, but I hope I'd always put what was best for my kids ahead of what was best for me." The rush of anger that bubbled up out of nowhere took them both by surprise. "Sorry, I didn't mean to snap your head off. It was…"

"A sore spot?"

She had no fucking idea. "Yeah, a little."

"Want to talk about it?"

"No." *Hell* no.

"Okay." Her hands continued to play lightly on his chest, her breath slow, warm puffs of air against his skin. No pouting. No tantrums. No wheedling. None of the things he was used to dealing with whenever Dana didn't get her way. The things he knew how to combat.

Calm acceptance turned out to be a more potent weapon than tears.

Breaking all his own rules about never talking about them, he said in a halting voice, "I didn't have the best role models when it came to parenting. My grandparents raised me after my parents died and they, well, they weren't nice people." Understatement of the century. "They had very strict ideas about religion and behavior and...discipline."

A sharp intake of air preceded Cam's hug. "You don't have to tell me this. I understand. They hurt you."

"They did." Although 'hurt' seemed too mild a word for what he'd endured at their unforgiving hands.

"What happened to your parents?"

"They died in a car crash when I was ten." The lie had been told so often he almost believed it himself now. "My mom didn't have any family. My father's parents were my only relatives, so I was sent to live with them on their cattle ranch in Montana even though I'd never met them before."

"How long were you with them?"

"Until I was eighteen." And could legally walk out the door without them being able to have the sheriff drag their "wild and troubled" grandson back home.

Again.

"Oh, Judd." She pressed a kiss to his skin. Her mouth felt extra hot, which meant he'd probably gone cold, from the inside out. "Didn't anyone notice? Try to help you?"

"A few teachers noticed something wasn't right, but I told them what I was supposed to say."

"I fell down the stairs, I walked into a door," Cam murmured.

"The paddock gate closed on my fingers, I tripped over a feed bucket I left lying around in the barn," he continued, the lies told by rote still right there waiting to be voiced. He gave her a questioning look. "How did you…"

"I've been a teacher for over twenty years, and I do emergency fostering. I've heard more than a few excuses that didn't quite fit." She stroked where she'd kissed him as though in commiseration. "But your teachers believed all of yours? Even after it happened more than once?"

"They believed what was convenient. My grandparents were pillars of the community. Of the church. I was just some angry, sullen kid no one knew." He grimaced. "I did try to tell the doctor the truth once when he was setting my hand." After the third break on the same finger from a too-vigorous caning. "Too bad for me he was of the same Old Testament 'spare the rod, spoil the child' mentality."

An ember from the burning pit of anger that had sustained him as a kid started to glow again inside his chest when he thought of the five days locked in the woodshed. To "fast and contemplate" for breaking the golden rule of silence after the doctor informed his grandparents of what he'd said.

There had been a lot of visits to that woodshed over the years.

"After that, I learned to stop expecting anyone else to help me." Not even the one who should have. "I had to take care of myself. So, I did. When I got a little older, I tried to run away. I kept hoping they hated me enough to let me go. But it turned out they wanted to save my heathen soul even more, and kept having me brought back."

Cam reared up on one elbow. "Your *what*?"

He almost managed a grin at her outraged expression.

"Yeah, that's what they always said when they were doling out another 'lesson.' Although in hindsight, I think they hated my mother more for convincing their son to run away together at eighteen than they did for her being part Blackfeet and putting her 'Indian blood' in *their* grandson. That just gave them a properly righteous excuse to make me pay for my parents' sins. In their own minds, anyway."

He'd become their whipping boy for the son who'd gotten away. Literally.

"God." Collapsing back to his side, she laid a gentle hand over his heart. "I'm so sorry no one was there for you when you needed them. No child should have to endure that, especially at the hands of the very people who are supposed to love them and keep them safe."

Blinking back the sting in his eyes that *was not fucking tears*, he placed his hand over hers. They lay there, the beat of his heart as it slowed back to its normal steady rhythm a dull pulse through their stacked hands.

There was more, so much more he could tell her.

But there was only one thing that truly mattered.

"I swore if I ever had kids, I'd never do a single thing to hurt them. No spankings, no being sent to bed without supper. Even time-outs were hard for me to do." Too many bad memories of that damn woodshed.

"I've always tried to do everything I could to make sure they were happy. That the choices I made would never cause them a moment of doubt that I loved them. That it really was what was best for *them*." Not like his father, who'd only used the words to soothe his guilty conscience.

But Cam didn't need to know about that ultimate betrayal.

"I've seen the way you are with your kids. The way they are with you. Judd, those kids love you to death, and I know you'd die before you ever hurt them." Cam brushed her fingers over the tat resting over his heart again. "You are a wonderful father. Never let anyone tell you you're not, because they're lying."

"Even if I'm only a part-time, long-distance dad?"

Because these past few weeks had driven home to him just how much he hated missing the little things in their lives. Eating meals together. Hanging out watching silly cartoons. The soft kitten-snore his daughter made when she was sleeping.

Things no amount of Zoom calls could ever replace.

Her fingers stilled. "Do you want to be more than that?"

Heart giving a huge thump he knew she had to feel, he took a deep breath and put it out there despite the risks. "I think maybe I might."

Chapter 11

No man should look sexy riding a camel.

Arms folded along the wooden top rail of the ring where said man and beast were making another circuit at the end of a long lead, Cam barely held back the sigh wanting to escape.

Camels were dirty, smelly beasts. But cradling his daughter in front of him, Judd made this one look good. Spine straight, shoulders back, hair slightly tousled around his face by the wind. Put some robes and a headdress on him, and he could be a warlord chieftain riding into a desert camp to claim his Bedouin bride.

Or his Romani goddess.

Throwing the brakes on that train of thought, she forced her attention to the other two camels being led around the large ring. Her nephews Owen and Alex were on one, while Judd's son and her other nephew, Elijah, occupied the other. They all looked like they were having a blast.

Her nieces, Mary and Hazel, had already finished their ride and were currently in the restroom with her sister Lynne, washing their hands.

She wasn't the only one who thought camels smelled bad.

That left Cam with a few precious minutes for herself. Not having to watch and herd the mob of kids. Not needing to fight the tingles that raced under her skin every time Judd was within two feet of her. Not forced to deflect probing questions from her sister, who seemed to have developed a keen interest in the exact nature of Cam's relationship with Judd.

Which, she had to admit, was a legitimate question.

Too bad she didn't have an answer for it.

Three days had passed since he left her melted and sated in her bed. And she still wasn't sure if they'd made a huge mistake, or taken the first step toward something special. Judging by the slightly awkward start to their zoo outing this morning, she guessed he was having the same confused feelings on the matter.

Of course, the awkwardness could have also come from her darling sister being all up in Judd's business from the moment they got in the ticket line together.

And she'd thought Uriah had given him the third degree that day outside school.

Ha.

The sheriff didn't hold a candle to Lynne when she went into momma-badger mode.

"I still can't believe you invited him."

Speak of the devil.

Glancing at her sister who'd sidled up next to her at the fence, she did an automatic scan around them for the girls. They were on a bench under a nearby tree, shaded from the afternoon sun, heads bent over the brightly colored map of the zoo's attractions.

She hoped they were looking for the nearest food vendor, because she was starving.

"I told you. I thought it would be something nice for him and his kids to do that maybe he wouldn't have thought of on his own."

"Uh-huh."

Actually, it had been a semi-desperate bid to spend time with him after he'd turned down her offer of a lazy Sunday brunch the morning after their night of hot and sweaty sexcapades. She hadn't gotten the sense he was lying when he said he'd already promised to work on Mr. Garvey's roof all day. She already knew him well enough to understand his sense of honor concerning promises and obligations.

But she also hadn't wanted to let too much time go by before they saw each other again, either.

Absence did *not* always make the heart grow fonder. Sometimes it just allowed doubts to fester and grow into more than they should be.

Not that she was projecting or anything.

So, she'd mentioned her planned outing with her sister, taking the kids to the zoo, and asked if he wanted to bring his kids and come along. It seemed like a perfect way to see him again, but in a neutral, no-choice-but-to-be-platonic situation. Just in case he was feeling the same niggling uncertainty as she was about what they'd done.

And what came next.

"Are you upset I asked him to come?"

Lynne smiled and waved as the camel carrying Owen and Alex lumbered past before answering. "No, his kids are great. And having another adult to ride herd on these monsters is always welcome. Especially when the adult looks like he does."

"Lynne!" Even knowing her sister was happily married couldn't squelch the flare of possessive jealousy that swept over her.

"What? Oh please." She flapped her hand. "Yes, he's good looking, although not nearly as hot as Jamal. What I meant was the don't-mess-with-me vibe he gives off. It's like having our very own guard dog keeping everyone in line."

While she'd have to disagree with Lynne's clear bias toward her husband on the whole hotness matter, she had to admit she was right about Judd's slightly militant aura.

As relaxed and easy-going as he seemed with the kids—even the ones not his own—he still exuded an unconscious sense of command all of them were under the spell of. There had been markedly fewer arguments today than on most trips involving this many kids, and zero cases of anyone getting separated from the group.

He never tried to take charge from her and Lynne. When he said something, though, everyone listened.

"What I am is surprised," Lynne continued. "A week ago, I hadn't even heard you mention the man's name. And now he's here on a family outing. Call me crazy, but that means something."

"Okay, you're crazy." But not wrong.

"So, what's going on? Are you dating? Just friends? Friends with benefits?"

Heat flared up her neck and spread like wildfire across her face. "Oh, my god, seriously? You do recall I'm the big sister here, right?"

Lynne made a sound like a leaking tea kettle. "The family's worried about you."

The family.

Of course, they'd all know she'd asked Judd and his kids to come along. Lynne would have been on the phone to their mother the minute she hung up with Cam about the addition to their outing. Like an emergency call daisy-chain, mom would have called her daughters-in-law, who would have in turn told their husbands, who would have gone straight to their father.

She cringed inside.

It was only a matter of time before her dad decided to poke his nose into things. And where Uriah and Lynne hadn't managed to scare Judd off with their dogged inquisitiveness, he just might.

"They're especially concerned after what happened on Saturday," Lynne added, waving again as Elijah and Boone passed by.

Cam's hand froze mid-wave. "Saturday?" she croaked, visions of a sweaty, groaning Judd flashing through her brain in a scorching rush.

"At the bake sale? When you showed up with him? And he hovered all over you the entire time before you left with him again?"

"Oh, right." The bake sale. Not the hot sex afterward. Of course. How would anyone know about that?

Although it looked like her sister might have some suspicions after her less-than-innocent reaction.

At least now she knew why no one in the family had bothered to call and grill her Saturday night, or any of the days since. They must have decided to leave it to Lynne to handle in person, when she couldn't escape.

And she'd inadvertently handed her Judd on a silver platter as a bonus.

Should have thought that through more.

"Well, you can tell everyone they have no reason to worry. Whatever is going on between Judd and I is our business, not theirs." Not that that would ever stop them.

"Aha! So there *is* something going on!"

Wanting to beat her forehead against the railing for her poor choice of words, she didn't reply. Instead, she turned her attention to where the riders were offloaded from their respective camels. Part of her cringed as she watched how awkward it was for Judd to dismount onto the high platform. But another part was proud of him.

When Carly had balked at getting on the giant animal with anyone other than him, he didn't hesitate to agree. Despite the concerned pinch of his lips as he'd studied the logistics of the deep two-person seat he needed to swing his leg over.

Uncomfortable or not, he'd done it.

I'll always put what's best for my kids ahead of what's best for me.

If anything could make her fall a little bit in love with someone on such short acquaintance, it was a statement like that. Which probably should have worried her a lot more than it did.

Because she had.

Just a sliver, but it was enough that she was vulnerable to getting hurt in a way she hadn't allowed with any man since her divorce.

Lynne looked from Cam's face to where Judd was walking toward the exit gate with a skipping Carly's hand firmly in his. She smirked. "Oh, yeah. There's definitely something."

"Leave it," Cam warned.

Lynne made the leaky kettle noise again, but held up her hands in surrender.

Right. Like she was buying that. Butting into each other's business was her siblings' favorite pastime.

"Did you see, Miss Richards?" Carly asked in an excited voice. "I rode the camel all the way around. Twice!"

The girl's exuberance was contagious, bringing a smile to her face. "I did. You were wonderful." Her gaze drifted up to Judd's face, including him in that assessment. Their eyes snagged and held. Her breath caught in her throat as a tiny spark of heat flared in the indigo depths, an answering glow lighting in her belly.

The boys erupted through the exit gate, all talking and laughing at once, shattering the moment. And not a second too soon. Cam put a hand to her stomach as she glanced away, a little shaken by the strength of her reaction to just a look.

Lynne, bless her, took charge of the horde, announcing everyone needed to go wash their hands before they did anything else.

"I'll take the boys." Judd's voice held a hint of gravel in it, telling her he'd felt it, too. "Can you bring Carly to the little girl's room?"

"Of course."

She made short work of the task. Working in an elementary school had given her a master's degree on how many ways little girls could dawdle in a bathroom rather than taking care of business and getting out.

Did Judd realize the same about the boys? As she and Lynne waited with the girls back at the bench, she had a moment to worry he might have bitten off more than he realized when he took charge of all four of them at once. Not that they would cause any trouble. They were all good kids. But they were young, hyper, and in the care of an unfamiliar adult whose boundaries of control they might just be tempted to test.

A concern that dissipated as they all came streaming out the bathroom door single file, Judd bringing up the rear like a diligent sheepdog herding his flock.

The image made her grin.

It also made her realize she missed Cooper padding along at Judd's side. She'd gotten so used to him always being there, it was like a part of Judd was missing.

Did he feel the same way?

It had been his decision to leave the dog at home with Mr. Garvey, but she had the feeling he was more uncomfortable about it than he let on. Cooper was more than a physical aid for him. There was also the psychological benefit of the security he represented.

Because she was watching, she noticed the small hitch in Judd's gait. When he got closer, she could see the lines of discomfort bracketing his mouth, even though he was still talking normally to the boys about something to do with baseball.

When they reached the bench, the boys immediately began arguing with the girls over whose turn it was to pick what they did next. Cam stepped closer to Judd with the backpack he'd left in her care when he got on the camel.

"Is everything okay?" she asked softly.

His mouth drew into a grimace as he shouldered the pack. "I need to go take care of something. I might be a few minutes, so if you want to head out to the next attraction, I can catch up when I'm done."

Having deduced whatever was in the backpack he always carried had something to do with his prosthesis, that meant whatever he had to 'take care of' did as well.

She shook her head. "That's okay, we'll wait for you. Besides," she added, glancing at the debate going on over the map with a wry grin, "you'll probably be done before they agree on something, anyway."

When Judd got on the short line for the family restroom, with its single occupancy and locking door, she knew she'd guessed right about his prosthesis. Hopefully, it wasn't anything serious.

Her brain started working out different contingency plans for the rest of the day if he had to leave, both with and without his kids staying. Seven children to two adults would be tricky, but not impossible. It was more delivering Boone and Carly home afterward that might get a little sticky.

Explaining to Dana Aiken how she'd come to have the children in her care when they'd started the day with their father wasn't something she wanted any part of.

"Wouldn't it be faster for him to use the regular men's room?" Lynne asked five minutes later, sounding slightly aggrieved at the delay. Cam couldn't really blame her. The kids were becoming restless.

"I don't think it's the toilet he needs to use."

"Then what—oh!" Comprehension lit her sister's eyes. "Got it. It's a leg thing."

"I think so."

"Daddy pro'ly needs to fix his socks," Carly said, startling them both.

She looked down at the girl, who leaned against her leg. "His socks?"

Carly nodded, eyes trained on her father as he entered the restroom as though afraid he might disappear forever. "His leg socks. He has to change them a lot, 'cause his leg sweats and changes size, and his pro...pro..."

"Prosthesis," Cam supplied.

"Prosisis can rub and make a blister." She rested her head against Cam's hip as though it were the most natural thing in the world.

With a lump clogging her throat, not certain if it was from the girl's words or her actions, she ran her hand over Carly's head in a gentle stroke. Her hair was much lighter than her father's, but had the same texture, silky and thick. "Thank you for telling us."

She had no idea if Carly understood what she'd said or was just parroting something Judd had told her. Either way, it was good he'd been open with his children about his injury and prosthetic limb. They were young, yes. But the young were sometimes a lot better at dealing with new and strange things than many adults were.

Well-established ideas and prejudices could be tough to break.

"Mom, can we go? I'm hungry."

Cam and Lynne exchanged a look. Both were familiar with that particular tone from Owen. It was a stepping stone to whining, which was only a pebble's throw from full-on brat. "In a few minutes, honey," Lynne said. "We're just waiting for Mr. Aiken."

"Okay."

This time the look Cam shared with her sister was one of shocked surprise. "*Okay*?" Lynne whispered. "That's it? Oh, we have *got* to bring your guy with us next time we take the kids anywhere. He's like a freaking Pied Piper. They'll follow him any-where!"

She probably should have protested that Judd wasn't 'her guy,' but it might have sounded like a case of the lady protesting too much.

Besides, she kind of liked the sound of it. And, if she wasn't mistaken, her tough-to-win-over sister had just given Judd her tacit stamp of approval.

Would wonders never cease?

Of course, there was still the rest of the family to deal with. But one was a good start.

As Judd emerged from the restroom, a man waiting in line hold-ing the hand of a girl slightly younger than Carly said something to him. They were too far away for the words to carry, but the body language was clearly angry.

Judd replied, but whatever he said didn't placate the man. He jabbed a finger in Judd's direction, then pointed from the family restroom door he'd just exited to the men's room entrance on the left.

Before she could catch her, Carly bolted in the direction of her father.

"Carly, no! Stop!" Cursing herself for not being quicker to react, she ran after the girl, who was dodging people a lot more fluidly than Cam could.

For someone with little legs, she was *fast*.

She arrived just in time to hear the girl admonishing the stranger with, "It's not polite to point your finger at people, you know."

The guy, who was probably in his late twenties, looked a little taken aback at being lectured by a child. "You're right," he conceded, then looked back to Judd, annoyance still stamped on his face. "But it's also not polite to use restrooms designed for *families* who need them when you're all by yourself and don't need to."

Muscle flexing along his jaw as he clenched it, Judd muttered, "Sorry," before putting a hand of Carly's back. "Come on, let's go."

As they turned to leave, the guy gave a parting shot. "Selfish jerk."

She had a feeling Judd would let the insult slide because of the kids. But she found she couldn't. She turned back, ready to give a piece of her mind despite the squirmy feeling in her belly public scenes caused.

Only Boone beat her to it.

Racing up, he planted himself between the man and his father and sister, eyes blazing.

"My daddy's a war hero, and he lost his leg fighting for his country. You shouldn't be mean to him!" He crossed his little arms over his chest, chin thrust out like a bulldog as he glared up at the man.

Carly mimicked her brother's stance. "Yeah! Don't be mean."

Mouth opening and closing like a hooked trout, the guy had the grace to look first embarrassed, then ashamed. "You're right. I'm sorry." He swallowed his pride and repeated it to Judd. "I am sorry."

Judd gave a tight nod. "Let's go, kids. Everyone's waiting on us."

Boone took one of his father's hands, Carly the other. Before they moved, though, Carly turned to the younger girl holding her shamefaced father's hand and said, "You should ride the camel. It's lots of fun."

Eyes wide, the other girl nodded, a shy smile on her face. Carly waved goodbye with her free hand. The girl did the same. Just like that, they were friends, conflict forgotten.

If only it were as easy for adults to manage.

Lynne had the other children either sitting on the bench or touching it. An old trick their mother had used to keep her own brood in one spot on penalty of losing dessert for a week. As they made their way the short distance back to them, Carly reached out and took Cam's hand in hers.

She'd had lots of children hold her hand over the years. It's what they did, what they were taught. Hold a grown-up's hand to be safe.

But this time, this child, felt different. Judd already had a firm grip on his daughter. She didn't need to take Cam's hand to feel safe. She'd taken it because she wanted to.

A fact that pleased her on a deep, visceral level.

"Sorry, he got away from me," Lynne said, giving an exasperated look at Boone, who was smart enough to appear contrite.

"Sorry," he mumbled.

Judd gave Lynne a rueful smile, then asked, "So, what did we decide is next?"

In unison, the shouted reply was "Ice cream!"

He grinned. "Sounds good to me."

As she and Judd brought up the rear, Boone and Carly once more a part of the eager pack, she asked softly, "Are you going to be okay with a couple more hours of walking?"

He hitched the backpack higher on his shoulder in what she was coming to recognize as one of his few tells for being uncomfortable. "All taken care of, thanks. I'm good to go."

The faint lines still at the corner of his mouth said something else, but she didn't call him on it. Instead, she angled her path so she was walking close enough for their arms to brush. "I know I'm not Cooper, but if you need to, you can always lean on me."

Voice rough but gaze tender, he took her hand lightly into his. "No, you're definitely not Cooper. You're something much, much better." Leaning in for a clandestine kiss on her cheek he whispered, "Plus, I bet *you* don't hog the bed."

A zing tickled low in her belly at his words. She knew they were meant playfully, but still couldn't stop herself from upping the stakes, just a little.

"Well, I guess that's something you'll have to find out for yourself, now, isn't it?"

The rumble of a low groan escaped his throat.

"Do me a favor? Get your ice cream in a dish? I don't think I could handle watching you lick a cone right now." He shot her a pleading look filled with barely banked heat.

Given how easily their meal at The Shack had turned into an hour-long act of non-contact foreplay, she was quick to agree. "Same goes."

"Deal."

"But after we get home—" She bit her lip, knowing it drove him crazy.

"All bets are off," he growled.

The bass in his voice sent a shiver of delicious anticipation through her. Threat? Promise? Who cared. Either one ended with the two of them quenching the steady heat that would stay stoked but contained until then.

She could hardly wait.

Chapter 12

AFTER PULLING HIS TRUCK into the diner's parking lot, Judd turned off the ignition and sat, drumming his fingers on the wheel in a nervous beat. It was late morning. Judging by the almost-empty lot, he'd timed it right and the breakfast rush should be over. That meant a better chance of stealing a few minutes of Dana's time to talk.

And ask for a favor.

Just thinking about it made his fingers pick up tempo. She'd been pretty good about giving him as much time as he wanted with the kids during the week. When her folks weren't laying claim to them, anyway. Which had been more often than he would have liked, but so far hadn't been excessive. Just frustrating.

But he was about to ask her to break the one rule she'd set down when he'd gotten to town. And he had no idea how she was going to react.

Which was why he was doing this in person rather than over the phone. It was easier to read an unstable situation and adjust tactics when it was done face-to-face. It was also harder for someone to say no.

That was the plan, anyway.

Not that any of his plans had gone the way he expected lately. Or wanted. Starting with the evening of hot, sweaty sex with Camille he'd spent half the day fantasizing about as they tromped around every inch of the zoo on Tuesday.

He hadn't been honest with either her or himself about the painful rub on his residual limb. Adjusting the sock thickness and adding a bit of padding to the sore spot had helped, but by the end of the day he knew he'd been a stubborn idiot.

Thankfully, the rub hadn't turned into a blister. But it had needed time to heal properly without further irritation or it would have. Which meant being unable to wear his prosthesis, which meant no time with the kids. Or Cam.

And definitely no sex.

All of which had put him in an extremely foul mood the past two days.

Camille had been nothing but understanding and concerned when he'd begged off of their planned evening after the zoo. She hadn't even given him an "I told you so" look, even though he deserved one.

Instead, all she'd wanted to know was what she could do to help.

Which was nothing. All he'd needed was time to heal.

Most of which he spent in dread fear she might show up at his door anyway while he was sitting there with his stump swinging in the breeze.

To his undying relief, she hadn't. Although she had called and texted several times.

No, it had been Uriah who'd invaded his space, barging into the camper the next day like he had the right. Even after Judd told him to fuck off and get lost.

Uriah's reply had been for him to suck it up, get over whatever pity party he was having, and bring his pansy-assed self up to the house. Because he sure as hell wasn't replacing the rotten spindles on Wilt's staircase all by his own damn self.

Judd grinned at the memory.

Uriah on a rant was a sight to behold. And while he'd been pissed at the time, it had been just the kick in the ass he'd needed to stop acting like a bashful teenager hiding out until the zit on the end of his nose was gone to be seen in public again.

This was who he was now, zits and all. And the time would come when he'd have to come out from behind closed doors without his prosthesis and the illusion of normalcy he'd come to depend on.

So, he'd sucked it up as instructed, grabbed his crutches, and made his way to the house. His basketball shorts were long enough to cover the end of his elastic bandage-wrapped stump. Still, he'd spent the first five minutes in Uriah and Wilt's company feeling like his dick was hanging out in public.

Neither man gave the empty leg of his shorts more than a curious glance. The prickly feeling of being exposed faded, and he'd been able to almost forget about it entirely as they got to work.

Sliding out of the truck, he stepped gingerly on his left leg, testing for any signs of discomfort. Nothing. Not even any lingering tenderness. Which was a good thing, because otherwise he wouldn't be here doing this.

He shook his head at his own vanity. He might have been able to handle Uriah and Wilt seeing him sans leg. It didn't mean he was ready to start showing up in public that way.

But maybe he could finally bring himself to share it with Cam.

The thought jumped in out of nowhere, freezing him. Should he?

More importantly, *could* he?

A question for later. He shoved it aside, needing to focus on dealing with Dana. Given her feelings about Cooper, he left the dog in the truck, windows opened halfway. He'd be fine for the short time Judd would be inside.

Still, just like at the zoo, he hated the feeling of not having him at his side. Looking back, he caught the mournful expression on the dog's face as he watched Judd walking away, and felt even worse.

"Sorry, buddy," he muttered as he yanked the door open. Steeling himself, he went inside. As he'd guessed from the parking lot, the place was mostly empty. Only two booths were occupied.

Perfect.

He was only standing there a few seconds when Dana came out of the kitchen carrying a tray with three steaming coffee mugs on it. Her eyes widened when she saw him. But she breezed past to one of the booths, where she set out the mugs and accompanying condiments with a smile Judd knew from experience was patently false. Only then did she come back to him, smile fading into a scowl.

"What are you doing here?"

"And good morning to you, too." He winced when her scowl deepened. Okay, not in the mood to tease. "I need to talk to you about something."

"Can't it wait until after I get off work?"

"It would be better if we could talk about it now. It should only take a few minutes. *Please*," he added when it didn't seem she would say yes. Chances were Dana at the end of her shift would be tired and cranky and a lot less willing to be agreeable than she was now.

Although now wasn't looking all that promising, either.

She relented with ill grace. "Fine. I have a break in about ten minutes. I guess we can talk then. But you can't just hang around in here, waiting. My boss won't like it."

"How about if I order a cup of coffee?"

She looked as though she wanted to argue, then sighed and spun on her toes. He followed her around to the far side of the dining room, past empty booths a much more uniform shade of blue than the ones The Shack boasted. Her rubber-soled shoes made a soft squeak on the tile floor with every hurried step.

He couldn't remember a time he'd seen her in anything other than a pair of heels, even when she'd still been waiting tables when they first dated. It seemed practicality had finally won out over image.

Hoping that was a sign of maturity, his spirits rose as he waited for her to bring his coffee. Out of habit his eyes drifted over the room, automatically assessing the space and the people in it. He recognized most of them from the bake sale.

Miss Inez and Miss Thelma sat in one booth facing one another, chatting quietly.

The clipboard-Nazi, Heidi, sat several booths away from them with two other women. They looked somewhat familiar, though he didn't think he'd actually been introduced to either. Or maybe it was just that they all looked so much like one another. The way they dressed. The similar styles of their just-been-to-the-salon perfectly done hair.

It was like a mini Stepford-wives convention.

Since Dana had led him the long way around to his booth, he wasn't sure if any of the women had seen him. He was still debating whether manners dictated he go over and say hello or pretend ignorance when Dana came out with his coffee on a tray.

As she passed by her booth, Heidi's hand snapped out into her way, causing Dana to do a quick side-step to avoid it, almost upsetting the tray in the process.

"Oh, Dana…"

"Just a sec, I'll be right with you," she chirped brightly. When she got to Judd, the pasted-on smile she wore did little to hide the embarrassment in her eyes. Or the resignation. She delivered the coffee and little metal pot of milk, and was gone before he could say anything, heading back to the other booth with a slight droop to her shoulders. Like a dog heeling to a master it expected a scolding from.

Judd straightened, eyes narrowing.

What the fuck?

Empty tray clasped against her chest like a flak jacket, Dana asked, "Can I get you ladies something else?"

"Some coffee that isn't cold would be nice." Heidi shoved her mug toward the edge of the table with a manicured finger.

Dana grabbed for it before it tipped. "Of course. Sorry." She put the mug on her tray, then added the other two as the Stepfords mimicked their ringleader. "Anything else?"

"That'll be all."

The dismissive reply and accompanying hand wave clearly found their mark. But Dana managed to keep her smile as she headed for the kitchen.

He knew for a fact their coffees had been piping hot just five minutes before. He'd smelled it as Dana went by with them when he came in. Seen the mugs literally steaming.

What was their game?

Dana returned with a trio of fresh mugs in one hand, and a glass carafe in the other. She placed each mug before the women and poured.

He grinned. There could be no disputing they were getting fresh, hot coffee now.

Good for Dana.

But before she could escape, Heidi said, "This is regular. Mine was decaf."

Dana stopped. "No, everyone had regular."

"I said, mine was decaf."

Dana's lips tightened, the smile now more grimace but still hanging on.

By a thread.

"Of course. My mistake." With careful movements, Dana removed her mug and retreated once more to the kitchen.

Heidi didn't wait for her to be out of earshot when she said, "I mean, honestly, how hard is it to get a simple thing like coffee right?

If she can't even remember that, it's no wonder she never made it as an actress."

As the women tittered, Judd's temper began to rise. True, Dana hadn't achieved the success she'd been seeking in Hollywood. But that had absolutely nothing to do with the crap these three were pulling now.

They were purposely yanking her chain. He just wasn't sure why.

"I heard the only part she could get was in a hemorrhoid commercial," one of the Stepfords said in a mocking tone.

The other added, "Well, I guess that says a lot about her *crappy* acting skills." They both laughed, the sound more vicious than merry.

Heidi clicked her tongue. "Ladies, no need to be catty." But she said it with a smile that said she was laughing right along with them.

Dana returned, filling the new mug she brought from the carafe whose orange rim marked it as being decaf. "Will there be anything else?"

The long hesitation made it clear Heidi was trying to come up with something, but in the end, she said, "Just the check. We have things to do, and we've wasted enough time here already."

As if that was anyone's fault but their own.

Taking their check out of her apron pocket, Dana placed it on the table.

"Have a nice day, *ladies*." The slight emphasis she put on the word made it clear she'd heard everything they said. And why not? It wasn't like they'd been trying to keep their voices down.

Heidi had one last parting shot before Dana could escape into the kitchen.

"Oh, and Dana? *Love* the shoes."

That set all three of them tittering again as Dana fled.

Okay, that was it.

Judd was halfway across the diner before he realized he had no idea what he could say or do that wouldn't make things worse.

Don't be mean. His daughter's words came to mind, but somehow, he didn't think they'd have the same effect on these three cackling hyenas as they had on the guy outside the zoo bathroom. They enjoyed publicly shredding their prey's pride far too much.

Hmm...

Rather than continue to his original destination, he stopped at the booth where Miss Inez and Miss Thelma sat. Both somewhere in their seventies, the women had taken obvious care with their hair and makeup. Their 'going to town' faces, Cam called it at the bake sale.

Personally, he thought they were a lot prettier than the younger Stepfords, whose 'going to a magazine photo shoot' look made them seem like plastic dolls instead of flesh-and-blood women.

Or maybe it was just the ugliness on the inside leaking through.

"Good morning, ladies. May I say, the both of you are looking positively radiant today." He didn't bother to modulate his voice. He wanted to be heard.

Miss Thelma's wrinkled cheeks pinkened. "Flatterer."

"Nothing but the truth, ma'am."

"Hmph." Miss Inez pursed her lips, but there was a twinkle in her dark eyes that said she appreciated the compliment. "So, young man, how are you enjoying your stay in our little town so far?"

"As a matter of fact, I'm finding small town life surprisingly pleasant. Very different from the city."

"How so?"

"Well, I'd have to say the main difference is the people. Everyone here is so nice. I guess maybe because they all grew up together. They know each other's families, watch out for each other's kids. There's a real sense of community here."

Something like understanding sparked in the older woman's eyes. And approval. "Yes, well, we do pride ourselves on how well we take care of our own."

"And it shows. I mean, I've only been here a short time, but I can already tell no one in this town would be petty enough to use their own social position to try and tear down another hardworking person. Or take pleasure in their discomfort."

"Of course not. We raise our girls up to be ladies here." The way Miss Inez raised her voice, Judd knew she wasn't any happier with the way Heidi and crew had been behaving than he was.

"Inez is right," Miss Thelma added, thin lips pursed as though she'd tasted a lemon. "No *true* lady would ever behave that way."

He wanted to kiss them both. Nothing he said could have cut as deep as that rebuke from two of the town's matriarchs.

"I'm glad to hear it. It's good to know my children are being raised around those kinds of values."

"And such lovely children they are!" Miss Inez smiled. "I hope your little girl enjoyed the cake."

Judd grinned. "She did. Even more so when she found out the inside was just as pink as the icing." Carly had since acquired a new obsession for strawberry everything, insisting that it "tasted" pink. "Well, I've taken enough of your time. I just wanted to be sure and say my hellos before you left."

"What lovely manners you have, dear boy." A sly expression came over Inez's face. "It's almost as though you were raised up here and were one of us yourself."

Not sure what to make of either the look or the comment, he dipped his head. "Thank you, ma'am. That means a lot coming from you. Now, you ladies have yourselves a wonderful day."

Not casting so much as a glance in the direction of the Stepford booth, he retraced the path to his own and sat sipping his coffee.

Waiting.

It took less than thirty seconds for the three women to vacate their booth, silent and stiff as they paid their bill and left. The tinkle of the bell as the door closed behind them was like a little victory dance. He smiled into his mug.

Bye-bye bitches.

A moment later, Dana slipped into the seat opposite him. Her light blue eyes, so similar to Boone's, looked bruised and unhappy. "I can't believe you just did that."

His sense of righteous conquest began to fade. "I didn't mean to make it worse."

"Worse?" She huffed out a disbelieving laugh. "Judd, that had to be the nicest thing anyone's done for me in...well, a really long time. The way you set them all down like that? And Miss Inez and Miss Thelma, too? It was..." She shook her head, a small smile curving her mouth. "Perfect. Thank you."

Relieved he hadn't read the situation wrong after all, he returned the smile. "You're welcome. But tell me, was there a reason for all that, or are they just always nasty?"

Dana sighed, shredding the edge of the paper placemat in front of her. "Heidi and I were friends in high school. Best friends, or so I thought. But looking back, I guess I just took it for granted she was okay with the fact I was the one in the spotlight, and she always came in second."

"What do you mean?"

"Well, when I was Homecoming Queen, she was in my court. I had the lead in the senior musical, she was my understudy. I dated the captain of the football team, and her boyfriend was only second string. No matter what it was, what I did was always a little bit better."

Thinking back, he remembered how self-absorbed she'd been when they first met. "I'm gonna go out on a limb here and say you probably weren't exactly considerate of her feelings about that?"

She made a face. "I was a teenager. What do you think?"

"Fair point. But you're both adults now. And parents. She can't still be holding a grudge about petty high school crap after what? Ten, eleven years?"

"Almost twelve, and oh yes, she can." She shredded the pieces of paper she'd ripped off into even tinier bits. "There might have been...something else that happened. After we graduated."

When she didn't go on, just kept shredding the placemat, he pushed. "Dana?"

Her breath whooshed out, sending the pieces of placemat confetti scattering.

"I always knew what I wanted to do. Go to Hollywood and become a star." She grimaced, but continued. "And I made sure everyone else knew it, too. Or, at least I thought they did. Kyle, my boyfriend, decided all I needed was a good reason to stay, so he proposed the day after graduation. He had a ring and everything."

"Obviously, you said no."

"Oh, I did more than say no. I made it clear I couldn't wait to shake the dust of this town off my shoes. That Slow Creek was too small for me. And so were all the people here, and their small-town dreams."

"Ouch." He winced in sympathy for the guy.

"I'm not proud of the way I acted. But I basically told him he couldn't give me what I wanted, so no, I wouldn't marry him. And the next time anyone saw me back in this town, I'd be rich and famous and they'd all be asking for my autograph."

Wow. When Dana burned bridges, she used napalm.

"But that didn't happen."

"Not even close."

"Okay, so you were shitty to your high school boyfriend. What does that have to do with Heidi?"

Dana gave him a twisted smile laced with bitter irony. "Who do you think she married?"

Ah.

"She stayed, and ended up with the life I threw away. The guy, the house, the money, the perfect little family. For the first time, she came out on top, and she can't seem to stop rubbing my face in it every chance she gets." The smile softened. "Although maybe now she'll give it a rest, since you took her and her little wanna-be posse down a few pegs. Thank you again for that. You have no idea how much it means to me."

The adoration in her eyes made him almost as uncomfortable as realizing he was what she'd ended up with instead of that perfect, pampered life. The complete opposite in every way. "Sure. No problem."

Biting her lip, she concentrated on gathering the torn paper bits into a pile. "So, what was it you wanted to talk to me about?"

If it had been Cam sitting across from him, watching her teeth press into the plump flesh of her lower lip would have driven him wild. With Dana, the sight only made him miss Cam more than he already did.

"I actually wanted to ask a favor. About the kids." Dana raised an eyebrow encouraging him to continue. Mentally crossing his fingers, he got the rest out in a rush. "I just found out last night the San Diego Padres are going to be playing the Royals in Kansas City this weekend, and I was hoping I could take the kids to one of the games."

"This *weekend*?"

"I know we agreed my time with the kids wouldn't impact your days off with them, but this is a special circumstance. And I'm hoping you'll be willing to make an exception, just this once."

"Why can't you take them to a game during the week?"

The fact she didn't say no outright was encouraging.

"I would, but this is interleague play. It'll be the only time the Padres come to Kansas City this year. And I'd really love to take Boone to another one of their games. Even if he does root for the wrong team now," he added with a wry grin, thinking of the Royals pennant hanging over his son's bed.

Dana's mouth softened into a fond smile. "He was so excited when you took him to his very first game. I remember when he came home, his little teeth blue from cotton candy, talking non-stop about everything he saw."

"And so exhausted he fell asleep in his dinner, right in the middle of a sentence," Judd added with a laugh. They'd spent ten minutes cleaning mashed potatoes out of his hair before putting him to bed.

Looking over at Dana, he could tell she was remembering it, too. Things hadn't always been horrible between them. There had been some good times.

Especially with the kids.

"Anyway, I know it's a lot to ask, but I'd really appreciate it if I could take them. It's just one day. Please." He wasn't above groveling if needed.

Dana sighed. "Well, you did just do me a good turn."

"That had nothing to do with this." He didn't want her to think he'd only interceded on her behalf to garner brownie points.

"Oh, I know. But still, I kind of owe you one. So...I'll say yes, on one condition."

"Anything," he said instantly.

"I go with you."

He did a slow blink. "But...you hate baseball."

"I don't *hate* it. I just never obsessed over it the way you and your friends did. Besides, this way will be easier for you. You won't have to worry about dragging both kids with you when one needs to go to the bathroom. And with Carly, that's a *lot*."

Now didn't seem the time to mention he'd been planning to ask Cam to go with him. Although not for her bathroom duty skills.

"I guess there is that." The zoo trip had proven his daughter had a bladder the size of a hummingbird.

"Admit it, it's the best compromise to the situation. You get to take them to the game, and I don't have to give up my day with them. It's a win-win for everyone."

Not for him. He'd have to spend the whole day with *her*.

And without Cam.

"If you're sure..." He gave her one last chance to change her mind.

Which she didn't take.

Damn it.

He managed a smile. "Okay, I'll get the tickets for the four of us for tomorrow, if that works for you. It's an afternoon game. The drive should be less than two hours, so we won't get home too late."

"Sounds perfect. Text me what time you'll pick us up." Scooping up the remains of the shredded placemat, she smiled and slid out of the booth. "Don't worry, it's going to be great."

He brooded as she walked toward Miss Inez and Miss Thelma, a bounce in her step that had been missing before. Great?

No, it was going to be a fucking disaster.

But she was right about one thing. It was the best compromise he could hope for under the circumstances. And to share this experience with his kids, he could put up with just about anything.

Even her.

But what was really going to suck?

Telling Cam he was spending the day with his ex.

Chapter 13

She couldn't believe how much she'd missed him.

It was silly, really. It had only been a few days since she saw him at the zoo. Days in which they'd spoken on the phone and texted several times as his leg healed. There shouldn't have been time for her to miss him.

And yet, the second she heard the truck pull into her driveway, her heart began to race and her palms went sweaty like a schoolgirl anticipating her prom date.

Very mature, Camille.

That was the problem, though. Ever since she'd started this relationship—she could finally admit to herself that's what it was, or at least, what it was becoming—she'd felt younger and freer and just more *her* than she had in a very long time.

It was both liberating and a little scary. She wasn't sure she remembered how to be this version of herself anymore.

But so far, she liked it.

Being with Judd had reminded her that underneath the daughter, sister, auntie, friend, and principal, there was a living, breathing woman named Camille. One who had hopes and dreams that had nothing to do with any of those roles and everything to do with her own desire for happiness.

In trying to fill the voids in her life by being all things to all people, she'd lost sight of that fact. Until now.

Until Judd.

Still, there was a fine line between eager and embarrassing. Smoothing a hand over her giddy stomach, she forced herself to wait until he actually knocked before getting up to open the door. Jasper let out a plaintive meow of displeasure and stalked past her down the hallway to his hidey-hole in her closet.

Well, at least he wasn't running there in a panic anymore whenever Judd came over. That was something.

She opened the door and smiled. "Hi."

He smiled back. "Hi yourself."

And it was like no time had passed at all.

She stepped back to let him and Cooper in, then closed the door and stood there staring at him like a kid with a crush. "You look good."

Judd's smile broadened until lines crinkled at the edges of his gorgeous eyes. "Thanks. So do you."

Realizing how the comment had sounded, she stammered, "I meant, you look like you're feeling better. Not that you *don't* look good. You always look..." She bit her lip as she looked him over head-to-toe with greedy eyes. Lord have mercy, the man was incredibly edible. "Delicious," she finished on a breathy sigh.

Desire flared in his gaze. Making a low sound in his throat, he stepped toward her, cupping her jaw with one hand.

"God, you're dangerous," he muttered before taking her mouth with his own. The kiss was fast and demanding, sending her already twitchy body into sexual overdrive as his tongue delved between her lips. Dueling with hers in the most carnal sort of parry and thrust until every bit of her was tingling in anticipation.

She was dangerous?

The man obviously didn't know his own power over her.

Ending the kiss with a sigh, Judd leaned his forehead to hers, thumbs stroking along her cheeks as though he couldn't bring himself to stop touching her. "God, I missed you."

I wasn't the one who went into hiding for two days.

The petulant thought wasn't fair. She'd known from the start the man came with emotional baggage. Mountains of it. If she wanted him, she'd have to be patient and deal with the occasional boulder when it rolled down into their path.

Eventually, hopefully, he'd feel comfortable enough to trust her with the things he still struggled with.

"I missed you, too." She took a reluctant step back. If she didn't, she might end up stripping him right there in the entryway.

Again.

"I picked up a bunch of cold cuts for sandwiches and that bread you like. I thought maybe we could pack up a hamper and go have a picnic out by the lake." Something that wouldn't involve a lot of walking, just in case his sore leg wasn't as healed as he said it was.

The last thing she wanted was to lose any more time with him. The summer break was counting down quicker than she was happy with, and she planned to make the most of every day they had left.

Judd picked up a lock of hair laying over her shoulder and played with it. "Or we could stay here and work up an appetite first, then have a picnic in your bed instead." He gave a light tug on her hair, urging her closer.

She went willingly, caught between his arousal and her own.

It was impossible to fight both.

"I guess we could do that." A small gasp punctuated her words as he pressed his mouth to the tender spot below her ear, his tongue tracing a hot line down to her collar bone. "We could definitely do that."

"Good. I'm feeling greedy. I don't want to share you."

Because no matter where they went, they were likely to run into someone she knew. Or he did. And honestly, she wasn't in the mood to share him with anyone right now, either.

They had two whole days to make up for. She didn't want to waste a second.

Hand clasped around hers, Judd stalked to the half-closed bedroom door. It wasn't until he shoved it open and stopped in his tracks that she remembered the disarray her bedroom furniture was in.

"I forgot, everything's still a mess from painting."

"You had someone come in and paint your room?"

"Of course not. I did it myself." She'd needed to stay occupied the last few days. Otherwise, she might have done something stupid like drive over to Judd's camper uninvited.

"You did?"

"No need to sound so surprised," she said dryly.

He had the grace to appear apologetic. "Sorry. It's just...this is a pretty big project to take on all by yourself. Especially moving the bed and dresser."

"Not really. I pick one room every summer to paint and change the furniture and accessories around a little." All those years of home shows had given her more ideas than she'd ever have time to use.

A small line formed across his forehead. "You could have asked me to help, you know. I would have been happy to do it for you."

Something about the way he said it rubbed her wrong.

"Thanks, but I didn't need anyone to do it for me. I think I did a pretty good job on my own."

"No, you did! Of course you did. I didn't mean to imply you hadn't, or that I could have done it better. It's just that...I would have helped if you needed me to. Which you obviously didn't. It looks great."

He was clearly backpedaling, but at least it sounded sincere.

She gave a tiny sniff, mollified. Painting the small bedroom hadn't been difficult at all, aside from working around the plastic-covered furniture heaped in the middle of the floor. Which she moved using the little glide discs she'd ordered online.

Easy peasy.

On a whim, though, she'd changed things up from her usual mellow tones and gone with a bold accent wall opposite her bed. And she was pretty darn pleased with how it turned out, if she did say so herself. The luxurious deep blue would be the first thing she saw when she woke in the mornings, and the last thing she'd see at night.

A dark blue, she just now realized, that almost perfectly matched the color of Judd's eyes when they darkened with arousal.

The way they weren't any longer.

She bit back a groan of frustration. It was her own fault the mood had slipped away. If she'd just remembered about the bed being inaccessible and steered them toward the living room in the first place, they'd probably both be halfway to naked by now.

Maybe even three-quarters.

Well, that she could fix. Sliding her arms around his neck, she pulled his head down for a kiss. He was passive for a few seconds, allowing her to take the lead as her tongue ran along the seam of his lips, begging entry. But as soon as she stroked her tongue against his, the leash snapped.

He pulled her flush against him, hands on her rear, kneading and caressing and generally driving her lower half wild through her shorts with every dip of his fingers between her legs. The promise of heaven *right there* but never quite connecting.

She returned the favor, pressing her hips to his in a slow grind that mimicked what they could be doing if only they were wearing a few less layers. The hard press of his erection said he was all for it.

Yes!

Breaking the kiss with a gasp, she grabbed his hand and practically dragged him back to the living room.

"Sofa sex," he purred, snuggling up behind her to press the insistent ridge in his pants against her rear. "That could get a little tricky, but I'm game."

"Actually…" Reluctant as she was to lose contact with his hard body, she stepped forward and yanked the cushions from the sofa, startling Cooper as they hit the floor near where he'd laid down.

With a disgruntled snort, he got up and moved into the kitchen.

Sending the dog a silent apology, she pulled the exposed strap and made a *ta-da!* gesture at the queen-size sofa bed that unfolded. "Better?"

"Sweetheart, any surface I can lay you down on makes things better," he said, backing her toward the mattress so she had no choice but to sit. "The sofa, the bed, the kitchen table…"

"It was the patio table, actually. We haven't tried the kitchen table yet." She let out a gasp as he dropped down beside her and urged her onto her back.

"An oversight which definitely needs to be rectified."

Any reply she might have made was swallowed up by the kiss he swooped down to give her. After that, the man was everywhere. Devouring her mouth, nibbling her neck, licking his way down to the top edge of her blouse. The tiny buttons slipped free beneath his shaking fingers.

Cupping her breasts through the lacy bra she wore underneath, he gave them a gentle, reverent caress, thumbs running over the hard points of her nipples.

She moaned at the sensation that zinged through her body like a streak of lightning in a summer storm.

When he did it again, harder, she writhed, wishing the bra gone so she could feel his hands on her bare skin.

That wish came true a few minutes later, the bra disappearing along with her blouse and Judd's polo shirt. His belt hung undone, cargo pants hanging open at the zipper as her hand delved beneath his boxer briefs to explore the hot, hard length of him.

He sucked in a sharp breath as she spread the small bead of moisture she found at the tip along the sensitive edge of the upper crown.

"You have very talented fingers, Miss Richards."

She grinned and gave a gentle squeeze, eliciting another intake of breath.

"It's all that knitting. It keeps them nimble." She gasped as his hand snaked into her shorts and beneath her panties. "You're pretty talented yourself, Mr. Aiken."

"I'm highly motivated to please."

The moan he drew from her as he slowly circled her clit with a fingertip wet with her own arousal had a primal growl to it. "It's working." Her hips bucked. "*God!*"

Needing more, she frantically shoved her shorts down her legs, kicking them off before rising to her knees beside him. "I bought condoms, but they're in the other room."

Judd caught her arm before she could climb off the mattress. "So did I, and mine are closer."

Pleased he cared enough to ensure they didn't repeat their previous recklessness, she waited with growing impatience as he fumbled his wallet from his pocket and fished out two foil packets. "Only two?" she teased.

"The rest of the box is in my go-bag."

A shiver rippled through her at the gravelly words. "That should do."

"For now." The promise in his voice was underpinned by the darkening of his eyes, the blue so rich and deep it was like a midnight sky in July.

Getting to her feet, she shimmied her panties down, loving the way his gaze devoured the sight of her naked body. She knew it was far from perfect. Her breasts were too small, her hips barely there, and her stomach had a definite over-forty pooch starting. But with Judd, none of those imperfections mattered.

He made her feel beautiful.

"I guess you'd better dress that bad boy up so we can get this party started."

Wallet thunking to the floor, Judd reached for the open waistband of his pants, lifted his hips, and shoved. Pants and briefs were all the way to his knees before he froze. Something she'd never seen from him before flashed across his expression.

Panic.

Her heart squeezed in her chest for him. Ignoring the black top of his prosthetic that was exposed, she made sure to keep full eye contact as she crawled back onto the mattress beside him.

"We can do it like last time. Or whatever way you want." She kept her voice soft. Not wanting to push him into something he didn't want, but not willing to let him shy away from that next step if he was ready to take it, either.

It was a dangerous balancing act.

"I can even go get that skirt out to wear again if you like," she offered when he didn't say anything. "But just so we're clear, it would be for you. I have no problem with seeing your prosthesis. But I'll do whatever you want to make *you* comfortable."

Seconds ticked by.

There was a war going on inside his head. She could tell by the tightening of his jaw and the way his hands trembled. As though he was struggling not to yank his pants back up and run for the door.

The need to reach out, to touch him, comfort him, was almost impossible to resist.

But she did.

Whatever he decided, it needed to be his choice. Without any influence from her.

Her stomach sank when Judd sat up abruptly. But rather than bolt, he worked his pants and briefs off his legs in jerky movements. Kicking them away, he perched on the edge of the thin mattress, shoulders hunched, gaze fixed on some distant point across the room.

Or maybe someplace deep inside.

Because he expected her to look, she did. She'd seen the bottom part of the prosthesis before when he'd worn shorts. The short silver rod leading up from his still shoe-clad foot—she'd figure that out later—led up to a thicker black piece that somewhat resembled a calf, ending at a metal knee joint.

It was the part above that she'd never seen before. The knee portion connected to a black plastic-looking shell which encased most of his left thigh. A strip of milky-white material showed from under the top of it, right before the crease of his groin. And somewhere under there lay what remained of his leg, although there was no telling exactly where it ended.

She was human. The sight of Judd's body, damaged and permanently altered, sent a shaft of intense emotions through her.

Pain for all he'd had to suffer and endure from his injury. Sorrow for what he'd lost because of it. Guilt because when this had happened to him, she'd probably been sleeping soundly in her bed, blissfully unaware of the sacrifices being made by men and women just like him all around the world. Who were still making them, every day.

It was a humbling realization.

"And now you're disgusted," he muttered. "I knew it."

Of course he'd draw the worst conclusion from her silence.

"Judd, look at me. Do I look disgusted?"

Like a man asked to face his executioner, he slowly turned his head.

Whatever he saw in her expression sent first a flash of disbelief and distrust through his eyes, followed by something else.

Hope. Fragile, painful hope.

"You're not...disappointed with what you see?"

"Disappointed?" She rolled her eyes.

Silly man.

"The only thing disappointing is that someone isn't as enthusiastic as he was a few minutes ago." Taking his no longer erect penis in her hand, she added with what she hoped was a seductive grin, "Although I think I can take care of that."

Not giving him time to reply—or think—she leaned down and brought him into her mouth. It took a minute of careful attention, but then his body was right there with her again, hard and ready.

She let out a soft mewl of disappointment when he gently disengaged her.

"I want to return the favor," he said hoarsely, "but I need to have you first. Now."

"Any way you want me."

She wasn't expecting him to pull her to her feet. As she opened her mouth to ask why, he moved them both to the thick, rolled arm of the sofa and had her face it. It only took light pressure on her upper back urging her to bend forward for her to catch on.

The chenille was cool and soft against her naked belly, but not as cool as the air on her bare butt. There was the crinkle of foil being ripped, and before she had time to be self-conscious about her exposed position, Judd was there, pressed against her back.

Covering her. Warming her.

His breath tickled along her spine as he kissed his way up to her neck, sending shivers across her skin.

"I'm not sure how well this is going to work," he muttered against her ear as he spread her legs with his knee. "Tell me if I hurt you in any way."

"You won't."

"Promise me."

She whimpered as the hot press of his erection slipping between her legs halted. He was seriously going to stop? *Now*?

"I promise. Please, just—*ah!*" Her ability to form words was stolen as he sank deep inside in one quick thrust, leaving her with only moans and sighs as he settled into a slow, steady rhythm. His hands found her breasts, adding to the onslaught of sensations as he stroked and tweaked and caressed.

She wanted to touch him, too. Kiss him. Something. Anything. But being in this position kept her from doing any of that.

It also kept her from seeing him.

Or his leg.

Which was probably the point.

That was okay, though. Judd had come a long way toward trusting her with something very personal and painful. This was one more step on the path to the time he'd finally feel completely at ease with who he was when they were together.

She'd savor every small victory she got until then.

The rhythm of the steady strokes eventually changed. Judd's hands left off their exploration of her sensitized body and settled on her hips, where they held on for dear life as he began to thrust harder and faster. His grip shifted.

Whether by accident or design, so did the angle of her lower body. She let out a gasp of pleasure as he sank even deeper.

Arching her back, she pushed back at him with every thrust. Doubling the sensation. Reaching, stretching for the starbursts of impending orgasm tightening low in her belly. Until finally, they exploded in a kaleidoscope of pleasure that flowed out to every part of her body, right down to her fingertips.

It went on and on, until Judd's body shuddered against hers. His groan was low and long as he pressed as deep inside as possible as he found his own release.

It was a good thing it took several minutes before she was able to string any words together, or she might have said something incredibly stupid.

Like, "I love you."

Instead, she let out a contented sigh. "That was amazing."

Breath still coming in warm pants against her back, Judd let out a low chuckle she could feel deep inside. "I'll second that."

They both made sounds of disappointment and residual pleasure as he slowly withdrew. It took no urging at all for her to collapse onto the sofa bed mattress, limbs flopping like overcooked noodles. She expected him to join her.

He didn't.

"I need to go take care of the condom. And...some other things. I may be a few minutes."

Much as she wanted to ask about those things, she just cracked an eyelid and flapped a limp hand in his general direction.

"Go. Do whatever you need to do. I'll just lay here, being a puddle."

A tiny grin twitched on his lips. "A puddle, huh?"

"Uh-huh. A very happy, thoroughly sated puddle." She flapped again and closed her eyes, only to open them again once she knew he'd turned and walked away. Lordy, he was as much a treat to watch going as he was coming, the dimples above his taut tush teasing her with every step.

He detoured to grab his backpack, which he'd called his go-bag, and disappeared into the bathroom with a soft snick of the door.

It was only then she realized the entire time she watched him—okay, drooled over him—she'd barely even registered his prosthetic leg. Oh, she knew it was there. It was hard to miss. But it was just another part of him, like his tattoo or his butt dimples.

One part which in no way defined the incredible whole that was Judd Aiken.

Her heart still hurt for him, for what he'd suffered. But the high-tech limb in no way detracted from the man who wore it.

Not to her.

Hoping to discourage a repeat of last time, she slipped beneath the sheets naked and waited. She must have dozed for a few minutes, because the next thing she knew, Judd was sitting on the edge of the bed beside her. It was clear from his pinched lips as he stared down at the floor he was trying to decide if he should get dressed or not.

She lifted the sheet in invitation, hoping to tip the scales.

After a brief hesitation, he slid in next to her. He took her mouth in a soft, sweet kiss before curling his arm around her as she nestled against his right shoulder. There was still a sense of uneasy tension in him. She could feel it. But he was here, with her, and that was all that mattered at the moment.

She snuggled closer, inhaling the salty tang of perspiration and musk. "Well, that was a lovely way to work up a sweat."

"I hope it was okay."

"Okay? I think I already called it amazing," she said with a small laugh.

He didn't join her. "No, I mean, I should have asked before I just bent you over the sofa like that. I wasn't sure if I'd be able to manage any other position, but that's no excuse." He sounded annoyed with himself.

"Again, did you miss the 'amazing' part?" She pulled back a few inches so she could look him in the eye. "If I wasn't comfortable with it, I would have said so, Judd. And as far as other positions go, we can take our time figuring those out." She pressed a kiss to his chest, tasting the salt. "Lots" –*kiss*—"and lots"—*kiss*—"of time."

Her tongue swiped over his nipple to punctuate her promise, drawing a full-body shudder from him.

"Jesus, woman. Are you trying to kill me?"

No, I'm trying to keep you.

She patted his taut stomach before snuggling into the crook of his arm again with a contented sigh. "Don't worry, I'll let you rest up a bit first."

"How kind of you." His dry tone was laced with amusement.

She smiled against his chest. "I thought so."

Seconds ticked by. Then minutes.

The silence was comfortable, but his body still held a hint of stiffness. Biting her tongue to keep from asking what was bothering him, she waited for him to either bring it up or work his way through it on his own.

"I had to go dry off the silicone liner because of that sweat we worked up." The words were abrupt, with no preamble.

Unsure what landmines might lay ahead, she kept her response simple. "Okay."

"I had to do the same thing at the zoo the other day. Any time I'm out in the heat for too long, I have to stop what I'm doing and take care of it."

"Okay."

"*Okay*? How are you okay with that? Doesn't it bother you at all?"

"Does what bother me? That you were injured? That you survived? That the doctors were able to not only save your life, but give you a way to walk again?"

"That I'm damaged. Less of a man."

The raw pain in his words made her heart ache for him.

"Oh, Judd." She pushed up on her elbow so she could look him in the eye. "You're a lot of things. Brave. Sexy. Stubborn. Loyal. Kind. But what you *aren't* is any less than the man you were when you had two legs. Is your life different because of this?" She put her hand lightly on his left leg, ignoring the way he flinched. "Of course. But different isn't the same as damaged. In fact, I'd say you're a fucking miracle."

The surprise of her dropping the f-bomb did its job, distracting him from the fact she was touching his prosthesis, even if it was through the sheet. Amusement flashed in his eyes, wiping away some of the doubt clouding them.

He cupped her face and drew her down for a kiss. "No, sweetheart, that would be you. *My* fucking miracle."

Later, when their growling stomachs forced them to come up for food, they sat naked on the sofa bed eating sandwiches and watching tv. Judd still kept the sheet over his legs, but that was okay. He seemed more relaxed and at ease with himself than ever before, and she loved it.

She loved him.

There was no use denying it any longer.

What she was going to do about it was something she hadn't figured out yet.

Picking a grape from the plastic container between them, she said, "Well, since we had your version of a picnic today"—she shot him a look he responded to with a smug smile—"maybe tomorrow we can go to the lake and have an actual one?"

His smile leaked away.

"I meant to tell you. I'm taking the kids to a ballgame tomorrow."

"Oh." Pushing her disappointment away, she smiled. "Well, that should be fun. I'm just surprised Dana agreed to let you have them on a Saturday."

And maybe a little hurt he hadn't asked if she wanted to go, too.

She'd thought...well, it didn't really matter. Judd's time with his kids was precious to him. If he wanted them to himself for the day, she'd just have to understand and get over the sting of being left out.

"Yeah, that's the thing. She'd only agree if she went with us."

"Ah." Well, that explained why he wasn't asking *her*. Probably, anyway. There was still a niggle of uncertainty he might not have asked her even without Dana's ultimatum, and it bothered her more than it likely should have.

Judd frowned as though not sure how to interpret her response.

"Believe me, it was *not* my idea. We haven't spent more than an hour at a time in each other's company since the divorce. Spending a whole afternoon together is going to be...a challenge."

The way he said it made the word sound more like *disaster*.

Which shouldn't have made her feel better.

But it did.

"You'll have the kids there as a buffer. I'm sure you can both manage to be civil for a few hours for their sake."

"You're probably right. Still…" He caught her hand as she plucked another grape. "I'd have much rather had you there with me instead." Giving her deep eye contact, he guided her hand to his mouth and stole the grape from her fingers with his tongue.

His mouth against her skin stirred up the heat resting at a slow simmer in her belly.

She cleared her throat. "So, picnic raincheck until Sunday, then?"

A wicked smile bloomed. "Looking forward to it already."

The heat kicked up to a slow boil. "So am I."

But even so, a pinch of doubt remained. Some primal warning from deep in her lizard brain, screaming at her that Judd spending time with the young, beautiful woman who'd borne his children was a bad, bad idea.

For her. For Judd.

For whatever this was they were beginning to build together.

She might have fallen over the tipping point and into the first blush of love. But she still had no idea how much of that feeling was returned, and how much was just good, hot sex for him.

The first sex, by his own admission, he'd had in over a year and a half.

No. He'd broken down so many barriers with her. Opened his feelings, if only in tiny bits. They might be small achievements, but they were victories all the same.

So no, it couldn't just be all about the sex.

Could it?

Chapter 14

"You've got to be shitting me."

Braking his truck to a stop in front of his camper, Judd glared at the sight waiting for him. The man lounging in the folding camp chair under the fading sunlight was the very last person he'd expected—or wanted—to see. Then again, he probably should have expected something like this. The guy was an ass, but he also wasn't the type to give up easily when he wanted something.

And right now, he wanted Judd.

Muttering another curse, he turned the truck off and shoved the door open. "What are you doing here?"

"And hello to you, too, sunshine." Like a lazy snake soaking up the sun, Ray Zebrowski gave every appearance of having just been woken from a nap.

Judd knew better. The man might have left the Teams more than five years ago, but he still had the same watchfulness that had kept them all alive in places where a moment's inattention could get your throat slit.

"But to answer your question, I'm here because you haven't been returning any of my calls or texts. So, since we couldn't connect electronically, I figured I'd just have to come by and talk to you in person. The old guy up at the house said you were out at a ballgame. But that you were due back soon and I could wait here for you if I wanted, since I was a friend and fellow vet. Gave me a beer and everything." He nodded at the empty bottle near his feet. Which meant he'd been waiting for a while.

Stubborn bastard.

"Friend? That's stretching the definition a little, don't you think?"

Zee put a hand to his heart. "You wound me."

He answered that bullshit with a snort. "And not returning your calls meant I wasn't interested in hearing whatever you have to say. So aside from the free beer, you've wasted your time." He looked down at Cooper, who was leaning up against Zee's leg, eyes half-closed in ecstasy at the ear rub he was getting.

The traitor.

Not that he could really blame the dog, since he'd been left behind.

Again.

Because of Dana.

Again.

In an effort to help keep the peace, he'd instead relied on the hated folding cane as backup balance on the million and one steep steps at the stadium. Dana hadn't said anything, but it had been obvious when she got in the truck she was relieved the dog wasn't there, even if the kids had sounded their disappointment. She showed her appreciation the rest of the day by being on her very best behavior.

If he hadn't known better, he might have thought she actually *enjoyed* herself today.

"Come on, Judd, don't be that way." The smarmy charm which had served him so well procuring things for his Team in country—food, native clothing, information—was in full force as Zee leaned forward in the chair, hands clasped between his knees. "We're a lot more alike than you want to admit."

"Insulting me isn't going to help your case."

"We both got forced out before we were ready to go." Zee went on as though he hadn't spoken. "We're both highly trained, highly motivated, and exceptionally good at what we do. And that makes us very attractive commodities to my bosses and their clients."

Judd's lip curled back in distaste. "Private military contractors."

"Private *security* contractors."

"Call it what you want, they're still mercenaries. And by they, I mean you."

Zee gave him a frustrated look.

"Judd, come on, man. What else are people like us supposed to do? It's not like our skill set translates well into the real world. Nobody's advertising on LinkedIn for washed-up snipers and infiltration experts."

The 'washed up' part stung, no matter how true it was. As was the rest of what Zee was saying. They were both well trained, highly efficient, and almost completely unemployable in the civilian sector. Guys with computer and tech training had a built-in niche to land in. But the rest of them?

Not a lot of options.

Annoyed he was agreeing with anything Zee had to say, he unlocked the camper and went inside. After dropping his go-bag, he grabbed two beers from the mini-fridge and took them outside, not sure why he was bothering. Giving Zee another drink was like feeding a stray dog.

It would just make him harder to get rid of.

Handing over one of the bottles, he barked, "Get your ass out of my chair."

"Roger that, Bravo Two." With a smirk, Zee moved to the ground, tilting the bottle in salute before he took a long swallow followed by a satisfied *ahh*. "So, a sunny Saturday afternoon taking in a ballgame with your kids, huh? Doesn't get more apple-pie American than that."

Judd remained silent, taking a drink. Waiting for the pitch he knew was coming.

"You've got two, right? A boy and a girl?"

Hackles immediately snapped up. "You don't talk about my kids. Ever. Got it?"

Hands raised in a placating manner, Zee said, "No harm, man, no harm. I was just thinking stuff like that's got to get kind of expensive. Tickets, parking, food, a couple souvenirs for each of them. A jersey or hat or those stupid foam finger things or whatever." He shook his head. "It's gotta add up."

It had been a small fortune.

"It was a special occasion. A splurge." And definitely not something he'd be able to afford again for quite some time.

But it had been so worth it.

"True, true." Zee nodded. "But the other stuff. Clothes they grow out of every couple of months, doctor's appointments, after school crap like football and ballet—"

"Still talking about my kids." There was clear warning in his voice.

"My point is—"

"Oh, you have one?"

"—kids are expensive. All the time. And those cost go up exponentially as they get older and need more things. Bigger things. Cars. College. Where're you going to get the money for all that?"

"That's a long way off." But the thought did make his stomach grind as he stared down at the icy bottle he rolled between his hands.

Where *was* he going to get the money?

"Not as long as you'd think. And you may love your kids to death, man, but do you really think you'll be able to cover tuition to an even halfway-decent school by asking 'Do you want fries with that' for a living?"

Fucking Zee. He knew exactly what Judd's weak spot was, and he wasn't pulling any punches as he kept jabbing at it.

"I can find something better than that. If I have to, I can go to school myself, on Uncle Sam's dime. Earn a degree."

Not that he had the slightest idea in what. But it was an option.

"Sure, sure. Four years of school, then an entry-level job somewhere as a good little nine-to-fiver drone, and you'll only be what? Almost forty? Sounds great. *Or,*" he added with the flair of a game show host about to reveal what was behind door number two, "you can sign on now for a job you're already qualified for—over-qualified, really—and start raking in the moola from day one."

He named a salary that nearly had Judd's eyes bugging out.

"Nice, right? Helluva lot better than E-8 pay. And after those same four years, you'll have a hefty little nest egg in the bank. Plus something even better."

He shouldn't ask. But he had to.

"And what's that?"

"Breathing room to decide what comes next."

Well, fuck.

Taking a drink to buy time to think past that very excellent argument, he dropped his free hand onto Cooper's head. "You do know I'm down a leg, right?" He tapped his beer on his left knee, eliciting a dull clunk against the glass.

"Last time I checked, you didn't need a leg to shoot straight."

"But you do to hump in to your mission site and back." That fucking uneven terrain thing again. Not to mention sand and dirt and sweat.

"Maybe on the Teams. The beauty of private work is the missions are short and sweet. Go in, get the job done, back to base in time for dinner and a cold one." Zee held his bottle up before taking a long drink.

In no way did he believe the job was as clean and easy as Zee was making it out to be. But he was starting to wonder if he'd maybe been too hasty in his decision to reject even considering what he and his bosses had to offer.

Because fuck, that was a *lot* of money.

And as he'd found out today, doing even little stuff for Boone and Carly could add up fast. And college? Shit, he hadn't thought that far ahead. But now the idea was in his head, he couldn't *not* think about it.

Sure, there were scholarships and student loans. But he didn't want his kids to be limited in any way when it came to choosing what path their futures would take. He wanted to give them the options he never had.

He just didn't know how.

Zee was handing him one possibility. But did he really want to get tangled up with the kind of people Zee associated with?

It hadn't been much of a surprise when Zebrowski left the Teams five years ago that he'd be approached by one of the private contractor companies. It happened all the time. Providing security and other services in the crazy of the Middle East and Africa and other hotspots around the world was big business these days. Where better to staff your paramilitary force from than the actual military?

After that, Zee aggressively headhunted his former Teammates, as well as members of the other Special Forces communities. When their enlistment contracts were up, or if they were forced to retire for medical reasons like Judd.

No, the surprise had been when he started actively recruiting men who'd crossed a few lines of human decency in the name of duty. Who'd been forced out with discharges marked other than honorable. People no decent soldier would want at their side. Or their back.

And for that, nobody liked him much anymore.

Or trusted him.

Like him or not, though, he'd spoken nothing but the truth, no matter how self-serving. What he offered people like Judd, who'd outlived their usefulness to the Navy, was a chance to take what they knew, what they were good at, and turn it into a viable job again.

One that paid—*holy fuck*—a shit-ton of money.

He'd be lying if he said them still wanting him despite his disability didn't make the proposition all the sweeter. Finally, someone who acknowledged he still had some value. Could still be worthy of his job.

It was the validation he'd been needing this past year. The thing to prove he was still the man he was before that bullet sent his entire world spinning out of his control.

A chance to feel like himself again.

To feel *whole* again.

And the fact he wasn't jumping at it told him something had changed for him. Something fundamental. Two months ago, hell, *one* month ago, he'd likely have allowed himself to be sweet-talked into signing on. Seduced by the thought of strapping on his old life like a comfortable pair of boots and pretending everything was the same. That he was the same.

But it wasn't.

He wasn't.

In so many ways.

And the thought of heading off somewhere halfway around the world to do dangerous things for a paycheck no longer held any appeal. Not even for that kind of money. Not when he had so much right here worth so much more to him.

He'd had a taste of the family life he missed out on before, and he wasn't going to walk away from it a second time. He'd take watching Boone play first base and having pretend tea with Carly and her dolls over being shot at any day of the week, and twice on Sundays.

Not to mention having Camille in his bed, looking at him like he was the most perfect thing in the world to her.

"Thanks for the offer, Zee, but I think I'm gonna have to pass."

"Seriously?" He studied Judd a moment, then cursed. "Well, shit. I guess I waited a little too long. You went and did it already."

"Did what?"

"Dug in civilian roots." Zee shook his head, looking disbelieving. "You were on my 'least-likely' list for that. Always took you for a lifer."

He gave a small shrug. "So did I. Things change."

"Shit," Zee said again with feeling. "Well, at least tell me it isn't because of your ex. She was—"

"The mother of my children."

"—a lovely person," Zee finished smoothly. He offered a crooked smile. "But not the kind you up-end your entire future for."

No. *She* wasn't.

But that wasn't any of Zee's business.

"Have a safe trip back to...wherever, Zee."

"And I guess that's my cue to leave." He drained the rest of the bottle and got to his feet. "Thanks for the beer, man. It was good to see you again."

"Yeah, you, too."

Zee grinned, showing he knew a lie when he heard one.

"You take care of yourself, Judd. And if you ever change your mind, you just give me a call. We're always hiring." He started toward the house, where he must have left his car, then turned around and continuing to walk backwards as he said, "Hey, whoever she is? I hope she's worth it."

He called up the memory of pure acceptance and affection, maybe even—dare he think it—love he'd seen in Camille's eyes yesterday. Despite being face-to-face with the reality of his prosthesis and its limitations to his life. To his being a whole man.

A feeling of calm certainty settled over his normally cynical heart.

"She definitely is."

"I'm really sorry about this."

Judd grinned at Cam across the cab of his truck, where her expression of resigned exasperation matched her tone. "I told you, it's fine. I've already met your sister and most of the kids. The rest of your family should be a cakewalk."

"Hah! You poor deluded man. You have no idea what you're in for."

Maybe not.

When he picked her up twenty minutes ago and she'd informed him her family had invited themselves along to their romantic picnic by the lake, he hadn't gotten annoyed or disappointed.

Okay, maybe a little disappointed.

But he had decided rather than lament an opportunity lost, he'd embrace the one gained. Camille was clearly very close to her family. What better way to deepen their relationship than by making a good impression with them?

Of course, that was assuming they liked him.

Her sister Lynn had seemed to, after her initial interrogation period at the zoo. But the only set of parents he'd ever had to impress before had pretty much hated his guts. Nine years later, they hadn't thawed an inch. In fact, their animosity had only grown, especially since he hit town and started cutting into their time watching the kids for the summer.

Like he was cutting into Camille's summer free time. Time that might have—no, almost definitely would have been spent with her great big family.

Shit. Maybe he *should* be worried.

They let Cooper out and gathered their things from the back of the truck, then made their way from the parking lot to the picnic area. It was a beautiful summer day. Not too hot or humid, for which Judd was thankful. He might even get through the afternoon without having to go take care of his prosthesis.

Though for the first time since he'd hit Slow Creek, he wasn't filled with a sense of uneasy dread at the thought he might have to.

Cam's family had already staked out a good-sized area right near the water. Several wooden picnic tables were overflowing with wicker hampers similar to the one he was carrying. If they had even half the amount of food in them Cam had stuffed into hers, they were all going to be eating leftovers for a month.

Then again, her three siblings looked like they had most, if not all, of their children in tow today, so maybe it was just enough. As he'd recently discovered, kids ate like locusts when given the opportunity.

A high-pitched squeal as Judd was dropping off the hamper meant they'd been spotted. More specifically, Cooper had been spotted. Kids stopped what they were doing and came running.

He did a quick count. Yup, all seven of Cam's nieces and nephews were there. He braced himself. This might get bad. He was used to giving the short lecture about service dogs and how not to distract them unless they'd been released from duty.

He wasn't used to it meaning so much if anyone got their feelings hurt by it.

To his surprise, all the kids stopped short of dogpiling onto Cooper, forming a small semi-circular cluster a few feet in front of him instead. Their ages ranged up into the teens, but it was one of the youngest, nine-year-old Elijah, who seemed to be in charge.

"See? He's wearing his service dog collar, just like I said. That means we can't bother him, because he's working. Not unless Mr. Aiken says we can." He looked up at Judd. "That's what Boone told me. Right?"

"That's right." He exchanged a look with Cam, who appeared as baffled as he was. "You should always ask before you go up to any strange dog you see, but especially service dogs. Some have to pay very close attention to the people they're helping, and any distraction could be dangerous for them."

"Like for a blind person," Hazel piped up. Her desire to reach for the dog was almost palpable, but like the others, she was holding herself in check. Barely. "You don't want to distract them when they're trying to cross the street or something."

"Exactly. Very good, Hazel."

She beamed at the praise, but her younger cousin Mary chimed in, "But you're not blind, so what does Cooper do for you?"

"Mary, that's a rude thing to ask." Cam shot him an apologetic look.

"No, it's fine." But before he could formulate a kid-appropriate response, Elijah did it for him.

"Boone said his dad got hurt in the war, and now he has a superhero leg. But he doesn't always wear it, so Cooper helps him if he has trouble getting up or needs something he can't reach." There was a chorus of *oh*s as they all craned their necks to study Judd's prosthesis, partially exposed beneath his long, baggy shorts.

His stomach did a small somersault at the scrutiny, but he swallowed the discomfort and let them look their fill without shifting away.

Superhero leg?

That was new.

And maybe why the kids seemed more intrigued than freaked out by what they were seeing. Which was a relief, since wearing shorts had been a decision made when he'd thought it'd be just him and Cam.

She leaned against him and murmured, "Kids say the darndest things, huh?"

They sure did.

Recovering from his surprise, he nodded at Elijah.

"Well, that's basically right." In this case, simpler was better. "But, since I have lots of people here to help if I need it, I think Cooper can have a little free time. If there was anyone around who might be willing to play with him?" He grinned at the jumping and shouts of *me, me, me!*

After a quick check with Cam it was okay, he knelt down and carefully introduced each of the children to Cooper, making sure they were comfortable with him. Once that was accomplished, he unclipped the leash and gave Coop his release command.

Dog and kids ran off in a happy, noisy rush.

"Just don't let him go in the water!" he called after them. Coop loved to swim, but it was a bitch getting the wet-dog smell out of the truck.

One of the older kids in his mid-teens hung back from the pack, leaning against a nearby picnic table. He watched them go with a look halfway between disinterest and longing. Judd opened the backpack at his feet and took out a raggedy tennis ball and a frisbee pocked with teeth marks.

"Hey, John, right?" The teen nodded. "Maybe you could take these and help keep an eye on everyone for me? Make sure no one gets into something they shouldn't?"

John took the items with cautious hands. "Yes, sir."

"Good man."

Back straightening from the "I-don't-care-about-anything" slouch he'd been affecting, John nodded again and hurried off after the other kids.

Cam slid her arm around his waist. "Nicely done."

"What?"

"That. John's the oldest of all the kids. Sixteen is that awkward, in-between age where he's trying to distance himself from the younger ones because he thinks he's too old for them now, but at the same time I can see how much he misses being a part of the fun. Giving him a grown-up mission gave him the excuse he thinks he needs to hang out with them. To play with the dog, and just be a kid for a little while longer." She went on her toes and pressed a kiss to his cheek. "Thank you."

He raised a shoulder in a shrug. But her words created a warm glow deep in his chest.

"So, it looks like I was right all along."

Turning at the vaguely familiar voice, Judd found himself looking into sharp green eyes studying him with a combination of humor and triumph. He puzzled over that as Cam stepped from his embrace to give the older man a hug.

"Right about what, Dad?"

Dad?

A few things clicked into place in rapid order. Part of him wanted to laugh. The other part wanted to roll his eyes and groan at Fate's sick sense of humor.

He settled for shaking the man's hand. "Good to see you again, sir."

"Wait. You two have met?" Cam looked confused.

"A few weeks ago, at the fishing tournament. But I had no idea he was your father," he added, knowing what was about to come next.

Sure enough, Hank slapped a hand on Judd's shoulder. "Didn't I tell you she'd be perfect for you?"

Judd winced.

Not at the impact, though it had had a bit of force behind it, but at the dawning look of horror that bled across Cam's face.

"Wait, you're..." She shook her head and redirected her incredulous gaze. "Dad, *Judd* is the man you were trying to set me up with at the fish fry?" Her gaze shot back to Judd. "And you knew about this?"

"Hank insisted I should meet his daughter. I had no idea it was you. Just like I'm assuming you didn't know he was talking about me, either."

He hadn't caught a last name when they'd been introduced on the fishing boat. And even if he had, he probably wouldn't have guessed he was Cam's dad, given he was somewhere north of seventy to have served in 'Nam. Which meant Cam might be a few more years older than him than he'd estimated.

Not that it mattered.

Not to him, anyway.

But remembering the catty comment Heidi had made at the bake sale calling him a "young man" that might not be true for Cam. Was it possible his being younger than her had been an issue? He'd hate to think so. Cam was...Cam. The year on her driver's license meant less than nothing.

Slowly, the tension seeped from her rigid spine beneath his hand.

Which allowed his own body to relax as well.

Thank Christ.

"Okay. You're right. I didn't know he was talking about you, either." She shot an exasperated look at her father. "No more matchmaking, Dad. Okay? As you can see, things worked out just fine without your help."

"Whatever you say, sweetheart."

Judd bit back a grin. Clearly, Hank was going to take credit for bringing them together no matter what anyone said.

The humor drained right out of him as Hank locked onto him with the focused gaze of a father sizing up the man his daughter had her arm wrapped around.

"So, Judd. What are your plans?"

"Dad, you just promised two seconds ago."

"What? This isn't matchmaking. This is getting to know the man you managed to choose all on your own."

Judd bit back a grin when Cam muttered something that sounded suspiciously like "Christ on a crutch." He leveled Hank with the calm, respectful look he usually reserved for his superior officers.

"No concrete plans just yet, but I've recently begun to consider my options right here in Slow Creek."

"Recently, huh?" There was a wealth of unspoken question in his tone.

"Yes, sir. Very." He refused to look at Cam, not sure he'd be able to keep the heat from showing in his gaze. Not the type of thing you did around a woman's father.

Not without risking your balls being ripped off.

"I suppose that makes sense, your kids being here and all."

Shit. How much had he told the man about himself while they were trapped on that fishing boat? He couldn't remember.

"Yes, sir. But I've found there are even more reasons for me to stick around than I first expected." It was as much of a declaration as he was prepared to make.

Anything about his and Cam's relationship needed to be discussed with her first.

"Well, now, that's good to hear, son. Damn good to hear." He slapped him on the shoulder again. "Come on, then. My wife will have my butt in a sling if I don't bring you over to meet her before the rest of the kids grab you for a chat."

The good humor in the words didn't belie their underlying warning.

Sure enough, as they walked to where a petite woman with Camille's brown hair and eyes sat on one of the picnic benches, they passed two men who eyed him with the kind of distrust and challenge only brothers would display.

It looked like Hank wasn't the only one he needed to protect his balls from.

It was a long while before they were alone again. They spread a blanket under one of the trees a little ways off, and Cooper passed out in blissful exhaustion at their feet. Sitting there, watching the clouds blow across the late afternoon sky, breathing in the clear, fresh air scented with pine, the world finally shrunk down to just the two of them.

His back was pressed against the knotty trunk, probably getting sap all over his shirt, and he didn't care. Not with Cam between his legs, her back against his front, his arms around her as his head rested against hers.

A strange feeling settled over him. One it took a while to recognize.

Contentment.

Cam snuggled a little closer against him. "Did you mean it? What you said to my dad earlier, that you're thinking about staying here?"

"Yeah, I did."

"That's really good to hear." She paused. "But…Slow Creek is a world away from the likes of somewhere like San Diego. Are you sure it's what you want?"

At the moment, he didn't think there was anything he could want more.

But he put aside his current state of mind and chose his words carefully.

"Actually, I had a job offer last night, doing what I thought I wanted to do. But it would have taken me from home for long stretches. And I realized I didn't want to be that far away from the people I care about anymore."

That far away from you.

But the words stayed stuck behind his fear and his total lack of experience in how to be part of a normal, healthy relationship.

With Dana, it hadn't been a matter of wanting to be with her so much as feeling he had no choice once she told him she was pregnant. But with Camille, everything was different.

He was different.

He wanted to be with her more than he wanted just about anything except his kids.

And he wanted to do it right.

That didn't include making declarations about feelings and thoughts about the future in the middle of her entire family unit. Half of which were still on the fence about whether he was leaving the lake today with his junk intact.

No, when they had that particular discussion, the time would be right, and they were going to be alone. He just needed to work out the logistics. See the problem, work the problem. He wasn't a romantic kind of guy. But for this, for her, he'd figure out a way.

When he did it, it was going to be perfect.

He hoped.

Chapter 15

Judd had never considered himself a coward before.

But for the past week, he found there were two things he had a difficult time summoning up the courage to do.

Tell Camille how he felt about her.

And let her see him without his prosthesis.

There was no deny the first had a lot—if not everything—to do with the second. That deep inside, he wasn't as confident as he thought about how Cam was going to react when she saw exactly what she'd be getting.

Every scarred, damaged inch.

She might say she could handle it. But they wouldn't know until he actually worked up the nerve to test that theory.

It was Friday now, and he was still waiting for it to happen.

Not that there hadn't been opportunities over the last few days. More than a few. Ever since Sunday, every evening they spent together ended in her bed. Or her sofa. Or on her kitchen table, which they'd finally managed to try out not once, but twice after coming home from the picnic at the lake.

He still got hard when he pictured his sweet Camille spread out like a starving man's bounty on the polished surface. Those sexy little whimpers leaking from her throat as he feasted on her delectable body.

The very table they'd just finished eating dinner on now, as a matter of fact.

He shifted in his chair, adjusting for the sudden lack of space in his pants. As if she knew exactly what had happened and why, Cam grinned. And gave a deliberate lick to the fork holding the last of the lemon merengue pie she'd baked for dessert.

"You're just asking for trouble," he warned as his eyes tracked the extra tongue action she added to grab the last little bit of white.

Damn, but the woman had talent.

"Mmm, yes, I am." She put the fork down on the plate with a definitive click. "What are you going to do about it?"

Still leery of his balance, he couldn't throw her over his shoulder and carry her to the bedroom like he wanted to. So he settled for stalking her there instead, one deliberate step at a time. She played willing prey to his predator, dropping bits of clothing along the way like a trail of breadcrumbs. Just in case he needed any help following.

As if he ever would.

He could close his eyes and know where she was, even in the middle of a blinding sandstorm or raging blizzard. It was like she'd gotten into his blood. His soul.

And his heart, poor, shriveled thing that it was.

He would always be able to find her, and always know when she was gone. He felt it in the nagging sense of loss which dogged him every night when he left her warm, snug bed to go sleep in his cold lonely one.

All because he couldn't man up and take that final leap of faith.

Tonight, he swore as he stood at the bedside and stripped his clothes off while Cam watched with greedy intensity. Tonight, after they made love, he'd do it. He'd take off the prosthesis and let her see everything.

What happened afterward would be entirely her decision.

That didn't mean he couldn't stack the deck a little in his favor beforehand, though.

A good strategist always used every asset at his disposal.

With hands and mouth, he worshipped at the altar of her body. Bringing her to the brink of orgasm three times. Easing her back from the edge each time only to begin the buildup again. And again. And again, until she was a writhing, mewling bundle of sensitized nerve endings and was begging for release.

Which he gave her.

Then he started the cycle all over again.

After her second orgasm, he tore himself away to roll on a condom, resenting every moment they weren't skin-to-skin. Done, he urged her onto her side and positioned himself behind her, clasping her body against the front of his. She was warm, and wet, and inviting as he slid home with one sure thrust.

And that was exactly what she felt like.

Home.

With the same deliberation he'd already shown, he used his body to tell her what he wasn't able to say in words. He desired her. He needed her. He loved her. He wanted to build his world around her and his kids, right here in Slow Creek.

Which was beginning to feel like home to him, too.

His orgasm came not as a roar or an explosion, but more of a long, drawn-out sensation of perfection that started in his toes and spread throughout his entire being. The way Camille's body rippled around him with her own release only enhanced his pleasure. Drawing it out even longer for them both as he continued to stroke through the very last tremor.

By the time they were done, it was hard to tell which of them was more wiped out.

It took everything he had to withdraw so he could take care of cleaning up. The condom was quick and easy. His leg liner was going to need more than a tissue, though.

Do it.

The same little voice that had been urging him on all week whispered to him once more.

Show her. She can handle it.

Maybe so.

But could he?

"Mmm, missed you," she murmured as she rolled to face him. Her hands skimmed over his body in a welcoming caress, as though it wasn't mere seconds they'd been apart.

Skin warming under her light touch, he gently pushed back the lock of silky hair that clung to her damp cheek. "God, you are so beautiful."

She laughed. "So, sweaty women are your thing, huh?"

"When I've helped her get that way? Oh, yeah." He smiled when she laughed again, the sound like a velvet stroke deep inside him where usually there was nothing but a big pit of loneliness. An emptiness he hadn't even realized existed until Cam started to fill it with her warmth and love and acceptance.

Do it.

"Cam, I want to…" Fuck, why was this so hard? "There's something I've been trying to say, to do, all week, and…" He swallowed around the boulder in his throat as he stroked his thumb over her cheek again. "God, you are so special to me, do you know that?"

"I think you just did a pretty good job of showing me."

Her smile was infectious. His own lips curved in response despite the squad of infantry doing quick-march maneuvers in his stomach. "That was entirely my pleasure." Watching Camille come was his new favorite thing.

"Oh, no. It was definitely mine." She turned her head enough to catch his thumb with her teeth and give it a sharp nip. "And I plan to repay the favor. As soon as I can move the rest of my body."

"Which, if I did my job right, won't be until next week."

"Well, you *are* extremely thorough." With an exhausted sigh, she snuggled closer. "I wouldn't mind staying just like this until then."

Do it.

"Neither would I. But I, uh, need to take care of my leg first." The infantry went from maneuvers to full-out combat drill, making his stomach roil. He was really going to do this.

"Okay. Do what you need to. I'll be right here when you get back."

Do it!

He opened his mouth…

And couldn't do it.

Like the coward he clearly was, he slunk off the bed, retrieved his bag, and shut himself in the bathroom like he had every other time he'd needed to make an adjustment to his prosthesis.

Stripping it off as he sat on the lid of the toilet, he called himself every name in the book. He'd had his chance—the perfect chance—and he'd blown it.

But maybe not.

Maybe he could still do this. Find his balls, go back in, and try again. Only this time he wouldn't let himself get distracted by her touch. Or her scent. Or the taste of her, still ripe on his tongue like wild strawberries.

He shook the sensory image away like a dog shedding water. Falling down that rabbit hole again wasn't going to get him any closer to achieving his goals. It was Camille he'd wanted to lull into a mellow post-orgasmic stupor, not himself.

Unfortunately, he did his job a little too well. When he got back to the bedroom, she was asleep.

Wanting nothing more than to crawl in beside her and forget everything else, he sat on the edge of the mattress instead to consider his options. He could wake her up and follow through with his plan, half-assed as it was. Or he could say fuck it and wait until tomorrow to try again.

They had the whole weekend to themselves. No taking any kids somewhere. No interfering family sticking their noses into their business. No annoying ex-wife asking him to fix this or take a look at that because it's dripping or 'making a weird noise' every time he dropped the kids off at the house.

Just him and Cam, entirely alone. Together.

Surely, he could find the right moment to make his big reveal somewhere in those forty-eight hours.

Even knowing he was making excuses didn't affect his relief at the decision to postpone his little show-and-tell.

Tomorrow for sure.

You are so full of shit.

The urge to just get it over with swept over him again. But a tiny niggle of something—doubt? fear?—stayed his hand as he reached to wake her. He kept telling himself she'd be fine with what she saw once he took his prosthesis off. But what if she wasn't?

Worse, what if she wasn't, but being the kind, caring person she was, she pretended to be?

That would be a thousand times worse.

"You're back." The sleepy purr of her voice was accompanied by her hand sliding along the sheets to tug on his. "Come to bed."

He resisted. "I have to go."

"It's early still."

"I need to feed Coop," he lied.

"Oh." She released his hand and snuggled her face into the pillow. "His food's in the pantry."

Shit.

He'd forgotten. Earlier that week, she'd asked what brand he used. The next day, a bag of it and bowls for food and water had appeared in her kitchen. As well as a treat jar which now sat on the counter next to Jasper's.

The cat and Cooper had seemed to reach a détente of sorts, marked by Jasper eating out of Coop's bowl whenever he wanted, and Coop letting him.

Judd, however, was still viewed with acute suspicion.

But at least Jasper didn't bolt out of the room when he saw him anymore. It was taking time and patience, but Judd was slowly gaining the skittish tom's trust. It was a testament to Cam's compassionate personality that she'd left the shelter with the most broken-down wreck they had, when a normal cat would have made for a much easier pet.

It was just who she was.

Something in him froze.

Was *he* just another broken-down wreck she was trying to save?

His earlier feelings of doubt and fear grew until they were close to choking him.

"No, I think I need to go."

Whatever she heard in his voice had her opening her eyes to study his face with concern. "Is your leg bothering you?"

"Yeah." Just not the way she meant.

"Okay." Reaching out, she stroked his arm. "Anything I can do?"

Forcing himself not to flinch, he gave his head a tight shake. "No. I'm good. Thanks."

She didn't look convinced, but didn't argue. "Do you want to postpone tomorrow?"

Tomorrow.

They'd made tentative plans to spend the day walking around Kansas City playing tourist. Maybe try one of the food tours that led you through a sampling of the wide variety of cuisines the city had to offer. A few hours ago, he'd been looking forward to spending the day alone with her.

Now?

"Why don't we play it by ear?" he replied after a slightly too long hesitation.

"Of course. Whatever you want."

What he wanted was to not have these doubts suddenly swamping him. Not to question every word, every action that had passed between them from the start. Not to wonder if what he'd seen as understanding and caring was really just pity wrapped up in a bright shiny bow of compassion.

But those doubts and others plagued him throughout the drive back to the camper.

Was he misreading his own emotions as well? Was what he felt really love, or merely pathetic gratitude that a woman had actually let herself be bedded by a one-legged freak like him?

Had he allowed Cam to gentle him to her touch just like she had the fucking cat?

An anxious whine from the backseat drew his attention away from his spiraling thoughts and back to the road. Realizing he was going much too fast, he cursed and slowed.

"Sorry, buddy." He reached between the seats to Cooper, who licked his fingers and whined again, keying in on Judd's mood.

As soon as he was inside the camper, he dropped his go-bag and headed straight to the mini-fridge for a beer. By his second, he'd managed to stop the merry-go-round of doubt in his head about Cam's motives and accepted he was creating problems where there weren't any. Self-sabotage, his therapist had called it.

Just a fancy name for being a chicken-shit, in Judd's opinion.

He couldn't man-up enough to give her the full monty, so he needed the problem to be with her to soothe his asinine pride.

By the third beer, he decided there was no reason to expose Cam to the harsh reality of his stump. Hell, he'd been doing just fine making love to her with the prosthesis on. Why would he even want to take a chance on messing up the best thing to come into his life in years?

By the fourth beer he'd talked himself into going back over to Cam's and doing exactly that, right this minute. Show her everything. Because he needed to know if she could handle the true him.

By the fifth, he knew it would be a mistake to go see Cam again tonight, although he was a little fuzzy about why that was. He was pretty sure it had something to do with the damn cat, though.

By the time he drained the final bottle in the six-pack, it was all he could do to stumble the short distance to the bunk at the back of the camper, strip off his prosthesis and liner, and drag on the shrinker he wore at night to keep his stump from swelling with fluids. He had a moment to wonder why the room was rocking like a ship in high seas as he collapsed onto the narrow mattress before he was sucked into unconsciousness.

Hours later, the immediate need to piss clawed its way through his alcohol-induced slumber. Fumbling for his crutches, he somehow managed to get to the bathroom and take care of business without falling off the toilet.

Mouth tasting like something Jasper used for a litter box, he steered a course toward the fridge for a bottle of water. Better yet, a sports drink. Maybe the electrolytes would help stave off the impending hangover he could feel hovering at the edges of his still fuzzy brain the way dawn waited just the other side of the twilight pressing on the windows.

One second he was walking.

The next he was falling, the crutch going out from under him before he had time to compensate.

If he hadn't still been half-drunk, he might have had a chance to catch himself on the way down. But the only thing he managed before hitting the floor was to turn his head so he didn't land face-first.

Pain exploded through his skull.

Brilliant white tracers enveloped his vision before everything faded to a dull tunnel-vision. His ears filled with the muffled roar of the ocean. Underneath it all, there was Cooper whining and barking as he nudged at Judd's prone body.

It took precious seconds for his rattled brain to realize the dog was seeking a command.

"Phone." His voice sounded like it came from way down in a well rather than his own mouth. "Get...the phone."

Nails scrabbled against old linoleum as the dog headed for the bedroom and the small table Judd always left his cellphone on at night to charge.

Only, he couldn't remember if he'd bothered to take it out of his pocket before he'd pulled off his clothes and fallen into bed or not.

Couldn't remember much of anything through the throbbing that threatened to cleave his skull in half.

He tried to turn his head in the direction Cooper had gone, but the movement set off another detonation, making his vision go from tunnel-vision to almost complete black. He groaned and swallowed back the bile rising in his throat.

From somewhere far away, he heard Cooper barking again, but he just couldn't focus on what that was supposed to mean. It was all he could do to hang onto the last threads of consciousness he had.

A cold nose touched his face, followed by a whine and a quick lap of a wet tongue.

Get help.

He couldn't seem to make his mouth form the words. Couldn't hold off the inevitable any longer. One second there was only pain and darkness.

The next, there was nothing.

The phone rang as Cam walked into her bedroom, a towel wrapped around her wet hair. Normally, there would be a second one around her shower-damp body as well for modesty's sake.

But today, she'd felt confident enough to walk through her own house in the buff and not worry about her tummy or the hint of boob sag she saw in the mirror. Being with Judd had given her a new perspective on her body and all its little imperfections.

If he thought it was beautiful the way it was, then so could she.

Picking the phone up from her nightstand, she smiled at the name on the caller ID.

Speak of the devil.

"I was just thinking about you," she purred, laying back on the sheets that still had his scent clinging to them. "I hope you slept as well as I did, because you wore me all the way out last night."

There was the sound of a throat being cleared on the other end of the line. "Uh, Camille, this isn't Judd. It's Uriah."

"Uriah?" Cringing in horror, she bolted upright, grabbing the sheet to wrap around her naked body even though he couldn't see her. "But...what are you doing with Judd's phone?" The only logical explanation hit her like a freight train. "Oh, my god, is he hurt? Was there an accident? Is he okay?"

"He's fine. Well, mostly fine. He took a fall and gave himself a good lump on his head, but otherwise he seems all right."

She closed her eyes and breathed a sigh of relief. "Thank god." She opened them again, struggling to calm the frantic beating of her heart. "I'll be right there. Are you at the hospital or the doctor's office?"

"Neither. The stubborn ba—um, idiot refused to go. Which is why I called you. Wilt managed to at least badger him into a bed in one of his spare rooms. But I figured if anyone could talk some sense into him, it would be you."

Any other time, she might have asked why he'd think such a thing. But after what she'd said when she answered the phone, it seemed a little silly to deny they had *that* kind of relationship.

Still, it didn't stop a blush from heating her face to the temperature of a waffle iron.

"I'll be there as soon as I can."

After hanging up, she grabbed the first clothes she put her hands on from the closet and pulled them on. A quick rub with the towel was all the drying her hair got before she yanked it into a band. She was halfway to the front door before she circled back, chanting, "Shoes, shoes, shoes," under her breath.

The drive to Wilt's place was short, yet long enough for her mind to play out all kinds of horrible scenarios about what might have happened. Had Judd been up early doing another repair on Wilt's house and fallen from a ladder?

Or even worse, from the roof?

Her stomach was a queasy knot by the time she knocked on the front door of the old farmhouse. There were thunderclouds darkening Uriah's ebony face when he opened it and ushered her in. For some reason, that made her feel a little better. If he was angry rather than worried, Judd's injuries couldn't be too serious. Could they?

She hoped, anyway.

"How is he?"

"That man of yours could give a mountain lessons on how not to budge an inch." He scrubbed a hand over his face and sighed. "But besides being an ornery cuss, I think he's going to be okay."

The relief that swept over her left her a little light-headed. "What happened? Was he doing work in the house when he got hurt?"

"No, he tripped and hit his head early this morning while he was in the camper."

Wincing in sympathy, she asked, "But why did he call you and not nine-one-one?"

Or me?

"He didn't call me. Wilt did."

"So, he called Wilt?" That made even less sense than calling Uriah, who at least was strong enough to help him up if he'd been hurt. Then again, maybe he didn't have the sheriff's personal number. Just because everyone else in Slow Creek had it didn't mean Judd necessarily would.

But he had mine.

Again, she pushed the pinch of hurt aside as unimportant for now.

"No. Damndest thing I ever heard. The dog came and woke Wilt up right before sunrise. Sat on the porch barking and howling like the devil was after him until Wilt finally came out to see what the problem was. When Cooper practically herded him over to the camper, he found Judd all dazed and bloody on the floor."

Her hand went to her mouth. He'd been hurt enough to *bleed*? "Oh lord."

"It wasn't like he cracked his head open," Uriah said hastily. "Just a bump and a little gash right about here." He touched his left temple near the hairline. "Judd took care of patching himself up before I even got here. Man's first aid kit is bigger than the one I carry in my patrol car," he muttered, sounding a little envious in that way guys got when someone else had better toys than they did.

Men.

"Can I see him?"

"Sure. Just...don't take it personal if he isn't exactly happy to see you. He's not in the best frame of mind right now."

As she followed the sheriff to the bedroom at the back of the house, she could hear two male voices in heated discussion coming from inside. Uriah gave a perfunctory knock on the open door.

"Sorry to interrupt, but you've got company." He stepped aside for Cam to pass.

Her gaze went immediately to the man sitting on the edge of the bed. Short hair mussed, face stubble-kissed, dressed in a dark tee and shorts, he looked like every fantasy she'd ever had of him waking up in her bed.

Until he turned his head to look in her direction and she saw the angry red and purple lump on his temple, covered by two stark white butterfly bandages. She couldn't stifle a small gasp of distress.

The second he saw her, Judd cursed and grabbed for the covers that had been flung aside. Pulling them over his lower body, he swung himself back into the bed. "God *damn* it, Uriah! What's she doing here? I told you not to call her."

Wilt, who'd been the one arguing with him, gave a bark of cackling laughter. "Well, I guess that's one way to make sure he stays put."

Struggling to keep Uriah's advice in mind, Cam ignored the lack of welcome and walked to the bedside. It was totally understandable he wasn't in the best of moods at the moment.

That didn't mean the words didn't still hurt.

"Of course, he called me. Someone had to come talk some sense into that thick head of yours." She tried to keep her tone light and teasing, but from the chilly stare he gave her, it didn't have the desired effect.

She attempted a more direct approach. "Why don't you want to go to the hospital?"

"Because there's no reason for me to," he replied, impatience radiating from every stiff inch of his body.

"Okay, but why not go, just to be sure?"

"I'm not wasting a doctor's time on a bullshit head bump when he can be helping someone who really needs it. And I know that's all it is, because I have combat medic training like all SEALs do, in case you've all forgotten."

She hadn't known that, actually. But even so, she doubted Judd was exactly objective when it came to assessing his own injuries. "Okay. But—"

"Enough." He cut her off with a slash of his hand. "I'm not going anywhere except back to my camper. Now. If someone would just get me *my damn crutches*."

From the way Judd was glaring at Wilt, it was a safe bet that was what they'd been arguing about when she came in.

"You just hold your horses now, son," Wilt said, seeming unfazed by the icy death-stare he was getting. "You don't want to see the doctor? Fine and dandy. But that means your butt stays right where it is so I can keep an eye on you."

"I'm not an invalid," Judd ground out through clenched teeth.

"Never said you were. But the last thing I want is to let you go back out to that rattletrap camper and have something else happen to you and not know about it till it's too late."

"Nothing's going to happen. It was a fluke. I slipped in the dark. It's not going to happen again." The words were clipped so sharp they almost hurt to hear.

"Maybe not. But I don't want to take that chance. And since I'm technically your landlord, I'm revoking my offer to use the darn camper for the time being and moving you in here instead."

"You're evicting me?"

Wilt snorted. "No, dumbass. I'm offering you better accommodations, such as they are."

"And if I don't want to move in here?"

"Well, I guess you have a problem, then. It's not like you have yourself a whole lot of options."

But he did. Cam knew it, and from the way Judd looked at her, he knew it, too. She gave a small smile and a nod of encouragement, letting him know she was more than fine with him coming to stay with her. At least in the short-term.

He continued to look at her, his eyes darkening just before he looked away.

"Then I guess I'm staying here."

Talk about a sucker punch.

She didn't realize she'd wavered on her feet until Uriah's large hand closed over her elbow to steady her. She gave him a grateful look and did her best to ignore the pity she saw in his eyes. "Judd..."

"I don't need anyone taking care of me," he snarled, hands fisting around the blanket bunched over his legs.

The action drew her attention to something she should have realized from the start. That if he needed his crutches, it meant he wasn't wearing his prosthesis. And knowing Judd's aversion to exposing that particular weakness to anyone, including her—maybe especially her—his level of assholery suddenly made a lot more sense.

"No one here thinks you do," she said, trying to sound like she meant it. "We just want to make sure you're taking care of yourself." When Judd finally looked at her again, she was struck by the stark vulnerability in his eyes before he blinked and they were filled with winter chill again.

"No one asked you to."

"Actually," Uriah said with a deep, annoyed rumble, "I asked her. So, cut up all you want at Wilt and me, but show Camille a little respect, there, son."

Judd's eyes narrowed. "So, now you're not just telling me what I can do, but what I can say?"

"That's not what I said, and you know it."

"Sure sounded like it to me."

"Is that right. Well, then, maybe you need to listen a little harder."

As things seemed poised to take a turn for the worse, it might be a good time for a strategic retreat. Maybe if she gave him a little space, Judd's hackles would have a chance to go down about her seeing him in such a vulnerable condition.

"You know what? I think I'll leave you boys to figure this out on your own while I go make us some breakfast. If that's okay with you," she added hastily to Wilt, who grinned and nodded.

"I'll never turn down a meal I don't have to do the cookin' for. Besides, maybe eating something will help take some of the piss and vinegar out of that one." He hooked a thumb at Judd, ignoring the dirty look shot his way as he gestured for Cam to follow him. "Come on, I'll show you where everything is."

She hesitated at the doorway. "Do you want me to take Cooper out to do his business?" The golden retriever had been planted at the side of the bed since she got there, his attentive gaze never breaking from watching Judd. As if he was afraid something bad was going to happen to him if he did.

Again.

"He went a little while ago. But thanks," he added gruffly.

It turned out Wilt didn't have enough on hand for a breakfast for four, especially when two of those four were Judd and Uriah. When she got back from a quick run to the store for more eggs and bacon, there was an unfamiliar car parked in front of the house.

Maybe Uriah and Wilt had managed to talk Judd into seeing a doctor after all.

Or called in reinforcements.

She hurried inside with the groceries. The door to the bedroom was closed, and there was no sign of the men. So she set about whipping up a hearty, stick-to-your-ribs meal, complete with made-from-scratch biscuits and gravy. Something she rarely indulged in herself but knew Judd loved.

By the time everything was ready, she was considerably calmer. Cooking always had that effect on her. It gave her time to think things through rationally as she measured and kneaded and poured by rote. In this case, it gave her the chance to finally process everything that had happened since her phone rang that morning.

While she wasn't exactly thrilled about the way Judd had acted and spoken to her, she understood. And was willing to let it go because of the circumstances. He was probably embarrassed. Almost certainly in pain.

Definitely, it seemed, no closer to crossing the line he'd drawn in the sand when it came to sharing that final, intimate part of his life with her. Allowing himself to be around her without the prosthesis on.

In fact, judging by his reaction, this might set that goal back even further than ever.

Just when she thought she might need to put everything in the oven to stay warm, she heard the bedroom door open and close.

"Finally!" Wanting to catch the doctor or whoever it was before they left, she hurried around the corner.

And stopped short.

It wasn't the doctor, or even Wilt or Uriah coming out of Judd's bedroom.

It was Dana.

Chapter 16

"Dana." Cam hated the surprised squeak the name came out as. Even if she *was* surprised.

Shocked, actually.

"Miss Richards." At least Dana sounded as taken off guard as Cam felt. "I didn't know you were here. I didn't see your car." The last came out like an accusation.

"I was at the store getting some things for breakfast." The polite thing to do would be to invite her to stay and eat with them. But despite the fact her mother would be horrified at the lapse in manners, she couldn't bring herself to do it.

The morning was awkward enough already.

Floundering, she said, "I didn't realize Uriah had called you, too."

"Oh, he didn't. Judd did."

If she'd felt sucker punched earlier, this was more like a body slam.

"I see."

Dana's pink-glossed lips turned up at the ends. "He wanted to make sure he told me what happened himself. So I didn't hear it secondhand and worry."

"How thoughtful."

"Isn't it?" Her smile broadened. "Judd's always been like that. Always looking out for me, being considerate. A real gentleman.

And he always took *such* good care of me during my pregnancies. When he was there," she added almost to herself.

Wow, no subtlety there.

Yes, I know you gave birth to the children he adores. But you also threw him away. You lost the right to feel territorial, so back off.

"Anyway," Dana continued, "after all the times he took care of me, I'm glad to finally get the chance to do the same for him."

Ignoring her own territorial urges—namely, to shove the other woman right out the front door and bolt it shut behind her—she said, "Judd has plenty of friends already taking care of him."

And me. He has me.

"But no one who knows him as...*well* as I do."

Much as she wanted to, Cam couldn't dispute the claim. Five years of marriage, no matter how long ago, probably counted for a lot more than a few weeks of good sex.

Really, *really* good, but still just sex.

She'd thought they were making progress toward something more. But with Dana standing there in front of her, at Judd's own request when he very specifically hadn't called for *her* to come, her confidence about that wavered.

Time to move this along.

"Are Wilt and Uriah in with Judd now? I need to tell them breakfast's ready."

"No, they went to get some things from the camper." She plucked a wisp of fur from her dress with a moue of distaste. "I wish they'd taken that dog with them. Ugh."

Rather than be amused or even surprised at Dana's apparent dislike of Cooper, the dog *everyone* loved, all she could focus on was how absolutely put together she was. White summery dress with little black polka dots, white wedge sandals, blonde hair curling in thick waves around her artfully made-up face.

Her young, dewy-skinned face.

Next to her, Cam was painfully aware of her flour-dusted shorts, t-shirt, and flip-flops. Her wet hair had dried in the lopsided ponytail she'd put it up in. If she took it down now, she'd spend the rest of the day looking like she had a bad case of hat-head. And the only makeup she wore was the Chapstick she'd found in the car, in the hope it would keep her from chewing her lips raw with worry.

She couldn't have felt less attractive if she'd tried.

"*That dog* got help for Judd when he was hurt. He's a hero." And if he disliked Dana as much as she apparently did him, he was also an excellent judge of character.

Not that she was feeling catty or anything.

Dana rolled her eyes. "Whatever. Didn't you say breakfast was ready? I hate to keep Judd hungry and waiting while we stand out here talking about his dog."

That, at least, they could agree on.

Heading back to the kitchen, Cam set about making up a plate with some of everything from the stove. That went on the lap-tray someone, she was guessing Wilt, had left on the big wooden table. She added silverware and napkins, as well as salt and pepper shakers she'd bring back to the table for the other men to use when Judd was done with them.

As she went to the fridge for some orange juice, Dana grabbed the bottle of ketchup from the table and squirted some on the scrambled eggs. Her confidence took another hit. She hadn't known Judd liked ketchup on his eggs. Such a tiny detail, but one more bit of proof Dana really did know him better than she did.

The finishing touch was a big mug of coffee. That she *did* know how Judd liked it. Strong and black. Turning back to add it to the tray, a growl rose in her throat at the sight of Dana rearranging everything. As though she had every right to mess with the meal *Cam* had prepared for Judd.

I don't think so, missy.

Pasting on a smile, she plunked the mug down and picked up the tray in a firm, possessive grip. "Would you mind getting the bedroom door?"

Dana answered with a sugary smile of her own. "Why, of course, Miss Richards."

It was childish to shoot daggers at the woman's back and silently mimic her words as they walked. But it made her feel a little better, so she didn't care. When they reached the bedroom, Dana turned the knob enough to unlatch the door, paused, then turned back to look at Cam, effectively blocking the way.

"You know, I think having too many people hovering over him will just make him more agitated. He hates being sick."

Judd wasn't sick. But she happened to agree with Dana's assessment, so she didn't point that out. "I think you're right."

"Good. So why don't I just bring this on in to him, then." She put her hands on the tray as though to take it away.

Cam resisted. "I don't think so."

"Well, he did phone *me*, now didn't he?"

He had. A fact that still cut deeper than she wanted to examine at the moment.

Before she could formulate a reply, Judd's raised voice filtered through the barely open door. "Dana?"

Everything in her froze as the other woman shot Cam a triumphant smile. He must have heard them talking.

And he'd called out for Dana.

Not her.

With numb fingers, she released her hold on the tray.

With what was probably supposed to be a sympathetic expression, Dana said, "I'm sure he'll want to thank you for the food. If you want to pop your head in for a second..."

"No. That's okay. I have some things to take care of at home, so...I'll just stop back later."

"You know, maybe you should call first. To make sure he's up for company."

"Dana, what's taking so long?"

The sound of Judd's voice calling again for his ex made her flinch, but not as much as Dana calling back, "Be right there, sugar bear."

Oh, it was definitely time to go.

"Tell him…I hope he's feeling better."

Trying not to feel like she was running away, she beat a hasty retreat for the front door, only stopping to grab her purse along the way. She nearly ran into Wilt and Uriah as she clattered down the porch steps, flip-flops slapping against the mismatched wooden boards in an angry staccato.

"Need something else at the store?" Uriah asked.

"No, I…breakfast is ready. It's on the stove." And probably getting cold, since she hadn't taken the time to put it up in the oven for them. "You can help yourselves."

"What about Judd?"

She gave a smile so tight it felt like her face would crack. "Don't worry. Dana's taking good care of him."

Uriah's expression said what he thought of that. "Camille, it's not what you think."

"It doesn't matter what I think, Uriah. It's about what Judd wants. Now, I have to go." She pushed past the two men, glad their arms were full because otherwise she feared Uriah might have tried to stop her.

As it was, he called after her to wait a darn minute, but she ignored him.

Her body was quaking so badly she had trouble getting the seatbelt latched. But she managed to hold off the tears pressing against her burning eyes so she could see to drive. All she wanted was to go home, crawl under the covers, and block out the world while she licked her wounds and tried to figure out what the hell had just happened.

Then she remembered those covers still smelled like *him*. Like them.

Of the last night they'd spent together making mad, passionate love. Sheets she'd rolled on like a cat in heat just a few hours ago, reveling in the scent and the memories it brought.

Now, she couldn't stand the thought of being anywhere near that kind of reminder of what a fool she'd been.

Instead of turning into her neighborhood, she continued driving until she found herself pulling up in front of Joelyn's house. Her friend's surprise when she answered the front door quickly morphed to concern as Cam sniffled back one of the tears that managed to leak past her defenses. "Judd—"

"No." Joelyn held up a hand to stop her before she got any further. "Tea first, then talk."

After shooing her twins out into the backyard to play, Joelyn settled Cam and herself in the cozy sunroom and shut the door. It took two strong cups of chamomile tea bolstered with honey—and possibly a splash of something from the liquor cabinet—before the tremors faded and her brain started to focus enough for her to think clearly again.

In between nibbles of the muffins Jo put in front of her with the third cup, she told her about the early morning call from Uriah. Her frantic drive to the farmhouse. Judd's fall and injury.

Jo's brow puckered in confusion. "But wait, how did the dog get out of the camper to go for help?"

"I asked him about that once before, when he was describing everything Cooper could do. He's trained to use a rope attached to the door handle to pull down and unlatch it to go get help if there's an emergency."

Like falling and bashing his stupid head open.

The memory of those stark white butterfly bandages against his bronze skin still made her stomach cramp. Despite everything, she hated that he was hurt.

Jo looked impressed. "Huh. That's pretty remarkable."

"Cooper's a very smart dog."

With a very stupid owner.

An opinion reinforced as she told Jo about Dana's appearance, and the fact Judd had called and asked her to come. "I mean, why would he do that? He's told me, more than once, he doesn't have any feelings left for her except as the mother of his children. Why would he want her there when he had…"

"When he had you?"

She nodded and took another sip of tea, letting the warmth slide down her throat and loosen the tightness building there again.

"I have to wonder if it's because of the way we were trying to keep him in bed. Maybe he felt ganged-up on and called her figuring she'd be on his side. Do what he wanted and bring him his crutches."

Or take him home with her.

That was a possibility she hadn't considered until just now. And one impossible to ignore now that she'd thought it. The prospect left a sour taste in her mouth even the honey couldn't dispel.

"Well, what did Judd say?"

"About what?"

"About why his ex was there." Jo stared at her with dawning horror. "You didn't ask him."

"I didn't get the chance to."

Did she sound as defensive to her friend as she did to herself? Judging by Jo's look of exasperation, that would be a big, fat yes.

"I might have said something when I brought in his food, but…"

"But?"

"Dana took the tray from me and insinuated having too many people around was making him agitated, and it might be better if

I came back later. Actually, if I called later," she said, remembering the condescending little smile the other woman had worn when she said it. "To see if he was 'up for company' or not."

Company. That had certainly put her in her place.

"And you just let her get away with that?"

"What was I supposed to do, fight her for the tray?"

"Um, *yes*! Okay, no, not actually, but you're the woman with the Mensa vocabulary. You could have sliced her into tiny, quivering pieces with a few choice words and she'd never know what hit her. Instead, you just conceded the field to her? Are you crazy?"

Was that what she'd done?

"You didn't hear her. Miss Richards this, Miss Richards that. Like I needed the reminder she's more than a decade younger than I am." As if her poreless skin and perky breasts hadn't been enough. "And besides, he called for her."

"We already established we don't know why he did that."

"No. I mean, he *called* for her. From the bedroom. He heard us both talking outside the door, and he called for *her*." Twice.

"Oh, Cam. Sweetie." Jo leaned in and wrapped her arm around her shoulders in a hug. "Maybe it's not what it seems."

"That's what Uriah tried to say when I was leaving." And maybe she should have taken the time to listen to him. But facts were still facts. "They have so much history together. And their kids. How can I fight that?"

"I think the better question is, do you want to?"

Did she?

No matter how much she was hurting right now, she could still remember how wonderful things had been between them these past few weeks. How he'd opened up to her. About his family, his injury, his doubts and worries for the future.

He'd met her family. Told her father he was considering staying in Slow Creek. That *had* to mean something.

Didn't it?

But most of all, there was the fact she loved him.

If for no other reason, she couldn't just give up without trying to fix whatever it was that had gone wrong this morning. To give them a chance to make it work. To find out what it was, exactly, Judd wanted.

Even if it wasn't her.

"Here we go, sugar bear," Dana chirped as she set the food-laden tray over Judd's lap. "Breakfast is served."

God, how he hated that old pet name.

Almost as much as he hated ketchup on his eggs. He glared at the ruined mess of what had probably been a very tasty breakfast and was now just red-coated crap. But he was hungry, and he'd eaten a hell of a lot worse, so he grabbed the fork and tucked in.

"Who were you talking to out there?" he asked between bites. "Have Wilt and Uriah come back with my things yet?"

Like my leg?

Because he wanted nothing more than to be able to stand on his own two feet again. Even if one of them was carbon fiber instead of flesh-and-bone.

Of course, the bastards wouldn't even give him his crutches, so he doubted he'd be getting the leg anytime soon, either. If it hadn't been for the knowledge Camille was outside that door somewhere, he'd have had his ass out of bed and hopping around the house looking for the damn things in a hot second.

Which was probably the whole reason Uriah had told her to come in the first place.

Manipulative asshole.

As he ate, he started to feel a little better. The nagging throb hitting his skull like a gong since he found himself laying on the floor in his skivvies had lessened to more of a bass drum. The strong, smooth coffee took care of the cotton-mouth, and the food stopped most of the angry churning in his gut.

The embarrassment, however, was still raging at full force.

Even so, he was starting to get a little edgy about how long it was taking Cam to come in and see him again. Yes, he'd been unnecessarily surly to her before. But she had to know it was the pain and mortification talking. Otherwise, why would she have bothered to stay and cook for him?

Which raised another question.

"Why did you bring the tray in and not Camille?" He forked up a piece of gravy-soaked biscuit that all but melted in his mouth. God, that woman could cook.

"You mean Miss Richards?" A funny look flashed over Dana's face. "Oh, she left."

The fork stopped mid-air as her words hit him. "She left?"

"Mmhmm." She smoothed a hand over her dress, drawing attention to her curves, as intended. She'd been using the same trick since he first met her.

The curves he ignored. But he did note how well-dressed she was. Dress, heels, makeup. Not Stepford wife perfect, but pretty damn close. And not likely her normal Saturday-morning-with-the-kids look. It was obvious she'd taken some time with her appearance before coming over.

Unlike Cam, who'd looked like she got dressed in the dark with her paint-stained tee and faded denim shorts. Things he knew damn well she'd normally never wear out of the house. Her public image was too important to her.

But she'd rushed over like that anyhow, caring more about getting to him than how she looked.

And then he'd gone and been a dick to her.

Asshole.

"Did she say when she was coming back?"

Because he owed her an apology. Maybe two.

Dana paused again, then shrugged. "She said something about having things to do, since I was here to take care of you. Oh, she did say she'd try to call later, though," she added after a second, offering the information like a consolation prize or something.

No, what it was, was a wake-up call.

He'd been wondering and worrying, and now he finally had his answer. Proof Cam couldn't handle the reality of him without his leg. She'd taken one look at the empty space under the blanket and bolted.

Okay, yes, he'd been intentionally nasty, trying to get her out of the room because he was embarrassed. But she'd taken it a step further and left the damn house altogether.

But she'd try to call later.

Right.

He dropped his fork to the plate with a clatter, unable to eat another bite of food that suddenly tasted like goodbye. Damn it! He'd really thought she'd be different than Dana. That she wouldn't let his defect keep her from seeing him as a whole man, rather than someone she couldn't bear to look at, much less touch, when he wasn't hiding behind his prosthesis.

Too bad he hadn't shown her the truth of himself last night as planned. Maybe it would have saved them both a lot of grief.

And him a lumped-up head.

Then again, he probably would have still gotten drunk and fallen on his face. Just for a different reason. But maybe then she wouldn't have felt obligated to show up and kick him while he was down.

"Don't you worry, sugar bear," Dana purred, perching her hip on the edge of the bed next to him. "I'm still here for you."

Yes, she was.

Of course, she was conveniently overlooking the fact he'd never asked her to come in the first place. All he'd wanted to do was head off the usual small-town gossip mill. Make sure his kids knew he was okay before they heard some distorted version of the truth that had him losing an eye or in a coma, or worse.

But Dana being Dana, had taken the call as an open invitation to insert herself into the situation. Even though he'd never even hinted he wanted her there. Now, though, with the pain of Cam's desertion still raw, he had to admit it felt good having her hovering over him.

She might not be able to look at the evidence of his missing leg either, but at least she'd never been anything but honest about her squeamishness.

Unlike Cam, who'd sworn it didn't matter.

Until apparently it had.

Needing to focus on something other than the disappointment and betrayal cutting him up like a pair of rusty knives inside, he asked, "How did the kids take it when you told them?"

"They were understandably worried, but I told them I'd bring them over later so they could see for themselves you were okay."

He nodded. That was just the kind of distraction he needed. And it gave him the perfect excuse to be let out of the damn bed.

"Good idea. Thanks. And I'm sorry you're wasting your day off like this." He cleared his throat. "Thank you for coming to check on me."

With a smile that used to signal he was about to get lucky, she said, "Of course, I came, silly. I'll come any time you need me to."

The promise made him feel both better and worse. It was nice to know someone cared enough to be there for him. He just hadn't expected it to be her.

Hadn't *wanted* it to be her.

He wanted it to be Cam, damn it.

Dana lingered a few minutes longer while he finished his coffee, then whisked away the tray with the promise to come back in a few hours with the kids. The door had barely shut behind her when it opened again and Uriah strode in.

"Scare another one away with your sparkling personality?" he asked, hooking a thumb over his shoulder with his free hand. The other held a blanket-wrapped object that could only be Judd's prosthesis.

"Hilarious." Agitated, because the joking question had some real sting, he flipped back the covers and shifted his weight to the edge of the mattress. "It's about time. Give." He held out a demanding hand.

"Got someplace to be?"

"Yeah. Out of this fucking bed." Sucking in a breath, he fought for a calm he wasn't close to feeling. "I spent *months* confined to a bed in the hospital. Trust me, you don't realize how much you take being able to get up and walk out of a room for granted until you can't do it anymore."

That lack of control over his own life had been sheer hell. It was what had motivated him to progress to first crutches, then the prosthesis, long before the therapists had thought he was ready.

With a sigh, Uriah laid the prosthesis on the bed, then shrugged the backpack off his shoulder. "We just wanted you to take more than a minute to recover before you went tearing off somewhere like nothing happened."

He understood their motives.

It didn't mean he had to like them.

"You held my crutches hostage. That's unlawful confinement. Not to mention a pretty shitty thing to do."

"That was friends looking out for a friend. A damn stubborn one."

He couldn't really argue. He *was* a stubborn bastard when he got his mind set on something. "Yeah, well, your methods suck. Especially calling Cam to come over."

Just saying her name made his heart hurt.

Uriah gave a smug grin. "Now that I won't apologize for. It worked, didn't it?" The grin faded. "Look, it's really none of my business, but—"

"You're right. It's none of your business."

"Remember that part about being stubborn?"

Judd massaged the bridge of his nose. The bass drum was starting up a new set in his skull.

"Uriah, I appreciate you trying to help. Honest to god I do. But just *leave it*." There was no way he wanted to get into a discussion about Camille.

The gut-wrenching disappointment and betrayal were just too fresh.

"Fine." Hands held up in surrender, Uriah walked to the door, but stopped and turned back before going through. "No, you know what? It's not fine. I've known Camille a lot longer than you have. And more than that, you didn't see the look in her eyes when she got here this morning. I did. That woman was beyond worried about you. I guess she didn't realize how thick that head of yours actually is."

"Funny."

"No, son, it's not. It's not funny at all. Because that little lady flat out loves your stupid, stubborn ass. It was there in her eyes when she got her first look of you sitting in that bed, alive and well. So, whatever happened, whatever stupid thing you might have said—"

"I didn't say a damn thing," Judd muttered.

"—you need to figure it out and fix it. Soon."

"It's not that easy."

"What's that saying you SEALs have? The only easy day was yesterday?" Uriah gave him a meaningful look. "Don't screw this up, Judd. Women like Camille don't come along more than once in a lifetime. You won't get another chance."

With that bit of advice he left, closing the door behind him with a soft *snick*.

Hours later, sitting on the porch with Dana watching the kids run around the yard with Cooper, Uriah's words still spun through his mind like leaves caught in a windstorm. Cam loved him? She cared?

What a bunch of bull.

You didn't abandon the people you loved, no matter how hard things got. You either stuck it out, or you never really love them at all.

His father had taught him that.

And yet, a part of him still wanted to believe. Wanted there to be another reason for Cam's abandonment. To have hope for the future he'd only just begun to envision for the two of them.

Stupid, fucking Hope.

"More tea?"

He tore his thoughts away from the problem of Cam and focused on the smiling woman sitting next to him, holding out the pitcher of sweet tea. "No, thanks. I'm still good." He rattled the ice in his half-full glass to prove it.

"Are you hungry? I could go ask Mr. Garvey for a sandwich. Or maybe some cookies?"

He swallowed down his annoyance. She was only trying to be helpful.

Maybe if he reminded himself enough times, he'd stop feeling like he wanted to crawl out of his own skin to escape.

"No. Thank you."

He could tell she was gearing up to ask if she could do something else for him. Just like she had since the minute she arrived.

Thank god the kids chose that moment to run up on the porch. Boone came to a stop beside the rocking chair, while Carly climbed into his lap like a little spider monkey.

"Dad, did you see?" Boone bounced up and down excitedly. "Cooper caught the ball every time I threw it!"

"I saw. You've got some arm there, son." Seeing him puff up his chest at the compliment made Judd grin.

From his lap, Carly examined the lump on his temple and reached up as though to touch it before remembering she shouldn't. "Does it still hurt, Daddy?"

He took her wavering finger and gave it a smacking kiss. "Not since you kissed it better when you got here, sweetheart."

Dana poured two more glasses of iced tea for the kids. "You see? I told you your father was fine. Just a teeny, tiny little bump. He'll be all better in no time."

"Will you be better by next weekend?" Boone asked.

"Oh, way before then." He paused. "What's next weekend?"

"We're going to Worlds of Adventure!" Boone bounced on his toes in delight.

"It's a theme park," Dana explained.

"They got rollercoasters and a Ferris wheel and bumper cars even!"

"They have," he corrected with a gentle smile at his son's enthusiasm. "And that sounds like a lot of fun." Not to mention expensive. He gave Dana a curious look.

"I won the tickets at one of the school raffles. The kids have been pestering me all summer to use them."

"And since you'll be better, you can come, too!" Boone nearly crowed.

Judd winced. "Oh, buddy, I don't think so." The last thing Dana would want was him horning in on her big trip with the kids.

"*Please*, Daddy?" Carly begged.

Caught between a rock and a hard place, he looked to Dana for some support in letting the kids down easy. But rather than seeming annoyed as he'd expected, there was a small smile playing at the corners of her mouth.

"I did win four tickets," she said with a tiny shrug.

"Oh. Still, are you sure you'd want me along?"

"Well, things went pretty well when we went to the ballgame as a family, so...why not? It'll be fun." Wearing the same expectant, excited expression as the kids, she asked, "So, what do you say?"

As much as he'd love to spend another day with the kids, it was the Dana part of the equation that had him hesitating. Yes, they'd managed to rub along pretty well at the game last weekend. Very well, actually.

But that little outing had bothered Cam. A lot. Oh, she hadn't come right out and said anything, but he knew spending the day with his ex had rubbed her on the raw. Doing it a second time might be pushing his luck.

Of course, Camille had left when he needed her, while Dana had stayed. She still hadn't been back, or even called the way she'd said she would to check up on him. And Dana was right back here with the kids, as promised.

Maybe it was time to stop worrying so much about what Cam might think.

"I say yes."

Chapter 17

"MISS RICHARDS! FANCY MEETING you here."

Cam looked up at the woman whose shopping cart had just bumped hers in the market's produce section the next afternoon. And put down the melon she'd been sniffing before she gave in to the sudden urge to launch it at her head.

"Dana. Hello." Her tongue automatically wanted to tack on 'nice to see you,' but she tried not to lie if she could help it.

She also tried not to be rude, either. Especially to parents of her students.

It was a conundrum.

She settled for asking, "How are the kids? Enjoying their summer?" There. Polite, yet neutral.

"Oh, very much. Having their father around so much has been wonderful."

The mention of Judd sent a needle through her heart. Even after having a day to regroup and really think about things, she was still uncertain where the two of them stood.

Wanting to be sure Dana was gone, she'd waited until last night to call and check on him, but it went straight to voicemail. When she called again this morning, he claimed he'd gone to bed early and must have not heard it ring.

Plausible. But she had her doubts.

Doubts that were magnified when he'd turned down her offer to cook dinner tonight, claiming he just wanted to take it easy and rest for another day. The words had sounded strange coming from a man who'd almost needed to be bungee corded to the bed to keep him in one place only twenty-four hours earlier.

What had probably hurt the most, though, was when he told her no when she'd offered to bring dinner to him instead. Only the fact he asked to raincheck the meal until tomorrow had kept her from losing all hope. Maybe he really did just need another day to get his bearings again. She wasn't ready to call him a liar about it.

Yet.

Pushing her chaotic thoughts aside, she pasted on her best principal smile.

"I can imagine. And I know Judd's been thrilled to have this time with them as well. It's easy to see how much he enjoys being with them. He's a wonderful father."

Okay, that wasn't exactly neutral. But darn it, it was the truth.

Dana nodded.

"Yes, he is. After seeing how happy the kids have been the last six weeks, I'm starting to think I made a big mistake."

The fine hairs on the back of Cam's neck stirred in warning. "Mistake?"

"Bringing them home to Slow Creek. Where we'd be so far away from him."

"Oh." Relief swept through her. Although the 'we' was still a little concerning. "Well, you did what you felt best at the time. And you've done a wonderful job raising them," she added grudgingly. "They're lovely children."

"Thank you." Dana preened a moment, then sighed. "But still, not having a complete family unit has been hard on them, even with my parents helping out. I can see that now. And since Judd's out of the service, he's able to spend the time with them he never could before. The kids are *so* much happier now. Actually, we all are. Which is why I'm so thrilled he's planning to stay."

Cam did a slow blink. "He told you that?"

Before he told me?

Last he mentioned, he'd merely been thinking about it.

"Oh, not in so many words, but...I'm hopeful. Everything just seems to be falling into place for us to fix the things we got wrong the first time. That's why next weekend is so important."

"Next weekend?" she repeated stupidly.

"Well, things went so well when we took the kids to the ballgame as a family, we decided to take them to one of those big family theme parks. Two days isn't long enough to know for certain, but, well, I'm pretty sure things will go the way we're hoping. I mean, between the history and the chemistry...it'll be just like before. Only better."

A chill settled deep in her belly. Two days. That meant overnight. Together. With Dana. In a hotel. With all their history and chemistry. Only better.

God, she wanted to vomit.

"That sounds...lovely," she said faintly. Because what else could she say? If it was true, if Judd had decided to go away with Dana to see if they could rekindle their marriage, even if it was for the sake of the kids—

The kids.

God. What would Judd do in the best interest of his kids?

The answer was immediate.

Whatever it took.

She knew that. It was a quality she'd admired.

Until now.

Dana made a show of looking at her watch. "Oh, dear, I need to run. This food isn't going to cook itself, and you know how men can be when their dinner's late." She gave a tittering laugh as though sharing an inside joke.

Knowing she probably shouldn't, Cam glanced into the other woman's grocery cart anyway. And immediately regretted it. Pot roast, green beans, baking potatoes. All the makings of one of Judd's favorite meals.

Lots of people's favorites.

But the glint of malicious challenge in Dana's sky-blue eyes made it impossible to lie to herself. The woman was having Judd over for dinner, and she wanted Cam to know it.

So much for wanting to stay home and rest up another night.

The fact Judd had chosen to lie when he turned down her dinner offer rather than tell her flat out he was already eating at his ex's hurt almost more than the fact he was doing it in the first place.

Okay, no. That definitely hurt more.

Her heart might feel like it was being shoved through a cheese grater, but she gave Dana a chilled smile, masking the pain.

"Yes, I know *exactly* how they can be." She took petty pleasure in seeing the other woman's smile slip at the reminder Cam had intimate knowledge of the very same man she was trying to reclaim. "You have yourself a nice night, now."

She was congratulating herself on having the perfect exit line when Dana went and topped it.

"And you get your own family, Miss Richards. Stop trying to steal mine."

Ignoring the items left on her grocery list, it was all she could do to stand on line at the check-out and pay for the things already in her cart. The ride home was made with the whip of Dana's words lashing at her, over and over again.

Get your own family. Stop trying to steal mine.

Your own family.

Steal mine.

Steal, steal, steal.

As the words repeated, a dawning sense of dismay grew.

Was that what she'd been doing? Yes, she'd enjoyed the time she spent with Judd's children. They were great. Polite. Smart.

Inquisitive and eager to learn. Just like her nieces and nephews. Why wouldn't she like spending time with them?

And yet...

Part of her had to admit it had been different. With her nieces and nephews, she was always Auntie Cam. That was her role, and it would never change.

But with Boone and Carly, she may have started out as Miss Richards, their principal, but on their outing to the zoo, things had begun to shift. She'd started becoming something else to them. Something more. Just as they'd started to feel like more to her.

More important. More personal.

But that was only natural, wasn't it? She'd become involved with their father. And as she and Judd drew closer and deepened their relationship, how could she not become more involved with his children, and they with her? She'd known going in the three of them were a package deal. If she wanted Judd, she'd be getting Carly and Boone as well.

Oh, God.

She *had* known that.

Was that the reason she'd so easily ignored her own rules about casual affairs and gotten involved with Judd despite not knowing his long-term intentions? Because as long as she was with him, she'd get the kids, too?

Her very own ready-made surrogate family, just like Dana accused?

Horrified at the possibility, she sat in her driveway, groceries melting in the trunk as she replayed every interaction she'd had with Judd that involved his children. Besides the zoo, over the last two weeks they'd also played mini-golf, visited the interactive children's museum, and gone to see the latest Disney release down in Lawrence, followed by a stop at The Shack for a messy bbq dinner.

Just like a family.

No. She refused to believe that even in her subconscious, she would have ever been so desperate. To become involved with Judd, or any man for that matter, for the sake of the children he had. She'd enjoyed being with them, yes. But she hadn't been trying to pretend they were hers.

The act of putting everything away in its place and setting the kitchen to rights was a familiar task that was both soothing and distracting. Her mind still whirled, but slowly the shock was wearing off and reason returned.

Dana's accusation was baseless. Other than the zoo, Cam had never been the one to suggest she go anywhere with Judd and the kids. She'd been content to let him have his days with them, and then come see her at night after he'd dropped them back at home. Joining them on those outings had been at his suggestion.

And she'd never, ever crossed the line. Never thought of them as hers. Only Judd's.

But would that change if she and Judd stayed together?

It was agonizing to think in terms of *if* rather than *when*. But after everything that happened yesterday, and what Dana said today, she had to face the very real possibility Judd was at least considering a reconciliation.

And if he was, who was she to stand in his way?

The thought burned like acid through every fiber of her being. But she forced herself to rely on her analytical mind and not her aching heart to think it through.

Fact one. Judd loved his children with all his being.

Fact two. His kids loved him just as much.

Fact three. Judd would do anything for Boone and Carly. Even let them move a thousand miles away from him so they could have a better life.

Fact four. Judd may have told her father he'd found a reason to stay in Slow Creek, but that didn't mean it had anything to do with Cam. She'd just assumed. It very well could have been entirely about the kids.

In hindsight, it probably was.

Fact five. While she'd been falling in love with him, Judd hadn't given the slightest indication he was doing the same. Oh, they'd gotten closer, and enjoyed each other. *A lot.* But while there had been words of affection, sometimes raw ones of pure sensuality, they'd never crossed that final barrier into true, open intimacy. Never talked about the future.

Maybe now she knew why.

Fact six. It didn't matter how she felt, or what she wanted. The only thing that really mattered was that Judd deserved a chance to be a real father to his kids. He'd been cheated out of so much time with them. And now he had the chance to get back the life he'd missed out on. His family. His *whole* family.

Everything just seems to be falling into place for us to fix the things we got wrong the first time.

Much as the words had made her want to claw Dana's eyes out at the time, thinking back now she could hear the wistful hope they'd been spoken with.

The kids are so much happier now. Actually, we all are.

All, including Dana?

Or including Judd?

A horrible thought struck. Had Dana been hoping for a second chance with Judd from the very start? Had she planned to use his summer visit to entice him back into being a family again? Was *that* why Dana had acted the way she did the previous day? So territorial? Because Cam had been throwing a monkey wrench into her plans to reclaim her husband's affection?

She lifted a hand to her mouth in horror.

Was *she* the bad guy in all of this?

Was she...the other woman? The homewrecker?

Her stomach gave a mighty heave.

No. She refused to think that way. Everything that happened between her and Judd had been entirely mutual. She wasn't some kind of sex siren who'd seduced him. The mere thought made her want to laugh.

But...

The memory of their last night in bed rose in her mind. He'd been so serious, so dedicated to making sure she was satisfied. Beyond satisfied. At the time, it had almost seemed like he was afraid it would be the last time he got the chance to touch her.

There's something I've been trying to say, to do, all week.

Judd's words after they'd made love came back to haunt her. He never had gotten around to finishing that thought.

She'd wondered—hoped—he might have been working up the courage to tell her he loved her. But what if that wasn't it at all.

What if he'd been trying to tell her it was over.

What if his almost manic lovemaking had been goodbye.

The thought made her ill. But it forced her to put her emotions aside and reexamine everything that had happened since Judd came to town in a new light.

If they hadn't become involved, might he have been more inclined toward a reconciliation with Dana? He said he had no feelings left for his ex, but that was before he started spending time with her. The ballgame. Dropping off the kids. Calling her to come to him when he'd been hurt.

Maybe it wasn't so much 'absence makes the heart grow fonder' as, how had Dana put it? History and chemistry?

And even if he wasn't falling back in love with her, there were still the kids to consider. It went without saying Judd would do anything for them. *I'll always put what's best for my kids ahead of what's best for me.* When he'd told her that had been when she first started losing her heart to him.

So, what was best for the kids?

If Judd and Dana reconciled, Boone and Carly would have a whole family again. Not to mention Judd wouldn't be relegated to weekly visits and every other holiday with them. He'd get to be a full-time dad. Maybe for the first time ever.

But they couldn't have that as long as he was with her.

He couldn't have that if he was with her.

The dinner hour came and went. She heated up a small ramekin of baked mac and cheese. But when she thought about Judd sitting down to a nice home-cooked pot roast with his kids and Dana as one big happy family, what little appetite she had fled.

She managed a few tasteless bites before scraping the rest into the trash.

With one of the home shows playing on the tv, she curled up on the sofa, dragging the throw over her even though it wasn't cold. Sometime in the fog that followed, Jasper appeared at her feet. He stared up at her a moment before he leapt onto the cushion next to her with a curious meow. When she didn't react, he walked up her body so he could push his little face into her neck, his purr growling like a lawnmower beside her ear.

The out-of-character show of affection broke the last hold she'd had on her buffeting emotions. Grabbing onto the cat with a sob that felt like her lungs were being ripped loose, she cried.

For herself. For Judd. For what might have been. For what would never be.

And when she was done, she didn't feel better.

She felt empty and hollow and all used up.

But she knew what she needed to do.

Nerves jittered through Judd's stomach as he pulled into Cam's driveway. It wasn't a sensation he was well acquainted with, and one he was finding he didn't much like. Nerves had no place on a mission, and he'd long ago learned to eradicate them with thorough reconnaissance and solid planning.

Know what you're doing. Go in and do it. Get out.

That was the problem, though. He didn't know what he was doing.

Any more than he knew what was waiting for him on the other side of that door. When Camille had called him a little while ago and asked him to come over this morning, she'd sounded...odd. Calm, yet a bit distant.

Getting out of the truck, he grimaced.

He couldn't really blame her for that. He'd been a shit to her the day he'd been hurt. Then ignored her call when it finally came later that evening. When she'd called again yesterday, he'd blown off her dinner offer with only the vaguest of excuses.

In his own defense, he'd still been dealing with a pounding headache, as well as a lingering sense of hurt and disappointment. He really had wanted a little more time to try and get both his head and his emotions straightened out.

Wilt had called it sulking.

And yeah, okay, maybe he kind of had been. But with pretty damn good reason.

There had been an upside to all that alone time—and it certainly hadn't been chowing down on sloppy joes with Wilt last night rather than whatever culinary delight Camille would have whipped up for him. No, what all that thinking had done was let him reach a place where he could forgive Cam for bailing.

He'd judged her pretty harshly for that, but realized it was unfair.

She just hadn't been ready. Something he must have known, deep down, since he'd agonized all last week over removing his prosthesis in front of her. So, when she'd come into the bedroom and seen him without it, no preparation, no warning, it must have been a shock.

And that had been with his clothes on.

How much faster would she have run if she'd gotten an eyeful of the naked version?

To be fair, though, she hadn't actually run. It had been more of a quiet retreat. And she'd stayed to make him breakfast first. If there was one thing he'd figured out about Camille, it was that food was her love language.

The more she fed you, the more she cared.

Opening the rear door for Cooper to jump out, he found himself poking at Uriah's words for the ten thousandth time. That Cam cared for him. Was in love with him.

God, how he wanted that to be true.

Especially since he'd been pretty certain he was falling in love with her as well.

But the same barrier between them and their future remained. If she couldn't accept who he was, as he was, then nothing else mattered.

Not even love.

As he walked to the front door past those precise rows of flowers, Coop pranced excitedly beside him, tail wagging at full-mast. It seemed he wasn't the only one who'd missed their daily dose of Cam.

He reached down and ruffled the dog's soft ears. Despite all the training for exactly what had happened, it still amazed him. That when the time came to do it for real, Coop had been smart enough to find a way to get help.

There weren't enough dog treats in the world for that.

Not that Coop expected any. A few words of praise and his squeaky toy were all the reward he'd wanted. Although getting to play with the kids for a few hours had been a fun bonus. He needed to make sure that happened more often.

And if his plans worked out, it would.

But part of those plans—a big part—depended on the woman on the other side of that door, and what she'd asked him here to talk about. Whatever it was had been important enough for her to not wait until he came over for dinner as planned. He was hoping for an apology, but he'd settle for an explanation.

Either would let them put the entire weekend behind them and concentrate on where they went next.

From the look on Cam's face when she opened the door, he wouldn't be getting that apology anytime soon. She looked much too calm for that. In fact, she looked much too everything.

Calm. Reserved. Distant.

As messy as she'd been dressed when she rushed to his bedside on Saturday, today she was the epitome of professional elegance. Lightweight trousers, mandarin-collared blouse, sensible pumps. A slightly softer version of what he'd come to think of as her principal armor.

Kind of like him choosing pants over shorts this morning despite the heat.

"Judd."

"Camille."

Wow, they were off to a great start.

He cleared his throat. "Did I get the time wrong? Were you on your way out to a meeting at school or something?" She'd mentioned there would be several as the start of the new school year approached, but he hadn't thought they'd begun yet. Maybe he was wrong.

"No, you're right on time. Please, come in." She opened the door wider.

A chill worm its way down his spine at her formal tone.

He went in, pretending not to see the smile she gave Cooper as she snuck him a treat. At least one of them was still in her good graces.

"You're looking better," Cam said as she walked to the sofa. The stiff way she perched on the edge of the cushion reminded him of a gazelle prepared to bolt.

Not certain why she seemed so edgy, he gave her some space and took a seat on the opposite end of the sofa. Something inside him withered when a hint of relief flickered across her face.

"Feeling better, too." He raised a hand to his head. The lump had receded, leaving behind a small cut that was already scabbing over, surrounded by a rainbow of bruises his skin tone did a good job of masking. "A couple of days, and it'll be like it never happened."

"That's good."

Hello, awkward silence.

"Thank you, by the way. For coming to check on me. And I'm sorry if I acted like an ungrateful ass when you did." He found himself fumbling for the right words. "I was just..."

"It's okay. I understand."

"You do?" Good. Then he wouldn't have to actually say it out loud.

Cam's head dipped in a small nod, but her eyes never met his. "I wasn't the one you wanted to be there for you."

He hadn't wanted anyone there, but at least Wilt and Uriah had already seen him legless. "That wasn't the way I wanted you to see it."

Cam's entire body went rigid before she visibly forced herself to relax. "So, that *is* what you were trying to tell me the other night."

Tell. Show. It didn't matter. He hadn't been able to do either.

Coward.

"I'm sorry if it caught you off guard."

"It did, but...it's fine. I completely understand. And..." She took a deep breath. "I'm okay with it."

Not exactly the unreserved acceptance he'd been hoping for.

"You are? Because you don't really sound so okay with it." More like she was forcing the words out through a vise.

"I am. Not that you need my approval. But if you feel you do, then you have it."

"Who else's would I need?" The sudden sensation there was a huge miscommunication happening hit. "Wait, what do you think I'm talking about?"

"That you're getting back together with Dana."

"What?" He couldn't have been more surprised if she'd started juggling flaming chainsaws. "Why would you—"

"And I think it's a great idea."

His words stumbled to a halt before he repeated, "You...think it's a great idea."

"Yes."

"That I get back with my ex-wife."

"Yes." A strained smile tugged at her lips. "It's not like you haven't been getting along well with her. I mean, you've been spending so much time together lately. Plus, you're going away this weekend with her and the kids."

"How..." He shook his head. It wasn't important how she knew about that. "It's just a trip to an amusement park. She won four tickets, so she asked me if I wanted to go along."

Damn it. He'd known it would cause problems if he said yes.

"Of course you should go. It's important for you to be doing these kinds of family things together. It'll mean a lot to Carly and Boone."

"You keep coming back to this 'family' thing."

"Family's the most important thing there is. And they're yours."

None of this was making any sense.

"Let me get this straight. You think I want to get back together with Dana." His stomach pitched when she nodded. "And what about you and me?"

Cam's expression turned sad. "Oh, Judd. There should never have been a you and me. It was a mistake we made in a moment of weakness."

She was still talking, but it was all white noise. The only words he heard were the ones rocketing around inside his head.

Should never have been? *A mistake*? She could actually say that?

Suddenly, one phrase cut through his disassociation like a blade. "What did you just say?"

She blinked at the harsh demand. "That ending things now is for the best."

Every demon from his past came howling back to laugh and scream inside his head. For the best. That wonderful phrase that always seemed to pop up whenever someone wanted to screw him over, yet make it look like they were actually doing him a favor.

"For the best?" The words came out as a harsh lash. "Why not just come out and say what the real problem is here, Camille? You realized you couldn't deal with having only three-quarters of a man in your bed, so you're taking the easy way out by so graciously doing *what's best* for me."

The surprise on her face wasn't feigned, but he chalked it up to her not expecting him to call her on her bullshit excuse.

"What? No! That never..." She shook her head. "Your injury has nothing to do with my decision. Honestly, I hardly even think about it anymore."

He gave a cynical laugh. "Right."

"I'm serious. This has nothing to do with us—"

"It has *everything* to do with us!"

"It's about you having the chance to be a part of a family again. *Your* family." She gave him a pleading look. "Trust me, it really is for the best."

"For god's sake, stop saying that!" He jumped up and stalked a few steps, hand tugging through his hair in agitation before turning back.

"No, you know what? You're right. Maybe this is for the best. Maybe I'm getting a lucky break here. Better to find out how you really feel before I get in any deeper than I already am, right? Even if this does have nothing to do with my leg"—which he didn't believe for a fucking minute—"knowing you can so casually say it's over, just like that, that it should have never happened in the first place..."

He shook his head. "I guess I don't know you as well as I thought."

Suddenly, he couldn't stand another second of that kind, slightly sad *I'm doing this for you* expression on her face. The face he'd wanted to have waking up on the pillow beside him every morning.

He snapped his fingers and stalked to the door, Cooper on his heels.

"Have a good life, Judd."

Her soft words almost stopped him.

But there was only so much a man could take.

He closed the door behind him with a harsh click and walked away, those bitches Fate and Hope laughing harder with every step he took.

Chapter 18

"Is there something wrong with the beans, Judd?"

"Hmm?" Blinking, he looked down at his plate and the last of the green beans he'd been pushing around his plate rather than eating. "No, sorry. They're fine."

He speared a few with his fork and shoved them in his mouth to prove it. Actually, they were slightly overcooked and mushy, which sapped most of the flavor. If Camille had made them—

He shut that line of thinking down before it could get started.

Something he'd been doing a lot of the last thirty-six or so hours. Walking away from her had been the hardest thing he had done in a long, long time. But it had either been that, or drop to his knees and beg her to change her mind.

To want him. Choose him.

Fight to keep him, when no one else in his life ever had.

Instead, he'd left with his dignity intact, even if his heart wasn't.

He still wasn't sure he made the right choice.

Picking up the glass of milk beside his plate, he drank it down to the bottom, grinning into the empty glass when Boone tried to do the same across the kitchen table. He only managed about half before he had to come up for air. Judd winked at him, making his son grin before he went back to finish the rest.

"Are you sure you don't want a beer?"

"No, I'm good with the milk, thanks. It makes your bones strong," he added for the kids, flexing an arm.

This time it was Carly who grabbed her glass and drank it down in noisy gulps.

"You were always so good at that," Dana murmured when the kids were excused and dashed off to the living room, where Cooper had been banished for the duration of the meal.

"At what?"

"Getting them to do what you wanted without them realizing it."

That had to be the third time tonight she'd paid him some kind of unexpected compliment. Talk about weird.

"I guess it's just my ninja parenting skills at work."

Dana laughed a bit too loudly for such a lame-ass joke.

Yep, definitely weird.

As he got up with his plate, Dana popped to her feet. "Sit. I'll do that."

"You cooked. The least I can do is help clean up."

"Don't be silly. I've totally got this." She patted his arm before whisking away both plates with an efficiency that reminded him what she did for a living. Which only made him feel worse about letting her wait on him in her own kitchen.

But short of grabbing the dishes out of her hands, there wasn't much he could do but sit and watch her bustle around, scraping plates and stacking them in the sink.

He should probably go.

Hell, he probably shouldn't have stayed in the first place.

When Dana had asked if he wanted to join them for dinner as he was dropping off the kids, he'd been prepared to say no. Even when she said they were having pot roast, which was admittedly one of his favorites.

But then the kids had started clamoring for him to stay, too. And the next thing he knew, he was seated at the kitchen table with a plate of tough beef and mushy green beans in front of him.

"We've got apple pie for dessert," Dana said, ladling grounds into the coffeemaker basket and swinging it shut with a snap. "And ice cream. Vanilla bean."

Two more of his favorites.

His radar immediately started to hum. Put together with the out of character compliments and the way she kept smiling at him and laughing at his stupid jokes, that was just one coincidence too many to swallow.

Something was definitely up.

It didn't take long for the tantalizing coffee aroma to permeate the room as the machine gurgled and hissed through its brewing cycle. After Dana brought two steaming mugs to the table and sat, she smiled at him again as she raised hers to her lips. "This is so nice."

"This?"

"You know, us all having dinner together like we used to. The two of us sharing a cup of coffee afterward in the kitchen while the kids play before bedtime." She took a sip, her eyes never leaving his. "Nice."

Raising his mug, he broke the not-so-casual eye contact.

What the hell?

"The kids are really looking forward to this weekend." Dana reached over and touched his arm, her fingers lingering on his skin longer than they should. "So am I. I'm really glad you're coming with us."

"It should be fun," he replied in a carefully neutral tone.

"Oh, it will! You know, I was thinking..."

It took a few seconds for him to realize she was waiting for him to say what he always used to when she fed him that line. But they weren't a couple. There was no place for any teasing "uh-ohs" between them anymore.

"Well, it's kind of a long drive to the park," she finally continued, seeming to figure that out when he stayed silent. "And to get in a full day there, we'd have to be on the road really early. Which means getting the kids up before the crack of dawn. And *that's* going to be a lot harder than it sounds."

He shrugged. "So, they'll sleep in the truck on the way there." He knew they could. They'd both conked out on him coming home from the zoo.

"*Or*," she said the way she always did when she'd already discounted what someone else said, "we could drive there the afternoon before and spend the night at one of the hotels nearby. Then we could all get up at a normal time, have a leisurely breakfast, and be at the park gates right when they open. All bright-eyed and bushy-tailed for a full day of family fun." She leaned forward, an eager expression on her face. "What do you think?"

Ignoring the way her breasts pressed against the thin material of her top in that position, he said, "I think it sounds expensive. Especially when just getting up early is free."

"I checked, and we can get a room for like seventy-five dollars. Plus free breakfast," she added.

Like powdered eggs and cold bacon were a big enticement.

"Double that, for two rooms." He could probably swing the seventy-five for himself, but he had a feeling she'd be expecting him to pick up the room for her and the kids as well. She certainly hadn't offered to pay for anything on their baseball outing.

"*Or*...we could just get one room."

Okay, that one stopped him cold.

"We could what?"

"Get one room. It might be a little tight with the four of us, but it should be fine for one night."

No, it would be a disaster.

Share a hotel room with his ex-wife?

He could think of a quick dozen ways that might blow up in his face. And that didn't even take into consideration how he'd manage his prosthesis with zero privacy. Especially if he had a bout of phantom pain like he had last night, leaving him curled on the bed moaning as molten streaks of agony burned through a limb that no longer existed anywhere but his fucked-up brain.

"That would be a really bad idea." Extraordinarily bad, in fact.

"We've done it before."

"Yeah, when the kids were little. And we were married."

And I had both legs.

Dana waved that away. "You and Boone can take one bed, and Carly and me the other. Think about how great it would be for the kids. Seeing us getting along. Going on a trip like a regular family again."

"But we're not a family anymore, Dana. Divorced people don't do family vacations together."

"They can if they're getting along." This time she reached over and put her hand on his. "Like we are."

Things had just moved from bizarre into What The Fuck territory.

After staring at Dana's hand on his for a few long, disbelieving seconds, he carefully extricated himself and sat back in his chair. "What exactly are you suggesting here?"

"I'm not suggesting anything," she said, toying with her mug while not meeting his gaze. "I'm just saying, well, things have been going pretty good with us these past few weeks, and maybe that's something we need to explore a little more. To see if *maybe* we were a little hasty when we decided to break up."

We hadn't decided anything.

Dana had done that all on her own, having divorce papers served before he even realized she'd been talking to a lawyer.

Before she'd ever talked to *him.*

Just one more person who hadn't loved him enough to stick around.

All of which was pointless to the current situation, so he packed it away unspoken.

"We have been getting along," he acknowledged. "Which is a lot better for the kids than if we weren't. And for us. But it doesn't mean the next logical step is trying to recapture the past. We're both very different people now."

Him more than anyone.

"Exactly! That means we won't make the same mistakes."

"Or we'd make even worse ones."

She made a frustrated little noise. "Judd, why do you have to be so difficult?"

"I'm not. I'm being practical."

"Okay, how's this for practical. If we were a family again, things would be a lot easier for us both. You could be with the kids all the time. Be a full-time dad." Her expression softened. "You really are a terrific father. They both love you so much. They'd be ecstatic to have you home again."

He ignored the pang that came with the reminder of how far he was on the periphery of their lives. Once they went back to school, it would be even worse. When would he get the chance to see them then?

"And what about you, Dana? Would you be ecstatic to have me back, too?" Because despite her words, something wasn't ringing quite true about this sudden desire for a reconciliation.

"Of course."

"So, what? I just move in here with you, and we pick up where we left off three years ago?"

"No, of course not." She made a face as she glanced around the cramped kitchen. "Even with all the little fixes you've made, this place is still a dump. But with the extra money you've been spending on rent pooled with mine, we could afford a much nicer house. Bigger. Three bedrooms. Maybe even four."

Ah. The pieces started to fall into place.

"Four? Why would we need four?" He lifted an eyebrow. "Were you thinking we'd have another baby?"

The look of horror on her face was priceless, if a little insulting.

"No! I mean, no, I hadn't really considered..." She swallowed hard. "Do *you* want another baby?"

"I don't know. Maybe. There's so much I missed out on with Carly and Boone, both when I was deployed and then after you moved away. It might be nice to get to experience some of that."

He'd said it to needle her, but realized he also kind of meant it. He'd missed out on a lot in his kids' lives. But he had zero desire for Dana to be involved if he ever did have another child.

An image of Camille flashed through him so hard and fast it hurt.

Not just because she was gone from his life. But because he knew she'd make an amazing mother, and she'd probably never get the chance. Not with him. Maybe not with anyone.

The unfairness of that made his next words a little harsher than they probably should have been.

"But I'm guessing from your reaction you were thinking the extra bedroom would be for me." The guilty expression was answer enough. "So, let me get this straight. You want us to be a family again, for me to live with you, pay the bills, but you weren't planning on sharing my bed."

"Well, it's been a long time, but...maybe we could eventually do...things..." Her voice was so faint it faded off into nothingness.

The fact she could barely acknowledge his injury by looking at his leg was nothing new. But her obvious disgust still hurt. "Or maybe we wouldn't."

She gave a small shrug. "I hadn't really thought that far ahead."

"Clearly. So why would you even bring the idea up in the first place?"

"I was just...you were so..." She mumbled something he couldn't hear.

"What?"

With obvious reluctance, she repeated herself.

"You stood up for me. To Heidi and her friends. And I liked it. I liked having someone in my corner for a change. Coming back here the way I did, no job, divorced with two kids, after what I said to everyone when I left... I've spent the last three years feeling like everyone here was judging me. Laughing at me. Enjoying my failure. But then you came, and you fit in so easily, and everyone looks at you like, I don't know. With respect."

"And you thought if we were together again, maybe some of that respect would spill over onto you as well."

She winced. "It sounds bad when you say it like that, but, yeah, I guess I did. But I really was thinking about you, too. About being able to be with the kids more. And since you're living in a crappy place, and I'm living in a crappy place, I thought we could, like, combine our resources. Then everyone would get what they wanted. Especially the kids."

Much as he wanted to deny it, her plan actually made a modicum of sense.

And if she'd made the offer a month ago, he might have even been tempted to go along with it. What Dana was suggesting was more than he'd ever thought he'd get as a life, being the broken mess he was now.

But his time with Cam had shown him he should expect so much more.

That he *could* have more.

Not that it meant he was going to get it. Not from her. That much was clear since she'd shooed him off to another woman with a shrug and a smile. Even so, he found he was no longer willing to settle for less than he deserved.

"The kids wouldn't benefit from us living a lie. And that's what it would be, Dana. A lie. I do still care about you, but I'm not in love with you anymore. And I know you don't love me, either, so don't even try to act offended by that statement."

She looked like she wanted to argue, then deflated. "I didn't think this through very well, did I?"

"Not really, no."

She gave him a rueful grin. "I think I miss the old days when you would have sweetened the truth some to make me feel better."

"Sorry, but this truth is a little too important to sugarcoat. People should be together for the right reasons, not the most convenient ones."

"I know. You're right." She toyed with her mug again. "So, I guess that means you and Miss Richards have the right reasons, then?"

By accident or design, she'd managed to scrape the scab off that barely healed wound. "No."

"No, you don't have the right reasons?"

"No, we're not together." The admission tasted like ash on his tongue.

"You're not?" Dana's eyelashes fluttered in a series of fast blinks, usually a sign of nerves. "That's...recent, isn't it? I mean, you were still together a few days ago when you were hurt, and she seemed..."

"Seemed what?" It was probably masochistic to care, but he couldn't seem to help himself.

"Invested. In, you know, you." She added a lame little hand wave in his direction.

He snorted. "Not enough to stick around for long." He caught Dana's wince. "What?"

"Um...do you want some more coffee? I think I'd like another cup." She jumped to her feet.

"Dana." He froze her with a stare until she wilted back into her seat.

"Okay, I *may* have let her think you wanted me there more than her."

"What? Why would you do that? And why would she believe you?"

"Well, you did phone me and not her."

"But I didn't ask you to come." He hadn't asked Cam, either. But truth be told, as pissed as he'd been at Uriah for calling her, a part of him had been soothed by the way she'd rushed right over.

Dana, not so much.

"Well, I might not have mentioned that part," Dana mumbled into her coffee.

"And she just accepted it, without coming to talk to me about it?" That didn't sound like Camille at all.

"I may have kind of gotten in her way when she was maybe going to do that."

It took a few seconds to untangle her knotted-up sentence. "You stopped her from coming in to see me? For god's sake, why?"

"I don't know. I...I think I was a little intimidated by her. I mean, she's smarter, and more mature, and has this great job she's really good at. She's so put together, and I'm this big, hot mess. I guess I just didn't want you to see the two of us together and figure that out."

Remembering how the two women had been dressed that morning, he would have said it was Cam who'd been the hot mess. But he had a feeling Dana wasn't talking about appearances. Although since she'd taken all that extra care...

"You were already thinking about this plan of yours by then, weren't you?"

Thinking back now to how attentive she'd been, so insistent about staying, how could he have missed it?

Dana nodded.

He wanted to get mad, but he was more interested in understanding. Because it still felt like there were pieces not quite fitting together.

"Okay, that explains why you did what you did. But why would she let you stop her?" Cam wasn't exactly a pushover.

"Actually, I think that was you."

"*Me*?" He reared back in surprise. "What did I do?"

"You called my name, remember?"

He vaguely recalled doing that. But it was because she was supposed to be checking on where Uriah and Wilt were with his prosthesis, not because he'd been missing her. Then he remembered.

"That's when you came back into the room with the tray." A boulder landed in his gut. "Cam was right outside the room then, wasn't she? And she thought, what? That I wanted you and not her?"

"I kind of helped her think it," she whispered.

"Damn it, Dana!"

"I'm sorry!" She shot him a pleading look. "I know it was a crappy thing to do, but I was jealous, okay? I admit it. I was jealous of you and her, especially when I was hoping I could convince you to be you and me again."

"So, you lied to her?"

"No, I never actually *lied*. I may have exaggerated and hinted, but I didn't lie."

It was so like Dana to split hairs thin enough to see through.

"Well, whatever you did, it was still wrong."

"I said I was sorry."

And surprise, surprise, she actually sounded it.

He sighed, anger trickling away. "It doesn't matter. Not really, anyway." All of that may have given Cam the excuse she needed to leave, but it hadn't been the real reason. "None of that's why she called us quits, so..." Another round of nervous eyelid flutters made him stop. "Unless there was something else?"

Looking miserable, she told him about running into Camille at the grocery store and everything she'd said. As she talked, he pinched the bridge of his nose, wishing he'd accepted the beer she offered earlier.

"So, that's how she knew about the trip to the amusement park," he muttered when she got to that part. "But it's still not—"

"I told her to go get her own family and stop trying to steal mine," Dana blurted, then covered her mouth as if horrified by her own words.

He stared at her as all the anger that had drained away flooded back with a deafening roar. "You said *what*?" Only the kids being in the other room kept him from shouting, though it was close.

"I know," she groaned, dropping her face into her hands. "It was an awful thing to say."

"Awful? Try cruel." Despite not knowing about Cam's fertility problems, Dana's words couldn't have been more hurtful if she tried. They'd struck right at the most vulnerable part of Camille's tender heart.

"I didn't mean to hurt her. But I know I did. God, the look on her face! All I could think of was how I wanted to take it back. But then she was gone, and..." Her hands lifted in a helpless gesture. "I'm so, so sorry."

"Yeah. So am I."

Because suddenly he was sure he'd made a huge, glaring mistake.

He'd been so caught up in feeling hurt and betrayed by Cam's sudden decision to end things between them, he hadn't bothered to examine all the inconsistencies. Question her reasoning. Push back and fact-check the things that didn't make sense.

Not performing those kinds of oversights were what could tank a mission.

Not doing them now had done far worse.

It had put his entire future in jeopardy.

Damn me for a fucking fool.

And he was one. Because the one thing he knew about Cam above all else was that family came first for her. Not just her own. Every family. Including his. If she thought for an instant she was standing in the way of him and Dana having a second chance together...

She would do exactly what she'd done. Bow out gracefully, without making him have to choose.

"How could I have been so stupid?" he muttered.

"Judd?"

He met Dana's concerned gaze and shook his head. "Never mind. I need to go see if I can figure out a way to fix things before it's too late." As he pushed his chair back and stood, Dana gave him a look he could only describe as wistful.

"Just tell her how you feel about her. It's pretty obvious," she added when he looked at her in surprise.

"Evidently not to her."

"Then make her see, no matter how many times you have to try. What's that SEAL saying? 'Never give up, never surrender,' right?"

He didn't have the heart to tell her that was the tagline from a sci-fi movie, not a SEAL motto. There were a lot of reasons they'd never been a good fit. "Right."

If only it were that easy.

But as he left Dana's house after saying goodnight to the kids and collecting Cooper, it was clear he had a massive uphill battle ahead of him. Not only did he have to convince Cam he had zero interest in reconciliation with Dana. He also had to figure out how to take away the shadow of doubt Dana's accusation cast on any relationship he and Cam might have going forward.

But most of all, he needed to make her understand why he'd walked away after she said the magic words that never failed to flip his switch.

It's for the best.

He'd once told her his feelings about that self-serving sentiment, but never explained the why behind his deep-seated aversion.

Maybe it was time he did.

Chapter 19

Of course, to tell her, he had to find her first.

A task easier said than done, even in the small confines of Slow Creek.

After driving by her house enough times the next day that one of the neighbors probably called the police about a suspicious vehicle casing the neighborhood, he still hadn't managed to track her down.

No car in the driveway. None of his calls being answered. The same for his texts.

It was like she'd dropped off the face of the planet.

By the following day, she and her car were still MIA. A clandestine scouting mission around the perimeter of the house showed nothing but vacant rooms. The only thing he could see out of place were Jasper's bowls missing from the kitchen. Judd concluded she must have gone to stay with someone for a few days in order to avoid talking to him.

She'd obviously forgotten what he used to do for a living.

SEALs never gave up. They merely thought outside the box to find new and creative ways to overcome the insurmountable.

Eliminating her brothers from the mix of potential landing spots was easy. If she went to either of them, they would have already shown up on his doorstep to beat the shit out of him. Actually, having spent a lot of time in her sister's company, he decided he could probably put her on that list as well.

So, if not her siblings, who else could she hole up with on a moment's notice?

He knew she was best friends with one of the teachers, Joelyn Baker, but couldn't see her going there. Or to any of the other friends she'd mentioned. In a small town like Slow Creek, that would be tantamount to taking out a front-page ad announcing their breakup.

Which left only one other place for him to try.

"Good afternoon, Mr. Richards," he said as the door opened.

Hard green eyes glared at him from under bushy white brows. "You've got balls coming here, I'll give you that."

Oh yeah, Cam was definitely here. Or at least had spoken to her parents, which meant they'd probably know where she'd gone.

Whether they'd tell him was another matter.

"Big risk, big reward, sir."

"Big reward, huh? And what might that be?"

"A chance to make Camille listen to my side of the situation." He stood unflinching under the piercing gaze. Only letting the slightest droop of relief hit his shoulders when the other man uttered a *hmmph* and opened the door to let him in.

"That may take a bit more effort than you think." Hank's cane thumped on the hardwood floor as he led the way to the den, which held the lingering fragrance of old pipe tobacco. "My daughter is a bit headstrong. Takes after her mother that way." It might have sounded like criticism if not for the wealth of affection in his tone.

"Nothing wrong with a strong woman." He took the chair opposite the recliner Hank lowered himself into. "In fact, I admire that about her. Among other things."

"Really? Then why the hell would you go and break her heart?"

Pain sliced his own heart at those words. "Actually, sir, it was more the other way around."

"Come again?"

"I take it Camille didn't share the details of what happened between us?"

The older man's face puckered into a frown. "All she said was things between the two of you were over, and it was for the best."

He flinched at that fucking god-awful refrain.

"A decision she made on her own, based on faulty intel." He paused. "No, that's not fair. I was working on my own faulty intel as well, which just compounded the problem."

"And what intel was that?"

Not blaming the other man for the skepticism in his voice, he said, "Camille was under the impression our relationship was impeding a possible reconciliation with my ex-wife. Which it wasn't," he added when Hank's frown turned to something harder. "There wasn't, isn't, and won't ever be any reconciliation there. *Ever.*"

"Then why would Camille think there was?"

"Let's just say my ex gave her ample cause." Dana had done a foolish, hurtful thing, but he didn't want to tar and feather her for it.

"And is she going to continue to give her cause in the future?"

"No, sir. That issue has been dealt with, and she's extremely sorry for her part in the whole thing. I know she'll be apologizing to Camille, as will I. Once I find her." He pushed a little on the last words as a reminder of why he was there.

"Hmmph." Hank's finger rubbed across his lower lip as he stared at the floor, lost in thought. Judd's usual ability to wait anyone out was put to the test before he finally spoke again. "Did Camille ever tell you the story of how I came to marry her mother?"

He almost snapped back he didn't really give a shit about that right now. All he wanted to do was talk to Cam and straighten out his own issues. But some last shred of caution had him swallowing the impatient words.

He was the penitent here. He'd pay whatever price was required.

"No, sir, I don't believe she has."

"Oh, you'd remember it if she did. Like I said, Camille is very much like her mother." He gave Judd an enigmatic grin. "I met Anh while I was serving my second tour in 'Nam. She was this shy little thing who worked in the laundry on base, but she had the biggest smile. When you could coax it out of her, of course. Which wasn't too often, seeing as we were in the middle of a war and all."

Having met Cam's mother, Judd knew the "little" descriptor wasn't hyperbole. Mrs. Richards topped out at about five-foot nothing, if that. Everyone in the family except the youngest kids towered over her. Yet he'd seen her take charge of the entire clan with nothing more than a few soft-spoken words.

"I'll spare you the story of our long and rocky road to romance," Hank said, as though sensing Judd's growing restlessness. "Suffice it to say, by the time we decided we wanted to get married, I was coming up on the end of my third tour, and I was done with war. I wanted to go home. Start a family. And I wanted that with Anh. But to do it, I needed the Army's permission, and the wheels of military bureaucracy ground damn slow back then."

"Still do," Judd said with a grimace, remembering more than one instance of bureaucratic constipation that had nearly sandbagged a time-sensitive mission.

Hank nodded as though he'd expected as much.

"It was looking like we might not get all the paperwork done in time for her to go back to the States with me before I was shipped out. So I went up the chain of command, trying to get things expedited.

"I finally got to this one guy who really seemed to take an interest in my situation. A general's aide. Real sympathetic. Promised he'd do everything he could to cut through the red-tape and have my approval fast-tracked in time to catch that Freedom Bird home."

From the sour look on the old man's face, Judd had a feeling he hadn't kept any of those promises. "He was just blowing smoke up your ass?"

"Worse. A few days later, Anh suddenly tells me she's changed her mind. Doesn't want to marry me after all. Says she realized what a mistake it would be, going to America, leaving her family and culture behind. That I should go home and find myself a nice American wife."

He shook his head.

"Took me a couple of days, but I finally got her to tell me the truth. That the prick had gone to see her after I talked to him. Filled her head with all these lies about how awful it would be for her in America, how no one would ever accept her, would shun her. He basically painted a picture of hell on earth if she went home with me."

"Good enough reason to get cold feet." He could sympathize with the scared young woman she must have been, faced with such huge, life-altering decisions.

"Yeah, but my Anh's made of sterner stuff. She didn't care. She was willing to put up with all of that, and worse, because she loved me. When Captain Dickhead realized it, he changed tactics. Told her how damaging it would be to *me*, coming home with a Vietnamese wife. How it would get me ostracized by my family and friends, maybe even keep me from getting a job. A house. What a horrible life our kids would have. How they'd be treated like garbage for being of mixed blood."

"What a bastard."

"Oh, he was that," Hank agreed with a nod. "Unfortunately, a very believable one. It took me a long time to convince Anh everything he told her was a lie."

"But wasn't at least some of it true? I mean, it's before my time, but wasn't public sentiment kind of negative toward the

Vietnamese during and after the war?" Not to mention toward the men who'd fought in it.

"In some places, sure. But don't forget, this is Slow Creek. We take care of our own here. If I came home with a wife, no matter her nationality, you could be damn sure people would accept her."

Having met some of the judgy women in town, he had his doubts it had been quite that easy for either Anh or Hank. But he let it go. The sooner they got to the end of the story, the sooner he got to Cam.

"So, what happened after you convinced her to still marry you?"

"I found someone else to help with the paperwork who actually did what he was supposed to do. It was close, but it all worked out in the end despite everything the Army tried to throw in our path."

He had to know. "Whatever happened with Captain Dickhead?"

A scary smile crossed Hank's wrinkled face, showing a glimpse of the young soldier he'd once been. "Beat the snot out of the arrogant little prick the day before we went wheels up. Nearly got myself a court-martial instead of a discharge." He flexed his fist. "It would have been worth it, though."

A sentiment Judd understood fully. You just didn't mess with a man's family.

"Sir, while I appreciate you telling me your story—and I'm glad everything worked out the way it did—I'm afraid I don't really understand why you picked now to share it."

"When I said Camille took after her mother, I wasn't just referring to her stubborn streak. Although have fun with that one, it's a doozy," he added as an amused aside. "But they're also both alike when it comes to putting the people they love above their own self-interests, even if it costs them dearly.

"If Camille thinks being with her was interfering with you getting back with your ex, you're going to have a hell of a time convincing her otherwise. I gave you the short version, but trust me, it took a lot of talking and pleading to get Anh to believe she'd been fed a pack of lies. Camille being her mother's daughter, I don't see you having any easier time of it."

"Well, then, I'll just have to keep at it until she believes me."

Never give up, never surrender. Dana had actually gotten it right after all.

"And after she does, what if she still doesn't want anything to do with you?"

A possibility he didn't want to consider, but had to.

He gave the best answer he could, no matter how much it hurt.

"If after she has all the facts she still wants me out of her life, then I'll abide by her wishes, of course." Honesty made him add, "But I'm going to do my damndest to convince her otherwise first."

Hank seemed pleased with his response. Both parts. He grinned and nodded. "Fair enough."

That sounded like approval to Judd.

"So, is she staying here?"

"No. Her mother wanted her to—you might want to avoid my wife for a few days, by the way—but Camille said she needed some time alone. To think and come to terms with things. She borrowed the keys to the family fishing cabin up on the lake."

He was already rising from his chair. "And where is that exactly?"

"Whoa, whoa, hold your horses there, son. We're not done yet."

It was tempting to just leave and try to find the place himself. But the lake had a lot of shoreline. And likely a lot of cabins.

Battling every instinct screaming at him, he subsided into his seat.

Hank gave a satisfied grunt. "We've discussed Camille's part in this supposed big misunderstanding. But you never did say what that faulty intel *you* were working with was. I'm going to assume it's the reason you let my girl go without a fight?"

For the first time, he realized Hank wasn't as calm and even-tempered as he appeared. There was fire burning behind those eyes. The fire of a pissed-off old war dog ready to maul someone to defend his young.

Major miscalculation, Aiken.

And as much as he'd like to tell the old man it was none of his damn business, he figured this was still part of that penance he had to pay.

"I thought the real reason she wanted to end things was because she'd finally gotten a look at me without my prosthesis on a few days before. That she'd been disgusted by it. By me." He swallowed, but the familiar punch to his pride didn't land as hard as it usually did.

Especially when he remembered the look of honesty on Cam's face when she denied the accusation.

"And you figured she was just using what your ex said as a convenient excuse."

He nodded.

"If you knew my girl at all, you'd know she isn't like that. She's never judged anyone by their appearance or abilities. Not even hot-headed young fools who should know better."

Oh yeah, he was definitely pissed off.

"I do know that, sir. The issue with my leg is my own. It's something I'm still coming to terms with."

"I'll assume you've already slept with my daughter? Oh, don't look at me like that." Hank rolled his eyes. "Camille's a grown woman. What I'm asking is, how is it she hadn't seen you without your prosthesis before then?"

Because I'm a ball-less wonder who couldn't seem to pull that particular trigger.

"I was working my way up to it."

"Hmmph." Hank went back to rubbing his finger along his lower lip as he thought. "Seems to me you made an awful big assumption based on very little fact."

"In all fairness, sir, so did she."

Neither of them was blameless in this mess.

"Yes, well, she already had one selfish asshole leave her for a woman who could give him children. Why wouldn't she expect you to do the same?"

Too annoyed at being compared to Cam's douchebag ex to think before he spoke, he snapped, "Because I love her."

Holy shit.

Had he just admitted that out loud?

To Cam's father?

The slow smile spreading over the old man's face said yes, he had. "Well, now. You finally said the right thing, son."

Maybe he had. Maybe those were the words he'd needed to say to Cam three days ago.

If he had, none of this might have happened.

Or maybe it wouldn't have made any difference at all.

She might have still pushed him away, thinking she was doing the right thing. Growing up on her parents' love story would have given her a benchmark for the kind of sacrifice you would make for the ones you loved.

The thought of Cam recreating her own worst scenario for his benefit, seeing him happier with another woman and the children they'd made, left him humbled.

And angry.

She deserved more. So much more. Didn't she realize that?

Didn't she know how special she was? How precious? How in-credibly amazing? She should never have to settle for mere crumbs of affection from anyone, just the way she'd taught him that same thing.

And he was going to be the one to prove it to her.

Thick, black clouds crowded the sky over the lake, warning a storm was coming.

A bad one, judging by the wind kicking up small white-tipped waves on the normally placid water. It tore leaves from the trees, spinning them through the air around the wood cabin like green confetti.

Probably time to go inside.

In this part of Kansas, sudden, severe weather was no joke.

But the dark skies and thick atmosphere suited her current mood. So Cam continued to rock in the chair she'd dragged onto the back porch two days ago. Watching. Feeling.

Remembering.

She hadn't planned to leave town like a frightened rabbit.

Right after she'd done what she had to, letting Judd walk away with a clear conscience, she'd worried he might come back to try and change her mind. It was obvious he was conflicted. And honorable. And that he felt something for her that went beyond the physical, just as she did for him.

She hadn't realized how weak her own resolve was, though.

Not until she'd found a part of her hoping he *did* come back. That he'd choose her. And she knew if he showed up on her doorstep, she wouldn't have the strength to send him away a second time.

She just wasn't that good of a person.

Leaving town for a few days to remove the temptation had seemed for the best.

But spending all this time with only her thoughts and regrets for company had left her mired in an ocean of doubt and self-pity. She knew she'd done the right thing for Judd. He deserved to be able to enjoy his family without having to feel guilty about it.

But what about the right thing for Camille? When did *she* finally get someone who'd make the same kind of sacrifice for her? Who'd love and want *her*, flaws and all?

"Damn you, Judd Aiken." The words were ripped away by the wind, but she meant them. She'd been happy with her life until he'd come along and turned everything on its head. Okay, maybe not *happy*. Not very, anyway. But content. Comfortable.

Numb.

Yes. That's what she'd been. Numb.

After the gaping hole left by Ty when he abandoned her for Sally and their baby, she'd let her heart ice over to save it from bleeding all the way dry. And it had worked.

But the ice had migrated to the other parts of her life without her realizing it. Like a glacier taking over a valley, inch by inch, her entire life had slowly come to a frozen standstill. She had her family and her job, but nothing else could touch her.

Until Judd.

"And look how that turned out."

Once again, she hadn't been enough for the man she loved. At least this time, though, the choice to end it had been hers.

Not that it hurt any less at the end of the day.

Doing the right thing didn't keep her company when she ate her solitary dinner, or hold her close when she climbed into her cold, lonely bed. Alone was alone. Made all the worse by laying where Judd had made such wild, passionate love to her.

Warmed her back to life.

Every time she closed her eyes that first night after he'd gone, she remembered the feel of his hands. The scent of his skin. The taste of his mouth. It had been so real she woke up reaching for him more than once before remembering he wasn't there.

Wasn't going to be there again.

Ever.

She turned her face up, letting the buffeting winds cool her suddenly burning cheeks and stinging eyes. That had been the other reason she needed to get away for a few days. Judd had never been to the fishing cabin. There were no memories here to taunt her. Tempt her. Make her remember every moment they'd spent together.

Every word. Every gesture. Every look.

The cabin was a blank slate. Safe.

That had been the plan, anyway.

The problem with memories, though, was they were portable. No matter how far or fast you ran from them, they went right along with you.

A low rumble of thunder, the kind that seemed to roll on and on forever, echoed around her. With a resigned sigh, she got up and dragged the rocker inside before the rain started.

Normally, she liked to sit and breathe in the clean scent of the storm as it raged all around. The scoured-clean promise of new beginnings. But with the wind whipping the way it was, not even the porch would protect her from getting soaked.

Just like the cabin couldn't protect her from her torrent of memories.

Jasper let out a plaintive meow as he stropped through her legs the second she was inside. She picked him up and cuddled him under her chin. "I know, sweetie, you hate thunder. Let's find you a nice place to hide, okay?"

The cat usually burrowed deep into her closet at home whenever a storm rolled through. Improvising, she put his pet carrier in the small utility closet next to the kitchenette and covered it with a blanket. With the closet door left barely cracked, he should be able to get in and out at will, but still be mostly insulated from the worst of the noise.

"So, what do you think? Will it do?"

Jasper gave her an inscrutable look before sauntering away, tail twitching.

Great. One more male in her life she couldn't satisfy.

With no television in the cabin for distraction, she picked up the book she'd tossed in her bag before leaving home. Not that she expected to make much progress. The bookmark hadn't moved far despite the hours she'd sat on the sofa with it the night before.

She was right.

By the time the room grew too dark to see the words clearly, she hadn't gotten more than a few pages. Nor could she remember any of what she'd read. Disgusted with herself, she tossed the book aside and moved to a chair near the front window to watch the approaching storm instead.

The wind had begun to howl, which was a little unnerving, but the rain had yet to fall from the blackening sky. Lightning strobed through the clouds, followed by the increasingly loud drum of thunder.

Oh yes, the storm was almost there.

Headlights pierced the darkness through the trees along the narrow road which serviced this section of the lakefront. She felt bad for whichever of her neighbors had gotten themselves caught out in this. Hopefully they made it home before the deluge began. Which, by the thickness in the air, would be any second now.

But the headlights didn't turn into any of the nearby driveways.

They turned into hers.

No. Surely her mother wouldn't have broken her promise and come. She had been very specific about wanting to have some time to work things out. *Alone.*

Then again, it had been two whole days. That was probably one day more than she should have expected to get before the maternal interference gene kicked in.

"Damn it, Mom." Getting up to pace, she considered her options. There really weren't any. This was her parents' cabin, after all. She couldn't very well throw her mother out of it. Not that she would anyway, given the weather. Sending anyone out into this storm would be way too dangerous.

With a resigned sigh, she answered the knock at the door.

Only it wasn't her mother on the other side.

"Judd."

Chapter 20

"Hello, Camille."

The low rumble of his voice skittered across her nerve endings. Reigniting fires she'd spent the past three days trying to extinguish. Damn him for coming here!

And damn her for being weak enough to be glad he had.

"Can I come in? Please?"

She wanted to say no.

She *should* say no. Should slam the door in his face and walk away, just like he had. Petty and unfair, yes. But it would feel oh, so good. Cathartic, even.

The storm chose that moment to finally break.

With a vengeance.

A jagged flash of lightning lit the sky, followed by an almost immediate crack of thunder loud enough to feel in her bones, and the skies opened. The deluge hitting the metal roof made it sound like they were under a waterfall.

How could she, in good conscience, send him out in that?

But how could she let him in?

Another boom of thunder rattled the windows. Cooper gave a soft whine and pressed against Judd's leg, looking miserable and sealing her decision.

She sighed and stepped back. "I guess you'd better."

"Thank you."

"So we're clear, I only let you in because of the storm. As soon as it's over, you're leaving." She closed the door, resisting the urge to slam it because what was the point now? He was already on the wrong side for it to do her any good.

"I know you didn't expect me to show up here, but—"

"Wait, how did you even know where I was? Only my parents..." She let out a frustrated growl. "My father told you, didn't he?"

Judd nodded. "If it makes you feel any better, he didn't give the information up easily. He made me work for it."

Still matchmaking.

Thanks a lot, Dad.

"He shouldn't have bothered. *You* shouldn't have bothered. We already talked about this and decided it made the most sense for you to concentrate on rebuilding your family." Chest tight, she stalked to the sofa so she wouldn't have to look at him.

Because he looked so, so good.

And she was feeling so, so weak.

"Actually, you decided that before I ever got to your place that day." After dropping the backpack off his shoulder, he joined her on the sofa, flicking on the floor lamp beside it to dispel the gloom. "And I *was* rebuilding my family. With you."

Damn him for the ridiculous specter of hope his words raised. She quickly squashed it by reminding them both, "I can't give you a family, Judd."

"Maybe you can't give me *children*—"

"Definitely can't. Besides, I'm forty-two."

"So what? Age is just a number."

His quick dismissal of their age disparity was soothing, but didn't erase the bigger problem. "Pregnancy at my age, even if it was possible by some miracle, wouldn't be practical. Or especially safe."

Though a risk she'd take in a heartbeat, given the chance.

"That doesn't matter to me."

"Because you already have children. With Dana."

Get your own family.

The accusation still haunted her.

"No, because a family isn't just about having kids. Family is about surrounding yourself with the people who mean the most to you. For years, the guys on the Teams were my family. Not an ounce of blood shared between us except what we spilled in the line of duty."

"It's not the same thing."

"No, you're right. It's not. I loved them like brothers, but that's not even close to the way I feel about you."

Her heart stuttered. "Stop."

"Cam..."

"Don't say it."

"I love you."

The words hung in the air between them.

Right there, where she could almost touch them.

She squeezed her eyes shut for a second so he wouldn't see how deeply shattered she was by his declaration. "You don't mean that."

The faint lift of his lips might have been a smile if he hadn't looked so serious. "I think I know how I feel, Camille. And I'm telling you. I. Love. You."

Oh God, oh God, oh God.

The combination of pain and euphoria whipping through her was enough to make her dizzy. "You can't love me. You love Dana."

He sighed. "Listen to me. I don't love her. I haven't loved her for a long time. And I never felt a tenth for her of what I feel for you. I love you, Camille Richards, every stubborn, head-strong inch of you. And I should have told you that days ago."

Did he have any idea how much his words were shredding her up inside?

"You just think that's what you're feeling because I was the first woman you had sex with after your injury."

He gave her an incredulous look. "So, your theory is what? That I imprinted on you like a freaking duckling?"

Well, when he put it that way...

"Of course not." Maybe. "But there's no question being with me is complicating your relationship with Dana, and getting in the way of what the two of you—"

"Dana lied."

She stuttered to a stop. "What?"

"Dana. Lied." He enunciated the words slowly and distinctly, the blue of his eyes looking almost black as he held her in his steady gaze. "We were never getting back together, no matter what she tried to make you believe. I swear it."

"But the morning you got hurt...you called for her from your room. You wanted her with you. Not me."

That still had the power to jab a knife in and twist it.

"I had no idea you were out in the hallway just then. And I damn well would have preferred *you* keep me company while I ate the breakfast you went to the trouble of making for me. I know you may not believe that, given my unpleasant disposition when you first got there, but that was only because I hated looking weak in front of you." His gaze lowered. "And I hated knowing you'd seen me without the prosthesis."

"What?" She shook her head. "I didn't. I mean, I knew you weren't wearing it, but you were under the covers. And I was focused on your poor head." She'd barely registered anything else.

Judd's gaze snapped back up. "You didn't see?"

She shook her head again. "Not that it would have mattered if I did."

"It would have mattered to me. It *did* matter to me." He let out a hollow laugh. "I thought that was why you were trying to convince me to get back together with Dana. Because you couldn't handle what you saw and were looking for the easiest way to get rid of me without having to admit it."

A swell of outrage flashed through her veins.

"What? No! How could you even think such a thing?"

"How could *you* think I'd just walk away from everything we had to go back to my ex?" Judd countered.

"Because you did." The words tore out of her in a pained whisper, nearly doubling her over as she remembered him walking out of her house. She'd done her best to put on a calm, confident front.

But inside, she'd been dying a little more with every step he took.

"Aw, Christ, Cam." Judd slid from the sofa to the floor in front of her on his knees. He took her hands in his. "I'm so sorry."

"You didn't even argue. You just...left." She knew it was unreasonable to be so hurt by that. Not when it was what she'd wanted him to do. But logic didn't play much of a role in injured feelings.

"You're right. I should have fought harder for us. But I'm here now. Fighting." Judd's grip on her hands became almost painful when she started to shake her head. "I should have stayed that morning until we either straightened things out between us, or you called Uriah to come kick my ass to the curb. But..."

He took a shuddery breath. "But you were so calm about it. So damn certain. And then when you said it was for the best...it was like you'd kicked over the biggest hornets' nest in the world inside me."

"But...why?" She vaguely remembered saying it. And the way he'd suddenly switched from denying he wanted Dana to accusing Cam of wanting a way out of their relationship without looking bad. She'd been too wrapped up in her own conflicted emotions at the time to question the sudden shift.

But now...

Judd took a few of those deep, measured breaths like he sometimes did. Something she realized only now was probably some kind of calming technique. Whatever this was about, it wasn't just a stupid choice of words. This went much, much deeper.

And somehow, she was responsible for the pain she saw in his eyes.

"My father didn't die in the car accident that killed my mother."

The words were low and monotone, and every one sounded like an unwilling prisoner being wrenched from his mouth. "He was hurt, though. Bad enough that I would have needed to be put into foster care for a few months while he recovered if my grandparents hadn't shown up and offered to take me in."

This time, the squeeze on her hands was hard enough to make her gasp.

The pressure eased immediately.

"Sorry. It's just, talking about them..."

"It's okay."

She wanted to stroke his face, his arm, something, to try and soothe him. But he was holding onto her like a lifeline, and she wasn't about to let him go.

His nod was a little jerky.

"I already told you what they were like. But as bad as it was at first, I knew I could endure it, because my father would be coming to get me as soon as he was able to. Then we'd go away and never have to see those horrible people again."

A tiny shudder ran through his body.

"It took almost six months before he came to the farm for me. I was so damn excited. I had my bags packed and waiting by the bedroom door so we could leave as quick as possible. Except he wasn't there to take me away with him. Instead, he told me I'd be staying."

She nodded slowly. "I guess that makes sense. After losing your mother, suddenly becoming a single father, he'd want some help raising you while he continued to recover." She paused. "But that's not what happened, is it?"

"No. I could have lived with that. Knowing he'd be there to keep his parents from finding reasons to berate and punish me all the time. But it turned out he didn't mean *we* were staying there. He meant *I* was staying."

"What? He wanted to leave you there? Why, for goodness sake?"

"Oh, he had a whole slew of good reasons. At least, he thought they were. But then he dropped the real bombshell." His grip tightened convulsively.

"As a condition of taking on the burden of raising me, his parents demanded he sever his parental rights. Give them legal guardianship. And he did it. Before he even came to see me, to talk to me about it. He just...gave me away."

Saying the words out loud made his stomach heave.

He'd never admitted that before.

Never told anyone his father had not only thrown him to the wolves, but legally bound him to them so he couldn't escape until he turned eighteen.

"The worst part was, he had to know what his parents were like. From things they said over the years, they'd been just as strict and harsh with their punishments while he was growing up. And he still left me there." A roll of thunder echoed through the cabin, hopefully hiding the way his voice broke a little at the end.

It was still difficult for a grown, battle-hardened man to comprehend what his father had done. For a scared ten-year-old boy, it had been unfathomable.

"Oh, Judd." Cam's fingers tightened around his. He squeezed back, conscious this time of the strength he used. He'd probably already bruised her delicate skin.

"I begged him not to leave me there. Not to abandon me. That I'd be good, do whatever he said, not make a mess or talk back or anything else I could think to promise him. But he just kept saying how it was for the best. That everything he was doing was the best thing he could do. Over and over, like he was trying to convince both of us it was true."

"Maybe he really thought it was."

He shrugged. "Maybe. Who knows what was going through his head at the time? All I know is, those were the very last words he said to me before he drove away. Not I love you, or I'll miss you, or even I'm sorry. But, it's for the best."

A tiny sob escaped from Cam's tightly pressed lips. "Then I went and said the same thing. Oh, god." Horror filled her eyes. "I *did* the same thing. I made you think I didn't want you anymore. Told you it was the best thing if you were with someone besides me, like I was giving you away, too. Oh Judd, I'm so, so sorry." She tugged her hands to free them.

He gave them up reluctantly, crowding in against her legs so she wouldn't bolt. To his relief, she didn't even try. She just wiped away the tears leaking down her face.

He groaned. "Don't cry, sweetheart."

"But I hurt you!"

He wanted to lie, but chose not to. "Yeah, you did."

"I'm just as bad as your father!" The tears flowed faster. "I never meant to hurt you like that."

"I know. And that's why you're nothing like him. He abandoned me for his own benefit. You were willing to sacrifice your own happiness for mine."

"That's what you do for the people you love."

The word hung between them.

"You love me?" This time she had to hear his voice break.

And he didn't care.

Leaning forward, Cam took his face gently in her hands. "Of course, I do. Silly man." She breathed the last words against his lips as she pressed her mouth to his. The kiss was soft, tender, and tasted like tears.

With a groan that was half relief, half impatience, he deepened the kiss. Begging at her lips before plunging his tongue between them to duel with hers. She met him with equal desperation, the sweet taste of her mixing with the saltiness of tears.

He groaned again. "God, I missed you."

"I missed you, too." The words came out as soft pants interspaced with the almost frantic kisses she scattered over his cheek and jaw. "Get naked."

The growled command made him laugh. "Bossy woman. I like that."

"I know." She gave him a cheeky grin, then turned stern. "Now strip."

"Yes, ma'am."

He made quick work of his shorts and tee, relieved to see Cam wasn't wasting any time removing her own clothes as well. His erection bobbed lightly as he freed it from his briefs. It drew her attention with the intensity of a raptor spotting prey. He hardened even more under her gaze, his balls pulling up almost painfully tight.

"Please tell me this place has a bed."

Cam's tongue ran along her lips as she gave him a head-to-toe perusal. Then she turned and sauntered toward the door opposite the kitchenette area, the rounded globes of her naked ass moving in an enticing rhythm as she walked. He followed, only pausing to snatch the strip of condoms from his go-bag.

He wanted to go slow. To worship every inch of her the way she deserved. But his lizard brain was too far gone for any kind of finesse, the primitive need to re-stake his claim driving him hard.

Still, he restrained the urge to pounce when she lay back across the bed in invitation.

Barely.

Instead, he leaned over her and took the time to tongue her nipples, drawing a moan, then a gasp as his teeth closed around each hard tip in a gentle tug. At war with himself, he bypassed the wealth of silky skin along her ribs and belly.

No more time for play.

He went right for the prize between her thighs. She was hot and wet and nearly bucked off the mattress at the first slow swipe of his tongue.

Cam's head thrashed from side to side as he drove her wild with his mouth. "Judd, *please.*"

The impassioned plea snapped the last threads of his control.

Standing again, he tore open a foil wrapper and covered himself with superhuman speed. As he positioned himself between her splayed legs, he looked down at her. His wanton little principal, lips parted, eyes glazed and wild with passion. And something clicked into place inside of him.

A rightness he'd never felt before. A sense of true belonging. "Say it again."

She didn't need to ask what.

"I love you." She gasped as he sank into her with a hard thrust.

"I love you, too." Another thrust. "You're mine." *Thrust.* "You're never leaving me again." *Thrust.*

Her eyes opened from the blissful half-mast they'd drifted to. "Never. I swear it." Her gaze was as solemn as her vow.

Their eyes remained locked as his tempo increased, as though neither wanted to be the first to look away. It wasn't until her body convulsed around him that her head finally fell back on a moan.

Mere seconds followed before his own orgasm came rushing up from the base of his spine like a stream of molten lava and erupted to the accompaniment of a hoarse shout.

He collapsed onto the bed beside her and cuddled her close. Enjoying the feel of her damp skin against his, her hot breath on his chest, her soft hair tickling his neck. Every physical reminder that this was real.

That they were okay again.

And yet, as sated as he was, as happy as he wanted to be—she loved him, for fuck's sake!—there was still one important thing they hadn't addressed. And until they did, everything else was simply balanced on sand that could shift beneath their feet at any second.

After taking care of the condom in the bathroom, he did a quick check on Cooper, who'd settled in front of a cracked closet door, nose resting on his paws. His tail thumped against the floor in response to Judd's head rub, calmer now that the storm had moved on, thunder back to low rumbles in the distance.

Something he'd had been too caught up in their lovemaking to even notice.

After one last pat, he grabbed his go-bag and returned to the bedroom. Cam was still sprawled just as he'd left her. She was either too boneless to move, or she'd fallen asleep. The temptation to simply crawl back into bed beside her was almost overwhelming.

But unacceptable.

Not if they were going to have a real future together.

Sitting on the edge of the bed, he cleared his throat. "You awake?"

"Mmhmm." Stretching like a cat who'd been rolling in a field of nip, she smiled and reached out to run her hand along his arm. "Why? You want to have your wicked way with me again already?"

"I'm glad you think so much of my recovery abilities, but no. I actually wanted to…" He took a breath. "Remember when I said I was trying to show you something, right before everything got all mixed up and went to hell?"

She lost a bit of her lazy smile and sat up. "Yes." Her gaze went to the backpack at his feet before widening in comprehension. "Oh."

Forcing himself not to shade that one little word with any particular meaning, he soldiered on. "I tried to do this the last night we were together, but I lost my nerve. Maybe if I hadn't…"

He shook his head, not willing to go down that what-if path again.

"I know you say you don't care, that it won't make a difference. But after you...once you see, I won't hold you to any promises you made if you..."

Cam laid her hand on his. He barely kept from flinching.

"Just show me. Please."

Swamped with nervous fatalism, he laid out his supplies and took himself through the process of removing the prosthetic leg, the damp sock, and finally the silicone liner. Dried the liner and his stump as though the woman who could decide his entire future with a word wasn't sitting a mere foot away, watching.

By the time he finished, his heartbeat was galloping so hard in his chest it threatened to beat straight through his ribcage. He didn't want to look at her, terrified what he'd see in her face. But he was done with being a coward.

"This is it," he said, forcing himself to meet her gaze. "This is the real imperfect me. Under the clothes, without the prosthetic, beneath all the other layers. This is what you get. What you'll be stuck with, if you decide you really do want me." His gaze dropped to the scarred, slightly swollen stump of his left leg. "I know it's ugly as hell. Like I said, I'll understand if you—"

"Oh, would you please hush."

Her brisk admonishment had him blinking at her in surprise. But not nearly as much surprise as when she reached over and ran her hand along the length of his residual limb. An odd shiver stuttered through him at her touch. "You don't have to do that."

"Of course I do. This is a part of you. I'm not going to shy away from it."

"I wouldn't blame you if you did." Even though it would still hurt.

"Judd, you need to get something straight. I fell in love with you, *all* of you, not just parts. And this part does not define you." She moved her hand from the stump to his dick. "Just like this part, as lovely as it is, doesn't define you either."

He let out a strangled laugh. "Lovely?"

"Mmm, very." She gave him a light squeeze before her hand moved again. This time to his chest, her palm pressing directly over his crazily thumping heart. "*This* is what defines you. This is who Judd Aiken is, who I fell in love with. A good man. An excellent father. A loyal friend. Someone kind, and loving, and—"

"God, stop." The words came out in a hoarse rasp. "I'm not that. I'm not some perfect fucking paragon."

"No. Just almost kind of perfect, remember?"

It took a second, but he did. It was what he called her on their first not-quite date at her place, out on the patio. The comment was only memorable because it came right before he'd kissed her for the first time.

That moment was permanently seared into his brain.

"Not even that, even if you think so."

"Then how about this. You're perfect for me, in every way possible. Every perfectly imperfect inch, scars and prosthetics and crazy ex-wives included."

He stared into her eyes, wanting to believe. "You really mean that."

"I really mean that." She crawled over and straddled him, her arms looped around his neck. "And I mean this, too. I am perfectly in love with you."

Closing his arms around her, Judd whispered, "What did I ever do to deserve you?"

"The better question is, what are you going to do now that you've got me?" Caught between them, his dick stirred with renewed interest, making her smile and wiggle a little closer. Predictably, he swelled even harder. "Good answer."

He couldn't help it. He threw back his head and laughed at the sheer joy this woman had brought to his life. Where there had once been nothing but endless, lonely days stretching out before him, he now saw endless possibilities.

And all of them started and ended with her at his side.

Tucking her more tightly against his fully revived erection, he said, "In case you haven't realized it yet, I'm perfectly in love with you, too. You've had your chance to run. From now on, you're stuck with me."

"That's good, because there's no place I'd rather be." The smile that lit her face came with a spark of mischief. "Now, are we going to keep talking, or are we going to see how well this position works without the prosthetic on?"

His smile held its own bit of devilry in reply.

"Yes, ma'am."

Epilogue

1 YEAR LATER

"Are they here yet? Are they here yet?"

Grinning at Carly's excited shouts as she danced from foot-to-foot beside him on the farmhouse's porch, Judd ran a hand over her head and gave one of her pigtails a small tug. "Not yet, peanut. Soon, though. Here." He fished a tennis ball out of one of the large cargo pockets on his uniform pants. "Why don't you go see if you can wear Cooper out a little for me. He was stuck in the patrol car all morning and probably needs to stretch his legs."

"Okay. Come on, Coop!"

As child and dog took off across the lawn, Cam came out of the house, wiping her hands on a dishtowel. The smudge of flour on her cheek gave away the fact she'd been baking. She smiled at Judd in relief. "You made it in time."

"I told you I would." He pulled her close for a kiss. "Mmm, peaches."

"I'm making a pie for dessert." A small pucker of concern appeared between her brows. "What if they don't like peach? Maybe I should have made apple instead. Or a cake. Maybe I should *mmmph*."

He silenced her nervous chatter with another kiss. "They're kids. They'll like anything you make as long as it's sweet." He gave her another quick peck and licked his lips. "Mmm. Just like you."

"Stop." The swat she gave him was half-hearted at best. Peering over his shoulder down the driveway, she asked, "Shouldn't they be here by now?"

"You're as bad as Carly. Relax. They're not due for another half hour. Why don't you go finish your baking while I get changed?" As much as he enjoyed being back in uniform, even though it wasn't the one he was used to, he knew how intimidating he could appear in it.

A definite plus while patrolling the streets as a newly minted deputy sheriff.

But not the first impression he wanted to make on their guests.

"You might want to have a talk with Boone while you're in there."

The hesitation in her voice was something he hadn't heard from her when dealing with his kids in quite some time. "Anything wrong? I thought he was okay with this."

"He is. I think he's just a little...unsettled, now that it's actually happening. He could probably do with a bit of reassurance from you."

"On it." After stealing one more kiss, he went inside.

It still felt strange passing through the living room and not seeing Wilt. Sitting there in his ratty recliner like a wizened little gnome perched on a toadstool, cackling over something on the television.

A familiar sense of sadness filled his chest.

The old man had gone the way he wanted, peacefully in his sleep, a few days into the New Year. That didn't make the loss any easier.

Wilt had claimed only days before he passed that he'd had the best holidays and ninetieth birthday a man could ask for. Surrounded by his friends, and filled up on Camille's home cooking. He'd never been happier.

Then one afternoon he'd taken a nap in his chair and just never woke up.

Six months later, and he still missed the crotchety old Marine like crazy.

With a silent *Semper Fi* for his departed friend, he went to the bedroom he and Camille had renovated into their master and stripped off his uniform. No one had been more surprised than him when he found out Wilt had left him the house and property in his will.

Except maybe Wilt's great-nephew, Nolan.

The weasel had been sitting through the estate proceedings with a smug, self-satisfied smirk on his face as the lawyer droned on through the legalese. Expecting to get it all as the old man's only living relative.

The explosion that came from finding out differently was a story still making the rounds through the gossip mill. Uriah had to be called to physically remove the man from the lawyer's office. Only the threat of getting his butt tossed in jail for disorderly conduct and trespass had gotten him to leave.

Not that he'd let the fight end there. Nolan had immediately contested the will, claiming his "feeble" great-uncle had been manipulated by Judd into changing it when he was too old and sick to know better.

As he worked his modified uniform boot off the prosthetic foot and replaced it with a sneaker, he grimaced at the memory of how much that accusation had stung. He'd worried it might carry some weight, too, since he was an outsider and Nolan a lifelong Creeker.

But worse, he'd hated having anyone think for a single second he would take advantage of not just an old man and fellow veteran, but someone he considered a friend.

Fortunately, Wilt knew his great-nephew a lot better than Nolan had known the old man. Foreseeing trouble, he'd had his new will witnessed by not only his lawyer, but his doctor and a judge as well.

Nolan's petition was over before it even got started.

He still might have turned the property over to Nolan out of guilt—because hell, sound mind or not, he'd only known Wilt for a little over half a year—if it hadn't been for the letter. It seemed Wilt had known Judd pretty well, too. Anticipating his attack of conscience, Wilt had left a handwritten note for him with the lawyer.

Dear Judd,

If you're reading this, I've gone to the big PX in the sky and you're dealing with my butthead of a great-nephew. Sorry about that. I bet you're both pretty surprised by me leaving you the house. Boy, oh boy, would I love to be there to see Nolan's face right about now!

I know my nephew thinks he deserves the place, but don't let him make you feel he got cheated somehow. He's only ever seen it as an old wreck past its prime and not worth investing a minute of his time on. Kind of like me. In his hands, it'll all be torn down and the whole spread turned into a cookie-cutter neighborhood inside a month.

Of course, once it's yours, you're free to do whatever you like with it. But I've seen the pride you've taken in fixing the place up, bringing it back to life. I know you see it the way I do, as a place for you to raise up a passel of kids and herds of dogs to play with them. Make it a real home. Stop your procrastinating and get to it, son!

I may be gone, but don't mourn me. I had a damn good life. Just raise a beer in my name and maybe share a few bullshit stories with the boys down at the VFW come Memorial Day. You've been a good friend to this old man, Judd, and I thank you for that. You're a man I would have been proud to call my son.

~Wilt

Judd swallowed the thickness in his throat Wilt's parting words always caused when he thought about them. He never would have guessed the old bastard had such a sentimental streak. But the honest truth was, he would have been proud to be called his son, too.

After yanking on a pair of cargo shorts and a fresh t-shirt, he made his way to the small bedroom at the back of the house they'd turned into a game room for the kids. Boone was hunched in a chair, eyes fixed on the tv screen as he played some world building video game he'd kicked Judd's butt at the previous night.

"Hey, buddy."

"Hi, Dad." Boone's eyes never left the screen.

As he lowered himself to the other chair, Jasper got up from the floor with a big stretch and jumped into his lap. "So, how're you doing?"

Boone's shoulders rose in a shrug that was becoming all too familiar as the answer to everything that could mean anything.

"Anything bothering you?"

Shrug.

"Want to talk about it?"

Shrug.

With a silent sigh at the reminder of exactly how much patience and guesswork went into parenting, he stroked the purring cat and waited as Boone played for a few minutes. Hoping for some kind of visual clue for how best to proceed.

He couldn't find any.

But his boy had definitely inherited his exceptional hand-eye co-ordination, that was for sure. Although it might have been better if he hadn't gotten his single-minded focus as well.

"Could you pause that for a minute, please?"

Boone's sigh was nowhere near as silent as Judd's, but he did as asked.

"Now, I'll ask again. Is anything bothering you? Like, maybe the boys coming to stay with us?"

Boone picked at the edge of the handheld controller with his thumbnail, not meeting Judd's gaze as he mumbled, "I don't know. Maybe a little."

"Buddy, we talked about this last night. I thought you were okay with it."

"I was. I am. I just..." He squirmed in his chair and finally looked up. A wealth of conflicting emotions shone through his wide eyes. "Things are just starting to feel normal with Carly and me being here with you and Cam. Having other kids living here, too..."

"You think it'll be too weird?"

"No. Yes." *Shrug.* "Whatever. It doesn't matter. They're coming anyway."

His heart ached at the resigned look on his son's face, which had matured so much since he first hit town a little over a year ago.

"Hey, of course it matters. This is your home, too."

"Only half the time."

"All of the time. Even when you're at your mom's. You know that."

Shrug.

Damnation. He and Cam might have made a mistake saying yes when they got the call about the boys yesterday.

They had sat Boone and Carly down and explained the situation to them. Neither had seemed bothered by the idea of having temporary houseguests, but maybe they'd thrown too much change at them too quickly.

It had only been a month since he and Dana started the joint custody schedule they'd worked out for the summer. They'd see how the kids handled it before they decided whether it would be in their best interests to make it a more permanent—and legal—change come the start of the school year.

Dana had been surprisingly accepting of the idea when Judd floated it to her. Inheriting Wilt's house had given him the space to let his kids stay over without them having to sleep on Cam's fold-out sofa. With their own bedrooms, they could stay for more than just an occasional night or two.

He wasn't sure if her willingness was because she was still trying to make amends for her part in the previous summer's disaster. Or because it would finally give her some breathing room in her own life.

Whatever her motives, he didn't really care.

Not when it got him more time with his kids.

That wasn't the only benefit to all of the sudden space. Extra bedrooms meant Cam could finally fulfill her long-held desire to be put on the regular foster care list with the county. Before, she'd only been able to handle emergency placements that lasted a few days at most. Now, she—no, *they* would be able to take on children for as long as they needed to stay.

Removing kids from bad, maybe even dangerous situations, was something he fully supported being a part of.

But between the house still getting some renovations, his new job, and having his kids staying with them on a semi-regular basis for the first time, they'd agreed to hold off on any fostering until life settled into some kind of normal rhythm again.

Best laid plans.

What theirs had failed to factor in was getting an emergency placement request in the meantime. Or the fact his kids might not be as okay with the idea as they initially claimed.

"Judd, they're here!"

Not missing the sour look that flashed over his son's face at Cam's excited call, he cursed the timing. "We're coming," he called back.

Wishing he had a little more time to talk things over, he set Jasper on the floor.

"We'll discuss this more later, okay? Because I meant it. This is your home, and we want you to be comfortable here. But for right now, these boys have no place else to go, and they're probably pretty scared and upset, coming to a new place where they don't know anyone. How about we try to make them feel at least a little bit welcome?"

"I guess."

The reluctant agreement was the best he could hope for at the moment.

With all the slowness of someone bearing the weight of the world on his nine-year-old shoulders, Boone walked out with him, feet dragging the entire way.

A dusty silver sedan with official plates on it was just pulling in behind his truck in the dirt driveway. Carly was on the porch with Cam, waiting. It was hard to tell which of them looked more excited.

Rather than join them by the steps, Boone veered over to pet Cooper. The dog had collapsed in a heap next to his water bowl, tongue lolling as he panted like a freight train going uphill.

Cam exchanged a worried look with Judd.

"Let's just see what happens," he said to her quietly. Despite the way Boone was acting, Judd had faith he'd be, if not entirely welcoming toward the boys, then at least civil. The rest they'd have to work out as they went along.

This was untrod territory for them all.

The red-haired woman who got out of the car was bird-thin. A pair of narrow black-framed glasses were perched on her nose. Which might have made her look a little stern if it hadn't been for the smile that stretched her lips as she walked toward them and up onto the porch.

"Miss Richards, it's good to see you again," she said, shaking Cam's hand. "Although I wish I wasn't, if you know what I mean."

"I do, and I couldn't agree more, Mrs. Powell."

So did he. Because her being there meant a child was in need of shelter, and that was always a tragedy.

"And this is who I was telling you about. My fiancé, Judd Aiken."

He could tell the woman was doing her best not to stare at his prosthetic leg as he shook her hand. Unlike a year ago, it didn't bother him in the least if she did.

"Ma'am, a pleasure."

"Yes, indeed, Mr. Aiken. A pleasure." Catching herself, she raised her gaze and cleared her throat. "And these must be your children."

"Yes. My son, Boone, and the jumping bean over there is Carly."

Cam had filled the social worker in on the new household dynamic the evening before. Normally, a new vetting process would be required before placing any children with them. But it seemed the situation was desperate enough that exceptions were being made.

Plus, having Uriah's personal stamp of approval carried a lot of weight.

Mrs. Powell smiled at the kids.

"It's so nice to meet you both. You look like you're very close to the same ages as Matthew and Levi. That should help make things a little easier for them." The last part was said more to Judd and Cam, and almost more like a hope than a belief. "If it's okay, I'll go get them now and introduce everyone."

As soon as the boys emerged from the backseat of the car, it was evident they weren't full siblings. The older boy of eight had blond hair cut short everywhere but the front, where it flopped over his eyes as he stared at the ground. The younger boy clinging to his hand was a scrawny-looking six, with hair and skin as dark as his brother's was light.

As they approached, though, it was clear there was a definite familial stamp on their features that marked them brothers.

He and Cam came down off the porch so they wouldn't be towering over the kids as Mrs. Powell nudged them forward like a mother goose with two reluctant goslings.

"Matthew, Levi," she said, touching the older boy's shoulder lightly, then the younger's, "these are Miss Richards and Mr. Aiken. The people I told you about that you'll be staying with for a little while."

Matthew used the hair over his eyes as a blind to partially mask the piercing look of distrust he gave them as he edged slightly in front of his little brother. Levi's big green eyes studied them more openly, but no less warily.

Neither did more than glance at Judd's prosthesis.

Despite the blatant mistrust radiating from the boys, Cam gave a warm smile. "It's nice to meet you both. Welcome to our home."

Judd squatted down to get more eye-level with the kids, and noticed one other thing besides their looks the boys shared.

As calmly as he could manage, not wanting to scare anyone, he asked Matthew in a soft but deadly tone, "Who hit you, son?"

The sullen yellow-green of the bruise on Matthew's face marked it as less than a week old. But there were other, more faded ones on both boys' arms that told him this hadn't been a one-time incident. The fact they were in need of emergency fostering meant the abuse most likely had occurred in the home.

The place they should have been the safest.

Which only infuriated him more. Because he knew exactly how it felt to have what should be your sanctuary become your prison instead.

He must not have tempered his rage as well as he thought. Both Levi and Mrs. Powell gave a small, involuntary movement. Like prey animals suddenly faced with a predator who might be interested in eating them.

Matthew, however, stood his ground. He picked his head up far enough to look at Judd without the cover of his hair, his gray eyes solemn as they studied him. As though weighing the meaning behind the anger and what it might mean for him and his brother.

Making an educated guess, Judd said, "I bet your hair used to be long all over, didn't it? Not just in the front. But you cut it short because that's the easiest way for someone to grab onto you when you're trying to get away."

"How did you—" The boy's mouth snapped shut.

"Because I learned the same thing. No long hair, no baggy clothes. You try to be invisible whenever you can be, and to move really fast when you can't. But no matter how hard you try, sometimes you just can't avoid the belt when it comes out."

"Gary used his fists." Anger smoldered in Matthew's eyes like a living beast.

Judd glanced to Mrs. Powell in unspoken question, making her start.

"Gary and Vicky Ward. They ran the foster home the boys have been staying in until their mother is able to resume her parental duties." Her lips tightened in displeasure. "Until yesterday, that is."

"He was always saying bad things about Momma, 'cause she's an attic," Levi piped up, edging closer.

Judd took it as a good sign that Matthew let him.

"Addict," Matthew corrected his brother. To Judd he said with a challenging air, "She's in rehab, though. She's coming to get us as soon as she gets better."

The words were like an echoed blow to a younger version of himself, who'd once had the same blind faith his parent would return to make things right. Hopefully, theirs was more deserving of it.

"I'm glad to hear it. But until then, what do you think about staying here with us for a while?" He jerked his thumb over his shoulder. "I'm sure my kids would love to have someone else to play video games with besides me. I kind of suck."

Matthews eyes lit up at the mention of video games before shuttering again. He shrugged. "Not like we have a choice."

Much as he wanted to say different, the kid was right.

They had zero say about what happened to them, entirely at the mercy of the adults in charge. Although, if he had to guess based on the bruise on his face, Matthew had found a way to exert at least a tiny bit of control over their situation.

Chronic abusers were very careful not to hit where it would show. Purposely taking a blow to the face would all but guarantee someone finally had to notice. Although, as Judd had learned, that didn't always mean they did anything to make it stop.

Luckily for these kids, someone had.

"You have a doggie?" Levi's words were soft but filled with excitement.

Following the boy's avid gaze, he saw Cooper had moved to the edge of the porch steps behind them to stand next to Carly.

Boone stood on the other side of the dog. His expression was less sullen than before, but Judd still couldn't get a good read on what he was thinking.

"That's Cooper. Would you like to pet him?" He grinned at Levi's enthusiastic nod. Matthew gave another shrug, but Judd could tell he was more interested than he let on. "Boone, would you mind introducing Cooper to Matthew and Levi?"

"I guess."

"Oh, is that a good idea?" Mrs. Powell fretted as the boys climbed onto the porch.

Judd gave a quick nod. "It'll be fine."

The adults watched as Boone told the brothers in a proprietary way about Cooper being a service dog and what that meant before letting the petting begin. There was one tense moment when Levi lurched forward into the dog to give him a hug, and Matthew started to reach for him in alarm.

Boone put a hand on his arm to stop him. "It's okay. Coop won't hurt him."

Sure enough, Cooper sat stoically under the enthusiastic attention. Then he gave Levi's face a few quick licks when he was released, making the boy giggle like a fiend. Only then did the tension ease from Matthew's small frame.

Boone gave him a friendly shoulder bump. "Told ya. Coop's great with little kids." And just like that, he'd aligned the two of them as the 'big kids' in the group dynamic. "Hey, wanna go throw the ball for him? He's really fast, and he can almost always catch it before it bounces."

"Sure!" Matthew hesitated and looked back at the three adults, eyes darting between them as though not sure who to ask. "Is that okay?"

"Of course!" Cam made a shooing motion. "Go have fun. But no one get too dirty, supper's in about an hour."

With a whoop, all four kids and the dog pounded off the porch, heading for the yard.

Watching them go, Mrs. Powell let out a small sigh of relief.

"Thank you again for taking the both of them. None of the other emergency placement homes were able to take two children on such short notice, and I really didn't want to have to split them up."

"And they shouldn't be," Cam replied.

"We'll try to find a more permanent place for them as quickly as possible. But we also have the other four boys who were in the Wards' care to find spaces for as well. And with the investigation that's sure to come from this situation....I'm afraid it might be a while."

Judd exchanged a look with Cam, who smiled and nodded. Good. They were on the same page on this.

"Don't worry about timeframe," he said, sliding his arm around Cam's shoulders and hugging her to his side. "The boys are welcome to stay as long as needed to get them resituated." And maybe longer.

But that was a discussion to be had later. Between the entire family.

He'd meant it when he told Boone what he thought mattered. His kids would never need to question whether anything he did was really what was best for them

Ever.

After retrieving the boys' meager belongings from her car, Mrs. Powell thanked them again and left, promising to check back the next day on how things were going.

Cam leaned against his side as they watched the kids playing. "You see yourself in them, don't you?"

Swallowing the roil of emotions clogging his chest, he pulled her in tighter. He'd never get used to the sense of peace just touching her could bring.

"More like what might have been." If he'd gotten out. If there had been people brave enough to stand up to his grandparents.

He pressed a kiss to her temple. "You're a good woman, Camille."

And she was all his.

Later that night, after the kids were finally wrangled into bed, he sat at the big kitchen table going over the papers a lawyer friend of Uriah's had helped him with. Setting up a non-profit to raise money for training service dogs for veterans had turned out to be a lot more complicated than he'd anticipated.

But if the Navy had taught him anything, it was how to tackle bureaucratic red tape. So, he'd be damned if he let this mess get the better of him.

His eyes were starting to burn when Cam came into the room and leaned over his shoulder to kiss his cheek. "It's getting late. You coming to bed soon?"

"Was that an invitation?"

"Always."

He turned his head to claim her lips, leaving both of them breathing hard when he was done. "And one I'll always accept."

"Good to know." She glanced at the legal pad on the table filled with scratched out names. All except one. "So, you finally decided?"

"I think so." He'd come up with dozens of options, but always seemed to circle back to the very first he'd written down.

"The Michael Winchester Legacy Foundation. I like it. Was he someone you served with?"

"He served, but not with me. Actually, he's the reason I have Cooper. He was an Army medic who was killed in action a few years ago. His family gave three puppies from his dog's litter to the

Another Step Forward foundation to be trained as service dogs in his memory. Coop's one of them. It was their way of carrying on his legacy of helping others, so I figured, what better way to keep paying that legacy forward than to name it for him?"

"I think that's a beautiful idea. And so was asking John if he'd design the logo for you. He was over the moon. Not to mention how it will look on his art school application." She slid her arms around him and gave him a hug from behind. "Now, enough work for tonight. Come to bed."

He didn't need to be told twice.

As they passed by the staircase, he paused to call up. "Everyone better be back in their beds in five minutes, or I'm coming up there."

There was a moment of dead silence, followed by the patter of little feet scattering and the thump of three bedroom doors shutting.

She grinned and shook her head. "Are you ever going to tell me how you do that?"

"Nope." He gave her a quick kiss before she headed to their room while he took Cooper out for one last pee break.

He leaned against the porch railing, where the newer wood had weathered up to match the old just as he'd predicted when he nailed it in last summer. A sense of complete contentment settled over him.

He'd spent so much of his adult life searching for exactly this without even realizing it. A place that felt safe, that no one could take away. People who loved him as he was, imperfections and all, real or imagined. A sense of purpose that went beyond the grand scale of his work with the SEALs to a more personal, visceral level. A family level.

His family.

Zee was right. He had put down roots here. Deep ones. Roots that were quickly becoming so entwined with this town and the people in it, he'd never again be able to rip free of them. And he was perfectly okay with that.

Because finally, he had somewhere he belonged. A place where he was whole.

This was home.

A Note From the Author

I hope you enjoyed Judd and Camille's (and Cooper's) story!

This series holds a special place in my heart. The inspiration for these books sprang from seeing guide dogs being trained all around my home town when I was growing up. And later, meeting a family who fostered guide dogs-in-training during their first year, teaching them basic social skills and commands. With all of that marinating in my brain, it was only a matter of time before the Wounded Warrior Legacy books were born.

I'd like to thank everyone who helped me with this book (and there were many!). First, my husband, whose understanding when I lock myself in the office to hit my deadlines is boundless.

Thanks to the folks at America's Vet Dogs, who graciously answered my one million questions when I was still fleshing out the idea for this series. And a huge shout-out to my sensitivity readers for the entire series, who kept me true. Any inaccuracies that remain are mine alone, and were sometimes necessary for the story.

I can't believe my time with this series is over. Well, for now, at least. I do have some ideas brewing for future service dog stories, but they'll need to marinate for a bit before they're ready to be served up onto the page. In the meantime, if you've missed any of the other books in the Wounded Warrior Legacy series, **Just the**

Way You Are or **A Light in the Darkness**, you can grab them by visiting my website (nikarhone.com). Just scan the QR code below.

While you're there, claim your FREE book just by signing up for my newsletter. You can also stay up-to-date on all future releases by following my author page on any of the major book retailer websites.

And finally, if you loved this book, please take a moment to leave a quick review at your favorite retailer. They're what feeds an author's creative soul. Thank you!

Resources

If you or someone you know is in crisis, please reach out:

Suicide & Crisis Hotline: (toll-free 24/7) call 988 and press 1
Suicide & Crisis Website: 988lifeline.org
National Call Center for Homeless Veterans: 1-877-424-3838(4AID-VET)

Americans With Disabilities Act: ada.gov

Please consider volunteering at or donating to your local service dog organization. If you don't have one, here are a few that I know of:

AmericasVet Dog: vetdogs.org
Guide Dog Foundation for the Blind: guidedog.org
Guiding Eyes for the Blind: guidingeyes.org
Guide Dogs of America: guidedogsofamerica.org
International Guide Dog Federation: igdf.org.uk
National Federation of the Blind: nfb.org
Paws of War: pawsofwar.org

Also By Nika Rhone

<u>Boulder Bodyguards series</u>
What the Lady Wants
Finding Forever
Can't Help Loving You

<u>Boulder Beaumonts series</u>
Worth Any Price
Never Let Me Go
All I Need Is You

<u>Wounded Warrior Legacy series</u>
Just the Way You Are
A Light in the Darkness
All Our Perfect Imperfections

About the Author

Nika Rhone spent her childhood wearing out library cards as she read her way through the extraordinary worlds far beyond her small hometown on Long Island, NY. By her teens, her imagination was taking her places all on its own, forcing her to learn how to type (badly) so she could get all the stories down on paper. After a long love affair with science fiction and fantasy, she finally discovered romance, fell head-over-heels, and now spends her days crafting happily-ever-afters for the characters who still tell their stories faster (and better) than she can type them. Her books include the Boulder Bodyguards, Boulder Beaumonts, and Wounded Warrior Legacy series.

You can keep up with all the latest book news, events, and giveaways by visiting her website www.nikarhone.com and joining her newsletter. You can also follow her on Facebook.